A Bitch for God
A novel by Clark T. Carlton

Copyright © Clark Thomas Carlton 2023

Cover design by David Colon

Publisher's note: This is a work of fiction. Names, characters, businesses, places, events, locales, and incidents are either the products of the author's imagination or used in a fictitious manner. Any resemblance to actual persons, living or dead, or actual events is purely coincidental.

Dedication

For Steve Schulte. I will never forget your competence, your decency and your integrity.

And in Memory Of
Tom Huckabee who should have been much more famous.

Gratitude

Thank you to Matthew Goodman, James David Martin, Tom Parry, Joseph Sierra, Michael Welch and Mike Werb for their careful reading of the early drafts and their suggestions. And thank you to my ever-loving partner, Mike Dobson, for his tolerance of my need to tap on a keyboard late into the night.

"No one who demands worship, however covertly, deserves respect."
— Wendy Kaminer, Sleeping with Extra-Terrestrials

"Therefore when thou doest thine alms, do not sound a trumpet before thee, as the hypocrites do in the synagogues and in the streets, that they may have glory of men. Verily I say unto you, They have their reward."
— Matthew 6:2

Chapter 1

From the sullen look on his face, I guessed that the youngish man to my left was a would-be actor anxiously awaiting his lucky break. He was a last minute fill-in for a dinner party in late October of 2013, the renter of the garage unit of a house perched high in the Hollywood Hills. Tuning out from the industry gossip and real estate chatter, he gazed through the sliding glass doors at the nightly spectacle of the Los Angeles Basin with its billions of lights and towers that glittered in the distance. Perhaps he needed some cheering up.

"It's beautiful," I said as I dipped my spoon into a pumpkin soup with a web of drizzled fennel oil and a spider-shaped crouton.

"What is?"

"The view. It's like diamonds scattered on miles of mink."

"Right," he said with the faintest smile.

"I'm Tyler."

"Keith."

"What brought you to Los Angeles, Keith?"

"Oh," he said, and fingered his mass of curly hair, his best feature, which was like some dense and lustrous butterscotch pudding. "Acting."

"How's that going?" I asked.

"Meh."

Bingo. A silence passed.

"Now it's your turn," I said. "You ask me a question, I answer it, and it might lead to a conversation."

"Sorry," he said. "I, uh...I broke up with someone today."

"Oh. Now I'm the one who's sorry. How long were you with him?"

"Her."

"Apologies... I... I thought you were gay... like everyone else here."

"I might be," he said. "I haven't decided. Which is what I should have told Lakshmi."

"Lakshmi? An Indian woman?"

"No. Lakshmi Steinmetz," he said. "Maybe you've heard of her. She's kinda famous."

"We're acquainted," I said. Years later, that name still made me wince. "Isn't she kind of..."

"What?"

"Um, you seem a little young for her."

"She's sixty-two and I'm thirty-four... for another two weeks. I just couldn't take that next step toward... intimacy. She just shit all over me, told me I'd let her down."

"It doesn't sound like she's changed much."

2

He shook his head and sighed through his nostrils. "She said it was the last thing she needed before her campaign, that I was sabotaging her."

"Her campaign?"

"She's running for Congress since the guy in this district is retiring— Hank Scharffenberger or something."

"Oh really," I said and felt a mix of anger and panic to learn Lakshmi would be running in my district. "Except she's not really running for Congress."

"She's not?"

"I'm sure she wants to be president."

"Right," he said, through half a laugh.

A moment later, I was the sullen one. It was not the first time I had thought of Steinmetz that day. That afternoon I had read an article about Robert Bravermann in the Los Angeles Times.

Bravermann was remembered by millions as one of the world's most beautiful men, the man that Tom of Finland had rendered in multiple portraits, someone whose photos were still attracting thousands of eyes fifty years after they were published. But those of us who worked with Bravermann remembered him for a hundred other reasons, including his clash with Steinmetz. He was running for office again, to be a member of the LA School Board. Though it was a little rude to do at a dinner party, I took out my phone and typed his name into Wikipedia to read his entry. I was astonished to see he didn't have one.

Miles, my partner, turned from his conversation and looked at me. "Where did you go?" he asked.

"1989," I said.

1989 was a time when the word "positive" meant the same thing as "death sentence." I had few memories of that year's clothes or music or any good times but I will never forget Robert Bravermann... or Ms. Steinmetz. The idea that she might be my congressperson had ruined my evening.

Could she win?

*

Wednesdays in 1989 were my days to spend with Allen, a friend from film school, who had full-blown AIDS. Sometimes that meant driving him to a doctor's office where he would sit in a glass booth to breathe in the mists of some potion that might save the sight in his good eye. "Health foods" like tofu, alfalfa sprouts and wheat germ were the last thing people with wasting syndrome needed, so whenever I went to pick him up, I brought him a cheesecake, a pecan pie or some Toll House cookies I'd made myself. It was too hot to bake on a sun-bleached day in July so I arrived at his apartment with a drum of caramel ripple ice cream only to find the door was locked.

"Don't come in, Tyler," he cried through the door. "It's a total mess on my floor right now. I didn't make it to the bathroom."

"It's cool," I said. "Shit happens."

"No. I don't want you to see this. Please."

"What can I do for you?"

"Just go," he said. "The ambulance will be here soon."

"I'll be right outside till they get here," I said. "Just in case you need me."

A couple of weeks later, I visited Allen when he was in the hospital for the seventh time that year. He was no longer able to eat so I brought him some photography magazines as taking pictures had been his hobby. His head was freshly shaven and at the crown was a circle of black stitches — it looked like a yarmulke of veal had been sewn to his head. I was told they had opened his skull with a rotary saw then scraped out some growth that clung to his brain and made his head pound in agony.

"Who is it?" he croaked out.

"I'm from Mary Kay," I said. "Here to make a more beautiful you."

"Hope you brought a few barrels," he said. Though it pained him, he smiled and revealed gums bulging with the purple lesions that covered his face and chest. On top of the mouth lesions were splotches of a dark yellow yeast infection. I had heard he looked like some withered, polka-dotted alien, but I was stunned and fighting every urge not to collapse in pity. It was pointless to ask how he was. It was hard to say anything.

"Sorry. I know I'm a mess," he said.

"No point in sorrow. I brought you some magazines."

"Give them to someone who can see," he said. "Please."

We were quiet again when horror and sadness crept up like a mugger and bashed me in the head with a crowbar. He heard me failing to stifle my sniffles.

"Don't cry, Tyler," he said. "I'm happy."

"Happy?"

"Everyone's stood by me. Friends and family. Total strangers. Makes me cry when I think about it. But it's happy crying."

Silence passed. The sun coming in through his window was an avalanche of brightness and it gave me a migraine.

"You should go," he said. "It's hard for me to talk."

"OK."

"Thank you, Tyler."

"It was just some magazines."

"No. I mean… thank you very much. For everything."

His arm extended in a strange, floating way, like a tree snake writhing toward an upper branch. His hand was alarmingly bony when I took it and felt like wet twigs in my palm.

"Bye," I said and patted his hand. I slowly set it back to his chest, afraid his arm might tear off like the wing of some chicken that had boiled too long.

*

Per his instructions, Allen's memorial service was held in his favorite movie palace, a revival house in Silverlake with an Egyptian theme. A harpist played Satie's *Gymnopédies* as we entered and the theme from *Dynasty* when we exited, which had been Allen's favorite TV show. In the lobby there was a table covered with flavorless cookies from Smart and Final and a coffee urn provided by his friends from Alcoholics Anonymous. I introduced myself to Allen's parents, a well-breakfasted pair from Iowa who stood at the end of the reception line. The father, wearing a polyester suit from the 1970s, seemed both touched and uncomfortable while shaking the hands of so many sad young men. His mother clasped my hand and meant it when she said, "Thank you for coming. I'm happy to see he had so many friends. I'm Gertie Stonehaus."

"I'm Tyler."

"Oh! Tyler St. George?"

"Yes."

"Allen asked me to give you this."

She handed me a large manila envelope. As I worked as a story analyst for production companies, I was pretty sure of what was inside and dreaded opening it. I was about to leave when I looked up to see Kevin Darrington, the cutest, blondest realtor in Los Angeles, waving at me on the other side of the room with a smile that belonged to happier days. After we had left film school, Kevin decided he could make more money selling houses in Hollywood than struggling in its film industry. He was wearing a light gray summer suit by Armani and wore a Patek Phillipe watch that cost more than what I'd made in the last five years.

"Tyler. Sorry to see you in these circumstances. It's either at a funeral or a fundraiser," he said as he handed me a plastic cup of what looked like ice water. "It's vodka," he whispered. "But don't tell the alkies."

"OK," I said and sipped. Usually when I saw Kevin it was at an AIDS event and I was serving him a drink instead of having one with him.

"How's Kyle? Is that going well?"

"Well, sure. Of course. We're fine. He's fine."

"He's a very lucky man. He should be here with you, don't you think? You will let me know if that ever comes to an end, won't you?"

"You're very flattering."

"Been keeping busy, Tyler? Writing?"

"Not much. It seems trivial to work on a screenplay when… when everybody's…."

"Dropping like flies?"

"I wouldn't use that expression."

"Of course you wouldn't. It's a cliché. You're better than that," he said and quietly laughed.

For some reason, my grief got the best of me and I wiped at tears.

"You OK, honey?" he asked.

"I don't know how I'm going to help now that Allen's gone. I've got to do something… for *some*body. I'm just sick of feeling so… so fucking helpless."

"Funny you should mention," he said, and patted my back. "We're starting a new service modeled on one in New York called God's Love We Deliver. They bring food to people who are homebound with the plague. You know, a hot meal delivered by a friendly face. My ski group's raised some seed money and we're looking for a somebody to lend a name to it."

"I'm good at baking," I said.

"You certainly are. I will never forget your tarte tatin with that crumbly pâte brisée instead of a soggy puff pastry."

Kevin noticed someone across the lobby and waved at him. "Excuse me, Tyler, but I've got to say hello to Brian Rosenman. I hear he's looking to unload that five bedroom up on Mulholland next to Carrie Fischer's place. We'll talk soon, OK?"

Kevin hugged me a little too intimately and I realized a rumor about one of his physical gifts was true.

I couldn't be at another memorial service for another moment so I quietly slipped out to my car and opened the envelope. I had guessed correctly that it contained screenplays. Like all of them, they were printed on three hole punch and bound with brass brads and had a cardboard cover. Clipped to the top one was a note from Global Artists Agency.

Dear Mr. St. George,

In accordance with my client's wishes, I am sending you some screenplays written by Allen Stonehaus who told me you are a talented screenwriter. Though I was unable to sell these screenplays, Allen wanted you to have them in case you saw something in them. You are welcome to rework them or borrow their ideas as long as you give Allen a cowriting credit and allow me to represent them. I think one of them would make a terrific monster movie. Please call me if you're interested.

Sincerely,

Gil Goldschmidt

"For Christ's fucking sake," I said out loud. For a moment I hated Allen for networking from the great beyond. A moment later I understood his need for taking one last stab at selling a screenplay. I started to laugh and couldn't stop. For a while I felt like two people, one laughing and the other crying. A moment later I felt crushed by a two-ton slab of grief then sank into a sleep so dark and deep it verged on death. When I awoke, the late noon sunshine was like knitting needles stabbing my eyes. I was late for a bartending gig at a gallery in Santa Monica, which was on the other side of town. Fortunately I was wearing a tie and was already dressed in the black and white of a server.

The Frederich Stumen Gallery was a vast space, a former warehouse, with a varnished cement floor and bright white walls and a vaulted ceiling with exposed steel beams. The paintings were by an artist whose show was called "Striation." Some of his canvasses were vertical, some horizontal, some were square and all were covered in rough black stripes that alternated with white ones. Hundreds of people showed up to drink wine and vodka and every last one of them was wearing black. The 80's had been a decade of bright, rich colors but it was ending in an obsession with tar-colored clothes.

As I looked at the crowd, I wondered if the clothing designers were all in mourning and perpetrating their grief as a dark joke on the fashion junkies. A pretty blonde woman was one of the last to arrive and she entered in a lemon and chartreuse mini-dress, something Marlo Thomas might have worn in *That Girl.* She looked like a crocus bursting through blacktop and made me smile for the first time that day. "You look fantastic," I said when she approached me for a glass of chardonnay. "Why is everyone else in black?"

"Cuz they're all fucking sheep," she said then cocked her head at the paintings. "Which is also why they're buying into this bullshit."

"I'm gay and I don't know you very well," I said. "But I think I'm in love."

*

When Wednesdays rolled around, I had a major case of the empties. I had stopped by Aids Project Los Angeles, Shanti and a couple of the hospices in the last weeks and all of them had miles-long waiting lists for new volunteers. "We're always looking for a monetary contribution," said a coordinator at the Necessities of Life Program.

"That is one area I definitely can't help," I said.

One Wednesday afternoon, I came home from the gym to find my partner cutting up his clothes. "Start a new screenplay," Kyle said as he ripped the sleeves off a flannel shirt then buttoned himself into some Daisy Duke shorts that threatened to reveal his testicles. I was too stunned to respond to his suggestion about writing. His muscular limbs were tan and shaven and popped from his outfit's ragged edges. The Doc Martins he was wearing had three-inch soles and made him unnervingly tall, at least six foot seven. As he admired himself in the mirror, he looked like Bruce Banner halfway to becoming the Hulk. This new look made me anxious — it didn't say "I'm spoken for" but was more of an advertisement, a neon sign of sexual availability. Nothing about it was appealing to me — it was blatant, a caricature, and bordered on the grotesque. Looking at him I couldn't imagine we had once been sexually obsessed with each other.

"What?" he said when he noticed me staring.

"Nothing. I'm just... getting used to your... new style."

"Did you hear what I said? Start another screenplay."

"I don't have an *idea* for a screenplay. These are not funny times."

"Then write a drama. Write *some*thing, Tyler. You're reaching the cutoff point."

"What cutoff point?"

"Thirty-five. If you haven't made it by then, you probably never will. There was a big article about it in *The Sunday Times*."

"I read it. Speaking of age, maybe you are a little too old for the Seattle grunge look."

"That's your issue. I'm Gen X. You're a boomer."

"You were born in 1960. Gen X is '65 and after. Are you sure you're not too old to be chasing the next youth movement?"

Kyle smirked and reached for a spray can of minoxidil on the dresser and spritzed his hairline. His head had been getting more egg-like. "I'm sure," he said.

"Where are you going?" I asked.

"Improv class."

"I thought that was last night."

"And tonight too. Different group. You bartending tonight?"

"No, I'm off," I said, wishing I was doing *something*. Once again, I was being left alone for the evening to wonder where Kyle really went at night.

"Write something. At some point AIDS will be over. And then where will you be?"

"I might be dead. If I am alive, I want to be able to say that I fought, that I helped."

"You've done plenty. Now do something for you."

Kyle had a point. And maybe — just maybe — my karma had changed. Perhaps all that helping energy I had put out there would return to me. Perhaps the souls of friends I had helped through this crisis were working together and lobbying God to shed his grace on me. Perhaps in one of the screenplays that Allen had bequeathed to me was some exciting seed that could grow into something strong and beautiful: a fruit-filled tree I could build a house in. I decided to sit down and read them.

The terrific monster movie, titled *Too Small to Keep*, took place on a catfish farm in Alabama. A genetic modification caused the fish to grow as big as whales but soon they were eating humans instead of the other way around. The next script was a buddy movie — very popular at the moment — called *Pre-op Cop* about a policeman who has to deal with his partner's sex change while they hunt down a serial killer. Guess who gets married in the end. The last one, a drama, was so weirdly awful it was fascinating. *A Hustle Here and a Hustle There* was a love triangle between a middle-aged Episcopalian priest, the priest's daughter and the man they both love: a male prostitute who went both ways. The hustler promises to love them both and swears off his profession but not before taking one last trick —with a serial killer called Inches who collected severed penises.

I was rolling up the screenplays as logs for the fireplace when the phone rang.

"Tyler! It's Kevin Darrington. Did I catch you at a good time?"

"An extremely good time. What's up, Kev?"

"We're up and running! We've found a kitchen and found a somebody to lend her name to our food service."

"Who'd you get?"

"Lakshmi Steinmetz."

"Who?"

"She's this new age speaker, one of the Four Metaphysicians. She lectures at theosophical lodges, places like that."

"Metaphysicians?"

"Also known as the Four Fag Hags of the Apocalypse. They're these women offering people with AIDS comfort through prayer and other New Age claptrap. Lakshmi's the standout. She's one of the cofounders of the Being Center, a place where you can get lunch and a massage, do some yoga and feel a little less alone. She said yes!"

"The *Being* Center? I used to take Allen there. One time I dropped him off at something called a Love-a-Thon. It was run by some kook named Eloise Clayman."

"Yes, I know all about the controversial Ms. Clayman and her claim that she beat her pancreatic cancer by praying it away."

"From what I've read, a cancer that was never medically documented."

"Correct. This is what we have instead of a cure, Tyler — glue guns offering hope."

"Glue guns?"

"Oh...it's a theater arts expression that's a little kinder than 'fag hag.' Every time you're building a set you turn around and there's a fat girl with a glue gun."

I was quiet for a moment.

"Tyler, I'm sorry, did I offend you?"

"No, not really," I said, as I thought about all the glue guns I knew and loved. "Is Lakshmi fat?"

"Used to be. She's kind of anorexic now. Thin as a licorice stick."

"Where do I sign up?"

Chapter 2

Manna from Heaven was coming together in the kitchen of a church built in the 1920s in the Mission Revival style. On one side was an old neon sign with broken tubes that spelled out West Hollywood Methodist. Outside on the sidewalk was a thicket of alcoholics and their lit cigarettes whose twelve-step meetings had ended or were about to begin. Inside the building was the faintly sickening smell of all old churches with notes of mildew, mustiness and mice. The dull wooden floors had not been waxed in decades and the stained glass windows were broken or cracked. I trotted up some creaking stairs to the spacious community room which had an impressive stage and velvet curtains covered in decades of dust. In the middle of the room was a circle of women glaring at me from their folding chairs as I walked past.

"Excuse me, sir," said their leader, a professional-looking woman with an asymmetrical bob as she stood and glowered at me in her skirt suit. "But this is a women's stag meeting."

"Sorry? I'm looking for Manna from Heaven."

"Over there," she said, pointing to a folding table outside of a kitchen near a swinging door and a wall of indoor windows. I looked from the leader to the faces of the other stag women as they stared at me in hatred.

"Thanks. Sorry. No intentions to interrupt your meeting. Hope you resolve all your issues," I said and heard them gasp and cluck their tongues and someone whispered "Rude."

I exhaled, shook it off and walked toward some much friendlier faces: a woman on the phone behind the table with a man my age who was ripping the edges from a dot matrix printout. He had a Kay-Pro computer circa 1984 that was somehow still working. "Hi, I'm here to volunteer," I said after the woman hung up.

"You *are*? Thank you!" said the woman in the upper register of a soprano as she rose up on three-inch spikes and clasped her hands. She was wearing a cobalt-colored blouse that enhanced the deep blue of her eyes and looked happily astonished, as if I had just brought a sack of gold to an orphanage facing eviction. Somewhere in her forties, she had a mass of blonde hair in a 60's flip-do, some pink lipstick from the same era, and she wore the kind of bra that made her ample boobs as pointy as torpedoes — very va-va-voom as they used to say.

"I'm Jonnie," she said. "Let's get you a name tag." She was reaching for some stickers that said "Hi, my name is" at the top when the man at the table swiped them from her. He was dressed in a black button-down shirt and glimmering from his thick chest hair was a string of pearls. His hair was an impressive globe of ebony curls that was almost as wide as his shoulders, which reminded me of Marc Bolan, the 70's glam rocker from

T-Rex. He scribbled on a name tag and handed it to me. It read "Cutie Pie Guy."

"Uh, actually my name is Tyler."

"Not anymore," he said and laughed. "So what's your boyfriend's name?"

"Kyle."

"Wrong answer. You're supposed to say 'I don't have a boyfriend' so we can go on a date." He laughed at his own joke, baring his teeth.

Jonnie looked comically pained as she playfully slapped the man's arm. "Just ignore Jericho," she said to me. "He's harmless… mostly."

"Jericho? Your name is *Jericho*?" I asked.

"Jericho," he said with his toothy smile and handed me a corrected name tag. "Let the walls come tumblin' down."

"Go on in, Tyler, tie on an apron and wash your hands!" said Jonnie. "Ask Tim what you can do! He's our chef!"

"Um, don't I need to sign in? Fill out some forms?"

"Just jump in! We're so very glad to have you! Later on if you want to leave your name and number with Jericho, you'll be welcome to."

Mildly stunned, I staggered through a swinging door into a beat up kitchen. A single fluorescent light fixture hung from dust covered chains and one of its tubes was out. The cutting counter in the center was covered with a warped particle board. The white walls and cabinets had not seen fresh paint in decades and had a patina of smoke and grime. The floor was a checkerboard of black-and-white linoleum tiles that were chipped and broken with muck embedded between their grooves.

Tim was pear-shaped and wore his shorts belted above his navel. He was in his fifties and more than fifty pounds overweight, but he scooted around the kitchen with the joyful vigor of a young man. "Where's rosemary? That bitch!" he said, giggling at his own joke as he looked through bottles of dried herbs in a spice cabinet. Standing near him were volunteers cutting slices of a raw brisket with an aqua-colored electric knife from 1965.

"Tim, I'm Tyler. How can I help you?"

He giggled. "I can think of all kinds of ways," he said. "But for right now, you can roll up some beef rouladen. I'll never forget the first time I made these," he said, suddenly girlish, his dyed lashes flapping. "After we threw on the cheese and threw 'em in the oven, Chef Carl threw me in the pantry and *raped* me — took him exactly twelve minutes. The oven timer went off just as we were pulling our pants up." He sighed wistfully as two younger, fresh-faced volunteers were giving him the sideways glare. Both were tall, blond and good-looking and were either brothers, lovers or best friends.

"Of course, I was young and pretty then," Tim said, coming out of his memory. "Like you, young man."

"Well, thanks for calling me young," I said.

People at Manna from Heaven were very flirtatious!

"Boys, let's wrap some brownies," Tim said to the volunteers. "Now we always wash our hands after touching raw meat -- pun intended — so let's all get over to the sink." As we waited to wash up, the blonds introduced themselves.

"I'm Jeremy," said the taller of them with a soft and aristocratic Southern accent. "Now, don't you mind Tim." he whispered. "He's always talking sex but he's no lech."

"I'm Joffrey," said the other, with a touch of a mid-Atlantic accent, as if he were talking over a pencil tucked in the back of his molars. "Tim reminds us that when we reach a certain age it is best we not recount our sexual episodes in public. But he is a very nice gentleman."

"With a good heart," said Jeremy.

"I can tell," I said. "He's a sweetheart."

"And right now he's doing this job for nothing. I think I know you, Tyler. Didn't you used to write for Galaxy Films?"

"I did. Wait, you're Jeremy Pindor. You wrote Snatcherella… about the talking vagina."

"Don't remind me. And you wrote Hell-a-Vision, about the demons that come out of a TV set and haunt people's toilets."

"Don't remind me. It's the last time I worked. Well, as a screen writer."

"We're in the same little boat."

I looked over to see Tim talking to the pans of rouladen as he slid them into a pink-colored, electric Kenmore oven with a cracked glass window circa 1962. "Don't burn," he said. "Stay nice and juicy!" He joined us at the sink and scrubbed up as if preparing for surgery. I felt a radiating warmth from him and liked him — even if he was baking pickles in meat.

While the rouladen baked in the oven, we focused on pans of something that looked more like rustic floor tiles than brownies. I was using a knife to cut around the brownies' edges when they shattered. Tim's pan of brownies shattered as well. "I don't think we can send these out," he whispered, not wanting to offend an amateur baker who had kindly done her best.

"I think someone forgot to add the flour," I said, "or got this confused with a recipe for peanut brittle."

When the rouladen were ready, we made an assembly line and slid them into aluminum containers with some hand-mashed potatoes and buttered string beans. The containers were sealed and then plunked into a grocery bag with an address list taped to its side. Jonnie hugged each one of the drivers when they arrived and they left her arms to pitch in with the packing. When all the bags were ready, everyone gathered in a circle and held hands, looking like the Whos in Whoville about to carol around the stump of what had been their Christmas tree. I went to the sink and started scrubbing pans.

"Tyler? Would you like to join us?" Jonnie called to me.

"For what?"

"Prayer circle."

"Oh... so this is a Christian group?"

"Christian and Jewish and Buddhist and whatever else. We're not religious, we're *spiritual*."

I joined the circle and took Tim's hand and that of a total stranger as Jonnie looked at each of us, smiling and bringing us to her attention.

"God has sent us new volunteers today!" she said. "Welcome to Noah, Lisa and Tyler!"

The volunteers broke hands to applaud us.

"And God has welcomed home some of our clients," Jonnie said, suddenly serious. "We say goodbye today to Anthony Granger,

Jimmy Lehrman and Carlos Portillo. God, let your angels take every shortcut through the clouds and bring them straight to heaven."

We were quiet a moment. After that, the volunteers mentioned the names of men on their routes or in their lives who needed some of "God's healing energy" or some "special prayers."

"And finally," Jonnie said, "For my own prayer, please God, our volunteer who drives to Compton has his own health issue today. Please send us someone to do that route."

"I'll do it," I said. "I've never been to Compton."

"You will? Thank you, God!" said Jonnie, looking up at the ceiling. "And thank you, Tyler!"

As I looked at the faces of the men and women in that circle I started crying. I tried to stop my tears but couldn't as a rush of feelings overwhelmed me. Here in this room were men and women who felt like I did, who were worried, grieving, and frustrated but determined to do *something* to make life a little better for those who were losing theirs.

"Tyler, are you OK?" Jonnie asked.

"I'm fine," I said. "These are happy tears."

I had an inner vision of my whole life taking a right turn. I was leaving some bleak, sunburned plain and in front of me was a curving, tree-lined road that climbed into cool and misty mountains.

Chapter 3

Compton was some place I had only ever driven through atop the freeway slicing through it. At eye level, it was a place of tiny Baptist churches, fried chicken outlets, wig shops and liquor stores. I parked and walked to my last drop-off, a neglected, low-slung bungalow with a grassless yard. Through the screen door I saw Kenny Calnan, a young and skeletal Black man lying on a mattress on the floor. He was watching a rerun of The Magilla Gorilla Show on an eight-inch black-and-white television and he only briefly made eye contact. The smell of the urine he was lying in hit my nose like a brick. I said hello and silently he took the container from me. Empty containers were scattered across and around the mattress. Wordlessly, he began eating with his fingers. He didn't respond when I asked him if there was anybody looking after him.

On my way back, I stopped at a payphone to tell Jonnie about Kenny's situation before I drove to the pristine grandeur of Beverly Hills to pick up eight scripts to read and analyze for Dino

De Laurentiis Productions. The first one was called *It's a Gas* and it was 104 pages of fart jokes.

A day after the scripts were synopsized and analyzed (I called *It's a Gas* a "real stinker") I returned to De Laurentiis where they had a new stack just waiting for me. In the last five years I had read perhaps five or six thousand screenplays and enjoyed fewer than fifty of them. The sight of eight new scripts was literally nauseating. Light in the head, I stumbled when Nancy, a D-girl (short for female development executive) handed them to me. I dropped on my knees to the ground, spilling them on the carpet. I had blacked out.

"Uh oh," she said. "You've cindered."

"Cindered?" I said.

"Burned-out. I've been expecting it. Happened to me a few years ago."

"It did?"

"Why do you think we hire readers? Take care of yourself, Tyler. You need some water? Some vodka?"

I went straight to Manna from Heaven to peel potatoes and carrots and cut hunks of beef for Irish stew. When that was done, Tim asked me if I would like to scoop the dessert, a berry crumble, into plastic containers. He handed me pans of purple sludge with what looked like hunks of plywood pressed into their centers. Whoever had made this thought somehow the crumble part would magically spread itself over the fruit in the baking process. The "crumble" upended when I stuck a spoon in it and looked like a goop-coated shingle.

"Tim, can I try baking something for tomorrow?" I asked when I showed him the mess.

"Why not?" he answered. "See what you can find up there."

I went up the flight of stairs to a pantry in the attic and found shelves that were stuffed with donations from the kitchens of people whose grandmothers had died. There were ancient cans of Vienna sausages, sardines, beets and jars of Mrs. Adler's Gefilte Fish as well as schmaltz, borscht, bread-and-butter pickles and some dented cans of Rotel diced tomatoes. I found a bag of flour, some baking chocolate, half a sack of lumpy sugar and an opened bottle of vanilla extract. I knew there was butter and eggs in the fridge downstairs and though I had no recipe, no measuring cups or even a mixer, I managed to make some decent brownies that were shatterproof. While they were cooling, Jonnie trotted up to me, her hands clasped together and looking at me with pleading eyes.

"Tyler, can you drive over to Roseanne and Tom's house?"

"Roseanne? Like Roseanne Barr?"

"Roseanne Arnold now. They've gone vegetarian and want to donate some frozen meat!"

"OK," I said.

"Thank you!" Jonnie said. "You're an angel!"

I figured I'd get a chance to see where Tom and Roseanne lived, maybe meet them when they invited me inside. It was a forty-five minute drive to Santa Monica in noon traffic before I reached the mansion the Arnolds were renting. I pressed a buzzer at the driveway gate and a Latina woman answered through the intercom.

"Yes?"

"Hi. I'm here to pick up some meat," I said.

"Some meat?"

"Yes. Frozen meat."

"One minute."

I heard her conferring with someone else in Spanish before the intercom cut out.

"I found it," she said a few minutes later. "I be right down." *OK, I'm not invited in,* I thought, expecting a team of domestics would be marching toward my car with fifty-pound boxes of frozen prime rib and filet mignons from Omaha Steak. Instead, a woman dressed in a polyester maid's outfit walked down the drive with a ziplock bag. Inside it were three frost-burned steaks and a pork chop. As I stared at it I thought, *Fuck you, Tom and Roseanne. Don't you have a dog?*

"Tell them thank you," I said.

When I returned, Tim was taking a break, sharing an extra brownie with a younger man wearing a T-shirt the color of salmon mousse that accentuated the pinkness of his skin — he was a "spring" in the Color Me Beautiful fad of the time. This new guy had blond, poofy hair that he lightened to a further degree and had eyes that were the faintest green. His demeanor was both diffident and haughty, and with his goatish facial features, he reminded me of the fay noblemen in a Fragonard painting. "Tyler, this is Gene. He's going to take over for me on Wednesdays, Thursdays and Fridays."

"Very nice to meet you," said Gene, extending his hand. "Gene Sitz. How do you do?"

"I'm very well indeed," I said, returning his formality. "Tyler St. George. How do *you* do?"

"You're a good baker, Tyler."

"You are," said Tim. "This brownie is delicious."

"We didn't have any baking powder," I said. "I whipped up the eggs with the sugar to get some air into it then folded in the chocolate after melting it in the butter. It would help if we had a mixer," I said. "And a measuring cup and spoons."

Jonnie entered the kitchen. I showed her the bag of meat the Arnolds had so generously donated.

"Where's the rest of it?" she asked. "Do you need a hand?"

"This is it."

"Oh, *seriously*?"

"Uh, it's the thought that counts?" I said.

"I hate to send you back out, but a production company called — just ten minutes away in Hancock Park. They just wrapped on a shoot and say they've got a *ton* of food left over. Can you do it?"

"Sure," I said. At least Jonnie was sending me to classy areas that day. I headed for Los Angeles's old money neighborhood where they were shooting a Halloween special at a grand Victorian mansion. I recognized people I knew from film school who were winding cords and breaking down lights and we pretended not to see each other while working in lowly positions. Someone with a clipboard pointed me to the set dresser who was supervising the gathering of at least fifty shriveled pumpkins that were charred black on the inside and had faces cut into them. "Hi," I said. "I'm here to pick up a food donation for Manna from Heaven."

"Are you by yourself?" the set dresser asked. His left sideburn was trimmed in the shape of a hammer while the right was in the shape of a wrench.

"Just me," I said. "Where's the food?"

"This is the food. Pumpkins. Did you bring any boxes?"

"Oh," I said. "I don't think we can use these."

"Why not? We figured you could make pies out of them."

"No, not really. These are ornamental pumpkins, not pie or sugar pumpkins. It's too labor-intensive. We'd have to peel and scrape and skin and puree after baking. Better just to open a can."

"Oh," he said, offended. "So you won't take them?"

"I really can't. But thank you."

The set designer was upset now, but I was not loading up my car with some fucking jack-o-lanterns.

"I have some food," said a voice behind us. It was the craft service guy whose job was to keep a supply of snacks and drinks available to the crew at all times. He boxed together a half-empty tin of Danish butter cookies, an opened bag of peanut M&Ms, some Mr. Salty Pretzels and one intact but cold pizza congealing in its box.

I returned with my treasures and told Jonnie, "I think we have to screen a little better. I would ask in a nice way just what they have to offer."

"You're right," she said. "But it's not just food they're offering. They're offering love, like we do! Speaking of which — and you can say no, Tyler — but on Saturday, there's this major food giveaway sponsored by Gary Arceneaux!"

"The music executive?"

"Yes! If you're not busy, can you help Tim out and drive downtown and help him load his station wagon? You'll have to get up good and early because it starts at seven. They've promised fifteen hundred dollars worth of food for us!"

"Well... sure."

"After that, you'll have just enough time to come to our pancake breakfast at Saint Stephens — if you like. It's our first official fundraiser and Lakshmi will be giving a lecture! Have you ever heard her?"

"I never have."

"You *haven't*? She's amazing! You will absolutely love her!"

Six a.m. is the middle of the night for me, but I met Tim on Saturday at his suburban tract house in the flats of Sherman Oaks. He invited me inside his conventionally decorated home with its broken-in Early American furniture and framed Currier and Ives prints. It looked more like a home in Fort Wayne than Los Angeles and it surprised me because he said he had worked as an interior designer. We drove in his old Buick station wagon with its peeling wood paneling deep into LA's warehouse district where there was a mile-long line of cars. The media was out in full force and on the lookout for sports and music celebrities who had all come to "pitch in." As we inched up to the head of the line, a TV reporter with platinum hair and a canary-yellow skirt suit knocked on our window. After Tim cranked it down, she thrust in a mic while a cameraman pointed his lens at us. "What organization are you from?" she asked with white teeth gleaming through painted lips.

"Manna from Heaven," said Tim.

"And who do you provide for?"

"People with AIDS."

Her face fell and they moved on.

At last, we reached the head of the line. When we stepped out of the car, some young Black men wearing USC letterman jackets threw heavy boxes at us. "Oof," said Tim when the first box hit his stomach, but he hustled and made the catch. Two lighter boxes were shoved at us and before we could say thanks, someone shouted, "You up!" to the next car. Gary Arceneaux, dressed in a three-piece suit, stood with Whitney Houston on a dais and shook hands with a city councilman, all of them holding up pretty, ribboned baskets bulging with fresh fruits and vegetables. The cameras rolled and flashbulbs popped.

"What do you think they gave us?" I asked Tim as we drove away.

"Not fresh vegetables in a ribboned basket. I think I broke my thumb catching that box." He held up his thumb, which had swollen.

Tim pulled over to an abandoned gas station and we got out and opened one of the cartons. Inside it were 144 tiny jars of some failed product called Wok Magik. I opened a jar and found a shriveled lump of garlic, chicken bouillon and salt inside.

"What the fuck?" I said.

We opened the other boxes and inside these were packages of Noodle Roni Parmesano. The picture of the Golden Gate Bridge on the front was faded and the expiration label read "Best Before June 1981."

"Eight years old! Useless," I said. "They may as well have taken a shit in this box. This is just some asshole making room in his warehouse and some other asshole promoting a record."

"Utterly useless," Tim said.

"Utterly fucking useless."

"UFU."

"Let's go back there and dump it out in front of the press. And then pelt Gary and Whitney with these little bottles."

"No," said Tim, trying not to laugh. "I think it's best we forgive and forget. C'mon, let's go and get some pancakes and see Lakshmi. I could really use one of her lectures this morning."

"Her lectures?"

"They always make me feel better. *She* makes me feel better."

We were quiet a moment, feeling foolish, as we drove through Little Guatemala where the streets were filling with Central Americans selling rags, old shoes and salvaged trash in piles on the sidewalk. Tim sighed and looked sad and worried.

"How'd you get involved with Manna?" I asked.

"I used to take Samuel to Lakshmi's lectures."

"Samuel?"

"My lover, Sam. I lost him last year. Now I'm about to lose my house."

"I'm sorry, Tim."

"I need roommates if you know anyone. And I'm sorry to say this, but it's got to be someone who doesn't have AIDS — and someone who has a job. Thank God they're going to start paying me for this one in a few weeks."

"They're still not paying you?"

"Not yet. It's OK... it's better that what money we have goes to food for the clients."

It is said that Episcopalians have more money than Methodists and that was definitely the case at Saint Stephens near WeHo. It was a well-maintained, gothic-style church with a gilded sanctuary, a comfy community room and a separate eating hall with windows that looked out on a rose garden. Tim and I were hungry and thinking we were too late for breakfast when we entered to find about a hundred gay men and a few women holding plates, looking at the kitchen door and quietly complaining. Everyone was wearing a name tag, half of which were upside down.

"What's with the upside-down tags?" I asked Tim as I slapped one on.

"It means you're single," he said. "And if it's on your right, it means you're positive." I could see an awful lot of those. As for the beauty quotient of the crowd, I thought it was exceptional, rivaling that of Studio One Disco on a Saturday night... before the plague took root.

Jonnie tottered over on her heels to us, trying to conceal her panic. "They might need a hand in there," she whispered, jerking her head toward the kitchen.

We entered and found some volunteers panicked in their failure to produce pancakes. No one was in charge. The batter in a large basin was so thick that it didn't pour and they were using a serving spoon to fling globs of it onto an ungreased griddle where it stuck and burned.

"They won't flatten!" said a guy at the griddle, trying to squash them with a spatula.

"The batter's too thick," I said. "Have we got a couple of gallons of milk? And a whisk? How about a ladle?"

"And somebody get me some Crisco," said Tim as he turned down the flame and scraped the grill clean. "And not for what you're thinking, tee-hee."

A short time later we had hundreds of pancakes. Without a batter chute, they were all different sizes, but when the first platter went out the door, we heard the type of cheering the Stones get when they take the stage. When everybody had a short stack, Tim and I made some for ourselves, competing to see who could make the most phallic flapjack. Tim went for a long erect dong in profile and I went for a flaccid, frontal approach that included testicles. "I have just the thing," Tim said after finding some chocolate sprinkles which he shook onto the balls to suggest pubic hair. We were laughing when Jonnie entered, hands clasped before her and her mouth agape. "You guys saved the day!" she said. "Come on out and take a bow!"

Jonnie, with her fists raised in triumph, led us out to the community room then picked up the microphone and said, "Let's hear it for the cooks!"

As everybody clapped, the other kitchen guys pointed to me and Tim, and two of them took clean plates and held them behind our heads as halos. I looked out on a sea of smiling faces as applause shot through us like warm bullets of chocolate-dipped love. We walked over to the community room to take seats for the main attraction, Lakshmi Steinmetz, where I had hopes of falling in love... or at least experiencing a little more dopamine.

Chapter 4

The expected way this story would go would be to tell everyone that when I first heard Lakshmi speak that a hundred thousand lights went on in my brain and that the psychic trash that crowded my head was recycled into a miraculous and liberating vision.

The truth is I was a little bored. And a little irritated. It reminded me of something I just couldn't place, something so embarrassing I'd forgotten it.

Jonnie, acting excited, sounded as strident as a piccolo as she stepped on the dais with a wireless mic and made the introduction. "Please welcome... Lakshmi Steinmetz!" A man at an audio board was out in the open at a folding table instead of in a booth. He played some peppy music that sounded like the theme for a game show.

During the sustained applause, a woman strutted across the dais looking determined and serious, an authority who came off as cold and reprimanding even before she spoke. She was wearing a well-fitting and expensive pantsuit on her trim frame and her dark hair with red highlights was the work of a well-paid professional. Some gold earrings of a South Asian design lent her a touch of the exotic and tied into the name she'd given herself: Lakshmi, the Hindu goddess of prosperity and love. Lakshmi had features that are often described as angular, but it was her long and pointy chin that kept her out of the beautiful column and put her in the kinda cute camp, a lot like Nancy Reagan. She pointed at the man at the audio board.

"Was that music?" she snapped at him. He reddened and shrugged. "I didn't ask for music. We'll talk later," she said. Visibly annoyed, she shook her head and exhaled. "Let's start over," she said with a forced grin and then started her lecture with a meditative prayer. "God has invited us all to a floating temple of silver and gold that glistens under a sphere of perfect light. Come with me to a place of pure love with steps to a door that opens to a vision of God where he reigns in peace in his perfect universe."

Her lecture that day, in observation of Yom Kippur, was pitched at the many people facing health crises and at others with the more typical dissatisfactions of life in Los Angeles. Her main message was the same as that of her friend Eloise Clayman: forgiveness of ourselves and others could heal illness, that the ultimate atoning was not in making amends for our own sins, but in forgiving those of others. She mentioned that for traditional Jews, the Day of Atonement commemorated when Adam and Eve were banished from the Garden of Eden.

"Let me explain what the same story means in terms of *The Way of the Miraculous*," she said, which I gathered was a book of modern prophecy. "The point of this allegory is that when God created the first humans, they were connected and one with God's love, the perfect Childrenhood. They were banished to the world of illusion for giving into the real temptation: ego, which was the forbidden fruit sold to them by a lying used car salesman of a snake. They were suddenly aware of themselves, seeing themselves as separate from creation, separate from God, separate from each other. And as for Eve, we can't blame her for the downfall of humankind — she was doing what any decent wife would do — she was sharing her food with her husband."

That was the first of a few laughs. She was kind of making sense and kind of making profound nonsense. Lakshmi spoke without cards, made dramatic use of her hands, strutted back and forth like a televangelist and had a presence that was Old Hollywood. She had some of Crawford's hardness and diction and some of Davis's superiority. Her haughty laugh and the upward tilt of her chin was a little bit of Hepburn.

The talk had no discernible structure but she presented her ideas with conviction, if not clarity, before she started to repeat herself. Some of what she said could be mistaken as Christian Science and its related system, New Thought, from the nineteenth century, with its infusions of Hinduism and Buddhism. Lakshmi told us that "sickness is *maya*, an illusion, something like a nightmare. The cure for sickness, physical and mental, is to ask God to remove the illusion. If you are sick, you are asleep and you are *dreaming* you are ill — you are having an *ill*-lusion. The best medicine is to ask God to wake you up, to join him in the reality of his unending love."

Lakshmi ended her lecture by asking those who had brought their copy of *The Way of the Miraculous* to turn to a passage on atonement. The man next to me offered to share and as I glanced over the pages, I saw the words "Jesus," "resurrection" and "Holy Spirit" as well as this thing called "the Childrenhood."

Just what was this reminding me of?

Lakshmi read aloud: "Atonement is the end of sickness for sickness is separation from God. Healing is to unite with God and uniting with God is atonement or at-one-ment."

As I read through other passages of *The Way*, I saw a lot of these circuitous sentences. "To love your Self is to love God who loves all his children. To hate your Self is to hate God and to hate all his children." "Be unashamed to be desperate for love, for love is desperate to be unashamed." "To know your enemy is to know your ego but ego is an illusion that can never know You."

She paused for a moment, set her chin on the back of her knuckles and looked thoughtful — a gesture that struck me as supremely affected — as her eyes flashed at inner visions. Her hands turned up and tensed as a tremolo entered her voice. "Webster defines atone as 'to make amends for.' But we deny the God that is both within and without us if we do not atone for our separation from him. When we do atone with God, we are *at one* with him, we are cured, in both body and spirit. The *real sin*, the real *dis*-ease is the enslavement to *ego*. Ego is *banished* when we accept that only love is real and *God… is… only love*! Thank you."

God is only love? I thought. *So he's made up of norepinephrine, dopamine, and serotonin?*

The audience applauded, long and hard, and for the first time since she'd taken the stage, Lakshmi smiled in a way that seemed real. She liked the rush of applause and the sea of faces that looked at her in awe and gratitude. I was feeling just the same way a short while ago when I was worshipped as the Pancake God.

Jonnie stood and entered the aisle to commence the second part of the show, the passing of the mic. I was sifting through memories, still trying to figure out why this all felt familiar when a young, fastidiously groomed man wearing a leather motorcycle jacket took the microphone. Though he was as pretty as any soap actor with an enviable head of coal-black hair, Wink's name tag indicated he was single as well as HIV-negative.

"Good morning, Lakshmi," he said with the trained voice of a Broadway actor. "I am in darkness over career frustrations. I have come so close in recent auditions only to learn I was the second choice, the backup. I have got so much to give and no one will let me give it. Hollywood is looking like an unhappy, unhealthy place... more like Toxicwood."

Lakshmi nodded as the crowd chuckled. "So you're thinking about leaving... on that midnight train to Georgia."

Everyone laughed, me included.

"But you know," she said looking left then looking right, playing the thoughtful coquette. "Something tells me you don't smack your head in the morning and think, 'I should have been a dentist.'"

Laughter again. "Correct," said Wink.

"You must honor yourself for pursuing your dream, Wink.

For every one of you who has come out here to act or sing or dance, there are ten thousand more who stayed at home and put that dream in a shoebox that gathers dust in the attic. If performing is what you love to do, you will find a way to do it. It may not be for an audience of hundreds of thousands, it may be just for a lucky few. But you *will* perform, and you'll know someone else is watching you and loving you for giving it your all… God."

The actor nodded and looked choked up as he brushed at a tear. A moment later, a lovely actress on the edge of forty told a similar story. After a series of national commercials — the kind that paid over $100,000 dollars with residuals — she was out of work. "My career has gone cold," said Melba. "The phone has… has…"

She looked around the room, her face an avalanche of despair as we waited for her to finish.

"It's stopped ringing."

"This is a time of uncertainty for you, of defeat," Lakshmi said. "But the last thing that will serve you is to wallow in negativity, to abandon hope. You've separated from God if you don't see his love now, if you see your recent disappointments as failures instead of stepping stones, if you don't see this time in your life as a transition, not as something that has passed. This is a time for you to count your blessings… and it's an opportunity to give. Can you give, Melba? For yourself and for your fellow humans?"

She nodded as she teared up.

Next up was one of several women in the audience who was dressed like Lakshmi and had borrowed her hairstyle and was also wearing *jhumka*-type earrings. Betsy had the look of the lovelorn with her stooped shoulders and downcast expression. She had the slow cadence of depression in her voice and it was obvious Lakshmi knew her, would have preferred to ignore her, and was impatient with her as she choked out her question.

"I... I met someone... new... recently... and... and he..."

"Where did you meet him?" Lakshmi asked.

"In a... bar," said the woman.

"Oh, this is sounding promising already," said Lakshmi to her biggest laugh that morning.

"No, no, he... he said he was *spiritual*," Betsy said, with just the slightest defensiveness. "And he mentioned coming from yoga and talked a lot about working on himself to make himself available."

"This is just getting better," said Lakshmi. "He's working on himself to make himself available. Any end date on that project?"

More laughter... I was feeling sorry for Betsy.

"How many drinks did you have with him?" Lakshmi asked.

"I... I don't remember."

"You don't *remember*? Everybody... whenever you drink, be sure to count them. When I started counting, that's when I realized I had a problem. Go on, Betsy, please."

"I've seen him a few times since our night together... and we... he wants to...just wants to..."

"Betsy, we know what he *just* wants to do. But one thing he doesn't want to do is take you out to dinner or to see a movie or to ever introduce you to his parents."

"But he *says* he does. The problem is..."

"Betsy, the problem is that you let him buy you a drink."

After another big laugh, Lakshmi looked straight into Betsy's eyes and said, "You are looking for a man to come along and complete you. But the only thing that can complete you is God. Look to him first for your perfect love and you won't be vulnerable to this kind of user."

Another woman reached for the mic, and in her own designer pantsuit, she looked like Lakshmi's younger, better-looking sister. "Lakshmi, I've got like, just the opposite problem. I'm with a man who totally wants to marry me but I don't know that I want to *be* married... at least not until I've got my career going and stuff. He's a really, *really* great guy, really cute, and a lawyer, but he doesn't work in entertainment. Does *The Way* have anything to say about my situation?"

Lakshmi looked surprised, as if the woman had told her that she had a ticket with all six numbers of Lotto America but was unsure about claiming the millions. "So, you have someone decent who wants to marry you and you're *not sure about it?*"

Lakshmi clutched her necklace, looked distant for a moment and then scoffed. "*The Way* says everything and nothing about what we should or shouldn't do. I would pray about this — and if you love him and he's the decent man you think he is, I would definitely consider accepting his proposal!"

Lakshmi turned to a man an aisle over who struggled to rise then leaned on a gnarly walking stick with a brass knob of a dragon head with red glass eyes. Legolas was single and his name tag did not need to be on the left to let you know he was HIV positive. He was emaciated and his mouse-like ears protruded through long and thinning curls. At the end of his leather necklace was a pewter miniature of the White Tree of Gondor.

"I been outta touch with my folks for the last five years," he said with a backwoods accent. "They rejected me when I tol' 'em I was a homasekshal. They tol' me to git out and said I should move to Hollywood if I wanted to be queer. So I did."

"I'm sorry," said Lakshmi. "I am so very sorry."

"So'm I. I called 'em last month to tell them I was dyin'," he said, then started coughing. "Scuze me," he said, and coughed some more. He sounded like he might blow his lungs out.

"Just take your time," Lakshmi said, and Legolas did. Everyone quietly waited.

"They wouldn't talk to me," he said, recovering. "But they sent me a letter. They spoke to their preacher who told 'em I should pray for forgiveness while I was alive, do what I *could* to git right with God — that he might let me in to heaven if I renounce my ways and repent."

"Sounds like you need to forgive your parents," said Lakshmi. "What would you like to ask me?"

"I don't know what to say to them," he said, and we watched as the cane he was leaning on trembled with the rest of his body. "Part of me wants to say... go fuck yerselves, ya stupid trash. Is this how ya show love to yer son?"

A heavy silence fell on the crowd. Lakshmi looked compassionate, gathered her thoughts, nodded quietly. "Of course you want to say that," she finally said. "They should be showing you compassion, Legolas, but they are victims of ignorance, and submerged in illusion. You can heal your own spirit by forgiving them and seeing this attempt to save you *is* love, *real* love, and it is a genuine concern for you. Write them and thank them for their concern. Then tell them you know that God loves all of us, unconditionally, and that he would never let anyone burn in a place called Hell after we shed this suit of flesh and bones. *The Way* tells us that our birth is one chapter and our death is another in the unending book of life. Ask God to help you write a happy ending for this particular chapter."

Legolas nodded, satisfied with her answer. He slowly set his bony bottom back on his chair with the help of neighbors who held his arms. Sighs of relief followed as everyone's breathing returned to normal. I was thinking that aging children had come to church that morning looking for love, guidance and discipline from a stern mother when a man took the mic and said it for me. "I don't have a question, Lakshmi. I just want to say that since I've been listening to your tapes and studying *The Way*, my life has turned around. It has been, well... miraculous! Now that I have this chance, I just want to say... I love you!"

The crowd gave a collective "Ahh," as if a hundred puppies had licked a hundred faces. "Thank you, I love you too," Lakshmi said after a melodious laugh. "I have time for one more question." She pointed to a young blonde woman in the back who had been sitting in the lotus position in her chair.

"Lakshmi, hello. Wonderful talk today, as usual. I have friends who I think would embrace your message, but they're scientists at Cal Tech and they're a very skeptical bunch. One of them said he rejected the very premise of *The Way* since it's rooted in prophecy. What can I tell them?"

Lakshmi's face froze in an angry smile. "I… I'm sorry," she said, as her voice went from alto to a sharp and squeaky soprano and a bit of a Southern accent slipped out. "I didn't hear you. I… I don't think anyone else heard you either. Could you repeat that?"

We had all heard the question, but the woman repeated herself as Lakshmi turned her back on us and headed to the podium to give her response.

"The best you can do for your *friends*," she said, as if she were spitting out some gristle, "is to pray for their peace. There's nothing unscientific about *The Way*. If we read the work of the physicist Fritjof Capra, we know that to explore physics leads us to metaphysics which leads us to God. Let us pray." She took a chair next to the podium and closed her eyes. A stranger to my left took my hand and Tim took my other hand and everyone closed their eyes. I kept mine open as I watched Lakshmi sink into communion. She took dramatic pauses as her voice deepened and grew trance-like.

"God... let our prayers... our awe... our desire for a better world... be the keys that unlock the cage... to where our greater selves can be free... and take up the joyous labor of freeing others... of vanquishing darkness... of building a world where love is king ... and the king is love... and the loving king is you, God. Help us help others... to see past illusion... to your perfect order and the beauty and peace of the Childrenhood embodied in your Son and servant, our brother, Jesus Christ."

She was slumping now, her head down, at one with her God. A long pause followed before she left her trance.

"Amen," she said.

"Amen" everyone repeated.

"Go out into the world, everyone, and remember that you are holy, worthy in and of yourself, a part of God, God himself, and a beautiful, beaming ray of his universal love. Let your love shine until next time."

How very flattering, I thought and realized I was smirking. *Everyone here, me included, is God*!

Soon after, Lakshmi was seated at a table next to cassettes and VHS tapes of her lectures, signing their labels for her fans as a chubby guy next to her accepted cash or imprinted credit cards on carbon slips with a roller. Standing behind Lakshmi was a tall, pale male in his mid-twenties with white-blond hair wearing paint-spattered overalls and high tops that were fashionably unlaced — a completely invented look. She turned and smiled at him between signings as he stood with his hands clasped behind him, his face an expressionless mask.

"Who's the guy wearing pants by Jackson Pollock?" I asked Tim.

"That's her latest, Kip. He's a painter."

"House painter?"

"No, portraits I think. Supposedly he's very talented."

"Looks fifteen years too young for her, don't you think?"

"Age is just a mindset. Let's just hope this one works out."

As I drove home I remembered what all this reminded me of.

Chapter 5

At fifteen, I was a lonely boy. My family had moved from a blue-collar melting pot in New Jersey to a white-as-Wonder-Bread suburb of Los Angeles which was a big step up for us. Arcadia was a safe, tidy town with an active John Birch chapter and a law still on the books that banned "Negroes" from remaining in town after sundown. On Saturdays, our neighbors washed their cars so that they would glisten in the parking lots of Protestant churches on Sundays. A quarter of Arcadians were wholesomely attractive members of the Church of Latter Day Saints, or Mormons, who worshipped at places called "stakes" instead of churches. Mormons may have been a controversial oddity for most of their history, but I found them an appallingly bland and conformist people who were opposed to expressing opinions. They smiled way too much.

Most of the kids at Arcadia High would register as Republicans when they turned eighteen, even the ones who smoked pot and listened to Bowie. They skied in Mammoth in the winters. In the summer they avoided the city beaches of Los Angeles and

Santa Monica to drive south to the ones in Orange County where they could tan with the other Caucasians. Their parents took them to orthodontists and dermatologists and very few had weight problems. Half of them were blond and blue-eyed and half of them were beautiful. At pep rallies, they loudly, proudly sang the school song while making what looked like a Nazi salute to the school flag with an extended arm. I was astonished to learn that in the sixth grade, a part of their education was taking cotillion classes, a tradition where they donned suits or white dresses and learned to waltz and pour tea while wearing white gloves.

The few acquaintances I had in 1972 were members of the McGovern for President Club. We were a tiny, mildly persecuted bunch of book readers, closeted homosexuals, Jews and hippie/freak leftovers. In the quad at lunchtime, our table had been overturned and our pamphlets tossed to the wind by handsome goons who would soon be heading to USC. When McGovern was crushed at the polls, so were we. His defeat meant the Revolution was dead, the Establishment was still in charge, and an era had ended. All over the nation, young people were trading rebellion for mellowing and looking inward. Rock was falling into glittery decadence or going soft. Banal acoustic bands like America and Bread were in vogue as well as the duos of Brewer and Shipley, Loggins and Messina and England Dan and John Ford Coley. The ferment, the energy, the tumult and color of the 60's had fallen away and in its place were Pet Rocks, granola, earth shoes and spider plants. It was not the time and place for me.

I was alone, eating a plate of Sloppy Joes in the cafeteria and reading Castaneda's *The Teachings of Don Juan* when a cute guy with naturally platinum hair approached. He was wearing a leather choker with a dangling charm of a fish symbol. "I know just what you're looking for," he said, "and it's not in *that* book. My name is Leif. And I love you." The card he left invited me to attend a Bible Study at a place called HiS HousE.

He loved me?

I had read about the New Jesus Movement in Rolling Stone: the Jesus Freaks who embraced Christ as a long haired revolutionary bent on overturning the Establishment, just as he had overturned the tables of the money changers. Some conjectured that Jesus was actually Black, an Ethiopian Jew who had been anointed with cannabis oil and "lived for today." Kris Kristofferson was singing that "Jesus Was a Capricorn" and a band called Ocean was telling us to "Put Your Hand in the Hand of the Man Who Stilled the Water." The Doobie Brothers had their first major hit with a remake of The Byrds "Jesus Is Just All Right with Me."

Maybe Jesus was all right with me too?

The middle-class flatlands of Arcadia were tracts of post-war ranch houses, but on one corner off of Duarte Road was a farmhouse from the late 1800s. It was something like a log cabin with a fireplace made from creek stones and its backyard had an actual well, not a decorative one. Outside in its grassless front yard under an ancient sycamore was a wooden sign with decorative burns along its edges — somebody's wood shop project — with letters burned into it that read HiS HousE. In the sign's corner was a fish symbol that looked as if it had swallowed the Greek letters ΙΧΘΥΣ.

I wandered into an open room where forty folding chairs were set around a stool before the cold fireplace. I took a seat and saw Leif across from me, waving and warmly smiling. A man in his twenties dressed in blue jeans and a flannel shirt took the stool. "Ah'm Vince," he said then started a song. Vince had a big smile, light blond hair and eyes as bright and blue as a gas flame. There was no guitar, just voices in unison. The first song seemed aimed at the newcomers: "He needs Jesus like we all do, must surrender to his will. She needs Jesus like we all do, to find a life fulfilled." The last song was sung like a dirge: "We are touched by his love, we are touched by his love, all we need, all we need, comes from Christ above."

When the room was filled, Vince said, "Let's join hands and pray." Two young men were seated next to me but they grabbed my hands without hesitation. It was strange and comforting to hold hands with men — something I had never done. "Lard Jay-zus, we thank you for all your blessings today, yer love, yer warmth, yer comfort," said Vince with his Western accent. "We dedicate this Bible study to you and in your name we pray. Ay-men."

Vince asked us to turn to pages in the Revised English Bible which was "more plainspoken" than the KJV or King James Version. Since I did not own a Bible, my neighbor shared with me. We started off, of course, with John 3:16 — "For God so loved the world, etc"— then read several more passages which all meant the same thing according to Vince. "Acceptance of the Lard Jayzus as your personal savior is the one and only means of gainin' eternal life."

The kids who attended this meeting went to all different churches on Sundays with their families. One of them, a likely Catholic asked, "So you don't need good works — or to be baptized or confirmed to get into heaven? No last rites before you die?"

"No," Vince said. "All you need do is accept Jayzus as your Lard."

I raised my hand. "And anyone can go to heaven? No matter what you've done?"

"Yes."

"So even Hitler could go to heaven?"

"Yes, Hitler would be in heaven if at one point he accepted Christ as his Lard and Savior."

I was stunned to learn that Hitler might be in heaven. I was trying to imagine him as an angel with wings and a harp and wondering if he still had bangs and that little mustache. After that, we sang a few more five note songs and then Leif walked up to me and asked me if I wanted a ride home.

"Well, sure," I said.

When we got to my house, he turned off the ignition of his parents' station wagon and looked me straight in the eyes. I was taken with his perfect complexion and the near whiteness of his hair that softly reflected the street light. His breath was sweet and his skin had a natural, pleasant smell like peeled apples in fresh milk.

"Can I ask you to do something with me, Tyler?"

I was nervous and a little excited.

"Sure," I said.

"Let me take your hands. I want you to ask Jesus Christ to enter your life and I want you to accept him as your Lord and Savior. Will you pray with me?"

"OK," I said, and we held hands. His were warm and firm. Moments later, I was saved for all eternity.

I attended a few more meetings, and Leif was always happy to drive me home. I liked the hugging and the hand holding, something Leif and I did frequently, but the meetings were getting stale and the only topic of discussion was "the Lord" which most people pronounced like "the Lard" with a hard California *r*. "Praise the Lard," we shouted whenever anything went right, including the turning of a red light to green. And we looked to him whenever something went wrong: "Please, Jayzus, help me find my car keys – oh, there they are. Praise him."

One night after the meeting, Leif drove a group of us up through the twisting, turning road of the local mountains to a stream in the forest of Chantry Flat. It was there that we shouted our praises up to the treetops and sang our simple songs. This was to the annoyance of some giggling stoners sitting at a picnic table in the distance who were there to smoke and play guitar.

"Smoke it!" one of them shouted.

"Do you know my Lord Jesus?" Leif shouted back.

"Do you know my Lord Hemp?"

I heard the laughter of the stoners then got a whiff of their burning pot. I was intrigued by that smell and wondered just how much fun they were having.

"Jesus loves you, brother," Leif shouted.

"Fuck off, Jesus freaks," a girl shouted back.

"Jesus can suck my veiny dick," shouted another guy to laughter.

"We are Christians, not freaks," Leif shouted. "Let's go," he said to us. "The Godless are in these trees now and smoking Satan's weed."

At school when I passed Leif in the hall he would say, "Praise him," and point to the sky. I would do the same, which meant "One way to heaven." One day at lunch we were sitting on the grass in the quad identifying the saved, the lost and the backsliders when Leif looked deep in my eyes. "Tyler, I think you're ready for Wednesday Night Prayer."

"Oh yeah?"

"Yes. I think that's what the Lord just whispered in my ear."

Wow. Leif was something of a prophet. Could I get messages from Jesus too?

Wednesdays were meetings where the Bibles were kept shut. It was "advanced"— for people who had already accepted the Lard. One at a time, people would speak aloud their requests or their thanks when they were moved. "Jesus, thank you for a B on that pop quiz today. I know you were helping me cuz, I'm kinda dumb," said one girl. "Too dumb to find the gosh darn pencil sharpener, but I did find you. I love you, Lard."

"Lard, thank you for helping me scrape enough money together for my car payment," said another guy. "I would have been one sorry mess this month if you hadn't blessed me. I couldn't have driven here. Praise, praise, praise you, mighty Jesus. My love burns for you."

"Jesus, I need your help tomorrow. I'm starting a new job at the McDonalds in Temple City and I've got the jitters," was the fear of another. "I know you'll help me find the other Christians who walk in your path and I know you won't let me walk alone. For you *are* the power and the glory and your love knows no end."

When the prayer-a-thon finally ended near midnight, the worshippers congratulated each other, discussed who had prayed best, and designated some unofficial winners. "Brother, you just about prayed yourself into heaven," said Leif to one young man who had pulled the loudest "amens" and the most approving murmurs.

"You too, Leif," he responded. "The Lard's ears are filled with your sweet praise." They were hugging when Leif noticed me, the only one not smiling.

"Tyler, what's wrong?" he asked.

"I don't know what's wrong, Leif. I... I accept Jesus as my Savior, but I just don't... don't *feel* it like you guys."

"Let's talk to Vince," he said, and put his arm around me and led me to the back door.

It was a dark and moonless December night and a cool breeze rustled the sycamores as Vince stood in the backyard of HiS HousE and looked at the stars with a beatific smile. When we approached him, he turned his smile on me, nodding knowingly as I explained my plight.

"Tyler, you have not been reborn," he said with unshakable confidence.

"Reborn? No, I guess not."

"Ask Jayzus for this blessing. Tell him you want to be born again. Leif and I will pray with you."

The three of us held hands. "Now, don't be frightened if you hear us speaking a strange language," Vince said. "Sometimes, when we are moved by our love for the Lard, we speak in tongues. At the moment you are reborn, you might speak in tongues, too. You might be on fire with Jayzus."

On fire with Jesus? Like the Human Torch? Yes!

Vince looked at me, started his prayer. "Jayzus, we bring you Tyler tonight, to fill with your spirit so that he may be reborn. Tyler wants to give himself to you, to surrender to your love, to live his life as your follower and serve only you."

"Fill Tyler with your spirit, Lard Jayzus. Take his old life, put it behind him and let Tyler be born again!" said Leif.

I looked up. I was waiting for the stars in the night sky to swirl and multiply before transforming into hosts of angels. I was expecting a warm ray of pure love to shoot down from the sky, set me on fire, and like a tractor beam, pull me up to heaven. Soon I would see the beautiful face of God that contained within it the infinite cosmos, and in his right hand, there would be Jesus, a being made of light and love. Maybe because I was hungry, I imagined that in his left hand, he had a five pound box of really good chocolates.

"Take me, Jesus," I said. "I am yours!"

Vince started speaking in tongues. It was convincing. I remember his "words" years later: "Leedo kreedo shadinar, shadinaro, Yeshua, shadinaro krido, ahshem, ashemela, Christos."

Leif attempted, quietly, to speak in tongues but he was more tongue-tied. Some of what he said sounded like "Abba Zabba" which is a kind of taffy with a peanut butter filling and later there was an "abba zabba doo," which made him sound like Fred Flintstone waking up from a nap.

I'd felt nothing, seen no vision. What I did see was someone's failed attempt to speak in tongues.

"So Jesus is God?" I asked Leif on an awkward ride home.

"Yes. And God is Jesus."

"But Jesus is also the Son of God."

"Yes. His only begotten Son."

"So God as Jesus sacrificed himself to himself in order to save mankind."

"Yes. You've got it."

"I do? Why did God need to do that in order to save mankind? Couldn't the Almighty God just have said, 'Mankind is saved, no need for me, as my Son, to suffer on a cross.'"

"Well... no... mankind had to... had to earn it."

"By accepting Jesus as Lord and Savior."

"It's as simple as that."

"But why was Jesus God's only begotten Son? Why couldn't he beget some more? I mean, God can do anything, right?"

Leif was quiet.

"And even if he was his only begotten Son, after he was sacrificed, God got him back anyway. Didn't he? He sits in his right hand."

"Well, I think so, yes. I'm glad to see you've been reading your Bible."

"But why do we need to be saved in the first place? Why does God allow Satan to have so much power? Why can't God just go down to hell and transform it into, you know, a second heaven and turn Satan back into an angel? Or is God not the Almighty? Is there a limit to his powers?"

Leif was quiet. "You have a lot of questions, Tyler. Maybe you should ask Vince."

"You know... it's just... I was watching the news tonight before we left. There's like, millions of people dying from starvation in India and Bangladesh and children who still have polio — people who will never see a doctor. How come we don't pray for them? Isn't that what Jesus should be taking care of instead of helping some guy get through his first day at McDonald's?"

Leif looked over at me and then blinked a few times. "Why, sure we can pray for them. We can do that right now."

"No, that's.... that's OK. I can do it later."

At the curb, Leif turned off the ignition, reached for me and hugged me. He stroked my back, which was new.

He pulled away then said, "I hope you know that whatever you're going through, whatever you struggle with, that you have a friend — in me, and in Jesus. Whatever it is, Tyler... turn it over to the Lard. Do you understand what I'm getting at?"

My heart was beating hard, in fear, not excitement. For the first time, I was being outed.

"I... I think I do."

"Jayzus loves you, Tyler. And so do I... in a Christian way."

That night in bed, I imagined what Leif and I might do if we could express that other love. After I cleaned up, I made this prayer to Jesus. "Jesus, I accept you as my Savior. I did not see you as I wanted to tonight and I do not understand your ways. But I promise I will never jerk off again if you will end these thoughts I have about other guys. Take them away and I will give my life to you."

I made that same prayer again and again for the next few weeks and patiently awaited my answer. I had abandoned hopes of seeing a Gustave Dore-type vision of Christ riding on a cloud in the company of a thousand angels. Instead I was waiting to hear what Vince called "a small, quiet voice."

The voice in my head that grew louder told me to stop going to HiS HousE, because for one thing, it was so fricking boring. One night I was listening to KLOS, a rock station that switched to leftist talk shows and public service programs on Sunday nights. After the usual "should we legalize pot debate" I heard my first lecture by Alan Watts, the great explainer of Eastern philosophy. I was captivated by his discussion of yoga, LSD and chanting all as a means of experiencing Oneness. I'd tune in again the following week.

On Wednesday I skipped HiS HousE and went instead to the religion section of the Arcadia library and found an illustrated book on world religions. The pictures, especially those in the chapters for Hinduism and Buddhism, were captivating and included elephant-headed and blue-skinned gods who wore a fortune in gold jewelry. The pictures of Krishna reminded me of both David Bowie and David Cassidy with their sexual ambiguity. Krishna, an incarnation of Vishnu the Preserver, the god who dreamed the world, wore strands of pearls, dangling earrings and a peacock feather in a tiara. And he did not skimp on the mascara and lipstick.

I went back for more books and lying on the shelf was a slim volume titled "Why I Am Not A Christian" by Bertrand Russell. That tiny, worn, leather-bound book scared me to the point of trembling but I sat down and read it then checked it out at the front desk to read again at home. "Religion is based, I think, primarily and mainly upon fear," Russell had written. "It is partly the terror of the unknown and partly, as I have said, the wish to feel that you have a kind of elder brother who will stand by you in all your troubles and disputes. Fear is the basis of the whole thing — fear of the mysterious, fear of defeat, fear of death."

*

Vince and Leif offered a simple solution to the fear of death with the call to accept Christ and a simpler solution to life's problems by "turning them over to Jesus." Lakshmi's solution was even simpler: death did not exist. As for dealing with our suffering, our loneliness, and our acquired immunodeficiency syndrome, it was even simpler -- it could be dismissed as unreal, dumped in the trash can of "illusion" for only God was real and God is only love.

I was never going to buy that. Part of me still believed in some entity, some source of creation, but what empirical evidence did Lakshmi have that God was real? What corroborated, peer-reviewed study at what accredited laboratory had proven that God was only love? If God is love, did she mean he is the biological mechanisms that promote the survivability of mammalian species? If God is only love, is he the norepinephrine, serotonin and dopamine released during romantic attraction? Is he also the oxytocin and vasopressin that are a part of family bonding and friendships?

Lakshmi would likely say no — her God was some benevolent being who had created the world as an act of cosmic kindness. His love is something bigger, something so incomprehensible that it overwhelms and confounds science and can only be pondered through metaphysics. But why did God/Love allow for the "illusion" of death and suffering? If God/love is the universe, why is illusion, or at least our vulnerability to it, a part of his creation?

I suppose Lakshmi might say that illusion is just an illusion too.

In the two hours of her lecture/mic session, Lakshmi had mentioned "ego" a dozen times, as something we must let go of to "end our illusions." This 'ego' was not the same one that Freud referred to as the "self"or "identity"and indeed, Steinmetz encouraged all of us to be "ingenious, beautiful, to prosper and shine with the light of God within us, to accept our own holiness as our means of transcending space and time and the limitations of the physical world. To do so is not egotistical, it is Godly."

This other "ego"of *The Way* was the "false self, the one that was not of God, but separated from him, that defended its survival like an addict who voraciously supports the habit that destroys him, who is addicted, also, to a belief in his own unhappiness."

My time as a Jesus person was just a few short months and I had never been convinced that Christ could enter into my life and transform it. Twenty years later, I was willing to be a "student of *The Way*" and consider that it was a more intelligent approach to faith. Perhaps I *was* attached to a false self, to an ego that separated me from seeing and uniting with a loving God. But over the next few months I would learn that if there was anyone who was enslaved to ego and addicted to a belief in her own unhappiness, it was a certain new age lecturer.

Chapter 6

The next time I returned to Manna from Heaven, I was tying on an apron when Jonnie entered the kitchen. "What did you think of Lakshmi?" she asked. "Isn't she fabulous?"

"She was OK," I said. "I liked what she said to that one guy whose parents are trying to save him from hellfire."

"Yes. It was miraculous!"

"It was?"

"Yes, as *The Way* describes miraculous — not like changing water into wine, but as a shift in awareness."

"Like... looking on the bright side?"

"OK... kind of. It's a little deeper than that."

"So who wrote *The Way*?"

"More like it was written down. It was channeled."

Oh, this is sounding promising already, I thought.

"Channeled? Like J.Z. Knight and Ramtha?"

"Yes, but by a Stanford psychologist. She told a friend of hers, another psychologist, that Jesus was singing in her ear."

Jonnie sang to me in what sounded like the same tune as *Ding Dong the Witch is Dead*. "Write down what I say, and I will reveal the way, the way of the miraculous, the most miraculous way."

"Jesus? Like Jesus Christ? He sang to her?"

"Yes... the Jesus that is the messenger of God's love. And all of us can be that messenger..."

"For all of us can be Jesus," I said with her in unison. I was getting good at predicting the end of passages from *The Way*.

"Yes, Tyler! We are all a part of the Childrenhood and members of the Siblinghood."

"All right. I'm always interested to know more about religions."

"Spirituality. *The Way* is a spiritual path, not so much a religious one."

"What's the difference?"

"That's a good question. You should ask Lakshmi about that."

I looked around the kitchen, which was bustling. A second oven — secondhand but gas and industrial — had been added as well as another refrigerator. Up on the wall was a marker board with the day's menu and the number of clients, which had jumped to thirty-eight. Gene was in charge that day and seemed happy to see me. "Tyler! You are just who I was hoping to see. Would you be able to make dessert for tomorrow?"

"I would... but for thirty-eight people?"

"This might help," he said, reaching under the cutting table for a KitchenAid standing mixer with a six-quart bowl and a rotating blade.

"Where do you get *that*?" I asked as I admired its classic, streamlined profile, a design that hadn't changed since the 1930s "Those are expensive!"

"Someone donated it! And look— new hotel pans and a measuring cup and spoons."

"Fantastic. Let me see what's in the pantry."

"We've got some money now. Whatever you can't find, you can go and buy. What can you make to go with chicken Marbella?"

"From *The Silver Palate*? I love that dish."

"I love that cookbook!"

"So do I! It was just what we needed after the 70's—the antidote to brown rice casseroles and steamed tempeh with miso."

"Exactly," he said and chuckled.

"Have you ever made Julee and Sheila's toffee bars?"

"I have and I love them."

"Fabulous. Do it. I just wish you could have made something for today's meal," he said, and pointed to some volunteers who were spooning out glops of bright green Jell-O with canned fruit cocktail suspended inside. Gene smiled at me and cocked his head. "So, Tyler... what's your sign?"

"Uh... Capricorn."

"At the far end of January?"

"Yes."

"That makes sense now — so you're kind of cuspy with Aquarius."

"I suppose so."

A few hours later when the toffee bars were finished, Jonnie pounced and asked me if I could do the route in East LA. "It's kind of far away. And a little…"

"Dangerous? No, it's not. It's cool. I've been out there a few times to see the murals."

"Tyler... you are just angelic! Do you have a cassette player in your car?"

"I do."

"Then take these. To help you on your *spiritual* path."

Jonnie handed me some cassettes with Lakshmi's picture on them, which I set in my delivery bags. I was bringing the clients yellow tail fillets with carrot and leek julienne and fresh asparagus in hollandaise. A new employee, a handsome bodybuilder, shook my hand and gave me a route sheet from Jericho's dot matrix printer. "I'm Nigel," he said with a posh English accent. "Thanks so very much, Tyler, for doing District 7. These are some explicit street-by-street directions in the most linear route possible so you won't have to fumble with the Thomas Guide."

Manna from Heaven was stepping things up.

*

When you exit off the Interstate 5 to Boyle Heights and East Los Angeles, you might think you crossed over the Mexican border. Suddenly, the buildings and houses are smaller, the streets are narrower, and the signs are in both Spanish and English. Psychedelic graffiti is everywhere, alternating with lurid, intricate murals with religious, political and ethnic themes. It always made me feel alive... and horny. So many caramel-colored Latinos with their shiny black pompadours in white ironed T-shirts.

I was removed from any sexual fantasies after meeting the clients face-to-face. The first stop was a makeshift hospice in a small apartment over a *carniceria* where the smell of blood and roasting flesh was in the air. The room was just big enough to accommodate four bedridden men in cots covered with children's bedspreads featuring My Little Pony, He-Man and the Smurfs. The men were small and gaunt and moved with tiny jerks. I felt like I was in a hospital for marionettes. One of them, with a lazy eye and puffing on a Marlboro, spoke to me in rapid Spanish.

"Por favor, hable más despacio," I said. "¿Hay aquí un hombre que habla Inglés?"

"Una mujer," said their caretaker, a transgendered Latina with *chola* make up who was stepping out of the bathroom. Her hair was receding at the forehead and the rest was in a sparse ponytail.

"What's he asking me?" I asked her.

"He wants Mexican food."

"Oh." I was stunned. Why hadn't this occurred to us?

"Nothing against White people food. It's just, like, the city is half-Latino. I can show you how to make if you want."

"What's your name?"

"Olga."

"Me llamo Tyler. Me gusto mucho la comida Mexicana y pienso que es un buen idea para los clientes. Voy a pedir. Te lo prometo."

"Tho cute when you thpeak Cathtiliano," she said while scribbling her phone number. "Maybe you could learn thome thpanish," she said, mocking the lisp I had learned from my high school language records.

I continued listening to Lakshmi's lectures as I drove the rest of the route through Boyle Heights. Jonnie had given me a holiday set in which Christmas, New Year's, Easter and the Fourth of July were all given new interpretations through the principles of *The Way*. The fit was sometimes awkward: square Christian and Hebrew allegories being jammed into the round holes of Buddhism, Zen and Daoism. Throughout the lectures, no matter what the theme, a personal strand was inserted about the follies of love. In the Christmas/Hannukah lecture was, "So to embrace this hope is defeating, like hoping that handsome guy who drifted away might call again. What we really need is a new string of Christmas lights or new candles for the menorah to light a different way."

In the New Year's lecture was, "We look to a New Year and a different future with better habits, a better job and more money like we look to some man, thinking that when he finally asks us to marry him, that life will start and we'll finally be happy. But he isn't going to ask, or if he does, we realize he's last year's bad news, that it's history repeating." And in the Easter lecture was "But we have to realize that our attraction to certain men is the attempt to annex something we should find or build in ourselves. Or it may be something we can never have, like blue eyes or a calm demeanor. When we lose that partner to someone or something else, our longing for those unattainable traits can return in a painful way. We feel like we are dying and in need of our own resurrection."

I started the Fourth of July tape in which Lakshmi stated at the outset that the Declaration of Independence was a "divinely inspired document." I knew Jefferson would have a problem with that since he was a deist who did not believe in divine intervention.

And he would not want to share credit for the founding documents of the United States with an entity he refused to call God. It was almost five o'clock when I was able to turn around and go home but I knew I was in for an hour of bumper to bumper on the freeway, so I veered off to the Los Angeles Central Library to wait it out in splendor. Built in the 20's, the LACL is an Art Deco palace with an Egyptian theme full of sphinx statues, celestial mosaics, murals and endless shelves of books. Atop its central tower is a miniature pyramid and at its peak is an arm holding a golden torch to signify the "Light of Learning."

 I wrote down info from the card catalog for magazine articles about *The Way of the Miraculous,* handed in my requests at the reference desk, and ten minutes later was handed some magazines. I learned that *The Way* was channeled by a secular, married psychologist named Nadia Karnowski. Her marriage, to a comparative religions teacher, was not a happy one. She was in love with her office mate, a young, gay psychologist named Stan Reilly. Somehow this detail did not surprise me, that there was a history of... glue-gunness within *The Way*.

 One afternoon, Karnowski told Reilly she had the sensation that she had tripped and was falling but Jesus Christ had caught her, righted her and stood beside her, and then sang into her ear. "'Write down what I say, for this is the Way of the Miraculous,' is what he said after he stopped singing," she told Reilly. For the next five years, Reilly wrote down Karnowski's "inner recitations" and then typed it up, cleaned up its grammar and added punctuation. At one point, the messages stopped and Reilly assumed the book was complete. Weeks later, he gave the completed manuscript to

Nadia to proofread. She handed it back to him and said, "I don't know why you're so interested in this. I don't know that anyone should be." The book was published after her death and promoted as a latter-day prophecy. It sold by the tens of thousands.

The library had a copy of The Way that I could spend some time with. The foreword stated that it was a "message from Jesus to complete the Gospels." As I read through its cryptic passages I was wondering why Jesus wasn't more plainspoken. He sounded a bit like an Elizabethan as nearly all these messages were written in iambic pentameter. Why had Jesus taken up a thousand pages to deliver a simple message? Where did he stand on abortion and birth control? On gay rights and women's equality? On the legality of pot? What did he think of slavery, rape, segregation and other difficult topics that are not discussed in the Old or New Testament or addressed in the Ten Commandments? Did he condemn the Vietnam War which was raging at that time of these new revelations? Where did he stand on the Israeli-Palestinian conflict? Did he agree with Saint Paul, the real founder of Christianity, that "Women should remain silent in the churches. They are not allowed to speak, but must be in submission, as the law says. If they want to inquire about something, they should ask their own husbands at home; for it is disgraceful for a woman to speak in the church."?

Some pupils of The Way called it a "challenging text"and if you are confused by it or refute it, you are told "your ego is getting in the way." But plainly, I could see that most of it was gibberish, malarkey, the disconnected ramblings of a mildly schizophrenic woman who had read a lot of books, some of them taught by her husband, and then she regurgitated them. It was speaking in tongues. The Way had some unifying principles with its biblical terminology, but it remade Jesus as a kind of Buddha who had achieved enlightenment. He was mostly a symbolic figure, but he was also something of a supernatural entity delivering a message from God. The Way reminded me both of the Book of Mormon with its colorless monotony as well as of English translations of the Koran with *suras* that alternate between poetry, common sense and impenetrable nonsense.

I turned to the last page in hopes of finding something that might summarize it.

"The angels of God are everywhere, all about, here to guide you. They are God's love, God himself, God's Son, the Light called Jesus."

"In all ways, on all Planes, Love surrounds you, Love will lead you."

"Turn to God, turn to Jesus, turn to Self for all are Love."

"Forgive yourself, forgive others, be forgiven, let others forgive."

"You do not walk in a loveless world, for I am the World, I am God and I am love."

I like to be 100 percent sure of something before I dismiss it as bullshit, regardless of its message of love and forgiveness. The

Way of the Miraculous did not teach anything that had not been said or written before. If Jesus Christ had something else to add to the Gospels, why did he wait two thousand years to deliver it? Why had he chosen to channel the rest of his message through a mentally tortured and agnostic psychologist where it would slowly reach an audience of a few million people? Why didn't God speak directly to all six billion of us? And as for forgiveness, should it really be offered to everyone, including genocidal tyrants? Did Hitler, Stalin and Mao deserve a pardon?

And what the fuck was keeping Jesus from making his return and appearing at an internationally televised press conference where we could all see and hear him for ourselves? But wait — Jesus was more of a metaphor, except when mentioning that he was the *real* author of The Way of the Miraculous, which is what makes it an *actual* revelation, something of a divine and a sacred text from the last prophet of the Hebrew god unless you are a faithful Jew or a Muslim. As for Mohammed, he had no mention in The Way — was he the last prophet or a false one?

I did not need this book in my life. What I did need was to let Manna from Heaven know that a third of our clients wanted Mexican food. A few days later I was back in the kitchen where Olga would teach me The Way of Enchiladas and Jonnie would ask me to do something which would bring me to my first meeting with Lakshmi Steinmetz.

Chapter 7

Tim had no objection to my attempting Mexican food but Gene was resistant. "It's kind of, I don't know... cheap and peasanty," he said.

"From a nutritional standpoint, it's got a lot of calories," I responded. "Very good for people with wasting disease. I figured for dessert I'd make a nice, rich flan with cream and egg yolks."

"Flan?" Gene asked.

"Well, you could call it crème caramel."

"Or renversée."

"Yeah. It's pretty much the same dessert. But I'd make it in loaf pans. Easier to slice and serve."

"Can you make enough for everyone? Caucasians too?"

"Sure," I said. "But most Mexicans are also of some Caucasian descent."

"All right then. A lovely crème renversée goes well with tomorrow's menu. *Très bien.*"

"Great. The uh... lady who takes care of these guys gave me a list of stuff to buy."

"The, uh, lady? So she's the *T* in LGBT?"

"Yeah, I guess."

"We have an account at Smart and Final now," said Gene. "Go and get what you need and just turn in the receipt."

On Friday, I arrived early to flip over and cut up the flan and make sure each slice was sitting in some caramel sauce. Olga arrived in drag *chic* and her wig was a big 60's updo. As I was giving her an apron, I realized who she was: the star of nightly drag shows at El Cielo, a Latino nightclub in Hollywood where they put on two different shows a night, six nights a week. And now she was taking care of men with AIDS! She stepped away to wash her hands.

"I hope you're flattered, Tyler. She dressed up for you," said Gene as he sneered and looked like a bleach-blond version of The Evil Queen in *Snow White*.

"It takes a real man to wear drag," I said, quoting somebody. "Olga's famous, ya know."

Olga taught me how to make a red enchilada sauce with a mild chili powder in consideration of the clients' sensitive stomachs. She poured several glugs of corn oil into a pot, finely chopped onions, salt and pepper and then minced garlic. Before the garlic could brown, she added flour to make a roux. "If the garlic burns, it's bitter. Add flour, quick. Stir until it's moist to get rid of the flour taste, but don't let it get too dark." She added half the jar of chili powder then just enough water to thin it. Olga did not measure her ingredients.

We scooped out some ripe avocados after that, chopped more onions and minced some garlic to make a chunky guacamole. We put the other volunteers to work grating Monterey Jack and cotija cheese. When the sauce was cooled, we dunked yellow corn tortillas in it, rolled them up with the cheese inside, then set them in rows in the hotel pans. Olga poured on the rest of the sauce then started some Spanish rice and made a fresh *pico de gallo* as garnish. Everyone with a Spanish surname got a Mexican meal. She autographed each of the lids with *"Buen Provecho! Con Amore, Olga."* On some, she drew a pair of heavily lashed eyes over her name.

  Fridays were also known as When Chefs Collide as Tim was there to supervise the prepping of the Sunday meal. As he got to work with his own coterie of older, chubby volunteers, Gene put finishing touches on his tarragon chicken salad with a side of pickled red and yellow beets topped with chèvre crumbles. The green salad was baby spinach and caramelized pecans with a raspberry vinaigrette. The dessert was the flan I had made, but Gene renamed it *crème renversée* when he wrote out the menu on the chalkboard for the drivers.

  When everything was packaged and prayers were over, Tim set to work making something he called Spanish meatloaf. It was pretty much meatloaf but with some pimento stuffed olives mixed into it and bread crumbs instead of oatmeal. Cans of Libby's Tomato Sauce would be poured over the top before baking with a scattering of bay leaves. He was using a big wooden paddle spoon to mix the ground beef with the eggs and bread crumbs in an aluminum basin when Gene stepped over. He looked down at the mixture as if it were vomit on his shoes. "I'm sure that's going to be just... marvelous," he said. "*Merveilleuse*... or should I say *maravillosa*."

  "Oh, it will be!" said Tim excitedly. He took a jar of stuffed colossal olives and threw them on top of the mixture. Lots of them landed with the eyes up. When Tim started mixing them in, it looked if he were bludgeoning the Muppets. "Chef Carl taught me to make this. The secret is to add some eggs. Gives it a smooth texture and a little body so it slices nicely."

"I'm just torn up that I won't get to try it. Where's the recipe from? Ladies Home Journal? Family Circle? The White Trash Cookbook?"

Tim took a moment. "I believe it's from Spain," he said.

"Yes, I'm sure it's an authentic recipe from the royal kitchens of Madrid."

Gene looked at me, his smirk turning to a warmer smile. "Tyler, can Jonnie and I talk to you about something?"

"Sure."

We stepped over to Jonnie's table where she was ending a phone call. "Well, don't stress, honey. God closes one door then opens another," she said. "Just throw it out to the universe and see what comes back — it might be a real boomerang of blessings. Love you too. Bye-eee!"

She clasped her hands and had that delighted, hopeful look. "Tyler, we have a big favor to ask."

"Compton?"

"No. That's covered. We're wondering if you could make a cake for next Friday."

"Sure. I've made a few cakes here."

"Not for the clients. Can you make a really nice cake, a decorated cake… for someone very special?"

"Who?"

"Lakshmi. We need something that will really cheer her up."

"Does she hate birthdays?"

"It's her fortieth and that's a tough one. The guy she was seeing is... well, he's seeing someone else now."

"We really think you should meet her," said Gene.

"Sure. I'd like to meet her. Why?"

"We think she needs to meet *you*," said Jonnie.

"You guys know I'm gay, right?"

Jonnie and Gene looked at each other and laughed in unison.

"You are just *darling*," said Jonnie. "That's not what we had in mind."

"Does she like chocolate or vanilla?"

*

On Friday, I was back at my weekend gig at JJ's Pub near South Central, a gay bar "Where Irish Guys Are Smiling." The manager, the bartenders, the cook and of course most of the customers were all "tramps" as the owner called them which was his euphemism for "alcoholics." The latter was Seamus who was better known as Legless or Shameless due to his constant inebriation. He was bracing himself to get through some paperwork with a shot and a beer when I arrived. I was tying on my apron when I noticed one of my favorite customers had a bandage over his upper arm.

"Duncan McKenna, how are ya? Another seven and seven?"

"Yeah, make it a good one. Just come from the tattoo parlor and it felt like a thousand bee stings."

"Oh yeah? What'd you get?"

He gingerly pulled back the bandage to reveal the image of an antique Underwood typewriter.

"That's amazing."

"Tomorrow it's going to be an amazing scab. This is how I spent my last paycheck from the Herald Tribune. Tomorrow's their last issue. I can't believe a city the size of Los Angeles will have only one newspaper."

"How's the job search?"

"Oh, guess I didn't tell you. I'm writing for… a magazine"

"Which one?"

"Well… *People*. I know, I know. But the pay's really good compared to a newspaper. Tomorrow I've got an interview with Vanilla Ice. And last week was Fabio. I can work on my book between assignments."

Our conversation was interrupted when the upper dentures of Oscar, the old man sleeping next to Duncan, suddenly fell out of his mouth and clattered on the bar. He awoke to jam them back in, closed his eyes, and went back to sleep. Duncan and I looked at each other, grinning madly.

"Now we know his drag name," Duncan said.

"What?"

"Polly Grip."

The stool next to Oscar was empty and in front of it was a drained plastic cup. Only one person ever drank out of those.

"Is that…"

"Yeah," whispered Duncan. "Here she comes. I can feel the tremors."

Rolling back from the bathroom was Two Buck Linda, a severely obese woman who had just been in the hospital. She only drank draft beer which was seventy-five cents and served in a humiliating plastic cup. Her usual habit was to drink up all of her public assistance checks then turn some tricks after that. She was proof that just about anyone can be a sex worker if your prices are extremely reasonable. She had never left me a tip. When she pushed her empty cup toward me I shook my head.

"No, Linda. I won't do it."

"Gimme a refill, Tyler," she said.

"Linda, you're not supposed to be here."

"I can go anywhere I want. It's a free country."

"I mean you aren't supposed to drink again. Ever."

"I got money."

"I don't care."

"You're fucking with my high!"

"I'm trying to save your liver. And your life."

Seamus looked up from his order sheet. "Give 'er a beer, lad," he bellowed in his County Cork accent. "And put it in a glass for the lady."

"Seamus, she has cirrhosis. She just left the hospital. If she wants to kill herself, that's her business. But I won't be part of it."

"Get out," said Seamus. "Leave your keys."

I pulled keys off my ring and dropped them in Linda's cup. Duncan followed me out to the sidewalk.

"Where you going, Tyler?"

"Where else? To get a drink."

"Let me buy you one."

Minutes later at Molly Malone's, I had a neat bourbon in front of me. It felt nice to be on the other side of the bar and through with JJ's Pub.

"Tyler, I always meant to ask you…"

"What?"

"Why were you working in *that* bar?"

I chuckled. "It was... pretty entertaining. Why do you drink there?"

"Because it's *very* entertaining."

We smiled, clinked glasses.

"What'll you do now?" he asked me.

"I'll just throw it out to the universe and see what comes back."

"Whaaat?" he said with a sideways stare.

"Oh, it's an expression I hear a lot at this place where I'm volunteering. You should come by sometime. It's the one organization where you can actually do something for people with AIDS."

"What's that?"

"Feed them."

I took a sip and wondered just what the fuck I'd do for money.

*

I had made a few specialty cakes for film productions. One of them was of the White House, another was of the Hanging Gardens of Babylon and my favorite was of the Starship Enterprise. I hated cakes that involved flowers and preferred architectural themes so for her birthday cake I decided to create Lakshmi's vision of a temple of silver and gold. Using a picture of the Temple of Seven Hills in Andhra Pradesh as my model, I stacked layers of frosted vanilla cake then carved them into a tiered, flat-topped pyramid. I tinted some marzipan a deep yellow and rolled it into a "sphere of light" as the top ornament. The sides were decorated with gold and silver dragées. I hand piped doors, gates and windows and some other temple decorations with a pastry bag and some different tips. The end result wasn't half bad.

As I was decorating, Gene walked over with his smirk preceding him by ten feet. "Tyler, that's enormous. That's a cake for fifty people."

"I figured whatever comes back we can send out to the clients."

"Is that the gold and silver temple?"

"You got it. Under a 'sphere of light.'"

"I was thinking of something more like this."

He showed me a picture in Gourmet magazine of an elegant mousse-filled cake in a chocolate shell.

"Oh. Well, I can make cakes like that too."

Jonnie walked over, mouth agape. "I think she's going to love it, Tyler. So much *love* went into it."

"Thanks, Jonnie."

"Can you bring it by the party?" she asked.

"Sure."

"Maybe you can serve it, too? We need a few people to help out tonight, you know, pass hors d'oeuvres, etcetera. Is it true you know how to bartend?"

"I do."

"You do?"

She clapped her hands under her chin and looked completely amazed.

*

Lakshmi's birthday party was being held in a house in the Hollywood Hills where the residents have the privilege of looking down on the rest of us. I had loaded the cake into the trunk area of my Honda Civic wagon and then carefully drove up the twists and turns of what are known as the "Bird Streets" with names like Thrush, Oriole and Blue Jay Way. I had brought a knife, some spare frosting in pastry bags and extra dragées to fix any damage.

The house was one of those flat-roofed, flimsy boxes built on stilts in the mid-60's. The housekeeper, Griselda, let me in and I set the cake on the table in the formal dining area of the great room. Typical of these houses, it had glass sliding doors to provide views of the LA Basin. I reset a few of the dragées, touched up some frosting and then looked around. This was a clean, colorless human container with no personality. I would never call it a "home." The Kreiss furniture was modern, white and blocky with Lucite end tables. The walls were empty except for a print of two soft rectangles of gray and blue by Rothko, that suicidal fraud whose only real talent was self-promotion. In this sterile room, the cake looked garish and alien and I felt empty and depressed, like I was in some hospital where both the patients and doctors had died.

I went home to change, eat and walk our dogs, Luna and Holden, before driving back. Kyle was gone, having left a note that said "Back around 12." Perhaps he had left for work at Ed Debevic's Retro Diner where he worked as the Kookmeister, a character that was a combination disc jockey and ringmaster of performances by the hammy waitstaff. But he might have been at a Groundlings class practicing his improv or he might have been with one of a few different writing partners, working on various screenplays. I never really knew anymore and didn't push him for details. When I did, he accused me of being controlling and suspicious and would only retreat further, and that left me with a deeper ache and a growing loneliness. I respected Kyle for his drive and encouraged his hustle, if that's what he was doing, but I imagined he liked keeping a secret life, that his illicit pleasures were sweeter for being hidden from me. I crumpled his note and threw it in the trash and was glad to have somewhere to go that evening.

When I returned to the house of the birthday party a couple of hours later, Gene and other volunteers were wearing dark green aprons. Gene was busy in the kitchen piping softened goat cheese onto leaves of endive. "Wash your hands and take an apron," he said to me. "I need you to spread the salmon pate on toast points and then insert a sprig of dill. Here's the example."

"Got it," I said. The other volunteers were busy chopping and peeling vegetables for a crudité and a green salad.

"After that, can you set up the bar, Tyler? You'll need to cut some limes."

"I'd be thrilled."

I was feeling a little miffed. I wasn't just dropping off a cake and helping out — I had become a cater waiter, cast in the role of a helpful homo. And it's not like this was a paying gig or a benefit.

I was setting up the makeshift bar on a card table when someone walked toward me, a short, semi-obese man with thinning hair in his late thirties whom I recognized as the cashier at Lakshmi's lecture. "I'm Jacob Hellman," he said and extended his hand. He was wearing black slacks, a white shirt, and a solid gray tie as uninteresting as the house so I figured he must be its owner. He had one of those faces where the lower half is larger and heavier and it gave him a resemblance to Mr. Toad from *Wind in the Willows*.

"Tyler St. George," I said as we shook hands. "Is this your house?"

"It is."

"Nice views." He was flattered and gave me a broad froggy smile. His lips were very red and resembled hot dogs straight out of boiling water.

"Thanks. Where do you live, Tyler?"

"We live in South Carthay Circle. Off of Fairfax."

"Oh, down there," he said, and the smile wilted. "You're a 'we'?"

"*Oui, monsieur,*" I said.

Jacob looked away from me, shook his head, and walked towards the dining room chairs. He pulled out each one until they were six inches from the table. "I don't know how many times I've told Griselda about this," he said.

Most of the arriving guests were men in their thirties and forties wearing slacks and ties and white shirts. I was serving them red or white wine, vodka, or club soda with lime – the same four drinks that are served at galleries. The doorbell rang again and Kevin Darrington entered with friends from his ski club and they appeared to have come from a tanning booth for five. Once again, here I was, wearing an apron and pouring Kevin a drink. "Tyler, how very good to see you!" he said and gave me a hug.

"Kevin. Got a nice glass of vodka for you with your name engraved on each cube of ice," I said, trying my best to smile. "I didn't know you'd be here."

"I'm on the board of Manna," Kevin said and nodded to his friends. "We all are. Cost a mere two thousand dollars of seed money for each of us. Like any good investment, you have to get in early." He laughed at his own joke then left to say hello to Jacob as Jonnie arrived, looking pretty in an embroidered Chinese dress of azure silk — she never wore any other color than the blue that reflected her eyes. At her side was a tall, older, and severe-looking woman with iron gray hair wearing black slacks and a man's button-down shirt.

"Jonnie, nice to see you."

"Tyler, thanks for your help," she said, giving me a hug and an air kiss.

"And is this... this is your..."

I was about to say "mom" and thought better of it.

"This is Doris," she said. "My *friend*."

"Hello," said Doris with a deep and musical voice that was like a bassoon. "Vodka on the rocks. More vodka than rocks if you please."

An hour later there was no sign of Lakshmi and the party stayed at a low simmer. Jacob had refused to play music and even turned it off when one of the cater waiters found a Bose radio/disc player on the bookshelf and tuned it to top forty radio. Kevin and his friends had been leaning on the dining room chairs, shifting them, and then stepped outside to smoke. Jacob trotted over immediately to reset the chairs as I went into the kitchen to get more ice.

"Where's Lakshmi?" I asked Gene, as he took mini-quiches out of the oven and slid them onto trays.

"She's notorious for being late to parties," he said. "Even when they're for her. She'll get here when she gets here."

"Who's that woman with Jonnie?" I asked.

"Her girlfriend. Sort of."

"Sort of?"

"Long story," he said. "Get these out there while they're hot," he said to the waiters.

When I returned to the bar, the doorbell rang and Jacob trotted over to open the door. In walked a tiny, plain woman without a bit of makeup. She was wearing flats, casual pants and a black hooded jacket that was monk-like. She lowered the hood to reveal hair that was flattened and pulled back by a cheap, plastic clasp. "Sorry I'm late," she said to Jacob and I realized it was Lakshmi.

"Happy birthday," he said, with a kiss to her cheek. Everyone converged on her.

"Thank you, thank you," she said, as if she were so tired. "Lovely to see you all, but I am so thirsty. Could I get a glass of white before I say hello?"

As soon as I had poured her glass, a waiter whisked it away. As Lakshmi drank, she accepted the birthday wishes of all but looked pained and brittle as she gave each person a shallow hug. "Jacob, can we have some music?" she called out. "Isn't this a party?"

Jacob walked toward the Boze and fished out Kitaro's *Towards the West* from a selection of six other CDs and soon cheesy new age muzak filled that bleakly ugly house.

Lakshmi headed for a dining room chair, which she pulled into a clearing. Jacob looked on, distressed by chair displacement, as other women followed her lead. Soon the birthday girl was surrounded by Jonnie, Doris and a few other women for a sub-party of females only. They were all watching Lakshmi, tuned to her every moment. The doorbell rang and a pretty, leggy brunette in her mid-forties entered followed by the exotic presence of a heterosexual male, a man so utterly straight-looking he looked like he'd come from the Republican Convention. The woman had a wrapped gift under one arm and a manila envelope under the other. I knew her from somewhere... but where? A television show?

"Happy birthday, Lakshmi!" she said extending the gift while cocking her head and smiling to reveal her molars. The wrapping paper was shocking pink and matched her skirt and nails. Her hairstyle was a wedge cut from 1976.

"Julie, please, I said no gifts."

"It's just a little something. This is for you too, the end of the week pouch," she said, and showed Lakshmi a manila envelope stuffed with mail and paperwork.

"Just hold on to it until Monday. I'm in no mood for work this weekend."

Lakshmi turned in my direction. "Can we get Julie something to drink? And a seat?"

""White wine, please," Julie said and I brought her that and a dining chair.

Lakshmi took a sip of her wine, her expression sullen as her eyes darted back and forth. The women were silent, waiting for her to speak. "I stopped by Kip's on the way here," she finally blurted.

"Kip, the painter?" Jonnie asked. "I thought you weren't seeing him anymore."

"I'm not but he invited me over for a birthday drink and to pick up my blow-dryer. I was just... *furious* with him."

"Why?"

"He pours me a glass of wine and asks me if I want to see the canvas he's working on. So I said yes, and he brought me to his studio and there was a painting of this... this attractive *woman* and I asked him who it was. He told me her name is Angela — and it's the woman he's been *seeing*."

"Why would he do that?" Julie asked, clutching at the healing amethyst around her neck.

"I have no idea. But I ran to the kitchen for a butcher knife and slashed that painting to ribbons."

Julie was raising her glass and halted. Jonnie was quietly blinking. I was pretending to tidy up in the area so I could eavesdrop. Silence passed until Doris spoke, leaning back in her chair and raising her chin for dramatic effect — an actress!

"Pardon me... Lakshmi," she said in her baritone. "But wasn't that a little extreme?"

"It was extreme of him to show it to me! Oh, I know, it was an emotional moment, all ego. But it was just *so insensitive*. I've got to forgive him but first I have to forgive myself."

Gene stepped over with some hot hors d'oeuvres.

"Happy birthday, Lakshmi. Asparagus wrapped in prosciutto?"

"No, thank you, Gene."

"Did you see your cake?"

Gene pointed to it and she stood.

"Wow! What is that? Oh, it's the temple of silver and gold! And it's even got the sphere of light on top!"

"Tyler made it — the bartender. He bakes."

I nodded at her.

"Thank you," she said and looked at me with her hurt expression and then a brief smile. "I love it," she said, flatly.

"You're welcome," I said. "Happy birthday."

As I returned to the bar, I watched the women focus on Lakshmi who did nearly all the talking, most of it a berating of this former boyfriend. When dinner was ready, Gene brought her a plate of rigatoni with a sun-dried tomato cream sauce and shredded chicken with a side of arugula salad. Lakshmi took one bite of each. When I approached to refill her glass she said, "No, I'm stopping at two."

Around the room the men in their slacks and ties were talking quietly with each other, and from their flat expressions it was about practical matters and money. Kitaro was repeating for the third time to make things worse. I was gazing out the window, wondering when I might be able to leave when someone almost shouted at me.

"Got any scotch?"

I looked up to see Julie's blandly handsome escort. With his furrowed brow and tight lips, he had the aspect of an arrogant predator.

"Just vodka," I said.

"That'll have to do."

I looked down to see something bulging at the bottom of his pant leg. Was that an electronic tag above his ankle? Was he a felon?

Behind him coming up for a drink was a portly man, the dreaded film producer Aaron Sibley aka Crazy Aaron. He was someone I pretended not to see on Tuesday afternoons at the Cocaine Anonymous meetings conducted in the community room while we cleaned up. With Aaron was a young man who was his latest protégé/office slave who nervously nodded his head. "Did you call him back? When?" Aaron asked his assistant, his eyes constantly darting. "Why are you waiting to tell me this now? What did he say? Did he really like it? Did he say 'like' or 'love'? Do you *really* think he liked it? Did he give it to Nick to read? Did he say when he'd get back to us?"

Aaron looked at me before his assistant could answer any of those questions. "Club soda. Same for my assistant, he's driving."

"Coming right up."

"Where do I know you from?" he said to me. "Are you an actor?"

"No, just frequently mistaken for one. I'm Tyler St. George… the screen writer. We had a couple of meetings when I was up for the rewrite of *Another Fifteen Minutes*."

"Right. Terrific script but I just couldn't get anybody to bite. How's the writing going… Tyler?"

"Well, here I am bartending," I said. "How are you doing?"

"I'm very well. I've got five projects in development and a green light on two."

"Congrats."

"Who's your agent, Tyler?"

"Shelly Blaustein."

"Shelly. Ugh! You need a new agent. I'm not talking to her."

The doorbell rang again and the room quieted as everyone turned to look at a woman floating in that I recognized as Eloise Clayman. Blonde, slim and in her late fifties, her face still had the compelling bone structure of a model and the telltale signs of plastic surgery and skin peels. She dressed for the part of a New Age priestess with a diaphanous scarf over a saffron-colored pantsuit. Lakshmi was flattered to see her and left the sub-party to hug her. "Eloise! You made it!"

"Well of course I did, Lakshmi," she said in a throaty voice. "Though I can stay just a very little while. So much work to do, another Love-a-Thon tomorrow."

"Of course."

Lakshmi tapped her wine glass. "Excuse me... could I get everyone's attention? Eloise can't stay long. Can we serve the cake?"

Gene rushed out with birthday candles, stuck in four and lit them. We sang "Happy Birthday," and with so many gay men there, there was no lack of harmonies. I cut the cake and its slices were passed. Most of the women took a single bite then set it down. Lakshmi and Eloise were speaking in whispers — a private conversation — when I noticed Doris staring at them in stony anger.

"Excuse me, Ms. Clayman," Doris said with thunder in her voice.

Eloise and Lakshmi turned and looked at her, miffed by the interruption.

"I don't believe I've had the pleasure," said Eloise.

"My name is Doris Zinman. And I'm a Jew."

"As am I," said Eloise.

"As a Jew, I resent you're telling me that the Jews were responsible for the Holocaust because of their past crimes — that they brought it on themselves."

"You're taking that out of context," said Lakshmi.

"You are," said Eloise.

"Bullshit," said Doris. "My grandparents were burned in Hitler's ovens and their only crime was running a fish market in Leipzig."

"Well, Doris," said Eloise, playing the lady. "It is a little more complicated than that. Something tells me you don't know how they lived in their *previous* lives."

"My God, woman," said Doris. "We're Jews, not Hindus."

Eloise stood, forcing a smile as she clutched the Hermes bag that matched her scarf. "I wish I could stay, Lakshmi — but I really must go. My chauffeur has left the car running."

"Actually," said Lakshmi. "I need to go too. Jacob, bring my jacket and walk me to my car."

As Jacob trotted for her jacket, Lakshmi addressed us all. We had quieted and were watching the act of her departure.

"Thank you all," she said. "It's been just lovely."

The door opened and I saw a uniformed chauffeur opening the door of a Rolls Royce, something that came off as weird, quaint and a little disgusting. Eloise and Lakshmi air-kissed each other before the chauffeur helped Eloise into her car and then shut its silver door.

Minutes later, the party was over. I was emptying the ice bucket in the kitchen sink when Kevin walked in.

"Tyler, how about a cigarette?"

"I don't have any."

"I'm offering you one."

"Why not?"

I stepped out on the porch and looked at the view as we smoked Marlboro Lights. As I was an infrequent smoker, the cigarette made me dizzy.

"How do you know Jacob?" I asked.

"He skis... or tries to. I sold him this house."

"It's an interesting group of people," I said.

"Is it now?"

"Eloise Clayman. Now that I've met her in person, I'm even more disgusted. A chauffeur-driven Rolls?"

"Paid for by people dying of AIDS," Kevin responded. "I told you that Allen couldn't stand her. He went to one of her Love-a-Thons and never went back. He said it creeped him out."

"I'm sure she charged him admission and told him he was responsible for getting sick and he just needed to love himself more, the way she did when she got over her so-called cancer. She's a phony, Tyler, a complete charlatan. She's trying to tell me the virus inside me is a manifestation of my own self-loathing, that I invited it in because of my fear of getting old and ugly. All that from someone who's had at least one facelift."

"I... I didn't know you were positive," I said, more than a little shocked.

"You do now."

We looked at each other and he sighed in what I can only describe as a very honest moment.

"I'm sorry," I said, and meant it.

"So am I." He took a drag of his cigarette then blew a long stream of smoke.

"So all of us are responsible for the bad things that happen to us?" I finally said, circling back to Ms. Clayman. "Because of what we did in our past lives?"

"Or our present one. It's all bullshit, Tyler. There's no such thing as karma. The other thing Clayman tells gay men is that they manifested this virus to correct their promiscuity. And the reason they're promiscuous is because they hate themselves."

"How come no one's taken her down?"

"We can't do that. What are we going to tell thousands of gay men with late stage AIDS who think they're being helped at a Love-a-Thon? That she's a bullshit artist who wants fame and book sales so she can fill her closet with Christian Dior?"

Jonnie stepped out on the balcony. "Tyler, we could really use your help in here."

"Be right in."

I looked at this other Kevin who had dropped his cheery facade and I felt strangely, deeply close to him as we looked with worry on the city below.

"Thank you for sharing that," I said, and regretted it. I was starting to speak in the language of all the 12 step-programs I was overhearing at the church.

"Thanks for listening."

We stubbed out our cigarettes and immediately I hated the taste of smoke on my tongue. It was bitter and underlining a sudden gloom.

Gene and I and the other volunteers cleaned for the next couple of hours. The last step was loading the mostly intact cake in my car to take back to the church to cut up and send out to the clients on Monday. It felt strange and surreal to climb up the darkened stairwell of the church. After I flipped the switch, the kitchen was shockingly bright and white under fluorescent bulbs and at the same time it looked so old and neglected. Outside, the Santa Ana winds were blowing, shaking the palm trees in a dissonant symphony. In my superstitious heart, I took that as an indicator of a coming change. The time flew as we cut up and packaged the cake as Gene was a terrible gossip and I was guilty of encouraging him.

"Where do I know Doris from? Jonnie's girlfriend?" I asked.

"Commercials."

"Which one?"

"The one where she plays a lady construction worker."

"Right! The one with a jackhammer who uses Silky hand cream to 'keep her paws pink and pretty.'"

"Yes. And before that, Jonnie was married to the guy who does the voice for Cocoa the Chocolate Chihuahua."

"For Cocoa Crunchies? The cereal?"

"Si, senor. He makes a fortune from it — over a million dollars a year just to voice a few commercials and sound like some sleepy Mexican."

"Was Jonnie an actress?"

"She was. For a while she was doing cartoon voices — for *The Archie Show* and *Josie and the Pussycats in Outer Space*. Silly trash like that. She won an Obie back in the late 60's for some obscure little musical when she could still play an ingenue. You can tell from her look that she's kind of stuck in that time. I've been trying to talk her out of that pink lipstick and bombshell flip-do for years. It's *très tragique*."

"When did she figure out she's a lesbian?"

"I don't know that she ever did. She's kind of bi. Emphasis on 'kind of.' As she got older, men lost interest, but when she waltzed over to the lesbian ball, well, Jonnie Lindley was the new girl in town. A femme in the lesbian world is worth her weight in platinum. If you ask me, I think she'd go back to men in a second if the right one asked her out."

"Oh. I guess that's why she asked me if I had a big cock."

"I'm not surprised. I can't imagine she really likes to lick an old, gray kitty. *Dégoûtante*," he said with a mock shudder.

"So how did Jacob Hellman get a house in the Hills?" I asked.

"He's done very well during the AIDS crisis. He has a home nursing business, and well... *lots* of sick clients. He used to be a nurse himself."

"How does he know Lakshmi?"

"He started going to her lectures after he tested positive. He probably got it from a hustler since he's the type that has to pay for it."

Gene was quiet a moment then looked at me with an admiring smile. "Tyler, you just have this... natural spirituality."

"I do?"

"It seems like you've hardly had to work at. But it's probably just... past lives." He looked lost in thought, taken with some profound realization. "Yes, that's it," he said. "It's your past lives."

"You believe in reincarnation," I said.

"Oh yes. I've been regressed several times by Thelma Moss, the parapsychologist."

"Interesting. She charged you money to do this?"

"Of course. It's a very valuable experience. You should try it."

"Were you anybody famous?"

"Yes," he said, with a prideful chuckle. "Theodora of the Byzantine Empire, Mary Queen of Scots and... Catherine the Great."

"Really," I said. "All queens." I worried about how that came out when I said it, but he didn't take offense.

"Well, technically Theodora was an empress." Gene added. "Oh, and I was also Bairavhi Brahmani who was a teacher to Sri Ramakrishna."

"Ramakrishna?"

"Yes. She was the one who taught him about the left hand path."

I busied myself with the boxing of cake portions and was struggling not to laugh at the image in my head of Gene dressed up like Catherine the Great and lying under a horse. He had stopped packaging and was looking at me again with those pale green eyes.

"You know, Tyler, I think she liked you."

"Who?"

"Lakshmi."

"Oh."

"Would you be interested in a job here?"

Chapter 8

The Being Center of Los Angeles was in a bungalow in a turn of the century neighborhood above Sunset Boulevard in Hollywood. In the late 80's, the area's charming houses with their sloped roofs, shady verandas, creek stone fireplaces and wood-paneled interiors were being rescued by aspirants of the film, TV and music industries. The house for the Center had been lent by its owner, a leather queen with AIDS, to Lakshmi and Eloise's organization. Before it was presentable, they had to decommission its sex dungeon and put a stockade into storage. The house wasn't exactly the Hollywood Hills, but it was upward, on a slope above the Flats. I walked up the cracked, concrete walkway to enter its homey space and just as before, it smelled of a baking Stouffer's lasagna that clashed with sandalwood incense. The receptionist at the front desk was a tall woman in her mid-fifties with short silver hair, a pretty face and a bubbly personality. She set down her knitting and gave me a warm smile.

"Welcome to the Center. How may I help you?"

"I'm Tyler St. George," I said. "I'm here to see Lakshmi and Terrence Stansfield."

"Have a seat, Tyler. I'm Vonnie," she said and offered me a handshake. I looked on her desk where there were a dozen framed photos of herself with a young man in various dance costumes, a mini-museum of her dead son. "Would you like some fudge?" she asked me extending a plate. "I made it myself."

"Maybe after the meeting," I said. "To celebrate if it goes well."

To my left in what had been a living room were some men who looked to be in good health as they attempted One-Legged King Pigeon on yoga mats. I took a seat on a sectional couch in what had been the dining room. Saucy cubes of cheesy pasta and a green salad had been served on paper plates to quiet, emaciated men and their companions. The yogis had commenced a loud breathing exercise, panting as they flicked their tongues, but over them I heard what sounded like an argument. The deeper voices of two or more men were muffled and unintelligible but above them was the sharp pitch of a woman. "I am very disappointed!" I heard through a door. "Don't you ever speak like that to me. Don't you ever speak to me again! You've never liked me! He's never liked me, Jacob! Get him out of here, he's fired! GET OUT!"

Sudden silence. Then a door opened and slammed and a man marched angrily out to the foyer clutching his suit jacket with one hand and holding a briefcase in the other. He turned briefly to look over his shoulder, his face red and sweaty with rage. I recognized him as one of the suits at Lakshmi's birthday party, someone who had chatted with Jacob Hellman for much of the night. The kitchen workers stepped out to see what had happened. The eaters set down forks and the yogis looked at each other in the awkward stillness. The receptionist set down her knitting again when the phone buzzed.

"Yes? Yes," she said looking my way. "OK. OK. Yes. Yes, I will."

Slowly, quietly, Vonnie returned the receiver to its cradle and stood as she spoke to me. "Tyler, our apologies, but we need to... reschedule. Something... *urgent* has come up. May we call you later?"

I was about to say OK when I heard more shouting behind the door and then a woman sobbing between hysterical shrieks.

My interview was rescheduled a few days later at what had been described in the press as Lakshmi's "modest" West Hollywood apartment. She lived in a well-maintained Colonial Revival, a fourplex with pink bricks, white trims and blooming flower gardens. While it was not luxurious, it was roomy and far from modest with its high ceilings, up-to-date kitchen and tasteful if unimaginative furnishings. The walls were mostly bare with surprisingly little artwork but they were painted the color of raspberry jam which was one thing I liked about it. Sitting at a desk in the foyer was a receptionist/personal assistant whom I recognized as the pretty brunette that had arrived at Lakshmi's birthday party with her mail pouch. The receptionist chatted on the phone and gave me a theatrical wave as I approached, smiling to reveal her perfect white teeth.

"Listen to me, sweetheart. It just gets better," she was saying to someone. "One door closes, one door opens. I am telling you, this little obstacle is actually a big step to something so much better, a ladder to the stars. I gotta go, sweetie, but we *will* talk soon and until then you just wait and see what the universe has in mind for you."

Wow, she spoke a lot like Jonnie. Maybe she was on the phone *to* Jonnie.

She hung up and turned her full attention to me, standing and throwing out her hand for a shake. In a white and pink skirt suit, she looked as bright as a bouquet of carnations. "You must be Tyler," she said.

"I am."

The phone rang again. "Office of Lakshmi Steinmetz. This is Julie speaking."

I looked at the wall behind Julie and saw her eight-by-ten with her agent's name and number in the lower corner and finally realized it was Julie Sainsbury, the model from *It's a Deal*, a Sixties game show where contestants in kooky outfits marched around giant hats. When the music stopped, they pulled out an envelope to reveal that they'd just won a new car, one that Julie would lovingly stroke, or they were zonked with a box of Sunkist prunes.

"OK, I'll tell her. Get here soon." Julie hung up and pressed the button of the phone's intercom. "Lakshmi, that was Derrick. He's going to be a few minutes late."

"Is Tyler there?" I heard faintly from the back of the apartment. They really didn't need an intercom.

"Yes."

"Send him back."

"You have been summoned," she said and pointed me to the bedroom with sweeping arms, as if showing off a new sailboat.

The door was partially open. I was a little tentative and felt like a male spider approaching a black widow in her web.

Lakshmi was lying in the center of a king-size bed, something that made her look even smaller and childlike. She was pouting, like a little girl who had been sent to her room. On her lap was a Ouija board and perhaps it had told her something she didn't want to hear. On her left was a pile of *The New York Times*, *The Los Angeles Times* and *The Washington Post*. On her right was a pile of magazines including *Time*, *Newsweek* and *Vanity Fair*. Her walls were covered with shelves full of books except for the one across from her which had a framed print of Maxfield Parrish's *Daybreak* in a chipped, antique frame. It looked like something bought for a few dollars at a garage sale that might have been in her college dorm. "I always loved that painting," I said.

"It's my favorite of his," she responded. She seemed sad and pensive yet eager to have me as company.

"Supposedly at one point one out of four American households had a copy of *Daybreak* — the most popular print ever. I always thought it was too beautiful."

"Too beautiful?" she asked, intrigued. "How can something be too beautiful?"

"It hurts to look at it — like someone who's too good-looking. And it's humbling. Parrish's mastery of technique is just astonishing, a real accomplishment, something that exceeded the old masters. If I was a painter, it would make me question my own abilities."

She tilted her head then nodded. "Interesting. Parrish was blessed with talent," she said. "And he made great use of it."

I looked around at her hundreds of books to see which ones we shared in common.

"You're a reader," she said.

"And a writer. Well, a semi-occasional screenwriter."

A few books caught my eye that were grouped together and all had the word "cult" in their titles including *The Psychology of Cults*, *The Mindset of Cultism*, and *Cults and Mind Control*. Next to these were books by Bhagwan Shree Rajneesh, a cult leader whose dissolution of his ashram and flight from Oregon was raw and recent history. Was Lakshmi planning on creating a new cult or attempting to avoid the appearance of one?

I looked on her bedside table and saw a familiar envelope, one with a picture of a smiling African child hugging a goat. "You're a Help a Child sponsor," I said.

"Only twenty dollars a month," she said with a glimmer of a smile.

"Just got a letter from mine in Bangladesh. His name's Sharmin. And his family just bought some new chickens. He said they're beautiful and one laid its first egg."

The smile broadened and she chuckled.

"Mine is in Sudan. Tyler, I remember you," she said with a hint of a Southern accent in what I could hear was her real voice. "You're the one who baked me that fabulous cake."

"Glad you liked it."

"What's your sign?"

"Uh, Capricorn," I said while wondering if this was an appropriate question at a job interview. And was this the interview?

"Capricorn! Of course you are," she said and her smile went incandescent as she cocked her head. "I get you, Tyler. I totally understand your energy."

The front door opened and we heard a theatrical male voice in the foyer as someone chatted with Julie, the two of them acting as if they were ecstatic to finally see each other after a decades-long separation by the Berlin Wall.

"Derrick's here," Lakshmi said in her deeper, more actressy voice, her face suddenly serious. "Go out and introduce yourself and I'll join you in a moment. Close the door on your way out."

"Why, hello, you must be Tyler," said the man walking toward me as he extended his hand for a vigorous shake. "I'm Derrick Vanderven."

I suspected Derrick had been in the theater at one point in his life from the way he sang his words and elongated his vowels. I recognized him as one of the guests at the birthday party, one of the Center's innumerable board members. He was wearing an expensive black suit and reminded me of Vincente Minelli with his bald head, pronounced teeth and stagey mannerisms. He was wearing what was called a "pizza tie," one with snazzy splashes of red, black and white.

"It's nice to meet you, Derrick."

"Are you an actor, Tyler?"

"No, but I'm frequently mistaken for one. I'm a screenwriter."

"As well as quite the chef we hear."

"Well, not professionally. But I worked in a lot of restaurants in my college years. And I believe *you* are the new CEO."

"Executive director," he said, smiling as he corrected me. "Lakshmi is the CEO. She prayed on it and it appears he approves of me for the position."

"Who does?"

Derrick looked up at the ceiling, toward heaven, and put his hands together in prayer.

"Oh. Right," I said and grinned. "He with a capital H."

Lakshmi emerged from her bedroom in one of her tailored skirt suits. She was three inches taller in her heels and had a fresh slash of red on her lips. "You're late!" she said and pointed at Derrick, her finger flicking like a switchblade.

"I apologize, Lakshmi," Derrick said. "But I thought we were meeting at the Center."

"Julie, where were we scheduled for this meeting?"

Julie flipped through her organizer after putting on her reading glasses. "Originally at the Center but then rescheduled for here. I... I can see why Derrick was a little confused."

"Tyler has the job," Lakshmi said to Derrick before she turned to me. "Tyler, this is an organization that is just scraping by. The pay is fifteen thousand a year and there are no benefits other than those that come from being of service to a very needy community."

Even in 1989, $15,000 a year was shitty money. The student loans would have to wait.

"I'm not here to get rich," I said. "I'm here to help."

Lakshmi was smiling again but looked on the verge of happy tears. "That is so Capricorn," she said, warmth in her voice. "Now if you all will excuse me, I've got to get back to my writing."

She froze for a moment. "Oh, Tyler, I forgot to ask. We're short of staff for tomorrow night's art auction at the Sarkisian. It may be just the *most* important night for our organization. Our survival might depend on it. I'm supposed to ask if you can bartend for us?"

"Of course I can," I said, knowing that Jonnie had put her up to this. "I'm a Capricorn."

Chapter 9

Hollywood showed up for Manna from Heaven. At one point, the fire marshals closed the doors of Larry Sarkisian's spacious gallery in Beverly Hills when it exceeded capacity. Angie Dickinson, Taylor Dane and Joyce DeWitt had to wait an hour before they were recognized as celebrities and secreted in through the back door. Just before the bidding commenced at 9 p.m., Lakshmi was introduced by Sarkisian, the "gallerist to the stars." Dressed in another of her "gently worn" designer pantsuits, she was cold and commanding as she took the microphone and treated the crowd as if they were her followers.

"Thank you all for coming, which is itself a gracious act. Now will you all please join me in prayer."

That was the moment a lot of people looked at each other to shrug or blink or make that asymmetrical expression of disdain. A few of the celebrities were her followers and they dropped their heads and closed their eyes in obedience. Lakshmi's eyes were closed as she streamed her consciousness and asked Jesus to reveal "the peace that comes out of chaos" then spoke of the "the love made pure when it leaves despair behind" and then, to prime the bidding, she mentioned the "freedom that comes when we let go of money, the release of which disintegrates the cage of our egos." Her trance was broken when many in the audience, not knowing who she was, lost patience and talked over her as she droned on and fell into Way-speak. "When our generosity flows, we have embraced the responsibilities of the Childrenhood and become one with all that is holy and become the Holy Spirit himself."

"Who is this chick?" muttered the man in front of me who had turned away from Lakshmi and handed me his glass for a refill. "Hell if I know," whispered his girlfriend, a notable television actress with a Texan accent. "Some sorta ooky-spooky Jew for Jesus." Somebody clapped three times and shouted, "OK, enough prayer!"

Lakshmi's eyes opened and flashed with anger as Sarkisian stepped toward her, nervously smiling as he reached to take the mic back. "Lovely, lovely, thank you, Lakshmi. Amen!" he said with a forced chuckle as the first piece was brought to the dais for auction. Lakshmi stepped away, fuming, as the auctioneer was handed the mic to describe a Hockney acrylic of a swimming pool.

Steve Martin and Victoria Tennant bid on several pieces and won them all including a picture of an angel painted by Keith Haring in the last month of his life. Brett Sommers outbid Jamie Farr for a rusted car muffler that had been affixed to a plank of wood by Noah Purifoy. Much of the art was the usual scribbles that Dali, Chagall and Picasso churned out by the thousands and that recycled through benefits like this one, but a few works made by volunteers and clients of Manna also came to the block. A blown-up and framed xerox of Madonna that a client had colorized with paint markers sold for $2,000. Other smaller works around the room were claimed in the silent auction and nearly everything sold, regardless of its quality. People wanted to help.

The party continued, but as usual, Lakshmi slipped out before everyone else. It was midnight when we ran out of liquor. The DJ ended the night with a nostalgia move, Donna Summer's *Last Dance,* a song with a special pathos that reminded us all of the carefree days, when sex and death were not so united. When the receipts taker told Jonnie we had made close to $500,000, she raised her hands and looked to the heavens. "Thank you, God!" she shouted. We celebrated the end of the evening with sips from a bottle of chardonnay I fished from the bottom of an ice basin.

The following morning, the event known as *Heavenly Objects - An Art Auction for People with Aids* was the lead story of the Calendar section of the *Los Angeles Times*. Pictures of the celebrities included "Ms. Lakshmi Steinmetz, lecturer and founder of Manna from Heaven."

After that night, the client list for Manna grew and so did the number of volunteers. Those early days were kind of like hosting a party every day and it was sort of like being a bartender. It was the job of the staff to make volunteers feel welcomed, appreciated and entertained as we set them to work at chopping, peeling, packing and driving. At eleven o'clock, we pulled pans out of the oven or pots off of the stove and the volunteers jockeyed for position, desirous of being the one to plunk in the mashed potatoes, splash sauce on the pasta or seal the lids of the containers, many of which were decorated with elaborate ink stamps and handwritten messages of love and support.

At eleven thirty, when all the bags were packed, everyone went into the community room to hold hands in an ever-widening prayer circle with ever-longer prayers, sometimes as long as thirty minutes. That annoyed me as it meant the food was getting cold. Jonnie encouraged the volunteers to pray aloud, to share their grief and their hopes, but it was also her daily moment, her own ministry, and her time back on the planks.

Occasionally Jonnie was upstaged by someone who requested to sing something a cappella or an actor or comedian who recounted a funny story. Once, a volunteer named Tourmaline entered the prayer circle with her ghetto blaster to perform a contorting, interpretive dance dedicated to the clients — something that would have to be described to them since they weren't exactly present. And then there was the day that two mimes in white face entered the circle to portray the encounter of a driver delivering food to a lonely client, each drawing a heart on his chest. When the "driver" left, he mimed a pair of angel wings and flew off while the "client" rubbed his tummy and licked his lips in anticipation of the delicious food. When he opened the bag, a heart-shaped balloon floated up that was tied to a candy apple. I had to literally bite my tongue to prevent myself from snickering.

Jonnie always wrapped up the prayers by looking skyward with some variation of "love and healing vibes for those who need them" and "peace and eternal bliss for those who have transitioned" and some variation of "thanks to God for his love, who is all love and made this day to love us all."

After the drivers left, if there were leftovers, we served them to the volunteers as lunch at some folding tables. These were some happy meals, full of laughter and jokes from the many performers and writers whose profession it was to entertain. The afternoons were harder and quieter and less well attended as they lacked the glamour and excitement of the assembly line. Post-lunch was often the monotonous "frenching" of thousands of green beans into slivers, the teary chopping of a hundred onions, the grizzly severance of meat from bones and the hard, messy work of scrubbing pots and pans by people we called "the suds saints" who got soaked at the shallow sink.

By four o'clock the chefs were beat, but every day ended with the sharp stink of bleach as we sanitized the counters and stoves and mopped the floor of corroded linoleum. Often enough, if someone flaked on a delivery, Johnnie would ask me to take the route which meant sitting in traffic coming back. I never turned her down and discovered a multitude of obscure neighborhoods in the Greater Los Angeles area. Deliveries were sometimes as far south as San Pedro where the dark silhouettes of cargo ships in harbor dwarfed the little bungalows. Sometimes the routes took me in the opposite direction to streets that ascended into Altadena and Sierra Madre and ended in the oak-forested canyons of the San Gabriel foothills.

I loved the waves of humanity that flowed through that kitchen, the constant stream of new groups and personalities. Some of the volunteers, the flaky ones, were the beautiful actors and actresses who attended Lakshmi's lectures. They were there to shift their karma in hopes of getting their big break and would parrot Lakshmi as they peeled garlic or grated cheese, saying, "We only receive as much from the universe as we put into it." They seldom returned for a second or third time.

The earnest and dependable volunteers were those who had seen a TV commercial starring a beloved comedienne who asked them to "put on their halos and come on down." Many of these were retired seniors and one group, who brightened every Thursday, was known as the Jewish Moms Brigade, a mahjong klatch who drove together from the San Fernando Valley and sometimes brought their adult children. Among other groups were some lesbian ex-nuns, some "differently abled" teens we were not to call "mentally retarded," several trans-youth runaways, an Asian sorority from UCLA and lots of Beverly Hills ladies who got all dressed up to pound out chicken breasts.

Some of the volunteers wandered over from a popular Alcoholics Anonymous meeting held in the community room that ran from seven to eight each morning. A few of these were celebrities and a couple were former customers of mine from JJs Pub. One morning we were thrilled when Elton John wandered over, shook a few hands then peeled a few potatoes. Gene or Tim and I would be setting up the kitchen as the twelve-steppers took the mic each morning to make their "shares" or elect officers or award chips to those marking a new period of sobriety. It made for some great eavesdropping with many gifted raconteurs reenacting the moment "they hit bottom." I will never forget the story of one very cute straight guy who talked about getting into a fight at Al's Bar over a woman he was interested in. He remembered getting punched in the jaw before a long blackout. When he woke the following morning, he was completely naked, in an alley and "wondering why my asshole felt so sore and greasy. I grabbed the nearest thing I could find to cover up my junk, a wrapper for some Hostess Ding Dongs."

Some of the volunteers were petty criminals completing their community service. Nearly all of them asked us to sign their cards that said they had completed their hours before they had done so. All of them promised to return — and not one of them ever did. A few of the volunteers were moochers who arrived late in the morning to tie on an apron, look pious during the prayer, and then treat themselves to some free lunch before sneaking away. Some were guys on the make having heard there were "lots of hotties" at Manna. Many of the people who came in were just lonely and had nothing else to do — they were supported by a trust fund or were comfortably retired with time on their hands. Some of the crazier ones were unemployable and supported by government programs and living in Section 8 housing. But most of the volunteers were there for all the right reasons. They felt for the suffering and wanted to do something, *anything,* to alleviate the pain and make sure that the sick got, as Lakshmi said, "a side of love with a hot meal."

Even with its grubby, stained walls and dirt-caked windows with their cracked glass, I remember that kitchen as a bright, sunny space and a cheerful refuge. I gladly ran up the steps each morning, eager to get to work and happy that each day would be interesting and different from the previous. I got to do something I liked, which was to make rich, caloric desserts as well as the Mexican, Chinese and Italian entrees. Volunteers popped cassette tapes of the latest music into a donated stereo and it often felt like a party. It was the making of many new friends and a series of invitations to dinners, fundraisers, bar and bat mitzvahs, cocktail parties, theater openings, weddings and afternoon teas most of which I felt too tired to attend but most of which I did. The work was getting harder and longer as the client list grew. We were poorly equipped, crowded, and in violation of health codes with a lack of refrigeration and storage areas safe from vermin. But instead of relocating to a professional facility, the flush of money from Heavenly Objects was being spent elsewhere.

Manna from Heaven was still under the umbrella of the Being Center, but the fame of the former was overshadowing the latter. Lakshmi decided it was time for the Center to leave its little, donated bungalow and take up residence on Robertson Boulevard in the heart of Boys Town. That meant paying an expensive rent. She chose a charming, pre-war building with two stories, a mansard roof and an extended first floor with rooms for yoga and seminars like "How to Find and Keep a Relationship" and "Recovery from Teasing and Emotional Abuse" as well as "Living Well with HIV."

Within weeks, the new Being Center was lovingly furnished with a saltwater aquarium and its walls were decorated with donated art. Lakshmi chose the largest office for herself, a sunny space on the second floor with French windows, a flower box and a view of the back of Studio One. Jacob Hellman took the office next to it. We held the first of what would be monthly meetings late in December of 1989 on the sectional couch of the reception room where Vonnie, the office manager/receptionist had completed the decoration of a Christmas tree and plugged in an electric menorah.

"Tyler St. George!" I heard as Derrick Vanderven stepped out of his first-floor office with its vintage furnishings. He handed me an opened envelope in front of the entire staff. "You need to pay your student loans."

I looked at the envelope, plainly addressed to me but with the Center's address on it — the long arm of the Federal Student Aid office.

"Why is this opened?" I asked. "It's addressed to me."

"If it comes here, we're going to open it."

"Well, I'm making less than three hundred dollars a week. The loans have to wait."

"Then you better arrange a deferral," he said.

So much for discretion, I thought.

The meeting began with everyone holding hands and Lakshmi leading a prayer. She looked different today — no make up — and she had stopped dying her hair its darker color with red highlights. She was wearing one of her hooded, flowing outfits that looked like the habit of a Coptic monk. Her angular face was plumper, softer. Had she gained weight? That was anathema to her as thinness was something she modeled, a part of her lectures, where she advised her followers to "reach for God instead of a cookie." Sitting to her right, in reverence, was Jonnie and on her left was Derrick, who sat up straight and quiet in his slacks and tie.

Jeremy and Joffrey, the handsome blonds, were now the Volunteer Coordinator and Applications Director, respectively, and each had a print out with them. "We are now delivering one hundred and seventy-three meals a day," said Jeremy in his soft Southern accent. "Up by 57 in the last week alone."

"And we have a waiting list of thirty-three more clients," said Joffrey. "Likely a lot more once I process some new applications."

"A waiting list?" said Lakshmi. "We shouldn't have a waiting list! Everyone who needs this service should get it."

"Lakshmi," said Tim, stress in his voice. "We've reached capacity. We reached it months ago. That tiny little kitchen is for serving cookies and coffee for church functions. It's not for serving two hundred complete meals."

"Tim is right," I said. "We don't have the storage space, the refrigerators, the stoves and the ovens to cook for any more people. The portions are getting smaller."

"We need a kitchen ten times the size of the one we have," Tim added.

Lakshmi looked at Gene. "How many more clients can we take, Gene?"

"Well," he said, hesitant to disappoint her. "We... we are running out of space."

"We need a professional facility," Tim said, his voice shaking with nerves. "And professional equipment."

"Like a commercial mixer," I said. "If I'm going to make cakes for two hundred people, I need a forty quart mixer. I'm having to work in batches with that little KitchenAid or hand mix in a basin."

"All right, all right. Let's pray on this right now," Lakshmi said, sounding annoyed. "Let's visualize with God what we want God to bring us."

"Let's visualize a new computer and a new printer as well," said Niles, the Englishman who prepared the route sheets. "Right now we've got a steam powered Kay-Pro that has not been working well since cockroaches took up residence inside it. And we need something better than a dot matrix printer if we're going to provide the drivers with some legible directions. I really should have my own computer."

"He should and I should get a new one," said Jericho, now the Director of Information Technology. "We're using my old one from five years ago which is a real POS."

"POS?" said Laskhmi.

"Piece of shit," said Jericho. "And we have no place to keep paper files. I'm overwhelmed with client and volunteer logs as well as the route sheets."

"And it would be nice to have a steady supply of new grocery bags," said Tinka, the newest to join the staff as the Delivery Coordinator, but colloquially known as the Bag Girl aka the Baguette. She had freshly shaven her head and her right arm was scabby from a new tattoo of a screaming baby. Tinka was wearing hot orange boxer shorts with purple polka dots and a tight wife beater with no bra. "It's just so tedious to have to reuse the same bags over and over again and to rely on donations from the volunteers. Please, please, please," she dramatized, "bring us your used grocery bags."

"Lakshmi," said Tim, working up his nerve. "I really think you need to come into the kitchen yourself and see what it's like now. If you knew just how difficult, how stressful, how crowded it is, you would...."

"OK, OK, OK," Lakshmi interrupted after looking at her watch. "I get it, we're going through some growing pains. Duly noted. Let's throw this out to the universe and see what comes back. Now since it is the holiday season, I've got a couple of surprises for you. Derrick?"

Derrick went into his office and returned with two blue-green shopping bags from Tiffany's. Inside them were little blue-green boxes, two for each of us. The men all got a black wallet and a black leather belt. The women got a black lizard clutch and a silver key fob. A belt and a wallet were practical choices and I could use them, but coming from Tiffany's, these had to have cost a hundred dollars each. If they had come with a gift receipt, I would have redeemed them to pay my rent. With what all these gifts cost, we might have bought a utility fridge, an industrial stove and a forty-quart mixer.

"Tiffany's," Gene said, touched by her choice. "Thank you, Lakshmi."

"We want you to know how much you're appreciated," Lakshmi said "Don't we, Derrick?"

"Why, yes," he said, a little startled to be invited into the conversation.

Lakshmi stood from her chair and smiled. "Now," she said. "You'll be seeing a little less of me for the next few months. I think you all know I'm working on a book but the more exciting news is..."

She looked around at all our faces, pausing to milk the moment.

"I'm pregnant!"

We broke out in applause and then shouted our congratulations.

"Wonderful news," said Derrick. "And who's the proud papa?"

Lakshmi was stunned, staring slack-jawed at Derrick.

"That's... that's none of your business!" she sputtered.

"I'm sorry," he said. "I didn't mean to offend. I was just hoping there was double good news... that you're having a baby as well as, um,... that you're serious about somebody."

"What are you implying?" she asked through indignant gasps. "I fully intend for my child to have a father someday!"

"I'm not implying anything," said Derrick. She stared at him, her heavy breathing the only sound in the long silence.

"Everybody, Merry Christmas and Happy Hanukkah," Lakshmi said, as if she was talking about a bloody car wreck. "Derrick, I need to speak with you in my office."

Derrick sighed and followed her up the stairs. None of us spoke as we heard the door slam and then the sound of Lakshmi ranting from the second floor.

"So," Johnnie said to Gene to fill the silence among us. "Are you still up for Dinesh?"

"I guess so," he said.

"What's Dinesh?" I asked.

"Not what," Johnnie said. "Who. He's an ascended master and he's visiting Los Angeles. You should see him, Tyler. We all should."

"Why?"

"To receive the blue light of cosmic transcendence, something he transfers with a breath."

"Is there a charge for this?" I asked.

"A donation. Lakshmi's going too."

Oh, this was sounding promising already.

Chapter 10

In the early mornings, Gene and I were usually alone in the kitchen to set it up. We pulled our pots and pans and utensils out of a tall, rolling cage that was locked up at the end of each day, which was a clumsy means of dealing with a complete lack of storage space. Nearly every morning, Gene had some grievance and after a "Good morning, Tyler" he spoke to me as if I were his therapist.

"I just hate my new car," he said on Wednesday.

On Thursday it was, "That cute Andy who comes in on Tuesdays *does* have a boyfriend. And he's black and a *Muslim*."

On Friday, it was "I'm just so sick of Anthony. He thinks he's *so spiritual*."

"And you don't think he is?" I asked. Gene was referring to a popular volunteer who had designed Manna From Heaven's logo: a smiling slice of bread with angel wings.

"I've been meditating *years* longer than he has. And I was a student of *The Way* before he ever came to Los Angeles."

"Are you competing with him?"

"No," he said and paused. "But he wants to go with us to see Dinesh."

"Why shouldn't he?"

"Because we're going with Lakshmi. And Anthony's just not on the same level as we are."

"You and Jonnie."

Jonnie entered at that moment, wearing a royal blue turtleneck as the weather had turned cooler.

"Good morning, gentlemen," she said as she did her usual shuffle on heels and looked at me with pleading eyes. "Tyler, we have a favor to ask."

"Yes?"

"What are you doing tonight?"

"I don't know. It depends on what you ask me."

"We need a designated driver."

"You're getting drunk?"

She and Gene laughed. "You are just *adorable*! No, we're seeing Dinesh! The experience can be intense! It's been described as an 'unfolding of the cosmos' and for some people it can be overwhelming. If you're one of the special ones who can see the blue light, it's advised that you shouldn't drive for at least a few hours."

"So you're too ecstatic to see straight?"

"Something like that. If it happens, you may not have complete control of your reflexes. All you'll want is to be with your bliss!"

"So this Dinesh is dispensing nirvana?"

"Not nirvana, but it's a 'beacon on the road to enlightenment,' a 'quickening of the process.' The blue light is the lowest level of the colors the Buddha saw before he reached eternal bliss... but it is progress."

"I would love to drive you," I said, and meant it. I wasn't going to miss this.

After work, I took my boxy, little Honda Civic wagon to a car wash and filled it with gas to drive to a hotel in Santa Monica where the guru of the hour, Dinesh Carvalho, would be giving a brief talk and then some "private sessions." With his magic breath, he would reveal the blue light to those he sensed had progressed enough to perceive it. I caught Kyle on his way out the door to work or somewhere. He was wearing the strange combination of short shorts with a leather motorcycle jacket and he had buzzed his hair to a tenth of an inch, a look that harshened his features.

"Why are you wearing shorts when it's cold out?" I asked.

"Why did you spend money getting your car washed?" he responded.

"I'm driving people from work tonight to a thing. Including Lakshmi."

"*Lakshmi?* Where are you taking Lakshmi?"

"*They're* going to get the blue light of cosmic transcendence from someone named Dinesh."

"The blue light of *what*?"

"Yeah, I know."

"Don't forget. Monday's my showcase at the Groundlings."

"I'd never forget that."

After I walked our dogs, I drove over to Gene's apartment which he said was in tony Hancock Park, and it was, sort of, an area near Melrose and Paramount Studios. It was a street of affordable, single-level duplexes just north of the city's oldest and most impressive mansions. Gene's neighbor had parked his truck on a grassless front lawn and I heard a rooster crowing from a coop in the back. The building was Old Hollywood Spanish and not without some charm, but inside Gene had a surprisingly empty apartment. He had worked as an interior designer so I was expecting a showcase of his talents, a place full of fine things he could get for a discount or were the discards of his rich clients. His spare furniture was sturdy but indistinct, mostly beige, and nothing he had was surprising, dramatic or whimsical. His walls were bare except for a picture of a young and beautiful Indian woman with a sizable dot on her forehead and wearing something like a red sailor's hat. She looked familiar.

"So you're a minimalist," I said as I looked around.

"No, I'm just very selective," he responded. "If I can't have what I really want, I don't accept any compromises."

At the end of the living room was an area with some canvasses, an easel and some oil paints on a palette. The canvasses were uninteresting with muddy colors and were neither abstract nor representational. The one he was working on was a loose grid of gray and white slashes on a background of muddy brown. The one brighter, colorful one was a clumsy series of closely packed squiggles. All of it was the work of an unpromising beginner.

"So you paint," I said.

"I'm just getting into it."

"Well you've got a lot of wall space for paintings," I said. "Did you study art?"

"No. I was a theater arts major."

"You *were*?"

"Yes, but I was just... too self-conscious to be an actor. I just couldn't do it. So I went into design."

"You and Tim," I said.

"Tim? A designer?" he said and scoffed. "Have you seen Tim's house?"

"Yeah. It's very... comfy-cozy."

"Let me be perfectly honest, Tyler. I have no idea who would ever hire *Tim* to decorate a house — maybe some elderly lady from Indiana who didn't know any better. Tim will also tell you that he went to UCLA, but what he won't tell you is that it was extension classes."

Just before we left, Gene lit a joss stick and set it before a small, porcelain idol of Kwan-yin before he rubbed a string of jade beads and mouthed a prayer. Then we went to pick up Jonnie from the bungalow in West Hollywood she rented. She was waiting for us on the porch swing with a friend, someone with a square jaw, broad shoulders and prominent biceps who wore Levi's and a blue work shirt. I thought he was a ruggedly cute blond and then realized *she* was a woman. She grabbed Jonnie by the shoulders and possessively kissed her before giving her a pat on the butt to scoot her on her way. Jonnie trotted to us on the toes of her heels, lugging one of her many oversized shoulder bags. "I am sooooo excited!" she said as she got into the car. "Aren't you excited, Gene?"

"I am," he said. "And a little... nervous."

"Nervous? About what?"

"I don't know. It's not like I haven't met an ascendant master before."

"You have?" I asked.

"Of course I have. I see one almost weekly. I've been doing Siddha Yoga with Chidvilasananda since she came here in June."

"With who?"

"Gurumayi," Jonnie said.

"She's the designated successor of Baba Muktananda," Gene said. "You *do* know who that is?"

"Oh, I do," I said, realizing the picture on Gene's wall was of his ascendant mistress. I remembered the story about her in Rolling Stone magazine — a rich and glamorous woman from India and the feud she had with her brother as to who would take over a multimillion-dollar business from Swami Muktananda. The swami was a man accused of rape and sex with underage girls.

"And her brother too," I added. "Swami Nityananda or something — who she accused of having sex with his disciples."

"He did," said Gene. "But Gurumayi has stayed pure. She's a pure being. I just... just..."

"What?" said Jonnie.

"I just can't imagine that Dinesh is more evolved than she is and that he can transmit that kind of... I don't know... *transformation* if that's what this is with a breath. Gurumayi meditated for years before she was ready to take over from Muktananda — before he could pass her his lineage."

"And how did he do that?" I asked. Gene scoffed, like I shouldn't be asking such a stupid question.

"With a few words."

"A few words?" I asked. "Like magic words?"

"A few *holy* words," Gene said. "And she was enlightened." He sighed with envy.

"Like I said, Gene, it's a beacon," said Jonnie. "Not enlightenment, not satori, and it's only for those who are ready for it."

Lakshmi was waiting for us in front of her building, dressed in an oversized cashmere sweater. She was chatting with a woman with a baby in a stroller who appeared to be one of Lakshmi's adoring followers. Gene surrendered the front seat to Lakshmi after opening the door for her. She scooted in ladylike, gingerly sliding her bottom over the seat.

"Tyler, thank you so much for driving," she said to me. "Is this OK with you? Are you disappointed that you won't be having a private session with Dinesh?"

"No, I'm not disappointed," I said. "But I am interested to find out about your experiences. I brought some work while I wait."

"Lakshmi, I meant to ask," said Jonnie, hesitating to complete her question. "Is this the right thing for *you*? At this point? I mean with the baby and everything?"

"You mean, would there be some danger to my fetus? No, not at all. I checked with Dinesh's wife and he's worked with plenty of pregnant women. Part of why I'm doing this is *for* the baby. It might give her a head start, put her on an early path to self-realization."

"I think you're going to make a wonderful mother," Jonnie said.

"Thank you. I think so too. So! Jonnie! How are you? I haven't talked to you in a while."

"I'm just fine," she said. "I'm wonderful."

"How are you feeling about Doris?"

"Well, sad. Not as sad as she is."

"You broke up with Doris?" I asked.

"Well, Tyler, it's complicated. We weren't really together in the first place so it wasn't quite a breakup. I've let her know she should look elsewhere — for someone who can give her more of what she needs."

"That's the most loving thing you could have done for her," said Lakshmi. "You've freed her to find someone right for her."

"Yes, I... I just need to be with someone who is a little more spiritual."

"Yes," Lakshmi said. "Doris was just so aggressive, all caught up in some self-defeating cycles. I always sensed some real ego addiction with her."

"Jonnie is already seeing someone new," Gene said, snideness in his voice.

"Do tell!" said Lakshmi.

"Nothing to tell," said Jonnie. "It's in the very early stages."

"What's her name? Or his name?" Lakshmi asked.

"Her. Sandy."

"She's built like Arnold Schwarzenegger," Gene said. "I'm jealous."

"Because Jonnie has a girlfriend or because she has muscles?" I asked.

"Both," said Gene, with a dour laugh. Lakshmi turned and looked at him.

"So, Gene. How are you? You sound kind of sad again."

He sighed. "I'm OK. I guess. But I'm thinking of changing my psychic."

"You are? Why?" Jonnie asked, surprise in her voice. "I think Rosalyn is very gifted!"

"Maybe she is. Maybe she isn't. But at my last reading, she saw no love potential for the next few years. The next few years! There was just a dark mist! And then she confirmed the whole thing with a tarot reading —the last card to come up was The Hermit!" He sighed again.

"Precognition is not a science," Lakshmi said. "Psychic readings and the tarot are never one hundred percent accurate. The best psychics I ever worked with were about seventy percent right. Once I got a reading that was completely wrong — but it came completely true for the friend I came with who sat in the lobby. He ended up getting my reading and I got his. It was just an accident of proximity."

Gene sighed once more. "I came alone to see Rosalyn. I don't know — maybe it was the reading for the woman waiting in the living room."

"Gene, you should look to God's love in the meantime," Lakshmi said. "God is better than any boyfriend."

"Yes," he said. "Yes, he is."

Over one hundred people were in a conference room at the Santa Monica Hilton where a dais had been set up with a large, throne-like chair. The crowd turned when the four of us walked in. Lakshmi had created a sensation just by her arrival and was converged on by a largely female crowd who were eager to get and give her attention. As she soaked it up and traded kisses and handshakes, Anthony, the graphics designer, walked over to us, dressed in a white cotton kurta over his baggy blue jeans.

Gene made the motion of smiling, but it was more of a torturous stretching of the lips.

"Anthony, you made it," Gene said.

"Of course I made it. I was invited," Anthony said after a derisive chuckle.

"By who?"

"By Dinesh. And I'm so glad that *you* made it, that you could ride in on Lakshmi's steam."

Gene pouted — he was incapable of concealing his emotions. An attractive blonde woman in her thirties tested the mic and asked us to take a seat after banging a little gong. Once we had, a homely South Asian man with long, greasy hair and a limp took the short flight of steps up the dais. He sat himself in the oversized chair, smiling broadly and cocking his head as he made eye contact with those in the front row. His way of speaking did not have the melodious formality of an Indian but was something more difficult to listen to, halting, and it created a strain. His teeth were a bright, bleached white and made a sharp contrast with the darkness of his skin and the blackness of his hair. Dinesh's smile never faded as he spoke and in his short talk, he hit the usual points about loving your self. "Let us recognize that self is not just *you* but all of existence," he said. He also spoke about ego, which he said was "sex, money and power, rolled into a big, shiny ball, but all of which can be vanquished with mindfulness." He praised the people in the crowd at the beginning of his talk and then again at its end.

"I have invited all of you here tonight because I believe each of you has the potential of seeing God within, the occupier of infinite space, and can open that door to him and get closer on your journey with a key I lend you. And this is not a key for adjusting your roller skates," he said and the crowd laughed as his head did the sideways bobble.

After the talk, Dinesh returned to his suite on the top floor as his wife and some other attractive women organized the individual visits. One of them accepted the $400 dollar donations in cash which had to be inserted, discreetly, into saffron-colored envelopes for a ninety-second encounter. A few in the crowd had brought Dinesh flowers and fresh fruit including mangoes and bananas.

"There's a pizza place that I like," I said to Jonnie as the three of them waited to surrender their envelopes.

"Pizza?" said Jonnie.

"Yes, while you're getting spiritual nourishment, I'll be getting some bodily nourishment. I'll wait for you in the lobby."

"All righty," Jonnie said, fingering the beads of her necklace and looking both excited and scared when they were signaled to come forward. "Oh my God, this is really happening!"

After a slice of plain and one of margherita, I opened a spiral notebook and reworked an old screenplay in the hotel lobby. I was making little progress as I was distracted by the opening of the elevator and the emergence of women and a few men who had come from their encounter with Dinesh. Some of them were quietly blissful with relaxed faces and a satisfied smile. Others were animated, looking at everything and everyone with renewed awe for the world. Two women were loudly laughing, linked in each other's arms, as if they had just shared the greatest secret ever. When Gene, Lakshmi and Jonnie appeared, they were a mix of expressions. Gene looked disappointed, Jonnie was euphoric and Lakshmi looked lost in other thoughts as the valet brought my car around.

"So, how was it?" I asked once we were in the car.

Jonnie struggled to speak and then finally blurted, "It was marvelous!"

"Marvelous?"

"Yes! I got a glimpse of the infinite — just a glimpse! — and saw what I can only describe as the *smile of God*. A true, true marvel!"

"Really," said Gene, with knit brows and a pout in my rearview mirror.

"Yes! I was resistant at first. I didn't like walking into a darkened room and being commanded by a man to 'lie down on the bed.' He looked me in the face with those big eyes of his and said, 'You are resisting this, Jonnie. You aren't ready.' And then he picked up a sword."

"A *sword*?" I said.

"A sword! A real one! With a jeweled hilt and a curve in it."

"A scimitar," I said.

"Yes! He stood over me, pointing the end at my stomach and said, 'Do you think I am here to hurt you, Jonnie? To make you bleed? To kill you when I cut your throat?' And then he raised the sword up to my throat. I said, 'No, you're not here to hurt me' which was the right thing to say. He smiled and dropped the sword. 'You are right,' he said. 'I am not here to hurt you. Now relax, let go of your fear and allow yourself to love yourself and take this next step.' And then he raised his arms and I saw it: blue light emanating from his fingertips! He dropped his head and blew on my face and I saw the blue light inside his mouth! And then behind him was more blue light and it raised up a kind of cosmic curtain to give me a glimpse of the beyond, the smile of God — and it was all... so... *beautiful!*"

"Really," said Gene again, in a mournful way.

"You didn't see it, Gene?" I asked.

"Oh, I saw the blue light," he said. "We all did. Dinesh looked at me, kind of cocking his head and then he reached out with his right hand to get a sense of my aura. He told me I was 'evolved' and ready to see the light but that I wasn't ready to see the place it came from, that I have some ego issues I need to surmount. I saw something like an aura from his fingers and when he blew on my face I saw it... I *did see* the blue light. Then he slapped me lightly on each cheek and told me I had to let go of my desires, that I was a slave to them, and that I should come back when I was *really* ready."

A silence followed that was awkward.

"How was it for you, Lakshmi?" I asked.

Lakshmi hesitated, wrinkling her nose and her mouth. "It was interesting. My experience was somewhere between Gene's and Jonnie's. But I don't know that Dinesh is really an ascended master. I think he's more of a magician."

"A magician? Like someone who practices sleight of hand?"

"No, he's someone capable of real magic. But I think he's more of a low-grade sorcerer than an ascendant master. He's willing to display his powers when he should be hiding them. I think he's kind of a benevolent trickster. For some, like Jonnie, he's a beacon, and for others, like Gene, he's a trickster who's trying to redirect and shake things up."

I could see Gene had slumped and looked even more dejected.

"Did he hold a sword to your throat?" I asked.

"Oh, no," she laughed. "He saw I was very relaxed when I came in. He knew immediately that I would see the blue light and that I didn't need to see beyond it."

"Why not?"

"He said I'd already seen it, that I'd seen God at least once already… which is true. He sensed that as soon as I walked in."

I heard Gene sigh through his nose.

"Gene," Lakshmi said, turning to look at him. "Don't be disappointed. Every step we take to be closer to God brings us closer to him."

"Yes, I guess," he said.

"It's early," Jonnie said. "Do you want to stop at Cafe Earth and get a tea? A little chamomile might help us sleep after all this excitement."

"I'd love to," Lakshmi said, suddenly serious. "But I still have some energy. I might write a little. And I definitely need to pray about something."

"Oh? How's the book going?" Jonnie asked, and I sensed a little hurt in her voice.

"It's getting there. Hmm," she said, having a sudden realization. She pulled out a notepad and a pen and wrote furiously in the dark until we reached her place. Jonnie and Gene remained silent, sensing Lakshmi was at work. She scrambled out with a perfunctory thanks, eager to get to her computer.

"Lakshmi's writing a book?" I said. "Fiction or non-fiction?"

"Non," said Jonnie. "We *were* writing it together but she's taken it over. Everything we worked on she would erase in the morning and then rewrite. So I got out of her way."

Jonnie's euphoria had vanished. It was tensely quiet when we approached her house.

"So, you're all right, Jonnie?" I said trying to remove all sarcasm. "You can walk to your door on your own?"

"I've never been better," she said. "And you are just an *arch*angel for driving, Tyler. Next time we go, we'll get a designated driver so you can meet Dinesh."

"Oh, uh... thanks," I said. She blew air kisses before she got out. I kept my foot on the brake and waited for her to get through her front door as Gene sat in the back, pouting.

"Why don't you sit up front, Gene? You're making me feel like a chauffeur."

"That's okay. It's just a short ride to my house. I'll just sit back here," he said and looked out the window. "I can't believe I spent almost my entire stipend on that."

"Stipend?"

"Oh, it's a little money my parents send each month." He was looking downward.

"I'm proud of you," I said looking at him in the rearview.

"Proud of me? Why?"

"Because you didn't fall for Dinesh. He may have fooled Jonnie, and Lakshmi thinks he's a sorcerer, but you're the one who didn't fall for his tricks."

"You're so sure it was a trick? That the blue light is fake?"

"I'm sure the blue light is real. But it's probably coming from some battery-operated device."

"So why did you take us tonight? If you don't believe in it."

"Because you asked me to. And I keep an open mind."

"Are you sure you aren't just being an ego tourist? That you aren't trying to prove your own superiority?"

"I make no claims to be superior."

He sighed again for what seemed the thousandth time.

"Can I ask you something, Gene?"

"What."

"Why was Lakshmi even interested? Hasn't she already seen God and the great beyond and battled and won against her ego?"

"She's... she's still on the path. She isn't there yet. She'll tell you that."

"She will?"

"She's fairly open about it. Lakshmi's not perfect, she's not a master. She knows she may never get there. She's compared herself to Moses — someone who's been appointed by God to lead his chosen to the Holy Land, but who will never enter it himself. She's said it again and again — she teaches what she needs to learn."

"But she's been at it for a while. Shouldn't she have learned it by now?"

"Her reward may not be in this life. Or even in her next one."

"She believes in reincarnation?"

"She thinks it's a possibility...but she's not convinced. That's a difference she has with Clayman."

One more sigh.

It struck me that perhaps Lakshmi did not want to openly differ with Eloise or with Dinesh on whatever it was they promoted because the three of them were all marketing their own brand of snake oil. They were not rivals so much as united charlatans who could milk each other's marks.

"I wonder sometimes," Gene said.

"About what?"

"Why God picked Lakshmi, why *she* got the gift."

"The gift?"

"Channeling. That's what she does, you know. She channels her talks — she has that connection to the beyond."

"Oh."

"And I wonder what she's praying on. That isn't good."

"She prays all the time."

"No. It's when she's praying *on* something. That's *never* good."

*

On Monday, Tim and I were in the kitchen readying his offering of something called tuna upside down pie for eleven o'clock assembly. As usual, Tim had some of his roommates and friends there, guys with pot bellies and the pale, papery skin of alcoholics, the men who Gene called Tim's Tipplers. They had brought a half-gallon bottle of vodka wrapped in a paper bag which they kept in the pantry upstairs. They hid their Dixie cups full of alcohol when Derrick Vanderven, to our surprise, entered the kitchen with a stiff upper lip on his face.

"Tim, Tyler," he said and we set down our knives as he came closer. "I wanted you to hear it from me first. I've come to say goodbye."

"Goodbye?" I said.

"Yes. I've been... let go."

"What?" I said. "Why?"

"I can't say why. But I didn't go without a fight."

"Who's taking over for you?" Tim asked.

"Jacob Hellman for now. They're looking for someone new — I feel sorry for whatever poor bastard they dig up. And as for Jacob Hellman, watch out for that one."

"Watch out for Jacob?"

"He's very... enterprising. He thinks it's acceptable to use Manna's client list to build up his home nursing business! As well as to run it out of an office at the Being Center! I do not."

My chin dropped and I struggled to find words.

"Why... why did she fire you?" I asked. "It was Lakshmi, right?"

"I'm sorry, Tyler. I can't tell you anything more because I've signed an NDA in order to get a severance fee. Don't worry for me. I'm quite relieved."

"You are?"

He cupped his hand and whispered in my ear.

"Believe me. I couldn't tolerate another minute of that cunt."

Derrick shook Tim's hand and when I offered him mine, he grabbed me at the waist and covered my face in wet kisses before planting one on my mouth. I was stunned by his news and numb to his unwanted affection. I reached for a kitchen towel to wipe my face as Jacob Hellman arrived, puffing after climbing up the stairs. He and Derrick stared at each other in silence, Derrick grimacing before he stuck his nose in the air then strutted off.

Jacob turned toward us with that yard-wide grin of his. "Guys, we want you to know that you don't need to worry. I'm in charge until we find a new director. Everything's fine."

"Everything's fine?" I repeated.

"Fine. One hundred percent. Now what did Derrick tell you?"

Chapter 11

I should mention that what Derrick had done in groping and kissing me was fairly commonplace. It was an annoyance, it was rude, but I did not find it to be a traumatizing violation of my person and it was certainly not my first experience of something like that. I never told anyone about it or complained. I wouldn't have called it an assault — he had slobbered on me — but I wondered if Lakshmi did have good reason to fire him. Mr. Vanderven had opened my mail about my student loans and embarrassed me in front of the staff. I didn't know how well he was doing in the day-to-day operation of the Center and Manna or if he was actually in charge. But even if his performance was poor, Lakshmi was the one who had hired him. She had done so after praying on it, and once again, God had given her some really shitty advice since he was her third director in the two years of the Being Center's existence.

And, to come clean on something, I would be lying if I said that when someone's shapely bottom appealed to me and I was friendly with the guy, I mightn't give it a grab. Back then, if no one was grabbing your ass, you worried you needed to get it to the gym. My apologies go to one volunteer who was offended a couple of years later when I ran into him at a bar. When I didn't ask for permission to stroke his appealing glutes, he was offended and everything between us soured.

Something else soured when I went to Kyle's showcase that Monday night. Like Kyle, I admired the gifted performers who had gotten their start at the Groundlings Theater. Many of them found success when they joined the cast of *Saturday Night Live* including Phil Hartmann and Jon Lovitz who were two current stars of SNL's second golden age. Paul Rubens, the man who would become Pee Wee Herman, was an idol and an inspiration and we loved Cassandra Peterson as Elvira, Mistress of the Dark and both were Groundlings alumni. At a recent Friday night show, we had seen Julia Sweeney doing her characters Pat and Mea Culpa. We knew she was destined for success and that Lorne Michaels would soon come calling. Kyle had succeeded in getting to stage three of becoming a Groundling — he had made it to the advanced class. The showcase he was performing in on a Monday night would weed out some and promote others to the Sunday show, where fledgling Groundlings might graduate to the official troupe and possibly to stardom.

I came home with the news that Derrick had been fired and Manna was in limbo but Kyle was too busy to hear me as he loaded up his Honda CRX with an array of the kitschy junk that was his performance trademark. Included in his ever-expanding collection were a plastic Jesus and Mary from an outdoor nativity set, lots of mangled and tangled wigs, some Mexican marionettes, squirt guns and rifles, a plastic ukulele, an old Emenee organ, as well as stacks of loud shirts, novelty aprons, a garish muumuu and an opera cape. When we were in film school, Kyle's film and video process was to throw together some junk that might have included several cockroaches dying after a recent spraying, adult diapers, a jack-in-the-box and a few marshmallow Peeps. He would then shoot a video or film around the stuff, a kind of Rauschenberg assemblage with me as a meat puppet for some live action. Sometimes it worked if he could think of a narrative with a payoff.

"Wow," I said as he threw in my Indonesian Ramayana puppets. "You're bringing all your stuff. And some of mine."

"Yeah. So?"

"So I thought your teacher said that improv isn't supposed to rely on props, that they're crutches. It's about what you make up out of air."

"So maybe that's why Steve's still teaching instead of acting. This is how I do it. This is me, my originality."

"All right, break a leg, buddy. You be you."

I meant that. I'd have been thrilled for Kyle to get into the Sunday show. I'd be ecstatic to move with him to New York when he was tapped for season 16 of SNL.

At the show, I sat next to Kyle's agent, Emily, who repped his screenplays, and in the audience were a number of our friends. The three-man band revved up the crowd with an ironic version of *In-A-Gadda-Da-Vida* followed by *Smoke on the Water* before the lights dimmed.

The skits were hit-and-miss. Kyle and his friend Kathy portrayed George and Martha from *Who's Afraid of Virginia Woolf* and invited a married couple in the audience to come on stage and play the roles of Nick and Honey. The married couple were themselves a pair of actors who hammed it up and got most of the laughs. Later, Kyle did a solo bit in which he put on some horn-rimmed glasses, a pageboy wig and a Mexican poncho to play a character whose job was to read Christmas letters from owners to the pets they left at a dog hotel. It didn't get a single laugh. When it was Kyle's turn to do some improvs based on audience suggestions, none of them worked, so he asked the audience for a "new one word suggestion" and someone shouted "next" to the biggest laugh of the night. The last skit he performed was set in a graveyard cluttered with Kyle's junk. I couldn't tell you what it was about or who the characters were and all it got were some sympathy chuckles. The skits that did succeed featured performers who had that natural ease on stage, who were good at both improv and written material. They were actors who had mastered accents and mannerisms and instantly sank into a variety of roles. They also took turns playing the straight man or woman to let somebody else shine.

It was around 2 a.m. when Kyle came home without a phone call — something that happened more and more and which had led to some ugly quarrels. I was up, reading *Men's Health* magazine, with our lovable mutts in bed with me. Luna and Holden greeted Kyle with wags of their tails and waited to be petted but Kyle was too dejected and more than a little drunk to react to them.

"I was at the wrong table," he said as he got undressed. His black motorcycle jacket dropped on the floor like a dead crow.

"The wrong table?"

"After the show we went to Tommy Tang's. Steve and Mindy invited Cristy, Jonathan and Barb to their table. The rest of us were at a different one. So no Sunday show for me."

"Take the class over. Try again."

"You can't. I knew Cristy would get in. Her husband's some big cheese. He wrote all her sketches."

"They were good sketches. She's funny. He's a good writer."

Kyle sighed through his nose.

"That last sketch was a disaster," he said.

"Yeah. It didn't work."

He sighed again and I could smell that he'd been smoking pot and cigarettes.

"Why didn't you run anything past me?" I asked.

"Past *you*? Because I know you. You would have criticized it."

"Yes, I would have. I'd have told you what I thought worked and what didn't. Why didn't you ask me to write with you? Or write you something?"

"This is my thing, Tyler. Not yours. And I don't need you. I'm a lot funnier than you are."

"So we're in competition? Why can't we do this together? When we were in film school, we used to be a team. We collaborated. It was fun. Cristy's not competing with her big cheese. They're a duo. He loves her and he wants her to succeed."

"But it's how you criticize. You're too honest. You're brutal."

"Too honest? I'll tell you what's honest — when no one laughs at your jokes. What's more honest than that?"

"Now you're being an asshole."

"Kyle, I support you. The best thing anyone can do for you is to tell you when your shit doesn't work. And you keep at it until you find something that *does* work."

"Oh really," he said, anger in his voice. "So just what do *you* think went wrong?"

I shrugged my shoulders, hesitated to speak. "You don't dig deep enough. Everything you do is on the surface. You go for the easy joke, the obvious pun, and you're *not selective*. There's nothing underhanded or textured, no subtext. And there's no vulnerability in any of it. Funny comes out of feelings... from darkness, anger, sadness."

He stood staring at me, tears in his eyes. "If funny comes out of darkness, anger and sadness, then you should be fucking hilarious. And a successful screenwriter."

He grabbed a blanket and sheets from the linen closet.

"I'm sleeping on the couch," he said as he left the room. "Oh, I forgot. Your agent called. Somebody liked your screenplay."

Chapter 12

"Would you quit working here if you get this writing job?" Gene asked me, tension in his voice, as I lay on the floor, my head under an oven as I attempted to relight its pilot.

"Yes," I said. "I mean, I like working here, the mission. But the pay is terrible. And the work is hard. And I'm going into debt. My credit's affected because I can't pay my student loans. I couldn't work here at all if I didn't have Kyle paying half our bills. And it's not like there are any benefits. What if I get sick?"

"Are you HIV-positive?" he asked me in front of multiple volunteers.

"I don't know," I said after a moment. "Never tested. But it's ironic that an organization that's about serving people with AIDS doesn't offer health care to its employees."

"We aren't the richest organization, Tyler."

"But why aren't we richer? The employees at California Aids Project got benefits after they unionized. And paid vacations! I think we're worth that. Don't you? Maybe money should have been spent on health care for the staff instead of rent for a fancy building. And when do we get a kitchen that can handle this workload? And the coming workload?"

Gene was silent.

"Shit, this thing just won't light," I said as I clicked the butane lighter again.

A blue light, like a tiny tsunami, rolled over my face and around my neck as I heard a loud *whoosh*. I clenched my eyes shut and when I opened them I saw smoke and smelled the sickening stench of burning hair. I stood and faced the volunteers as they struggled not to laugh. The explosion had burned my eyebrows, my lashes and the hairs in my nose.

"Fuck," I said. My meeting at Universal was that afternoon.

"Are you all right?" Jonnie asked.

"I think so."

"You're sure?"

"I'm sure. Just a little shook up."

"Well, good, I have a favor to ask if you're going to Universal. Can you deliver the Studio City route, Tyler? We're short two drivers today. Pretty please? With chocolate sprinkles?"

"The food'll be cold," I said. "But, sure. If no one else can do it."

"Thank you, thank you. You have just earned a thousand karma points," she said.

I ran down to the bathroom mirror to look at the damage from the blowup and make sure I didn't look too weird. My eyebrows were mostly there and my skin was pink with the faintest first-degree burn. I didn't see any blisters.

It was a terrible mistake to drive a piece of shit onto the lot so for the meeting I borrowed Kyle's Honda CRX, a new car he had bought with some game show winnings. I resisted the urge to dress up, which was considered a desperate move and wore some trendy Girbaud jeans with their label next to the center of the fly. For a top, I wore a burnt-orange, Italian T-shirt that made my blue eyes pop. On my feet were some expensive high tops with electric blue laces, borrowed from Kyle, that were two sizes too big but spoke of my casual, breezy life as a successful screenwriter who worked at home and skateboarded in his emptied swimming pool.

"Be your own charming self," I whispered as I walked into a waiting room decorated with the movie posters of a director whose work I admired. They were all jokey, imaginative fantasy and sci-fi movies with a little bit of darkness at their centers — the kinds of "popcorn movies" I imagined I would write.

"Hi, I'm Tyler," I said walking toward the exec, Don, and his D-girl, Sherry, with my hand extended for a shake. "Excuse my strange appearance," I said, getting ready to deliver a lie. "I was setting up my new barbecue when it decided I was its first hunk of meat to get grilled."

"You got burned?" Don asked.

"More like seared," I said. "To keep the juices in. It's OK, my eyebrows were getting a little bushy anyway."

They chuckled and pointed me to a comfy leather couch.

"So are you an actor?" Sherry asked.

"No, just frequently mistaken for one," I said, bored with my own repartee. Don picked up my script, *Sleepless Nights*.

"This is a terrific screenplay — scary and funny and hooky," Don said as Sherry nodded. "And the coverage is great. Please. Sign it for me."

"Like an autograph?" I said and chuckled.

"Yes," he said. "Someday I think this will get made. Joe liked it too," Don continued as I scribbled my name on the front of my screenplay. "He just doesn't know if the public's ready for a period piece with special effects. Joe does think you might be right to adapt another project."

Don reached for a copy of an illustrated children's book called *The Wishing Well of Weeping Willows* and showed its glossy front to me. On its cover, a boy and a girl in ragged clothing were hauling a bucket up a well in the darkness of night. The bucket held a glowing object that lit the kids' astonished faces.

I was intrigued — the image had drawn me in. I looked at Don's desk and saw that there was a stack of these books and realized I was not the only writer "taking a meeting" on the project.

"So, take this home, Tyler," Don said and handed me the book. "And come back in a couple of weeks and tell us how you would turn it into a feature-length movie."

"And at least four sequels," I said. They laughed.

The drive to drop off meals through Studio City was actually a route through the sprawling flats of North Hollywood, an area of bland, anonymous tract homes and cheap and ugly apartment buildings. That afternoon, NoHo had never looked more beautiful or exciting and the faces of the men who accepted Manna's offer of "love in a grocery bag" never appeared more noble and handsome.

"I will get this job," I said to myself as I drove home through rush hour traffic that seemed almost delightful. And just in case there was something to visualizing what you want for yourself, I imagined the millions of dollars I would get from a string of successful screenplays: a rainstorm of checks signed by Universal Studios. I would do what I loved and the money would follow in a tidal wave of crisp green bills that would raise my boat to Mount Ararat and a new covenant with a Benevolent Universe.

Didn't everything always work out for me?

Chapter 13

As part of his determination to get a boyfriend, Gene got a trainer at the gym we both belonged to. His straight, bossy trainer was tanned, pumped and veiny and he wore the latest in workout clothes: skin-hugging, translucent, Lycra short shorts with a matching tank top and a fanny pack. Gene had decided this was also a good look for him to wear to the kitchen even though he had yet to... show results.

We were at work finishing up Moroccan beef stew and couscous while the volunteers struggled to cut messy segments out of membranes for a grapefruit and fennel salad. As he often did, Jericho left his computer to refill his coffee mug and tease Gene or me in some public way. We were lifting a large pot of freshly steamed couscous from the stove when Jericho, with an envelope in hand, struck a pose and smirked as he stared at us. "Cute shorts, Gene," he said. "But you should be aware that when you bend over, you're giving us a free tour of your fudge factory."

"You're just jealous," Gene said. "Because I'm going to have a fantastic body. And you'll be stuck with a girly body that goes with your girly hair."

"My hair is a lion's mane," Jericho said and growled.

"Maybe it will come in handy at your next audition for Rum Tum Tugger."

Gene grinned in triumph as the volunteers laughed but Jericho was ready with a new offensive. "Oh, I almost forgot," he said, chortling before he continued. "Got a letter for you guys — it's addressed to the Chefs of Manna from Heaven. It's from some... *anonymous* clients." He set down his coffee cup and pulled out a sheet from the envelope and snapped it open.

The kitchen quieted as Jericho read through a smirk he could not contain, stopping every so often to register our faces.

Dear Chefs,

Please don't take this the wrong way and please don't think we are ungrateful for all you do. But a few of us were talking and we had some complaints about the food. We are interested in getting what we call comfort food. This would include beef stew, meatloaf, roast turkey, chicken pot pie, tuna noodle casserole, macaroni and cheese, ham and mashed potatoes, pot roast, etc. We also like the Wednesday enchiladas and the spaghetti and meatballs.

Things that do not work for us: weird chicken with prunes and olives, fish with gunky yellow sauce, beef stew with cinnamon and chickpeas, shrimp with apples and peas and anything with curry. As for the desserts, the cakes occasionally have burnt edges around the corners but for the most part, are very good.

Again, we don't mean to offend. We just thought you'd like to know our thoughts.

-- Anonymous clients

Jericho cocked his head then looked in the big pots of stew. "What's for lunch, Gene? Moroccan beef stew with *cinnamon* and *chickpeas?*"

I wasn't offended by the letter — it held up my end of the food, which were the desserts, Mexican Wednesdays and the Italian food. Gene's chest was heaving and his face had fallen. "That's just the opinion of a few people," he said, wiping at his eyes, his mouth quivering. He was so thin-skinned!

"Maybe we should send the clients a survey, see what they'd like," I said. "I think when people are sick, maybe they want the food they grew up eating. You know, what Mom made."

"I make a great mac and cheese," said Bryce, a new volunteer who was in his twenties and had livened every morning he showed up. He had been entertaining us that day with his imitations of Big Edie and Little Edie from Grey Gardens as he expertly chopped vegetables. "I make it with caramelized onions and a cream sauce. It's super caloric — it will completely enlarge your ass — so it's fantastic for wasting disease. It's so delicious you'll want to pull your pants down and sit in it to try and eat with your other end."

"So you were a cook?" I said through laughter.

"I was the cook at a dude ranch. In Texas," he said, putting on an accent. He swept up his shoulder-length blond hair and batted his eyelashes. "Don't you know a cowgirl when you see one?"

"That's where you learned to cook, Bryce? A *dude ranch*?" Gene asked with a scoff.

"Honey chile, I learned to cook at the Culinary Institute of America near New York City. How 'bout you?"

"I was a caterer," Gene said. "A *professional* caterer."

"What do you think, Gene?" I said. "Should we give Bryce a guest appearance? Mac and cheese this Friday?"

"Fine," Gene answered after some facial gymnastics. "I was planning on *paillard de poulet* with *sauce de moutarde* and a side of *ratatouille*. But if the clients want mac and cheese, then so be it. If they want a frozen Swanson TV dinner we can send that out too," he said, slamming a drawer shut.

"I'll go to Smart and Final after lunch," I said.

After we sent off Moroccan beef stew for its swan song, Bryce and I were writing down a list of items he would need when I felt someone's hand just below my butt. I turned around to see a short, pudgy man in his sixties with gray hair.

"Your butt is just so cute," he said. "It's like a peach."

"Uh, thank you," I said.

"I bet I could fit the whole thing in the palm of my hand. Can I try?"

"Uh, no," I said. "I'm busy. On my way to Smart and Final."

"Do you want some company?"

"I can handle it," I said. "Besides, I think you'd be of more use here."

"I'm Graham," he said. "Graham Stillson. I'm in casting."

"Well, I'm not an actor, Graham, but thank you for volunteering."

"You're not an actor? You should be."

I took off my apron and walked toward Jonnie and Jericho at their work table outside the kitchen.

"Jonnie, there's some guy in the kitchen who says his name is Graham Stillson. He says he's a casting director and he's, uh, he's coming on a little strong."

"Uh oh," said Jericho. "Casting Couch Stillson."

"Damn it," whispered Jonnie, her lips pursing in anger. "He *was* a casting director until he got run out of the business. He's showed up here because we've got such a good-looking crew."

"Should he be here at all?" I asked. "If he makes people uncomfortable?"

"We'll keep an eye on him," Jonnie said. "But if someone has come here out of love, we don't want to turn them away."

"I think he's come here out of lust," I said.

On the drive to Smart and Final, I rehearsed my pitch for the adaptation of *The Wishing Well of Weeping Willows* for my meeting on Monday. I was visualizing the laughs, the gasps, the smiles as I went through its three-act structure and the big event at its midway turning point. It was important, I knew from the times I had successfully done this, that I convey its emotions, that I get caught up in it.

The colorful details of the world I was evoking were in marked contrast to my shopping destination. Smart and Final was no Dean & Deluca. It was a chain of warehouse-style grocery and supply stores that was geared toward the lower end of the food service industry. I headed to one of its ugly, utilitarian boxes, this one on Melrose Avenue, and braced myself. Inside, it had an unpleasant, antiseptic smell that was more like a hospital than a supermarket. It only sold corporate brands and much of what they had was precooked foods in large plastic bags or gallon-sized cans. Low-end caterers could buy a fifty-pound bag of precooked fajitas, beef or chicken, to warm and serve - no prep or cooking involved. I loaded my cart up with a twenty-pound sack of white onions, eight gallons of whole milk, a forty-pound sack of macaroni and four ten-pound blocks of mild cheddar cheese as well as some hand graters.

The manager, Mr. Valchick, was manning the cash register, a short, bald guy with thick rimmed spectacles who I had never seen smile. He had never uttered even a perfunctory pleasantry and looked at me like I had taken a piss on his floor.

"Hi. This is on the Manna from Heaven account."

"You haven't paid your bill," he said.

"Sorry?"

"You heard me. Your organization hasn't paid its last three bills. You're three months behind. I told you the last time you came in here."

"Oh. Well, we'll take care of that right away."

"Until you do, you don't have any shopping privileges."

"I'll put it on my credit card," I said and handed Valchick my Visa. I hoped my limit was high enough. It wasn't.

"This is unacceptable!" I said to Jonnie and Gene when I got back to the kitchen. "I'm calling Jacob."

"Tyler, I'm sure this is just an oversight," Jonnie said.

"Once is an oversight," I shouted and signaled to her to hand me the phone. "Twice is negligence. Three times is bullshit." Jonnie gave me the phone slowly, reluctance on her face.

"The Being Center," said Vonnie. "How may we help you?"

"Hey, Vonnie. It's Tyler. I need to speak with Jacob."

"He's in a... a meeting, Tyler."

"Of course he is."

She wasn't lying — I could hear him arguing with Lakshmi in the background.

"Tell Jacob that they closed our account at Smart and Final," I said. "We owe them over twelve thousand dollars."

"Tell 'em to line up," she whispered. "Gotta go, call you later."

I went into the kitchen where the volunteers were at work peeling and chopping carrots.

"What's with the long face, Tyler?" said Ruth, the stout member of the Jewish Mom's Brigade as she swept up some carrot coins and threw them in the bin. She wiped a peeling off of her heart-shaped glasses and raised up my chin.

"We don't have money for tomorrow's meal," I said. "They kicked me out of Smart and Final."

"They did *what*?" said Goldie, the pretty blonde of the group. Her mouth was open in shock as she raised up and splayed her immaculate nails with cherry frost polish. "How much do you need?"

"About two hundred dollars."

"Two hundred dollars?" said Marlene who had a rust-colored perm. Around her neck was a necklace with a gold charm of playing cards that depicted a royal flush. "Two hundred *dollars*?" she repeated in disbelief.

"Yes. We owe them over twelve thousand."

"C'mon, Tyler," Marlene said taking off her apron. "We're going to Smart and Final. I'll buy the groceries."

"You will?"

"Of course I will. Two hundred dollars is peanuts. And I'll pay off the twelve grand. I just need a receipt for my tax guy."

She opened her shoulder bag and gave me a glimpse of wads of rolled-up cash.

"I was in City of Commerce last night," she whispered. "A good night at the pai gow tournament. Come on, honey. I'm driving."

On Friday, the volunteers set to work at grating cheese in tall piles of orange shreds around the kitchen island. The steaming pasta had been drained and was returned to its sixty-quart pot. Bryce had cooked twenty finely chopped onions (there was a lot of crying that morning when he pushed everyone for a finer chop) in eight pounds of butter until they were translucent. He added half a cup of salt, a half cup of white pepper and then eight cups of flour, stirring the mixture until the flour was cooked through. After that, he added gallons of milk that had been warming in a separate pot and whisked it until it was smooth.

"Double double toil and trouble, fire burn and cauldron bubble," Bryce said and then cackled like a witch. "Oh, we forgot an ingredient."

"What?" I asked.

"A small child. Have we got one?"

"I think we're out of them," I said.

"Gene will have to do." He called across to Gene who was chatting with one of the drivers, a chubby hippie girl wearing men's Levi's and a blue work shirt. "Gene! Your bath's ready."

Bryce turned up the flames of all four burners under the wide pot and stirred from the bottom with a large whisk.

"Do not let this come to a boil and do not let it skin," he said, "or all you're gonna have is a big ol' vat of Elmer's glue."

When the sauce started to steam and was "painful to the touch," we set the pot on the ground and then whisked in the grated cheese a pile at a time so that it would melt, not curdle. When the sauce was thick, smooth and glossy, we poured it over the pasta and stirred it with the paddle before setting it at the head of the assembly line. Everyone sampled a little as the volunteers plopped it into the containers with a bright side of buttered carrots sprinkled with Italian parsley. Gene flattered Bryce when his eyebrows rose in approval and he cleaned his plate.

"Not bad," Gene said.

"It's fucking sublime and you know it," Bryce said.

We'd had a few well-known chefs at Manna who came in and prepared their specialties, but most of them left after lunch was packaged and they'd taken their star turn. Bryce was different. He stuck around to do the grunt work in the afternoon and that day he helped Tim prepare his Sunday meal, pork a la king. Tim's usual crew was with him, the bloated and boozed-up guys, one of whom was an old customer of mine from JJ's Pub. As they chopped and diced, they quietly passed each other some Trader Joe's Vodka of the Gods. Gene, who had been sullen all afternoon, had taken note and picked up Tim's Dixie cup to give it a sniff.

"Really, Tim. And it isn't even four o'clock."

"Well, it is Friday," Tim said.

Jonnie entered with her happy surprised look. "Chefs! Just wanted you to know we got six calls from clients. The mac and cheese is a big hit!"

Bryce and I grinned as Gene sneered. "Well of course it's a hit," he said. "Just because something is pedestrian doesn't mean it isn't tasty."

"Pedestrian?" said Bryce. "Someone needs to come down from her high horse."

"I'm congratulating you," Gene said.

"I am too," I said to Bryce. "You should be working here. You could be the fun chef."

Gene's face fell and I realized I'd offended him — apparently he thought he was just as fun as anyone else. Jonnie tottered up to me, hands clasped in prayer-like fashion and I felt my stomach drop.

"Tyler, you can say no but I have a big favor to ask."

"Yes?" I said.

"Lakshmi's baby shower is Sunday. We forgot a cake. Well, we don't have a budget for a cake. Can you bake her one? And drop it off at Julie's?"

I hesitated. My pitch was on Monday.

"It's exactly what I wanted to do this weekend," I said.

And maybe, after Monday, it would be the last thing I would ever do for Lakshmi Steinmetz and Manna from Heaven again.

Chapter 14

If Gene had asked me to bake a cake for Lakshmi, I would have made some flourless gateau of ground almonds with a chocolate mirror glaze and a spattering of gold leaf as a minimal decoration. But Jonnie had asked me and I felt strangely motivated to go all out and do six tiers of something that would barely be eaten by Lakshmi and her weight-conscious friends. It would be something like her temple cake that I knew would be returned to the kitchen for the clients and volunteers. I brought home the KitchenAid mixer as well as all the ingredients I would need.

While the cakes were cooling, I went to the toy section of the 99 Cents Only Store and filled a handbasket with stuff made in China. I found something called Bag O' Babies and it was just what I wanted. They were sacks of tiny, rubber baby dolls that were in diapers and crawling on all fours with pacifiers in their mouths. As the top ornament, I found a larger, pink-cheeked doll that was lying in a rubber bassinet. Lakshmi was having a girl, so I used hot pink buttercream as my primary coating and then pressed the little crawlers into the frosting of the layers' rims, alternating their direction on the different layers. I filled the bassinet with some white frosting, pressed the doll inside it, then sprinkled white candy balls on top to make it look like a bubble bath. After that I piped decorative filigree in a contrasting, dark chocolate frosting. When it was finished, it was garish as hell and looked like something from a Busby Berkeley musical.

Kyle took a look at it and burst out laughing. "I'm jealous," he said, his highest compliment. He took pictures of the cake with his Polaroid One Step before he left to practice improv with his new group, the Comedy Omelette, which was made up of other almost-made-it-to-the Groundlings.

On Sunday morning, I set the cake in an open box and gingerly drove it to Julie Sainsbury's home. She lived in a mid-century single level, two doors down from Ray Bradbury's place in upscale Cheviot Hills. Using my elbow, I rang the doorbell and a man answered I recognized as one of the suits at Lakshmi's birthday party. Julie's husband was the serious-looking straight guy and he was, indeed, a felon. He was wearing an electronic tracking cuff around his ankle, something that was highly visible that morning since he was wearing shorts.

"Hi, I'm dropping off the cake for Lakshmi's shower," I said.

"Come in," he said, eager to get rid of me and get back to a baseball game. "Jules, got a guy here with a cake delivery," he shouted toward the kitchen. He went back to his TV den as I stepped into the combined dining and living room. The room was decorated with pink streamers and balloons and there was already a cake on the coffee table but it was made out of disposable diapers.

Julie stepped out in a bathrobe. "Hi, Tyler. So nice of you to bake for Lakshmi."

"I enjoyed it," I said and pulled down the sides of the box to reveal my work. Julie gasped and her jaw dropped. "It's… it's unbelievable!" she said and laughed. "That's like a fifty-pound cake!"

"Maybe forty," I said.

"You can just see all the *love* that went into it."

"Send back what doesn't get eaten to the kitchen," I said. "It won't go to waste."

"Andrew! Andrew come and see this," she shouted and her husband came out, reluctantly, but his eyes popped when he did.

"Wow," he said as he got closer. "Where's it from?"

"I made it," I said offering my hand for a shake. "I'm Tyler St. George. I'm one of the chefs at Manna."

"I'm Andrew Belfry, Julie's husband. Jesus Christ Almighty, Tyler. The hens are gonna love it."

*

"So Jim throws himself down the well and swims through the dark water, like Shelley Winters in the *Poseidon Adventure*, to the point where he can't hold his breath anymore. Just as he's sucking in water, he sees light and swims harder toward it until he breaks through, gasps for air. Jim is back at Sea Castle and his sister, Ginny, is still chained to the rock as the Harpies circle in their flight, their claws unfolding as they ready to tear her to pieces. King Delegock and his mage, Abra-Cadaver, sit with his subjects in the rafters, thirsty for a bloody entertainment.

'For my final wish,' Jim shouts to the skies as he raises the Ring of Thalamop, 'I wish to bring my sister home alive and well!'

"The Harpies screech as their feathers catch fire, and they fall from the sky, burning and crashing into piles of smoking ash. 'Kill him!' the King shouts and his soldiers raise their bows and arrows — but they turn into electric eels that electrocute the soldiers before they slither away. Abra-Cadaver raises his skeletal arms to cast a spell but his wand morphs into a massive tree trunk that falls and flattens him.

"Jim races to his sister and breaks her chains with the Mallet of Bilgoth as lightning tears up the sky and deafening thunder shakes the castle and tornadoes whip up the water. The sea swirls and gathers into a great wave that douses the sun before a tsunami rolls toward the castle, knocks it off its rock, and breaks it into a billion exploding pebbles. Everyone is sucked into the ocean as Jim grabs his sister, clutches her under his arm, and together they are rocketed through a watery chaos before they are shot out in a mushroom geyser that explodes the wishing well.

"The geyser recedes, sets them down on the soaked ground, and when they raise their heads, they look around, see they are home, back in Weeping Willows. A siren wails and lights strobe when a flashlight shines on their faces. 'They're over here!' the sheriff shouts and Mom and Dad run toward them, bursting into tears of relief as they sweep their children up into their arms."

I was out of breath as I finished my pitch. Caught up in the emotion of it, there was a tremble in my voice and tears in my eyes.

Don and Sherry looked at each other, quiet as they absorbed it all.

I had them!

The phone buzzed.

"Yes," Don said. "OK. Yes, yes. I think we both feel the same."

I realized then that I wasn't just pitching to them. I looked over at a dark window in the wall and realized it was a two-way mirror. Who was sitting behind it? The director? Lew Wasserman? Steven Spielberg?

"Tyler, I'm just speaking for myself but I... I'm blown away," said Don. "I'm just dust in the wind."

Sherry, the D-girl was nodding, hesitating before she spoke. "It may be a little too intense for a family film," she said. "But we can work on that and with a few nips and tucks we can keep it family-friendly."

"Absolutely," I said.

"Just one question," Don said. "Can I get his number?"

"Whose number?"

"The guy who sells you LSD."

I drove back to the kitchen to bake lemon meringue pies and was high on hope, something I couldn't contain, as I lined pans with dough and crimped their edges.

"How did it go?" Bryce asked me.

"Pretty well," I said, trying to fight back a grin. "No chicken counting."

When I got home, my dogs came to greet me and Holden licked my face but I could see Luna wasn't feeling well — her neck was low and stiff and she seemed to be limping. I was petting her when I looked over at the phone and saw the blinking light of the message machine.

Chapter 15

"This is a message from Bank of America," said an automated voice. "Your deposit of two hundred and thirty four dollars and six cents made on March 28 was returned for insufficient funds. You have a balance of twelve dollars and thirty-eight cents."

Fuck! My paycheck bounced.

"Assholes!" I shouted and realized I'd frightened my dogs. "Sorry, puppies," I said as I went to them and scratched their necks. "Let's go for a nice walk." Holden, our larger mutt, wagged his tail but Luna, a short-legged and older corgi mix was definitely not well. Had she eaten the wrong thing? We went halfway around the block before she stopped walking at all. I carried her home in one hand while I held Holden's leash with the other. When we got back, there was another message on my machine.

"Heeeey, Tyler, it's Shelley. Give me a call when you get a chance."

Shelley, Hollywood's cheeriest agent, did not sound so hopeful.

"The good news is that they loved you," she said. "They think you're an amazing writer. And it was a split decision. Three to two."

"Who was against me?"

"It was the big wigs. They thought you were too original, too ahead of the curve. They said the public needs to catch up with you. But keep in mind that these are the guys who passed on Star Wars. One of them called it 'cowboys and Indians in outer space.'"

"Too creative," I said. It wasn't the first time I'd heard that.

"They want to work with you, but not this project. And they asked for first look at your next spec. I know you've got one in you, Tyler, something that meets that middle ground between fresh and familiar."

When I set the phone back in its cradle, I had that feeling of a long, slow fall to a lightless place that has no bottom, where the air is so heavy it weighs on your limbs and it's like trying to breathe in molasses.

I've seldom taken solace in alcohol as drinking too early in the evening puts me to sleep, and when you wake up, you have a hangover as well as the problem you tried to drown. But down the street was a 7-Eleven with a pint of dulce de leche Haagen-Dazs that was screaming out my name. The ice cream was softened by the time I got it home and I made short work of it even as I endured an ice cream headache.

The short sugar high was followed by a deep and paralyzing nap. I dreamed of looking over the wall of a wishing well where a trio of witches bobbed in the water. They cackled as they demanded that I jump down to suck on their cold, flabby titties in return for fulfilling my wishes. When I resisted, my clothes burst into flames and I dove into the water to save myself from burning. The witches pressed against me, offering me their milk. The first nipple filled my mouth with ice-cold ammonia, the second one with hot diesel, and the third one gushed with airplane glue. The witches told me that I would have to bring each of them to sexual ecstasy, and if I did, they would get me a ten-picture deal at Paramount with five offers to direct and a shelf full of Oscars. The least ugly of the witches opened her mouth to kiss me, but her tongue was a slab of maggot-ridden meat. Her rotten teeth fell into my mouth, and when I swallowed them, like seeds, they sprouted into burning vines that snaked through my intestines. When the second witch poked out my eye with her long, pointy nose, I woke up clutching my face, relieved to find my eye was intact.

Luna was lying on the floor making a strange, whining noise. Her belly was now the size of a honeydew. I grabbed my keys and drove her to the twenty-four hour vet. The veterinarian, a young and beautiful Vietnamese woman, gingerly probed Luna's sensitive belly. "How old do we think Luna is?" she asked.

"She was maybe five when we rescued her. And that was about seven years ago."

"We will do an X-ray to confirm it but I believe her stomach has reversed. It is not something we can correct. She is suffering now and it is not going to get better."

"Can I take her home?"

"I would not recommend it. I am sorry. That is not best for her."

While Luna was being X-rayed, I called Kyle from a payphone in case he'd come home since it was after eleven. When he didn't pick up, I tried him at Ed Debevic's diner and the host, staying in beatnik character, said, "The Kookmeister's taking a sick day, daddio. Ya dig?"

A sick day?

I tried Kyle's writing partner, Annie, who sometimes worked late with him. "We didn't work today, Tyler. It's late. I'm in bed," she said, understandably annoyed. "And we never work at night."

"You don't?"

"No."

That was news.

"It's Luna," I said. "She's dying."

"Oh, I'm so sorry, Tyler. Tell Kyle to call me when you do get a hold of him. We need to finish our screenplay."

The X-ray confirmed the worst. Luna's whimpering was now marked by sharp yelps of pain and her breathing grew short and rapid. I lifted her, brought her to a black mat in a back room, and she licked my face as an intravenous drip bottle was wheeled out and a needle inserted between her shoulder blades. As I stroked her and said goodbye, a slow release of phenobarbital sent her into sleep and then a coma. I watched as all tension left her body and then she collapsed, like a puppet abandoned by its puppeteer.

"She is ready," said the doctor, and the assistant approached for the second, more lethal injection. That one I did not want to witness.

"Can I have her collar?" I asked.

My credit card was declined for a bill close to $1,000. "I'm sorry," I said through sniffles, embarrassed by a stream of snot. "I promise I'll be back tomorrow to take care of it."

"All right. We understand," said the woman at the front desk in all sincerity. "We're very sorry for your loss."

It was sometime around 2 a.m. when I heard Kyle come through the door. I was watching Headline News on CNN as they repeated the same stories every twenty minutes. My grief had given way to rage as Holden jumped off the bed, wagging his tail, to run out and greet Kyle which was something I felt he didn't deserve. He saw the look on my face and his own filled with fear as I walked toward him, my body tense with rage.

"Where the fuck were you?" I shouted.

"I was at work. And then I went out for a drink."

"No, you weren't you fucking liar, because I called Ed's. 'The Kookmeister is taking a sick day, daddy-o.'"

He backed away.

"Fine," he said. "I went with Barry to a club downtown. You wouldn't have gone so I didn't ask."

"A club? On a Monday night? What kind of club? A sex club?"

"It was just a club — a roving club in the warehouse district."

He was heaving as we locked eyes.

"Luna is dead," I shouted.

"*What?*"

"Something with her stomach — it reversed. It happens to older dogs. I had to put her to sleep. Without you!" I shouted. I picked up one of our vintage 50's dining chairs and smashed its legs on the floor, breaking them. "And then you fucking lie to me! What else are you lying about? What drugs are you on?"

"I smoked some pot. So what?"

"*So what?* You come home at two in the morning without a phone call?"

"Stop trying to control me!"

"Control you? Christ, you are so fucking blind! You don't see how this hurts me? How it makes me worry and wonder what dangerous shit you're up to?"

"You... are... fucking... crazy!" he shouted, sticking his finger into my chest. It was a move from out of some acting class, which made it all the more irritating. I had to restrain myself from putting my fist through his nose and out the back of his skull.

"I'm crazy to stay with you!" I shouted, my voice getting louder. I picked up the next chair and used it to bash in the dining table.

"Stop that! I love that table! I love those chairs!" Kyle shouted, a mix of crying and yelling.

"I don't love you!" I shouted as I bashed the table again and again before it buckled and broke in two. "You're a lying, fucking scumbag! And the best thing I can do for you is take one of these chair legs to bash your brain in and put *you* out of *your* misery!"

"This is why I don't tell you stuff!" he shouted back. "You get so angry!"

"I'm not supposed to get *angry*? When you lie to me? And why? So you can do crystal and give your asshole to everybody in Silverlake? When our dog is dying?"

"I said I'm sorry!" he shouted at me, but it was in pure contempt, mocking me with a squeaky voice, as if I were the asshole.

"That is not an apology!"

"I told you! I'm sorry!" he repeated in that same, infuriating tone, stepping toward me, no longer cowering, with his hands making fists.

"Go ahead! Take the first swing, Kyle! And then I will beat your face to a bloody fucking pulp!"

"You are totally crazy!" he roared back. "I can't discuss anything with you because you start tearing shit up!"

"You will not turn this around on me. If you don't want me and our *living* dog as your family, then *just fucking leave*. I want someone who wants me back — someone who isn't an addict. Someone who isn't in denial about turning thirty. Someone who doesn't *hate* me."

He was quiet a moment then looked at Luna's collar, which had fallen from the broken table to the floor. He picked it up and started crying.

"She's gone," I said. "Gone."

We were both sniffling in a horrible silence when he grabbed and hugged me. "I am sorry," he said and I felt his tears on the back of my neck. "And I'm sorry I wasn't there with you." He was shaking as he gripped me tighter but I wanted to pull away. My rage was like some repeating, nuclear mushroom cloud as all of Kyle's infidelities, his lies, his thieving and his abandonments from over the years exploded inside me. I wanted to yank down the bookshelves, kick in the television set, tear up his clothes and burn it all in a bonfire.

"If it makes you feel any better," I said. "I didn't get that job at Universal. So it's just a great fucking day."

When he heard that, Kyle was suddenly quiet and he pulled away and his face looked blank. As I thought it might, it comforted him. "Oh. I'm sorry," he finally said quietly, distantly, and then as if in a trance, he went to the linen closet and grabbed a blanket and a pillow and made up the couch. I went back to bed and after closing the door, I heard him turn on the television. Holden was frightened and shaking as he crawled up to me. He licked my face and then curled up inside my arms. I had never felt closer to any other being. A few minutes later, my head was a cyclone of rage. I couldn't sleep and was unable to read or watch TV. At three in the morning, I took a long walk from Pico Boulevard up to the Hollywood Hills in hopes that it would exhaust me. It was seven in the morning when I called Gene at home and let him know I needed a day off.

"A day off? Did you get that writing job?" he asked.

"I did not," I said. "My dog died. And Kyle... well, it's a long story."

"Universal may not want you, Tyler. But we do. We love you," he said sincerely. "Take the day off, of course, and Wednesday if you have to. I'll work for you today."

"Believe me, I will need to work on Wednesday. I will need to do something. Thank you, Gene." I was touched by his sweetness and his compassion and reminded that at one time I had liked him and thought of him as kind.

Later that morning, Kyle went to the vet's and paid the bill. We couldn't afford to cremate Luna, so he brought home her body. The vet had wrapped her in a plastic sheath and added a dry ice packet. We put her in the back of Kyle's car along with a collapsible shovel and then took a long, quiet drive with Holden on a too-sunny day into the mountains of the Angeles Crest Forest. Kyle pulled over at a remote place I used to camp in as a teenager where there was a shady density of ancient oak trees. They were covered in crusty, black bark and their crooked limbs looked tired from holding up their burdens for centuries. We walked to a clearing with a carpet of fallen, spiky leaves and hundreds of pointy acorns.

Animals die in the forest all the time, but I knew burying a pet was likely illegal so we took turns digging a deep hole and kept a look out for forest rangers. I removed Luna from the sheath and held her cold, limp body to my chest. I stroked her a final time in case I had somehow gotten the magic power to bring her back to life. When I started sobbing, Kyle took her from me, rocked her in his arms, then set her in the hole. Holden sniffed her and whined as he paced around the hole's edges. Kyle threw in the first shovelful of dirt. I threw in some acorns I hoped would sprout and grow strong from her remains. We reset some rocks then hid the scar we'd made in the soil with a thickness of leaves. On the drive home, Kyle placed his hand on my thigh.

"I really am sorry," he said as his eyes filled with tears. "I'm sorry I wasn't there for you... or Luna."

All I could manage to mumble was "OK." I cranked the chair back to the reclining position and finally fell asleep.

When we got home, I saw a grocery bag at the front door. Manna from Heaven had delivered lunch to us. Inside the bag was a card signed by Gene, Tim, Jericho and the rest of the staff. "Dearest Tyler. We are so sorry for your loss," read the note written in Jonnie's cute, feminine handwriting with little hearts over the i. "Know that Luna is in a better place. She is happy and knows that someday you will join her again."

Inside the bag were a couple of pieces of Lakshmi's pink frosted baby shower cake. The dark chocolate cake was a strange and violent contrast with the bright pink icing.

I went to bed at seven and woke up at six the next morning and forced myself to get to the gym to lift some weights. When I walked into the kitchen, Gene, Tim and Jonnie hugged me. "We are so glad to have you back!" Jonnie said. "It felt like a month without you!"

"Yes, Tyler. We missed your sunshine!" Tim said.

"I don't feel like I'll ever be sunny again," I responded.

"Of course you will be," Gene said, in all sincerity. "You deserve to be happy, Tyler. And you will be."

Gene looked so different that morning with a flush of red in his cheeks. He seemed to be an inch taller and his eyes seemed brighter and greener. Warmly smiling, he was both energized and happy as we opened up the cage of pots and pans. For the first time ever, I heard him humming and the song was *Whistle While You Work*.

Someone's luck had changed for the better.

The rest of the morning was an embarrassment of hugs and consolations from staff and volunteers. "I'm sorry you about your dog," said Jeremy. "And I'm sorry you didn't get that writing job. You don't have to tell me how that feels when you get that close. It's like someone ripped out all your bones and you wonder if you'll ever walk again."

"Exactly."

Since it was Mexican Wednesday, I needed to make fresh guacamole. At nine thirty, I was headed to the bathroom when Jacob Hellman raced up the steps, his belly flapping, with envelopes in hand and that enormous, red-lipped grin. "Angels!" he said, summoning the staff to the community room and away from the volunteers. "We apologize — it was an honest mistake," he said as he handed us new checks. "And it will never happen again. A check was written in the wrong amount to our leasing company and they cashed it and it wiped out our balance. It's all been corrected." He handed me my check and I noticed that this one was not signed by Andrew Belfry but by Jacob Hellman.

"Tyler, I'm so sorry about your dog," Jacob said.

"Thanks. You're signing the checks now?"

Jacob nervously grinned. "Yes, I'm expanding my duties. Hug?"

We did a manly faux-hug with pats on the back. The anger that had been choking me for the last twenty-four hours was giving way to grief. I was overwhelmed by all the warmth and support I'd felt that morning. Wiping at tears constantly, I had a strange moment while I made the batter for red velvet cake. The recipe, which I had to multiply by twelve, required six cups of red food coloring. It was an intense sight as I poured it over the yellow batter and it spread like a kind of fiery blood. I incorporated the food coloring with a hand mixer and with its bright gloss, it looked like gallons of spilled nail polish. Jonnie walked into the kitchen with that look of happy surprise, ducking her head and clasping her hands under her open mouth.

"Tyler! Phone call for you!"

"For me? Who is it?"

My stomach flipped. I hoped it was my agent, calling me to tell me that Universal had changed their minds and was hiring me to adapt *Wishing Well*.

"It's Lakshmi!" she said.

Oh. Lakshmi.

I went out to the community room where Jericho extended the phone receiver, his hand over the speaking end. "Well, aren't you special!" he said. Gene and Jonnie watched me from a distance but were listening.

"Hi Lakshmi."

"Tyler! I wanted to say thank you for that *amazing* cake!"

"You're very welcome. It was nothing."

"Nothing? It was everything! It was just so imaginative! You are *so* creative. When I walked in and saw it, I just burst out laughing. We took some pictures!"

"It was my pleasure. I had fun making it."

"I'm sure you did. So, how are you, Tyler? Jonnie told me you're going through a bad time."

I sighed. "My dog died. I couldn't have loved her more. She was family. And on the same day I had a major disappointment career-wise, the biggest fish to ever wriggle off the hook."

"Are you an actor?"

"No," I said, not surprised that she had asked me that again — there were so many frustrated actors among her followers. "I'm a screenwriter but one who's been off track for a while. I almost got this job at Universal and… well, it hurts worse when you fall off the top of the ladder. I'm feeling pretty… shattered today."

"I get you, Tyler. I completely understand that. I know that pain."

"Yes. Painful. But I need to start a new project… whatever that is."

"Have you asked God what he wants you to write?"

I was silenced when she said that. She had said it with such conviction and warmth in her voice that I considered it.

"I haven't," I said.

"You should, Tyler. God is waiting for you to ask, for you to serve him. And to be in service to God is to be in service to yourself and others. I'm praying for you, Tyler. Take care."

I hung up the phone and had a glow — finally, for the first time, I had been touched by Lakshmi in the way she touched others. I felt *loved* by her.

A few minutes later, the list of dead clients who had "transitioned" was posted on the cork board. I knew the names and the faces of some of these men and had even handed them grocery bags. Their deaths were all too real. My grief for Luna returned and as I stared at the blood-red batter of my cake mix, I realized something: I no longer believed in a caring God and doubted his very existence.

If God did exist, he had created a world of endless pain and suffering, a world of profuse violence where the survival of some relied on the bloody deaths of others. God was a cold witness to lions, cheetahs and wild dogs when they ripped out the throats of wildebeest calves and left their mothers grieving. He had ignored the prayers of six million Jews who had been exterminated in Hitler's camps. God had let twenty-seven million Soviets die as they fought the Nazis — and that was fairly recent history. He was just as cold in this present moment when the retrovirus he had included in his Creation was continuing to replicate itself and leave its human hosts vulnerable to endless diseases before they died in misery.

I suddenly hated myself for being self-involved and stupid enough to think that God would or should give a shit about something as trivial as my screenwriting career. And if he wanted me to write something that celebrated the return to him as someone who might solve my little problems — well, fuck that God. He was just another needy narcissist who was starving for attention.

Gene, and my favorite new volunteer, Bryce, were talking again with the volunteer I had noticed last week. She was making them smile as they spoke to her while she rearranged her bags for delivery. As usual, she was wearing a pair of baggy 501 jeans and a loose blue work shirt over her plump body. As she spoke to Gene, he looked even more glowing, his hand patting her back as they strolled off to join Jonnie in the prayer circle. Bryce took one of her hands and Gene the other and the three of them were smiling at something she'd said just before the prayer got started.

Who was she, this new source of joy?

Chapter 16

I didn't want to join the prayer circle that morning and made a show of tending to my cakes and flipping them around to the hotter part of our less-than-professional ovens. As the cakes rose and domed, I went to work at washing out the basin and my utensils which turned the dishwater a dirty pink. When at last the prayer circle dispersed, Gene, Bryce and their new friend dressed in denim walked toward me. She had long, curly hair, laughing eyes and a face not unlike the Mona Lisa but with a double chin. She smiled warmly when Gene introduced us. "Tyler, this is Magdalena."

"Nice to meet you, Magdalena," I said, wiping my hands on my apron before I shook one of hers.

"My friends call me Madge. Nice to meet you, Tyler," she said, and then cocked her head and looked concerned for me. "Gene didn't need to tell me you're in pain," she said. "I felt it before I came in. It's just radiatin.'"

"I'm fine," I said. "Time heals everything."

"Yeah, it does, but you need to take special care at this moment," she said. "I think we can help you."

"Oh?"

"Madge is a Reiki master," Bryce said.

"She's teaching classes at the Being Center," said Gene. "We're all learning how to do it."

"Reiki? I don't know that much about it," I said... but I did. Reiki was something Allen had tried a few times in search of relief from the pounding headaches and the endless diarrhea and other gastrointestinal disorders associated with AIDS. He made it sound like faith healing or "laying on of hands," something I had witnessed in my brief time as a Jesus person. After a while, Allen gave up on it.

"Reiki will help you," Madge said with the built-in indignation of a New York accent.

"Where are you from?" I asked. "I'm hearing East Coast."

"I'm from Florida," she said, pronouncing it *flaw-ri-duh*.

"Florida?"

"New York-y Florida. Miami."

"Right," I said and grinned.

"Tyler, we need a subject for Friday's class and I just *know* it will make you feel better," she said. "You run risks when you're grievin'. Your immunity is lowered when you don't sleep... and you haven't been sleepin'. And you become accident-prone. Grief is *terrible* for people who are HIV-positive."

"I don't know that I am," I said.

She looked at me again, running her eyes around my shoulders and my head.

"You're not," she said and smiled. "I don't see that, but your outer aura is black... so black. You're sad, very sad, but the other auric layers are still visible and the red is strong. That's good. You're a strong person."

"What would I have to do?" I said. I was not too terribly worried about my dark aura. I was sure I looked as sad as a basset hound.

"You wouldn't have to do anything," she said. "Just lie on your back and accept the energy."

"I think Tyler's done a lot of lying down and accepting the energy — with a little dab of Crisco on his sweet, pink bunghole," said Bryce and for the first time in days I smiled.

"I'm always open to trying new things," I said.

On Friday after work, about ten people sat on yoga mats in one of the back rooms of the Being Center in a semicircle around Madge and me. I was on my back on my own mat, looking up at the ceiling when she set a brass Tibetan prayer bowl on my chest and then ran a wooden mallet around it to make it sing.

"Let the vibrations of the bowl bring you into that place of oneness with the universe," she said as she looked out on her students. "It's good for your subject to feel that oneness, but it's more important for the master," she said. "It's comin' now," she whispered and then exhaled long and loud three times before she lifted the suddenly silenced bowl and handed it to Gene.

"We start with the crown chakra," she said and waved her hands with a little flutter until they stilled just above my forehead. "The crown chakra is also known as the Christ and Krishna Consciousness — the manifestation of God in a human form."

Madge worked her way down through the seven chakras, as well as some new ones which she retitled as the Galactic Highway, the Star Gate, the Core of Mithra, the Cosmic Garden, the Lost City of Atlantis, the Virtuous Cities of Heaven and the United Whale and Dolphin Queendoms. Her hands flew out, fluttering then opening, as if to scoop in some invisible force which she then compacted and concentrated over each of my chakras. She breathed out as a signal that the chakra had been activated before moving on to the next one.

When it was complete, she sat back on her haunches and nodded her head. "It's... it's good. The transference was very good, Tyler, and you were very acceptin' of the energy. The black emanation of your aura is a barrier to the good, a malignancy that's lettin' some dark entities and their miasmas near you. That's weakened you, but I think there's enough energy among the novices here to lessen if not disperse even more of that blackness."

Madge looked around the room at the circle of faces, all of which were entranced by her and absorbed in the demonstration. "Gene and Bryce, I sense that you are spiritual brothers with Tyler and that you have a strong bond with him. Do you feel the power to do a Reiki-meldin' to further his healin'?"

Gene and Bryce nodded and then knelt on the floor at the sides of my head. They pressed hands together and then clasped them above my Christ and Krishna Consciousness.

"When you feel the energy and the connection between you, begin," Madge said. The two of them looked into each other's eyes and nodded as they began a slow movement over my body, walking on their knees. After a long week of standing on my feet, I gave in to the pleasure of just allowing myself to lie on a mat and be the focus of so much attention. I realized I had been breathing in a shallow way and let myself take long, deep breaths. My mind emptied and I relaxed and felt sleepy.

Some have suggested that the benefits of Reiki may be attributed to a placebo effect: a kind of sugar pill that works with the power of suggestion. Some have asserted it's like going to any good doctor who shows concern for the patient's well-being, that the doctor's cure is both his medicine and his love. My little bit of bliss was interrupted when I started thinking that love was not enough to cure the gonorrhea that Kyle had given me when we were first living together, nor the second time. I was thinking about Christian Scientists, wondering if their response to curing gonorrhea and syphilis was to pray it away instead of a course of antibiotics. And then I was wondering if it was a good idea to have sex with Christian Scientists. I didn't think I ever had, but I had slept with some Mormons, and I started making a mental list of them and was trying to remember the details of their funny underwear. I remembered that the shirt had a plunging neckline.

"Sit up slowly, Tyler," Madge said after Gene and Bryce reactivated the United Whale and Dolphin Queendoms. "How do you feel?"

"Better," I said, and I wasn't lying. "I'm relaxed."

"Stop worryin'," she said. "Worryin' never helps. Besides, I'm only seein' good things for you. It's all gonna be fine, Tyler. More than fine."

The rest of the students took turns giving or receiving Reiki until it was six o'clock. The next class had gathered outside the door, waiting to take over the room, a seminar on Effective Visualizations for Relationship, Career and Financial Goals. Gene gave the three of us a ride back to our cars near the church in his Ford Taurus, which still had that nauseating new car smell.

"Why don't you like this car?" I asked him. "It's nice. It's new. I've never had a new car."

"Oh, it's *OK*," he said. "I just think I can get a better one."

"You will," said Madge. "In the next couple of years. Somethin' German."

"Really?" Gene responded. "Good."

"Madge, you talk like you can see into the future," I said.

She and Gene laughed. "She can," said Gene. "Madge is psychic."

"She is," said Bryce. "After I lost my wallet, she told me it was at the bottom of the washing machine. And it was."

"Do people pay you for readings?" I asked.

"They used to," she answered. "I worked for a psychic hotline in Fort Lauderdale. But then they brought in all these fake psychics. The fakes worked for a lot less money."

"Did you see that coming?" I asked.

"I did."

"Maybe you should have unionized," said Bryce. "The UPW... united psychic workers."

"You should ask Madge for a reading, Tyler," Gene said. "Though it may not be what you want to hear."

"What did she see for you?" I asked.

Gene tittered with pride.

"He's too modest to repeat it," Madge said. "Gene is going to have a famous lover. And they'll be livin' in some hilly place in Los Angeles, near Mulholland, I think, off of Laurel is what I saw. And someday, Gene will be a spiritual leader to hundreds of thousands."

"How.... interesting," was all I could manage to say after a long silence. "Did you get a reading, Bryce?"

"I did," he said. "Madge told me that one day I would meet Brad Pitt and Keanu Reeves and they would turn gay and we would be a threesome for about ten or fifteen years before I changed them out for Tom Cruise and George Clooney. And one day *I* will be a spiritual leader to hundreds of *millions*." He stuck out his tongue at Gene. "I actually didn't like my reading," Bryce said, suddenly serious. "But it doesn't mean it's not true."

"Bryce asked me about his actin' career," Madge said. "And I told him the truth, that I didn't see that, only gray clouds and fog. But I did see that he will be recognized, even celebrated, for other talents."

"And what are those?" I asked.

"It hasn't been revealed yet. Though I see this mountain of gifts for Bryce. Beautifully wrapped gifts that reflect his own gifts."

Gene pulled over when Madge sighted her car, a beat-up, blue Volkswagen Bug that matched her one and only outfit. The back of it was covered with a multitude of bumper stickers including a very faded McGovern/Shriver 72 and the classic, "My other car is a broom."

"Thank you again, Madge," I said as she readied to exit, hoisting up her fringed, macrame shoulder bag of natural fibers. "That was a really interesting experience."

"I knew you'd like it," she said. "Tyler, you didn't ask me, but I just have to tell ya because I'm excited for you. When it comes to your writin' career, you're gonna have a steady series of little successes. And then one of those projects is gonna blow up, big time, and after that it's all gonna explode."

"Really," I said. "Well... I look forward to that. Thank you."

We watched her get in her own car and she had to slam the door three times before it properly closed.

"So how is it you become a spiritual leader?" I asked Gene as we drove to Bryce's truck.

"That part was murky," Gene said. "But maybe, like the Buddha, I will have a satori moment and from there everything might just unfold."

I was quiet a moment as I put it all together. At last, Gene's real ambition was laid bare. He wanted to be Lakshmi.

"Take Madge's reading with a grain of salt," I said to Bryce when we got to his Toyota pickup that he called Miss Warwick. "If acting is what you really want to do."

"I was born an actress," Bryce said, doing a flawless impression of Gloria Swanson as Norma Desmond. "You see, this *is* my life. It always will be. Just us and the cameras and all those wonderful people out there in the dark."

As we drove away, I looked out the back window where Bryce continued his performance with his head thrown back, his eyes wide open and his hand swirling as he readied his close-up for Mr. DeMille.

"Isn't Madge amazing?" Gene asked as we drove to my car.

"She's... something else," I said as I got out, eager for some solitude. "Gene, thanks so much... for caring." I was opening the door of my car when I noticed Jeremy walking toward his. He looked tired and lost in thought.

"Hey Jer," I said. "You just leaving work?"

"Helping out Joffrey," he said. "We had about thirty clients fall off the list today and forty more come on. This little plague is unending. I wonder if I'll ever have time to write again."

"Speaking of writing… did you know Madge is psychic?"

"So she says. Did you get a reading from her?"

"I did, and you know, it's rosy. She said it would be slow but steady then something would take off and it would all explode. I'm gonna be huge."

"She told me the same thing. It's kind of sweet I guess. She may not be clairvoyant but at least she's rooting for us."

My stomach was rumbling with dread, not hunger, as I drove home in the darkness and the rush-hour traffic along Fairfax Avenue through Little Ethiopia. I wasn't happy to see Kyle's car parked in the driveway. When I walked through the front door, Holden, as he always did, ran up to me and put his paws on my legs and wagged his tail. I lifted him up to let him lick my face then turned to see that there was a glass vase of striking white flowers on the dining table: gladiolas, lilies and roses in what looked like milk instead of water. Kyle walked out of the bathroom and looked at me in contrition as I rocked our dog in my arms. He was dressed in a stylish white shirt with two oversized pockets and a collar with long, sharp points. The shirt was tucked into pressed jeans and the shoes he wore were black and shiny.

"Do you want to go to Vegas?" he asked in a quiet, tentative voice, as if I might say no. "I made a reservation at The Flamingo. They have rooms that are dog friendly. And I got us tix for Jubilee at the MGM on Saturday."

"OK," I said, taken aback. He knew that I loved those tits-and-feathers shows. "I need to take a shower."

"And how about counseling, Tyler? Do you want to get some counseling?"

"If you're paying for it."

Chapter 17

Over the next few months, Gene paid special attention to whoever famous walked up the stairs. The novelist David Leavitt was a driver for a few weeks while he was in town to work on a screen version of The Lost Language of Cranes. "Thanks for volunteering," Gene said as he introduced himself. Leavitt silently shook his hand when it was offered. I introduced myself as well and told Leavitt how much I loved his work. All he said was a quick "thank you" after making brief eye contact before turning to repack his bags.

"He's kind of shy," I whispered to Gene on the walk back to the kitchen.

"And he's not that cute," Gene said dismissively. "And besides... I heard he's here to complete some community service. Drunk driving or something."

Whenever any other unemployed actors popped in, including some from the canceled programs *Dynasty* and its spinoff, *The Colbys*, Gene would take a few breaths, work up his smile and then introduce himself. "Hello, I'm Gene, thanks for coming in. I'm the chef here at Manna... well, the head chef," he would say feigning modesty with a chortle. But so far there hadn't been "any chemistry" between him and the numerous celebrity volunteers. Every so often we had "fame alerts" which took on something of a teasing character when "the old queens of comedy" appeared, men like Charles Nelson Reilly, Alan Sues, and Dom DeLuise. Jericho walked into the kitchen one especially hectic Friday as we prepared for the arrival of someone whose own fame was increasing each day.

"Ohhh, Gene!" Jericho sang, hands on his knees with a mischievous grin. "Fame alert! He's heeeeeere!"

"Who's here?" Gene asked, smirking defensively as he scooped some shredded chicken and wild mushrooms into some buckwheat crepes.

"Your famous boyfriend! He's not very tall but, hint — he's *bigger than life* and just dying to meet you."

All of us stepped out to the community room to see the porn star Jeff Stryker, with an entourage that included some heavily made-up and silicone-enhanced young women wearing belly shirts and spandex. The women, perhaps, were the costars of Jeff's straight and bisexual work. Like so many stars, he looked shorter in person. He was signing autographs on dollar bills and random slips of paper as well as on the clients' delivery bags for some amused and delirious volunteers.

"I am going to have to pass on Mr. Stryker," Gene said to Jericho.

"Are you sure?" Jericho said. "I thought you said you could take ten inches. I mean, first you'd have to take that big stick out of your ass."

"The only reason I'd take that big stick out of my ass is to use it to beat your flabby butt. But you'd love that, wouldn't you? You'd beg for more until your buttocks were covered with bloody welts."

"Good one," said Jericho, laughing with the rest of us.

"Oh, and I forgot to tell you, Jericho," Gene said, stopping to pivot. "Gino Vanelli called. And he wants his hairdo back."

Jericho roared with everyone else. Bryce offered Gene a dollar tip, as if he were a stripper. "You got her," Bryce said.

Gene did not savor his victory for long and sighed and had his usual pensive look as he went back to work. Madge arrived, saw the look on his face, and stroked his back as she asked what was wrong. Gene muttered something and I heard her say, "Jericho has a lot of negative energy. But he's longin' for someone just as much as you are and he hides it with his sarcasm. He's out there, Gene— the one — but ya gotta let him come to *you*."

Gene nodded and looked comforted as we sprinkled grated Gruyere over hotel pans full of crepes and then slid them in the oven. At the stoves, Bryce was frantically blanching asparagus in batches and at the same time stirring a Meyer lemon hollandaise so it wouldn't curdle. I returned to slicing up the last tray of napoleons with a filling of hazelnut pastry cream. Using a yardstick, I measured the servings for uniformity and then cut them with a serrated knife for precision. Everything was supposed to be "perfect" that day, but as it was Friday, we had to finish up two meals, including the cold lunch for Saturday, the one day we did not cook and deliver. Earlier that morning, we had already made over three hundred tuna fish sandwiches, fruit salads and then cut up and wrapped some blondies which went into separate bags, before taking on our most ambitious meal ever.

Madge wandered over to the side counter where volunteers were helping me pack the dessert by setting each slice on a smear of chocolate to keep it secured to the bottom of the container. "Those are very professional-lookin'," she said. "They're perfect, Tyler... like you. You're the most perfect person I've ever met."

"I feel a lot less than perfect today," I said. For months, we were working longer and longer hours in a kitchen that felt smaller and smaller. I was exhausted and had a throbbing headache and felt like my leg bones were made of chilled steel. I'd had a cold for weeks that I couldn't shake. But that day, we had a show to put on, and for the first time ever, we were wearing old-fashioned paper hats that made us look like old-timey soda jerks. Gene and I had on special aprons with a Manna decal, the ones we'd worn for the TV commercials. He had told me to "wear something nice" so I had on some new black jeans as well as an ironed, teal-colored shirt with short sleeves that I rolled up to expose my triceps. At exactly eleven thirty, Jonnie came into the kitchen and loudly whispered, "She's here!" over clasped hands.

For the first time in months, Lakshmi Steinmetz entered the kitchen holding what was being called her "little bundle of bliss" since one of the many names she was considering for her baby included Ananda, which means "bliss" in Sanskrit. At Lakshmi's side was a smiley, sunny young nanny with a diaper bag in one hand and a baby carrier in the other. Coming up from behind Lakshmi was a well-coiffed woman wearing an ivory-white pleated skirt suit. She held a yellow legal pad and a pen at the ready.

"Lakshmi!" Jonnie cried out and everyone quieted and turned to look at Ms. Steinmetz. "Thank you for coming by!"

"It is *so* good to be here," Lakshmi said, working up a little Hepburn in *Stage Door* for us. "Everyone, everyone! If I could just get your attention for a moment. We know you are all so busy and doing such very good work, but please welcome Diane Toussaint. Diane is here from *Vanity Fair* magazine."

Diane quietly nodded and then scribbled something down as everyone gathered around Lakshmi to look at her baby. With her eyes closed, the girl who might be called Ananda looked pretty much like all babies, but everyone assured Lakshmi that her daughter was "precious," "gorgeous," "beautiful," and as Jonnie put it, "just the most darling little thing ever."

Lakshmi was touched. Motherhood had changed her, had softened her and given her a genuine femininity. Her face was rounder, less angular, and her smile was warm and genuine as the baby was admired. Jericho, having just gotten an autograph from Jeff Stryker, wandered over and made his way into the circle. "Lakshmi!" he said with a sarcastic grin. "The baby is just adorable. And she looks just like her father!"

Jericho laughed at his own joke as Lakshmi's jaw dropped several stories. She stared at Jericho, madly flapping her eyelids.

"Just who is the father?" Diane asked Jericho, her pen poised above her pad.

Lakshmi took a moment to compose herself, but she was heaving, and her shoulders looked as if they were flapping imaginary batwings. She cleared her throat and made one of her forced, angry smiles.

"That is not something I am willing to discuss," she said to Diane. "I believe we talked about that, didn't we, Diane?"

Diane shrugged.

"Now," Lakshmi said. "Let's talk about Manna from Heaven. Shall we? Gene, what are we serving the clients today?"

Nervous and self-conscious, Gene gave a perfunctory smile. "We're doing a French meal today," he said. "We try and do something special on Fridays. Along with *crêpes au poulet avec champignons sauvages,* we have a side dish of *asperges avec sauce hollandaise.* For today's dessert we have a lovely *millefeuille* with a *noisette praline crème pâtissière* and a *glacage au chocolat blanc.*"

"*Crème pâtissière au praliné noisette,*" said Diane, correcting him.

"Correct," said Gene as he blushed.

She spoke in French to him after that. I knew enough French to understand that she was asking him if we made our own crepes.

"I'm sorry," Gene said. "But I don't really speak French."

"Really? You don't speak French, Gene?" Jericho asked through a snicker. "Even though you lived in Paris and you toss around these French expressions all the time?"

"I never said I spoke French," Gene said.

"You are so busted. *Tu es tellement cassé,*" Jericho said then laughed.

"Gene, why don't you show Diane around the kitchen?" Lakshmi said as more and more drivers gathered in a noisy hubbub in the community room. "And then we'll meet for a prayer." Jonnie, the nanny, Lakshmi and her baby walked out to the crowd of volunteer drivers.

I followed them out with my first tray of packaged napoleons as a few in the crowd converged on Lakshmi. "Oh, we've missed you so much, Lakshmi!" said one of her fans, a tall, gawky man who went by the name Koala. He had a bald head that looked like he had shined it with Turtle Wax. "I've been listening to your tapes, but it's just not the same! When are you coming back to lecture?"

"Soon, Koala," she said. "But right now I have the greatest responsibility that God gives to women — motherhood." The crowd around her gave a collective "Aah."

"Are we ready for a prayer, Lakshmi?" Jonnie asked her.

"We are," she said, but Lakshmi was distracted and confused as she looked over at Jeff Stryker and his garish costars who were getting all the attention that morning. "Is... is that…"

"That's Chuck," Jonnie said.

"Chuck Payton," I said. "That's his real name."

"What's he doing here?" Lakshmi angrily whispered as she handed her baby to the nanny.

"He's delivering today," said Jonnie.

"But why today of all days?"

"We didn't know he was coming. And we couldn't turn him down. He's come here out of love."

Jonnie clapped, summoning everyone to the circle, and took Lakshmi's hand and then took mine. Making a beeline for Lakshmi was Madge who ran over, forcing herself into position to take Lakshmi's left hand.

"I'm Madge," she said to Lakshmi, grabbing her fingers. "Congratulations on your little girl. I'm sure you feel so relieved to have finally had a baby before the clock ran out... and such a healthy one."

"Oh," said Lakshmi, startled. "Yes, thank you."

"I've known we would meet for the longest time," Madge said. "I heard one of your very first lectures at the Theosophy Lodge when I first moved here."

"I appreciate your coming. And for volunteering," Lakshmi said, trying to cut her off.

"We should get tea sometime," Madge said, looking around Lakshmi's head to examine her aura. "I can see you won't be drinkin' alcohol for a while. You're breastfeedin'."

This was obvious from Lakshmi's fuller figure. She took a breath. "Yes…yes I am."

"It's not safe to drink now," Madge said. "Alcohol could be in your milk for hours once you've drunk it. But I can also see you don't wanna drink because of all the negativity you associate with alcohol in your past. You don't want to pass on that trauma to your newborn."

Lakshmi, at that point, could not hide her discomfort. "Excuse me, but just who are you?" she asked. Madge looked slighted as the two stared at each other in silence. Jonnie, trying to defuse the situation, jumped in. "Madge is one of our best volunteers!" Jonnie said. "She delivers twice a week! And when we really, *really* need someone, we just give her a call and she arrives with a smile and a week's worth of sunshine!"

"Wonderful," Lakshmi said, forcing a tight smile.

"She's also a good friend to Gene," Jonnie said. "And a very gifted psychic."

"A psychic. I see," said Lakshmi as her face stiffened.

"That's why we should get tea sometime," said Madge. "And see what's in the leaves… now that your daughter's been born. You're back to work on your book, aren't ya?"

Lakshmi cocked her head, took a breath. "Look," she said, dropping Madge's hand as the bitch stepped out. "I get you, girlfriend. I totally understand your energy. Now if you'll excuse me I've got a prayer to lead so we can get these volunteers on their way."

Madge looked offended as Lakshmi broke from the circle and walked into its center. She pivoted slowly to face everyone, her head nodding as her face took on that reprimanding look. Cold Angry Mom had appeared, ready to upbraid her offspring.

"Hello everyone," she said. "It is wonderful, a miracle, actually, to be back at this church and here at Manna from Heaven where I am sensing so much love and giving. You are all really just so extraordinary."

I looked over at Gene and the journalist from *Vanity Fair* who were walking toward the prayer circle. Gene joined joined hands with Madge and Jonnie.

"Our clients are so blessed to have you," Lakshmi said. "And how blessed you are to serve God and to…"

"Lakshmi, darling!" came a loud voice from outside the circle. Film producer Aaron Sibley was waddling in, out of breath from struggling up the stairs with a new personal assistant. He was another young, bespectacled male who looked as bedraggled as the last one.

"Aaron Sibley!" Lakshmi said. "What brings you here, Aaron?"

"We're volunteering today," Aaron said as he and his assistant joined the prayer circle.

"So lovely of you to take time out from your busy schedule. Don't you have a premier in a couple of months?"

"Yes, I do," he said. "My new film, *Stolen Thunder,* is coming out and it's…" Aaron had noticed Jeff Stryker and was distracted. It was hard not to notice Jeff since his most admired gift was bulging down the right side of his crotch. "… it's fabulous. It's a fabulous film," Aaron continued. "But there's much more important work to do *here*."

"There certainly is," said Lakshmi looking at Mr. Stryker again who had stolen *her* thunder. Jeff was looking back at her and wondering who she was. "Let us pray," she said and closed her eyes, slowly spinning like a dervish on downers as she entered a trance.

"God, you show us so much light today as we gather here to defeat this illusion of sickness that separates the Childrenhood from you, from your eternal love. Because of this virus, we can see our better selves, we can destroy our egos, we can get back to loving, can get back to you, Holy Father. AIDS is not the cover on a casket, but the lid of a beautiful jar that we can open to drink the ambrosia of immortality. Bless these volunteers, this staff and above all, the clients of Manna. Amen."

When the circle broke apart, Jeff Stryker was deluged by another wave of fans. Then he did that thing that was so rare in his videos — he smiled. A swooning and mustachioed volunteer had handed Jeff a Sharpie and made a request. Jeff uncapped the Sharpie as the volunteer, with little decorum, lowered his pants to get an autograph on his butt cheek. "I'm going straight to my tattoo artist," said the man in a loud, queeny voice as he waved over the signature with his hand to dry it. "So he can ink this in and I have it forever!"

"Diane," Lakshmi called to the journalist to distract her from the spectacle. "I think we're meeting back at my office at four?"

Diane nodded as Aaron Sibley approached her, shaking her hand and introducing himself. The two were chatting when Aaron nodded his head and Diane reached into her shoulder bag and took out a cassette recorder. They wandered over to the edge of the community room's stage where they sat for an interview. "Go wash some dishes or something," Aaron shouted at his assistant who looked startled and then did just that.

Closer to the kitchen, Lakshmi and Jonnie were in a corner, the two of them speaking in hushed tones. Lakshmi was glancing over at Jericho as he clowned for some new volunteers. While adding their info to his database, Jericho played with his pearls, wrapping them around the massive curls of his hair to make a strange and crooked bouffant. Lakshmi, wildly gesticulating, suddenly turned and stomped off, her face flushed with anger. The nanny, holding the baby in the car seat carrier, shrugged at Jonnie, then scrambled after Lakshmi down the stairs. The baby, who had slept through it all, finally woke and started to cry.

I went back to the kitchen to make lunch for the volunteers. There were no crepes left but there was some asparagus, some cheese and some shredded chicken and mushrooms in some congealing béchamel sauce. Bryce and I chopped it all up, stirred it together, then cracked open a few dozen eggs and improvised some frittatas.

I was irritated as well as exhausted. We had orchestrated a show for the glory of Lakshmi Steinmetz, one that had included the well-timed arrival of a Hollywood film producer who was no doubt promoting his latest movie as he talked up Lakshmi to *Vanity Fair*. But what really annoyed me was what Lakshmi had said about the virus, something that was an echo of Eloise Clayman's bullshit: HIV had been sent by God as a means of bringing us closer to him, of helping our better natures to emerge.

That was a God who could go fuck himself, I thought.

While we waited for the frittatas to puff in the center, Tim and the Tipplers arrived, out of breath as they struggled in with heavy cartons from Smart and Final. Gene folded his arms and smirked as the cartons were set down. Four of the cartons were cans of cling peaches. The other four were cans of Spam. There was also a jar of whole cloves and some boxes of brown sugar.

"Phew," Tim said wiping sweat from his brow. "I heard Lakshmi and the baby were here. I didn't know she was coming today."

"No?" Gene said. "I thought I told you."

"No! You didn't. I'd have come early if I'd known."

Gene shook his head and looked at the cartons as if a pig had just shit on the counter. "And just what are you making for Sunday lunch?" he asked.

"Fiesta Peach Spam Bake," Tim answered.

Gene openly scoffed and shook his head. "Fiesta... peach... *Spam bake?* Is that what I heard?"

"You've never had it? It's delicious," Tim said. "It's a great comfort food. The clients will love it."

"Oh, I am sure they will just adore it," said Gene.

"Spam is very popular in France," Tim said. "Ever since it was introduced by American soldiers in Dubya-Dubya Two. The French know a good product."

"You *do* know what Spam stands for," Gene asked.

"Spiced ham," Tim said.

"No. Shit pork all mashed. And just what is Tyler making for dessert?"

"Rice Krispies Treats," I said.

"Rice... Krispies... Treats? *Why?*" Gene asked, his voice tremulous with disgust.

"Tim asked me to. The clients will like them — childhood memories. I thought I'd do the peanut butter version with a chocolate icing for extra calories, kinda like a Reese's Cup."

Gene sighed in an exaggerated way. "Well," he said. "If we can have Mexican Wednesdays, I suppose we can have White Trash Sundays."

That landed with a thud. Tim gasped but said nothing. The Tipplers stared at Gene with contempt, silently shaking their heads. "Bitch," one of them whispered, a man who Gene called Wayne the Pain because he was always gender-fucking Gene and calling him Jeanette, Jenny or Jane.

"Uh, I don't think we have any Rice Krispies or mini-marshmallows," I said to break the tension. "I might need to get to Smart and Final myself."

"Mini-marshmallows?" Bryce said. "I'll go with you. Minnie Marshmallows is my drag name."

As we drove and shopped and loaded our cart, Bryce entertained me with stories about growing up gay in Midland, Texas. One of his first jobs was taking care of a wealthy neighbor's pet yak, also named Jericho, which allowed him to buy his first bong after a five-hour drive to Austin. We were unloading onto the conveyor belt when the sourpuss manager, Mr. Valchick, stepped over and gave me a grim stare. "Gigi, void all those charges, back them out," he said to the cashier. "No more credit for Manna," he said to me.

"Sorry?"

"Your check bounced."

"But someone was just in here."

"Fat guy who bought a lot of Spam? That was yesterday. I'm telling you, your check bounced. We just got notice."

"Not *my* check," I said. "I don't write the checks."

The manager picked up his intercom mic and his voice blasted through the store. "Samantha, bring me a copy of the notification of insufficient funds for Manna from Heaven."

I looked behind us and a line was forming. Suddenly I was a deadbeat who was making people wait. I knew it was pointless to try my credit card. Samantha appeared, an elderly, emaciated woman with a pencil in her gray bun. She looked at me as if I had killed her husband. She thrust a xerox of the bank notice at us and then shook her head in disgust.

"I'm sorry," I said to her and the manager. "We'll get this paid up."

When Bryce and I got back to the kitchen, it was strangely silent except for some muffled screaming from Lakshmi in the community room. Tim and his volunteers were quietly working as they drank from their Dixie cups. Tim put a finger to his mouth to quiet us. We listened to the screaming through the indoor windows as Tim's crew dumped out clumps of Spam to slice and then layer with peach slices before inserting them with cloves and sprinkling with brown sugar. I looked at Bryce who put his hands on his hips as the screaming continued. "Lord in heaven," he whispered with a Southern accent. "Sounds like somebody shit on Lakshmi's lasagna."

I quietly went to the landing of the stairs and spied on Lakshmi as she berated Jericho. Jonnie and Gene were standing near the two, stiff and silent, as Lakshmi lashed the air with her index finger. "Your behavior was disgraceful!" she shouted. "This story is a chance to grow this organization and instead you embarrassed me!"

"I told you, I was just joking!" Jericho shouted back.

"Joking? About the father of my daughter? You think that's a joke? And don't you *ever* shout at *me*, *honey*!"

"I'm sorry, Lakshmi. I didn't realize you were so sensitive about it."

"Sensitive? Don't you dare talk to me about sensitivity. You have been completely insensitive!"

"I said I'm sorry," he replied and there was a tremble in his voice. "Jonnie, Gene," he said appealing to them. "You know what I do here, how hard I work. Tell her, please, I…"

"It's not up to them," Lakshmi shouted. "You've never shown me respect! Everything is just a joke to you including my daughter! I told you, you're fired! Get out! GET OUT!"

"B…but Lakshmi, I…"

"I SAID YOU'RE FIRED!" she shouted pointing at the door. She caught me looking at them. "LEAVE! NOW!"

Jericho hesitated. He was sobbing, shaking and wiping at tears. "Please," he said, "I was… I was just…"

"You were JUST LEAVING!" Lakshmi screamed. "Jonnie, call the police. Get this tragic little figure out of here now! He's never liked me!" She pinned her eyes on me. "Tyler! What are you looking at?"

"I need to speak with Jonnie," I said. "And you. Our check to Smart and Final —"

"I DO NOT want to hear about it," Lakshmi shouted. "Not now, *honey*!"

Jericho was still for a moment, heaving, then found some resolve as his face went from sad to angry. He gritted his teeth as he went to the electrical socket and unplugged the ridiculously dated Kay-Pro computer then wound up its cable around the power strip.

"Just what do you think you're doing?" Lakshmi screamed.

"I'm leaving," he said as he attached the keyboard to the computer's front and snapped them together to make something that looked like a metal suitcase.

"Not with our computer! Call the police NOW, Jonnie! He's stealing from us!"

"It's *my* computer," he said. He put a box of paper under one arm and then held the printer with the other.

"It *is* his computer," Jonnie said meekly.

"It is," said Gene.

"But it has our information!" Lakshmi screamed.

"Maybe you should have thought of that before you fired me," Jericho said.

"But that's *our* intellectual property!"

"It's my intellectual property, *honey*. These are my programs that I developed, my data that I entered. Something that I did for *free* for this organization before they ever started paying me."

"You leave that computer here now!" Lakshmi screamed. "For the sake of our clients! How could you be so selfish?"

"I might ask you the same, *Miriam*," he said, using her real name.

Jericho awkwardly backed through the swinging door of the kitchen, struggling not to drop his cumbersome load.

"Goodbye, everybody," he said and then he started crying again. He walked past me, tears under his chin, and I watched him thump down the stairs when the printer slipped from under his arm and fell, cracking the plastic. "Fuck, shit!" he screamed, wailing as he slumped.

"I have it," I said and picked up the printer. We walked in silence to his car.

"Thanks, Tyler," Jericho said and hugged me after we loaded up his tiny, twenty-year-old Datsun Honeybee. "I guess Lakshmi can't take a joke."

"No, she can't. Look, Jericho, take a break," I said. "Have some fun. You deserve it. And don't worry. Something's gonna work out."

"Oh, I'm not worried," he said and grinned. "My stepdad's a lawyer."

I grinned myself when he got in his car and the globe of his hair get smushed by the low ceiling.

To my relief, Lakshmi had left the church when I got back to the kitchen. Tim and his friends were back at work and had popped in a cassette of Brenda Lee's greatest hits. I went through the pantry and saw we were low on flour. I found a few jars of Jif and realized I had enough supplies to make a few hundred peanut butter cookies if I added in some oatmeal as an extender.

I was more than exhausted when I finally got home. I was glad Kyle would be at work that night and the following one as I didn't want to go anywhere or do anything. I listened to my phone messages and heard that my latest paycheck from Manna had bounced. Sigh. I worried about some checks I'd already written on it, and thought about going through my stubs, but all I really wanted to do was lie in bed with Holden and watch television.

I was hardly refreshed on Monday morning when I walked into the kitchen and learned we were in even deeper trouble than I'd imagined.

And someone was blaming *us* for it.

Chapter 18

Tim had been planning on making meatballs with a combination grape jelly and barbecue sauce for Monday, but the counter was piled up with cold pans full of sliced Spam and peaches that hadn't gone out on Sunday.

"It was a complete disaster, Tyler," Tim said, a tremble in his voice, as I tied on an apron. "And there's no use in prepping anything for tomorrow until we can get that computer back."

"There's no paper backups? No files?"

"None! Jericho's got everything on his computer — client list, route sheets, volunteer phone numbers. It was a nightmare yesterday! All these volunteers showing up and no place to send them. And what about our mission? Our clients must be starving!"

I walked out to the community room and Jeremy, Joffrey and Nigel were standing and sipping coffee as the morning AA meeting dispersed. Jonnie was on the phone, turned away from us, muting her conversation.

"Good morning," I said.

"Tyler, it is morning but I am afraid there isn't anything very good about it," said Nigel.

"Jericho's still holding his little computer hostage," said Jeremy. "Until then, we're just about paralyzed."

"Is it true we don't have any paper backups? No files?" I asked.

"None. Welcome to the computer age," said Joffrey. "Everything's on Jericho's floppy discs."

Tinka the Bag Lady walked toward us with a huge bran muffin in her hand. Her right arm had recently been tattooed with a design of bees on honeycomb. "I better be able to lay some cable this morning," she said. "If we're going to endure another shitshow today, I'd at least like to do it with empty bowels."

Jonnie hung up and turned to us.

"We've had some progress!" she said. "The two sides are talking! Jericho's stepdad is cutting a deal for severance pay!"

"Severance pay? I thought we didn't have any money," I said.

"We don't but we're working on that too. I think what we need to do right now is pray."

"No," I said and felt my insides boiling. "I am *not* praying. What Lakshmi and her board need to do is to raise some fucking money."

"I am entirely agreed with Tyler," said Nigel. Jeremy and Joffrey nodded their heads.

"Yeah, I think for today we should ditch the fucking prayers," said Tinka.

"And maybe we need to call Vanity Fair," I continued. "And tell Diane Toussaint about this other side of Lakshmi Steinmetz."

Jonnie stared at me, her mouth agape. "All right, all right, I get it," she finally said. "Believe me, I am as frustrated as any of you."

"Jonnie, what has happened to all that money from the art auction?" Nigel asked.

"And when can we cash our checks?" asked Jeremy.

"Maybe I should just use my check to wipe my ass," said Tinka. "Then mail it to Lakshmi."

"I really don't know," Jonnie said when the phone rang again. "Lakshmi! Hi! You are? Really! Well, all right. That's very hopeful. See you then." Jonnie hung up the phone. "Lakshmi's coming by at eleven thirty... with the board!"

"We'll give them all some Spam," I said and walked back to the kitchen where Tim was fretting over the ruins of his Sunday offering.

"What do we do with all this lovely food?" he asked me. The Dixie cups were already out as the Tipplers had little to do that morning.

"I don't know," I said, then lowered my voice. "Uh, Tim... Lakshmi's coming so you might want to... want to…"

I pointed at his Dixie cup.

He gave me the slightest nod and they all drank up. Wayne the Pain took the bottle out to his car.

"Maybe we could take the Spam down to the LA Mission on Fifth," I said as they tossed their cups. "And I'll take some home with me," I added, knowing that the four-legged member of our family would wolf it right down.

"That's a good idea," Tim said.

"I'm sure one of the drivers will be glad to take it downtown," I said. "I'm gonna make a phone call."

I went down to the old glass and wood phone booth of the church's first floor where there were rooms that had been used for Sunday school. Now they were meeting places for twelve-step programs that ran from morning to night. The phone booth was in a hall between one room where the Sex and Love Addicts were meeting and another where Codependents Anonymous was underway. I looked at the room across from me where there was a meeting of Meetings Anonymous, a twelve-step program for people who were addicted to twelve-step programs. I pulled the booth's folding door closed and inserted a quarter.

"Tyler, always a pleasure in these unpleasant times," Kevin said on the car phone in his Mercedes S-Class sedan.

"So you heard about Manna? That we're broke again?"

"Of course I did. Lakshmi's been calling us, shaking us down for contributions. But I'm embarrassed to tell you I'm having some... some financial problems of my own, and strangely, it may be related to what's going on at Manna."

"How? What happened?"

"Oh, I'm just too embarrassed to tell you really. But don't ever let anyone talk you into investing in Mexican gas shares."

"Mexican *gas?*"

"Yes, and not the kind you get from eating frijoles. This may be the stupidest thing I've ever done. I'm talking about close to a million dollars. I may have to sell my own house. What I believed was the 'opportunity of a lifetime' was more of a get-rich-quick scheme... or I should say more of a get-poor-instantly scheme. And I'm not the only one who fell for it."

"Who convinced you to invest in this?"

He sighed. "Andrew Belfry."

"Andrew *Belfry*? That guy who's married to Lakshmi's assistant?"

"I think you mean the *felon* who's married to Julie Sainsbury. The *inside trader* who Lakshmi's been counseling since he left prison. The *embezzler* she's helping to rehabilitate by putting him in charge of the Center's finances — one of her more brilliant strokes."

I heard him scoffing as I took that in. "Of course I'm not implying *anything* about Andrew in our current situation," he said. "Or about Lakshmi. But I should have done a little more research and paid attention to somebody's ankle jewelry."

"Fuck," I said after a long silence.

"Yes, fuck, as in all fucked up. Fuck, fucked, fuckety."

"Are you coming to the church for this emergency meeting?"

"I have been summoned."

When I went back to the kitchen, Bryce had arrived and was entertaining the idol volunteers by lip-syncing "Too Much Heaven on Their Minds" to an old cassette tape of *Jesus Christ Superstar*. When he started doing the leap dancing to "Simon Zealotes," I had no choice but to join him. Though it was his day off, Gene arrived early for the impromptu meeting in his salmon-colored Lycra. He looked at us with haughty disdain as we went through the Pony, the Watusi and the Frug. "Dancing while Rome burns," Gene said then went to the pans of Spam and peaches. He lifted the aluminum foil off one and wrinkled his nose in disgust. "Well at least the clients won't have to eat this."

"Tyler, could we speak to you?" Nigel asked as Bryce and I did the Monkey.

"Sure," I said.

I followed Nigel outside to where Tinka, Jeremy and Joffrey were waiting for us near the steps. We stepped away from the clusters of alcoholics smoking among the yuccas that grew against the church's walls with their sharp, knifelike leaves.

"Tyler, we're thinking that each of us should be asking Lakshmi and the board some essential questions," Nigel said. "So that she cannot target any one of us as a ringleader."

"You mean we should all go on the attack so she can't single out one of us to fire."

"Exactly. All for one and one for all and all of that."

"Let's get Tim in on this too. I know what he'd like to ask her."

After we "sorted out" our questions, as Nigel called it, we went upstairs and waited for Lakshmi. She arrived on time with a baker's dozen of board members, all of them men in slacks, dress shirts and ties. Among them was Andrew Belfry who raised his chin and looked imperious as he stood at Lakshmi's right. At her left was Jacob Hellman who for once wasn't grinning that morning. Lakshmi called everyone to attention and with all these men behind her, I was reminded of how tiny she was, even in boots with two-inch heels. Her outfit was a bit Stevie Nicks-ish that morning: an ankle-length dress of black lace with a black velvet shawl. All that was missing was a top hat. Close to fifty people had crowded into our little kitchen to hear her speak including kitchen volunteers, drivers and staff.

"If I could have everyone's attention, please," she said to start the show. "As always, thank you, all of you, staff and volunteers for your work here, which is so deeply appreciated.

It's no secret that we're having some problems at the moment. I've come here to assure you that we are all working very hard to resolve them as quickly as possible. Until we do I am asking for your patience."

"But what exactly happened?" Nigel began. "I think we should start by identifying the problem in explicit terms, please. Besides this disaster with the computer, why have we run out of money again? That is the problem, correct?"

"Nigel, we are still a young organization," Lakshmi answered. "We are still finding our way. It's... *unfortunate* that we gave control of our one and only computer to one person."

"It was Jericho's computer, actually, and you haven't answered my question," Nigel said. "Why are we out of money? What happened to it? Why are our paychecks bouncing and why are we being turned out of stores?"

"We've, well... we've run out of money," Lakshmi said. "We've spent more than we have."

"We know that. But why don't we have professional fundraisers?" Jeremy asked.

"We don't need them... Jeremy."

"Yes, we do." Jeremy responded. "God's Love We Deliver has four professional fundraisers that do four events a year and each of them brings in multimillions of dollars."

"No!" said Lakshmi. "We are *never* hiring professional fundraisers. They take twenty-five percent of everything they make and they make millions for themselves!"

"But if they make a million, wouldn't we make three million more?" asked Joffrey.

"It's out of the question," Lakshmi said. "Making money from the AIDS crisis is exploitative."

"Maybe so," Joffrey said. "But God's Love doesn't shut down. And their checks don't bounce. Who is writing and sending out checks when we don't have money in our account?"

"Joffrey, it was an honest mistake," she said, glancing briefly at Belfry who was stony, his chin thrust out as he blinked over his folded arms.

"So was it an honest mistake to move the offices from a bungalow in Hollywood to a fancy building in Boy's Town?" Tinka asked.

"It was not!" Lakshmi said.

"What was the rent when the Being Center was on Curson Street?"

"Well, there was no rent. The house was donated."

"Right," said Tinka. "But the current rate for the Center on Robertson is eight thousand a month. Isn't it?"

"That's not something we should be discussing right now in this kind of setting," said Laskhmi.

"Why not?" Tinka said. "This is a nonprofit. Legally, aren't all expenditures supposed to be made public?"

"The new building is not for us!" Lakshmi shouted. "It's for the clients!"

"If the building is not for you and Jacob, then why does Jacob have an office in it?" Joffrey asked. "We know he runs his business out of it. Is that ethical?"

"That's not true!" Jacob shouted. "I do not run my business out of the Center!"

"Yes, you do," Joffrey said. "I hear your phone calls. And when I fill in for Vonnie, I transfer them to you."

"Jacob's work for the Center and Manna is essential!" Lakshmi shouted. "And it won't be questioned, *honey*."

Oops. The first "honey" had popped out.

"Yes, it will be," Joffrey said.

"Lakshmi, why does the Being Center have a fancy office building when we should have invested in a professional kitchen?" Tim asked, his voice trembling. "This kitchen isn't sanitary! We're leaving food out that can be infested by vermin. Last thing we need is for a client with a compromised immune system to eat rat poop or insect eggs… it could kill him! If the Department of Health were to show up, they could shut us down for lack of refrigeration!"

"I understand, Tim, really I do. But —"

"What you need to understand is that we need a new kitchen!" he shouted. "God's Love has a professional kitchen in what used to be a restaurant! What we need is a new kitchen, goddamn it, not some fancy office space!"

I looked at Tim with pride. Maybe it was the vodka, but he had finally connected with his anger and found his voice.

An uneasy silence was in the kitchen as Lakshmi shook her head, her mouth tightening as her nostrils quivered. "Look, that's how Ganja does it," she spat at us. "That's New York, we're Los Angeles, and the consequences of professional fundraisers who enrich themselves have yet to be seen. We *are* going to have another fundraiser and soon, one that *we* put on, not some opportunists looking to profit from a health crisis. In the meantime, God will lead us to our angels. Something the New Age community doesn't understand is *money* and how it's accumulated. God has a lot of money but we can't just expect it to be magically deposited in our bank account, we — "

"Lakshmi," I interrupted with a shout as my own anger exploded. "Not everyone here is a member of New Age community. I am not. And most of the people here are not students of *The Way of the Miraculous*."

"And your point is?" she shouted as she stared at me.

"The point is we can't rely on God," I shouted. "You're blaming us as the ones who have been impractical! We need a new kitchen and professional equipment and more computers and more employees. And we should never have moved the Center to a building we can't afford!"

"Look, *honey,* you have no idea how hard I work for this organization," she said, raising her voice with its ear splitting shriek. "And how hard Jacob works... and this board, I — "

"You have no idea how hard *all of us* work at this kitchen," I shouted back at her, "For *very little money* and for no benefits, *honey*. We're an AIDS organization whose own employees *don't have health insurance*. We have all...

"Excuse me," she shouted. "Don't interrupt me, Tyler, I will…"

"No!" I shouted over her, my voice reaching one hundred scary decibels. "This is *our* time to speak and *you will hear me*. We have all been doing our jobs here, *these volunteers* and *this staff,* which is to cook and deliver food to our clients. Someone has *not* been doing their job which is *you* and *your board!*"

That got cheers and applause from the volunteers. Lakshmi's face reddened then went the color of Muenster cheese. Kevin, standing with the other board members, was looking at me with raised eyebrows but an approving grin. Andrew Belfry was shaking his head, his arms uncrossing to point at me. "Sir," he shouted at me. "Don't you ever speak like that to Lakshmi!"

"Don't you ever speak like that to *me*!" I shouted back. "*You* don't tell *me* what to do."

"You watch it, mister!" he said, stepping toward me. "I don't have take that from a guy like you!"

"A guy like *me*?" I said stepping towards him as my fingers curled into a fist. "What kind of guy *am* I? And what kind of guy are *you*?" I said, and then lifted up my ankle. He stepped forward and we were inches close to each other, baring our teeth and having an ugliest face contest.

"You're fired!" he shouted and pushed me.

"I'll sue you, you piece of shit," I shouted back and grabbed him by his shirt front. I cocked my fist before Nigel yanked me away.

"Andrew! Andrew!" Lakshmi shouted at him. "Please, this is not the time and place! You cannot fire Tyler! No one fires anyone in this organization but *me*. And we will not tolerate violence at Manna from Heaven!"

Breathing heavily, Lakshmi had that look on her face when she entered into one of her prayer fugues. She closed her eyes for a moment and made the hand motions of stilling the waters as she looked up at heaven and exhaled. She opened her eyes. "Listen, everyone, please!" she said. "We must turn back to love now. We want you all to know that we have heard you today and sympathize with your concerns. I get you. God bless you all and thank you again for your love and good work."

Lakshmi looked at me in contempt as she led her board away, strangely taking them down the backstairs and past the trash bins. Kevin followed her out but not before giving me a wink. I realized I had spoiled Nigel's plan by dominating the last part of the confrontation, that I would be the target of Lakshmi's wrath.

Gene and Jonnie walked up to me, looking at me in silence and disbelief. "Tyler, you have a lot of anger," Gene said. "You can't speak like that to Lakshmi! Or the board."

"Yes, I can," I said. "And I did. I expect to get fired. And before I am, I spoke my truth to her... and to that scumbag she put in charge of our finances."

"Scumbag? Really, Tyler?" said Jonnie.

"I'm sorry. I meant to call him a *fucking* scumbag but criminal is more accurate. And I'm gonna speak honestly to whoever else might ask me questions, like certain Vanity Fair reporters. We are not the ones at fault here, Jonnie. The ones who fucked it up need to admit it and fix it."

Jonnie exhaled loudly and shook her head. "Mistakes have been made," she said. "But this is a time to be forgiving."

"This is the time to get a new board," I said. "And a new financial director. One who isn't a fucking crook."

"Tyler, you can't speak like that... that's slander!" she said.

"Look, Belfry has been doing a shitty job. And he's the one who pushed me. Maybe it's because I remind him of someone who used to fuck his ass in prison."

Jonnie looked around the kitchen to see if anyone had overheard me. They all had.

"Tyler, you go home," she said. "There's no meal going out tomorrow. Take a day off."

"Why, I'd love to," I said. I left knowing I was never coming back.

Holden was ecstatic to see me home early on a Monday afternoon. I took him to Runyon Canyon where I could blow off steam and he could socialize with a hundred other dogs. It was my favorite walk through the Hollywood Hills with spectacular views of the Los Angeles Basin, the San Fernando Valley and the Palos Verdes Peninsula thrusting into the Pacific. After we did the three-mile loop, I drove home thinking I should call De Laurentiis and ask them if they had any scripts for me, a thought that was sickening. When I got home, the answering machine was blinking.

"Tyler, it's Lakshmi. Please call my office, I would really like to speak with you."

Wow. Lakshmi was going to fire me herself.

"Hi Tyler," said Julie when I called, sounding as sunny as ever even though I had almost come to blows with her husband. "Lakshmi is right here and she's very excited to speak with you."

"She's *excited*?"

"Of course she is. One moment."

"Hello, Tyler. How are you?" Lakshmi said with a calm voice.

"I think you know how I am," I said. "So if you're firing me let's just get this over with."

"I'm not firing you. I understand why you're upset. You love Manna from Heaven as much as I do and you're just as invested in it. I don't appreciate how you and the staff spoke to me today but... some of your points are well taken."

"They are?"

"I think all of us need to step back and see that we're going through the kind of hardship that ultimately makes us stronger," she said, cribbing from Nietzsche. "With love and forgiveness, we are going to continue this project and it will thrive. I do understand how hard you work. And I won't lie to you — in the next week I'll be asking all of you to sacrifice even more for the sake of our mission. Will you consider that?"

I took a pause. "I guess. I'll *consider* that."

"One other thing," she said then paused.

"Yes?"

"No one is calling anyone at Vanity Fair to give them the other side of Lakshmi Steinmetz. No one is undermining my livelihood. Are we understood?"

I was hesitant. "We are," I said.

We had a deal. But in New York City, Diane Toussaint was getting an earful at the other Being Center.

Chapter 19

Jericho brought a magazine with him when he returned on Thursday with his Kay-Pro computer for what was being called "a special guest appearance." Joffrey, his replacement, was seated before a new Macintosh LC and checking out a game called The Secret of Monkey Island. Joffrey had been given a raise and the lofty title of Chief Officer of Technology, but it was Jericho who had a shit-eating grin that morning. As his dot matrix printer spat out the Kay-Pro's secrets, Jericho was singing, dancing and offering hugs and kisses to everyone who welcomed his return. "Love ya, mean it," he would say when they walked away. Joffrey began the tedious process of transferring the info on the printouts to files on the new Apple.

I set out a plate of leftover cookies by the coffee maker when Jericho wandered in to pick one up with his coffee refill. "Oatmeal raisin, my favorite," he said and took a bite. "Thank you, Tyler. These are the bomb, crispy edges and a chewy center."

"You're welcome. Can I ask you something?" I said in a whisper.

"Sure. It's six, maybe six and a half inches on a good day, with a head like a shiitake mushroom," he whispered back and then covered his mouth as he chuckled.

"Uh, better than a head like a portobello," I said. "But I was gonna ask if you've already been paid to surrender your computer data."

"Fuck yes," he said through a giggle. "Part of the deal was that it had to be a cashier's check. I cashed it as soon as I got it."

"And I suppose you can't tell anyone just how much you were... compensated."

He threw back his head and laughed, sending waves through the globe of his curly hair.

"Tyler, it's because I signed a nondisclosure agreement that there are *seventy five thousand* reasons I can't tell you what they paid me," he said. Jericho laughed some more and only pretended to try and contain himself. He got the reaction he wanted when Gene slammed down the lid on a stockpot and turned to glare at him.

"What's cooking, Gene?" Jericho sang. "It smells a little bitter in here, like you're cooking your own flesh or something. I've missed you, mean it!"

"Sorry I can't say the same," Gene answered as staff and volunteers turned their attention to what promised to be one of their kitten fights. "And I'm *not* sorry to hear that after today you are *never* to step foot in here again."

"Damn, Gene. I hope we can find some other place where you can still stick your tongue up my ass."

"Damn, Jericho. I hope you won't be riddled with too much guilt for extorting an outrageous settlement from a *charity*."

The kitten fight had turned into a catfight. The kitchen quieted as Jericho readied his response. He looked like a cobra with an afro as his head gyrated before the strike. "No, I won't be *riddled*," he said as his grin flipped to a grimace. "I'm not ashamed of *finally* being compensated for my work, or for standing up to Lakshmi instead of being a queeny little sycophant like you, one of her paper-trained teacup poodles. And I hope *you're* not ashamed of having rich parents you can always hit up for cash whenever you bottom out. Oh, I forgot. You never bottom out, Gene. Nobody wants your ass. I say all that in a loving way."

After low jeers, the kitchen went dead silent. No one laughed, not even Jericho, who always laughed at his own jokes. Gene was punctured, all too quiet as his face reddened and his head dropped. "My parents aren't that rich," he finally said, his voice breaking.

"Rich enough. I mean, who else can afford to blow four hundred bucks on having Dinesh blow blue light into him? Then again, that's probably the last time you got blown... maybe the only time. Speaking of Dinesh, *Gene*," Jericho said as he took out the magazine from his back pocket. It was a copy of *Manhattan Monthly* and on its cover was a picture of Dinesh Carvalho with a headline that read, Cuckoo for the Guru, Dinesh Cashes In. From the look on his face, it was obvious that Gene had already read the article.

"Allow me," Jericho said, opening the magazine and making a theatrical clearing of his throat before he read.

Dinesh Carvalho, Manhattan's guru of the moment, can quicken you on your path to enlightenment for a mere $400. His followers believe him to be a bodhisattva with the power to activate *the blue light of greater consciousness with his magical breaths, something Carvalho calls a "beacon on the road to enlightenment." Ex-followers say Dinesh is a fraud, a con artist and a sexual predator who has convinced thousands of people to give him millions of dollars and hundreds of women to have sex with him.*

"Dinesh's typical victim is a woman," said Jeanette Szostak, a psychologist, who has treated former cult members including followers of Dinesh. "And they are women with a history of physical and emotional abuse, women dealing with addiction or a psychological problem. They are lonely and vulnerable and easily convinced into giving away their money. They're also willing to have sex with a charlatan who promises it will make them more attractive to men or bring them closer to enlightenment.

Jericho looked up at Gene who was frozen, his face turned from red to the color of French vanilla ice cream. "I think that might apply to you, Gene," Jericho said. "For one thing, you're practically a woman."

The catfight had turned into a lion mauling a baby gazelle.

I heard the click of high heels and looked over to see Jonnie coming closer. She had been listening.

"That's enough of that," she said to Jericho pointing at him.

"Oh, I'm not finished," Jericho said. "And I think you in particular need to hear this, *Jonnie*."

Gene went back to his stockpot and pretended it needed stirring as Jericho resumed.

Touring throughout the United States, Dinesh hit veins of gold in San Francisco and Los Angeles where minions of spiritually hungry followers forked over their cash every ninety seconds to lie flat and have Dinesh blow on their faces. The breaths are believed to activate a blue light that is a transference of Dinesh's own enlightened state. "It's all sleight of hand," said an ex-follower who did not want to be identified for this article. "They're like the lights in a laser pointer and they're attached to the back of his teeth and at the back of his neck. And sometimes they fall off when he's doing his magic, like when he was trying to enlighten me.

And what does Carvalho do with the money?

"He takes it to Vegas and Atlantic City in suitcases with a harem of his favorite women," said the ex-follower. "After blowing the blue light, he blows the money on roulette."

Jericho was cackling, covering his mouth to mute himself as he lowered the magazine. "I can't go on," he said.
"Please don't," Jonnie said. "You're cruel."
"Oh, I'm just funnin' you, Jonnie," he said as his face went stormy and his tone turned angry. "But the two of you might have defended me when Lakshmi went on a fucking tirade and fired me because I made a joke about her baby's father."
Jonnie went silent, staring at him while shaking her head. Jericho had turned the kitchen into his stage and he was executing lines he had rehearsed.
"Just what is it exactly that Lakshmi does for this organization?" Jericho shouted, pivoting to make eye contact with

his audience. "I mean, besides taking credit and showing up once in a while to fire somebody?"

Jonnie was heaving. "She got the money to pay you off for one thing," Jonnie shouted, her voice getting shrill.

"Oh yeah? What millionaire did she beg?" Jericho said, cocking his head. "Was it David Geffen? Barry Diller? Sandy Gallin? Maybe she asked her father since he always used to bail her out. Whoever it is, let me know. I'd like to send them a thank you card, maybe a bottle of wine... or some lube and a dildo."

Jericho fanned himself with the magazine then turned a page to read again.

Carvalho, who claims his powers were bestowed on him by Vishnu after being hit by a car in Colombo...

"You stop that right now!" Jonnie screamed.

"Or what?" Jericho said, his grin turned malicious as he put his hands on his hips and cocked his head. "You're gonna fire me?"

"You vicious... asshole!"

"Speaking of assholes, what does Lakshmi's taste like?" he fired back. "Do you ever get tired of munching it? And as for munching, I always wanted to ask you... do you really munch carpet, Jonnie? Or are you just a fake lesbian, an attention slut... Gene seems to think so."

Joffrey stepped into the kitchen. "Jericho, the first file's finished printing. Can we start on the client list?"

"I'd be thrilled to," Jericho said before he dropped the magazine at Jonnie's feet. "A gift for you, Jonnie. Enjoy. Love ya, mean it."

Jonnie fumed in silence until Jericho was out of earshot. "That is one very weird man," she said, picking up the magazine and attempting to tear it in two. When she couldn't, she threw it in the trash. "And we thought he was spiritual!"

"He's obnoxious. But he was treated poorly," I said. "We all are."

"Are you?" she said to me, scolding.

"Yes, we are."

Jonnie sighed. "Lakshmi's called a meeting for today at five. She says she has good news and bad news. And she says you can all cash your paychecks."

"Hip fucking hooray," I said. "What's the bad news?"

"Likely that they are going to be some layoffs. And reductions to part-time."

"Layoffs. Really."

"And she wants to meet with you and Jeremy afterward."

"About what?"

"You'll have to ask her. Everyone must attend."

Lakshmi Steinmetz was a mistress of suspense.

That afternoon, Gene and I were tired from the peeling of over 1500 eggs for egg salad sandwiches that would go out as the Saturday cold meal. We had also prepped a Friday meal of chicken Kiev. My fingers were raw and I could still smell sulfur as I drove to the Being Center. The couches of the reception room were filled with the other staff who were grim and unsmiling. Tim had driven in from the Valley and looked worried and sweaty as he sat next to me wearing what were apparently the only pair of shorts he owned.

"You OK, Tim?"

"Fine. Just... my car's on empty. I can't drive it home."

"You can't fill it up?"

He shook his head.

"It's all right to cash your check," I said.

"I have and I've already spent it."

"Here's a ten," I said, reaching into my wallet.

"Tyler, no, I couldn't."

"It's just ten dollars. Get some gas. Pay me back... whenever."

"This is a loan," Tim said as he took the bill. "Thanks."

I could hear Lakshmi ranting on her phone on the second floor. "If you can't help us with this simple request then just lose my number!" she shouted before slamming down the receiver. After a series of screams she muffled with a throw pillow, she tottered down the stairs and looked exhausted. She exhaled as she rolled her shoulders and then struck a tragic pose. Instead of seating herself, she stood outside the sectional couches, looking down at the coffee table as if it were the burial hole for her mother's coffin. When she looked up, she pulled away the hair over her face and began speaking in a solemnly dramatic way as Jacob Hellman joined us on the couch.

"Everyone, thank you all for your patience," Lakshmi said. "The bad news first. As you know, we are short of funds again and we will need to cut back on hours and... some positions. We will be meeting with you individually to see just what you can do for our organization, to see what you can sacrifice."

She stopped pacing and gave us just a little smile. "Now for the good news. Just this morning we secured a venue where we will be holding a fundraiser, and I promise you it will be biggest event of the summer." Her smile was returning like the sun peeking out from rain clouds.

"When?" Jeremy asked,

"July 14. Bastille Day."

"Three months from now?" Jeremy asked. "Is that enough time?"

"Of course it is," she said. "We threw the art auction together in three weeks. This event is going to be called Celestial Objects, a Benefit for Manna from Heaven. It's going to be fashion and furniture, art and interior design, with donations from the most gifted people on the planet! And all of it for auction to benefit our clients. And of course, to benefit all of you, our wonderful staff that services them. We *are* concerned for your well-being and wanted to do this with some urgency."

Jacob nodded and was grinning, something that always made him slightly more sightly.

"There will be so much more to tell you about soon," Lakshmi said. "But for now we'd like to meet with you individually. Nigel, we'd like to see you first."

Nigel rose, adjusted his glasses and followed Lakshmi and Jacob up the stairs for a private conference. Once the upstairs door was closed, we whispered among ourselves.

"Have you figured out why she's meeting with us last?" I asked Jeremy.

"I don't know," he said. "Maybe we're getting fired."

"You're not, Tyler," Gene said, having overheard us.

"I'm not?"

"You aren't," he said, folding his arms and then looking away. Something about that was unsettling.

226

A few minutes later, Nigel came down the stairs. He looked at us and shrugged. "It's a good thing I'm not raising any children," he said and walked to the door. "They want to see Tim next."

Tim braced himself and I had a sickening feeling as I watched his plump bottom go up the stairs. I looked over at Gene who had the slightest smile.

"Is Tim getting fired?"

"No, I don't think so. But we... may not see him for a while."

"Oh *really*," I said.

"I think the clients can do without peach fiesta Spam bake until we get back on our feet."

Only two minutes later, Tim's face was wet with tears as he teetered down the stairs. He gave Gene a brief and angry look and then ran out the door without saying goodbye.

"He's so emotional," Gene said when Jacob looked down at us from the top of the stairs.

"Gene, we'd like to speak with you," Jacob shouted down and Gene dutifully climbed the stairs in his Lycra short shorts.

"Did they just fire Tim?" I asked Jonnie who was chanting as she fingered her sandalwood prayer beads.

"I don't know, Tyler," she said, annoyed by my question.

"Did Gene get him fired?"

"I don't believe so!" she said, even more annoyed.

"Tim was here first — volunteering for weeks before Gene showed up."

"I wouldn't jump to any conclusions."

Gene was trotting down the stairs just a minute later. "I'll see you tomorrow," he said to me on his way out. I was stewing, thinking of Tim driving home in traffic and wondering why he'd been treated so poorly. Tinka was up and then down just a minute later.

"They were already paying me horse shit," she said on her way out the door. "Now they want to pay me in rat shit. You're up, Jeremy."

From the coffee table, I picked up a copy of Psychology Today, addressed to L. Steinmetz, and read an article titled "How Sweat Keeps You Sexy." I turned to the classified ads in the back, nearly all of which were for astrologers and psychics offering their services. Someone else was offering to "rebalance your chakras," something they could do over the phone. Another ad offered the services of psycho-urinalysis.

A few minutes later, Jeremy returned shaking his head as he plopped down on the couch. "Your turn, Tyler. Then I'll join you in a few minutes for the mystery meeting," he said. "I hope your boyfriend is rich."

"Nope," I said as I took the stairs.

Lakshmi was at her desk holding a sheet of paper. Jacob was at her side and both of them looked terribly serious.

"Tyler, we know how hard you work and we know you're good at your job," Lakshmi started. "Gene speaks very highly of you and your abilities. And he says the volunteers just adore you."

"I love them too," I said. "Most of them."

"Until we're up to speed again, we'd like to ask if you can work part-time. Can you work mornings and take half your pay?"

"Did Tim get fired?"

"No. But he won't be coming in for a while. Not until we're in the black again. Gene will be working his days."

"So Tim won't be getting any severance? No retainer fee?"

"Not until we have money again."

"Listen," I said. "I'm the one you should lay off. I have a partner who works and I can go back to my old freelance jobs. Tim needs money a lot more than I do. He lost his lover a year ago and he's about to lose his house. He's got medical bills and expensive prescriptions. And he's been at Manna longer than anybody. When I first came here, he was working for free... for weeks."

Lakshmi blinked at me with a sad expression. There was a touch of shame about her as she reconsidered. "I wasn't aware of all that," she said. "Thank you, Tyler. So you would be OK if Tim worked part-time and you took a few weeks off?"

"I'd make the most of it."

She looked at Jacob who nodded his head.

"That's what we'll do," she said. "Have Jeremy come up."

"Jeremy," I shouted down to him with an English accent. "Mistress Steinmetz demands your presence."

Lakshmi was smiling sweetly when Jeremy took a seat next to me.

"So, gentlemen," she said with a smile and a touch of her Southern accent. "Some other good news is we've been invited to march in the Pride parade this June. It's a wonderful opportunity to promote our organization and raise some money."

Jeremy and I looked at each other, wondering how this pertained to us.

"Tyler, you're just so imaginative when it comes to cakes," she said. "Have you ever designed a float?"

"A parade float? No, I never have."

"But you could," she said. "And I'm just sure you could come up with something fabulous. You know Koala Cordanno, right? Koala's a florist who said he'd love to help, that he's built a float before. And Jeremy, you could organize this, rally the volunteers to help out."

"Uh, I suppose," Jeremy said. "I'm not sure we want to divert them from the more... uh, essential tasks at Manna right now."

"My idea is to have something with a little throne on top," Lakshmi continued, taking a rough drawing out of her desk. "And then a banner that stretches around the float that says "Lakshmi Steinmetz, founder and chairman of Manna from Heaven." And I think there should be room on the float for eight to ten cute volunteers to ride the float with me."

"Male volunteers," Jeremy said.

"Yes," she said. "Some of our more appealing guys, the type that could attract more volunteers. I think the two of you should be on it."

"That's very flattering," I said. "But a lot of our best volunteers are... not cute guys. It's a lot of women and lots of older folks and guys of average app..."

"I'm sure that's true," she interrupted. "But we're promoting the organization, bringing it some attention and we can do that with attractive people. Think about it and throw together some ideas while you have some time off, maybe work up a few sketches."

"Lakshmi, I think we're both flattered," Jeremy said. "But I don't know that I should enlist volunteers to build a float when we've run out of money for things like food and salaries... especially if it's a float that not everyone could ride on."

"Listen," she said, with a hiss as her mouth got small and her face got pinched. "The two of you get to keep your jobs. And I get the float I want. This isn't up for discussion."

Jacob gave a single nod.

"But it should be up for discussion," I said. "Jeremy's right, we—"

Lakshmi's phone rang. "Hello? Oh, hello!"

She mouthed "bye" and gave us a dismissive flick of her fingers.

Jeremy and I were unable to speak as we walked to our cars.

"I'm just fricking stunned," I finally said. "We're out of money but we're building a fucking float? I don't understand this at all."

"Well, I sher doo," said Jeremy, turning his Southern accent into full hillbilly. "Twenny years after high school, Miriam Steinmetz finally gits to be the homecomin' queen."

Jeremy and I would not be the only ones who had problems with a float for Lakshmi.

Chapter 20

Gene was hard at work on Monday when I came in to frost Rose Levy Beranbaum's banana cake with a lemon buttercream that I would need to make fresh that morning.

"You're late," Gene said to me. "And I need to know your menus for Sunday and Monday."

"I'm not late," I said. "I'm a volunteer today. I came in to frost my cakes."

"What are you talking about?"

"I was laid off."

"No, Tim is laid off. You're working part-time."

"I guess no one told you. I told Lakshmi that I could go back to my old jobs for a while so Tim could work."

"Why did you do that?" he said, looking as if he had just swallowed a spider dipped in snot.

"Because Tim needs the money. And he has seniority. This organization owes him for all the time he donated."

"Tim is also a drunk."

"Well... yeah," I said as I reached into the supply cage for an apron. *And you're a snotty little bitch.* "Gene, we're almost out of towels."

"I'll order some," he said, getting snippy. "If you aren't prepping this afternoon, then what marvelous dish is Tim working up for Sunday?"

At just that moment, Tim appeared with his boisterous crew hauling up bags and cartons from Smart and Final. The bags were bulging with loaves of white sandwich bread. "Tyler!" he said, coming to hug me. "I didn't think you'd be here."

"Just finishing up today's dessert," I said. "And then I'm off to pick up some scripts."

"Hello... Gene," Tim said, his smile flipped to a frown as he went to the cage to pull out aprons for himself and his crew.

"Hell-*low*," Gene responded, his voice low and ghoulish as he grimaced.

"We're really low on towels," said Tim, picking up one of the four that were left.

"I just told Tyler I'd order some!" Gene snapped.

"We'll need them for Sunday. We can't reuse towels, even if they look clean. They get moldy and mildewy."

"Mildewy? I don't think there's such a word as 'mildewy.'"

"You know what I mean."

"I will worry about the towels. Tim, if you're the chef here next week then I need your menus for Monday, Tuesday and Wednesday. Can you make enchiladas for Mexican Wednesday? How about *crème renversée*?"

"What?"

"Flan," I said.

"Um, no, but I can make Spanish meatloaf again, I..."

"It's Mexican Wednesday, not *Spanish* Wednesday," said Gene. "Or rather *pseudo*-Spanish Wednesday."

"I could probably make some nachos."

"*Nachos?*"

"Yes, you get a bag of Fritos and then grate some cheese and —"

"We are not sending out *nachos* to the clients! Nachos for lunch? What are you going to do, buy a hundred bags of Fritos?"

Gene pronounced it furritos, rhyming it with burritos.

"Doritos work too."

"No nachos!"

"You don't have to get upset. Maybe we skip Mexican Wednesdays until Tyler comes back."

"I am *not* upset. What's with all this sandwich bread? What are you making for Sunday?"

"Cowboy hamburgers."

Gene gasped and looked horrified.

"*What*, pray tell, are cowboy hamburgers?"

"They're fun and they're tasty. It's a baked, open-faced sandwich. We'll serve some pork and beans on the side and coleslaw for the roughage. It's very Western."

Tim's crew were setting out seven-pound cans of pork and beans as well as plastic-wrapped logs of ground beef. Gene, looking as if someone had just farted up his nose, went back to his lamb chops and using a paintbrush, he slapped them with black raspberry sauce. The volunteers were spooning a bulgur wheat and chanterelle mushroom salad into plastic containers while a guest chef from Chaya Brasserie pureed boiled carrots, sweet potatoes and caramelized shallots with his immersion blender as the side dish.

On the other side of the kitchen, Tim was ebullient as he went to work on his Sunday meal, happy to be back in the saddle. "Time to beat our meat," he said, followed by a trilling "tee-hee" as he picked up the wooden paddle. He pretended to propel a canoe before using the paddle to beat eighty pounds of ground beef divided into four separate basins. Once the beef was pressed along the bottoms and up the sides of the basins, he added cups of Hunts catsup, French's mustard, Heinz Sweet Relish then grated Kraft American cheese. He mixed the first basin until its contents were loose and shiny. "If only we had an industrial mixer," he said, wiping sweat from his forehead as he handed off the paddle to Wayne the Pain to take on the next basin.

"I've got a cement mixer at home," I said as I added chunks of butter to my hot syrup and egg yolks in the KitchenAid for the first batch of buttercream. "Should I bring it in?"

"Of course!" he said and giggled. "For one thing, it's just so butch."

The next step of cowboy hamburgers was taking slices of white sandwich bread, smearing them with margarine from a ten-pound tub of Blue Bonnet, and then setting them in rows on baking sheets. "Since they're not going to spread like cookies, you can pack them tightly together," Tim instructed. Once this was done, Tim used an ice cream scoop to plunk a hunk of meat mixture into the middle of each slice and then used the back of the scoop to flatten it.

"Is that American cheese in there?" Gene said, walking over to take a look after sliding his lamb chops into the ovens. His face had that vicious little smirk.

"Yes," said Tim.

"You know it's not really cheese," Gene scolded. "It's a cheese product. It's more vegetable oil than milk curds."

"Nothing else melts as smoothly," said Tim.

"Nothing else tastes like plastic. I don't know, Tim," Gene said. "I *really* don't know. What is this called again? Cow pie burgers?"

"Cow*boy* hamburgers."

"Well, yippee-yo-ki-yay. To be perfectly frank with you, it looks more like cow shit on a shingle."

Gene looked over at me, focusing his anger. "Tyler, what's your opinion? What do you think of cow pie, I mean, cowboy hamburgers?"

"Uh, the proof is in the eating."

"Then let's try one out. The oven's hot."

"I don't eat beef," I said. "But the clients might like it — it's kind of, ya know, comfort food."

Frankly, I was also put off by what Tim was offering for the Sunday meal. It reminded me of something my father, who had been an actual cowboy, might make when my mother was sick or too tired to cook. And I loathed pork and beans, a too-regular feature of my childhood, with its sugary tomato sauce, its mushy, melancholy beans and that weird little prize of a hunk of fatback that came in every can.

"Here you go. Over four hundred servings of banana cake," I said after I dragged my icing comb in a wave pattern over the last of twelve sheet cakes. "I hate to ice and run, but I've got an eleven o'clock appointment."

Gene glared at me as I took off my apron. "Tyler, thank you *so* much for coming in," he said with an angry scoff. "And for leaving us in such... *good hands* with Tim."

"Bye, Tyler," Tim said, trotting over to give me a hug. "And thank you for speaking up for me," he whispered.

"Don't mention it," I said.

Nancy at De Laurentiis was happy to see me when I walked into her cubicle. "Now are you sure about this?" she asked me as she pushed a foot-tall pile of scripts across the desk. "We're a little behind so I'm glad you could come in."

"Honestly, I need the work," I said. "Have you got a box for these?"

"If you're taking a box then you could take one more," she said and plopped thirteen scripts into a Kinko's box.

The hard part of being a script analyst is not in reading the scripts, which takes about two hours. The difficulty is having to synopsize their stories, which is a tedious labor when the script is shit and the vast majority of scripts are shit. Half of scripts are ho-hum, middling and predictable and half of them are just boring or poorly written. Very occasionally, there was a flashing nugget of gold and very, very occasionally, a sparkling diamond, and these scripts were a pleasure to write up. I preferred reading for De Laurentiis because they paid more than other companies but also because they got the weirdest submissions. After they had produced David Lynch's

Dune, and later *Blue Velvet,* every agent repping a quirky script sent it first to Dino D.

Of these thirteen scripts there were eleven forgettable ones but there were two that I will remember all the rest of my life One was called *Sledgehammer Freddy* and it was the story of an African-American man who worked in a slaughterhouse in Chicago during the Depression. The title character had a talent for stunning a cow with a single bash to the head with his sledgehammer. In under a minute, he could slit the cow's throat and hang it upside down to let it bleed to death, something he did better and faster than anyone in the meat industry. At one point, a rival shows up, Sharp Knife Shawn, a White man determined to prove that he is the world's fastest cow killer. Shawn is also intent on stealing Freddie's woman. The third act ended with a competition between the two men — a slaughter-off — in which hundreds of cows are killed and hung with their blood running into the sewer and turning the Chicago River red. And to show us that Freddie was deep down a nice guy, his pet at home was a sweet little cow named Buttercup that liked to lick his face. It was one of the weirdest scripts I had ever read and definitely the most disgusting.

The other interesting script was a murder mystery called *Honey.* The lead, Honey, was an ex-Green Beret suffering PTSD after his tours of Viet Nam. Once back in the States, Honey takes a job teaching synchronized swimming to wealthy young girls in their pools in Santa Barbara. No one could call Honey by his unknown first name, nor could they call him Mr. Honey. "It's just Honey," he insisted. One day a bus carrying one of his students and her swim team falls over a cliff, killing everyone. When Honey shows up to give his dead student her lesson, he witnesses her father, a wealthy developer, in a sexual kiss with a young man who turns out to be his own son. Honey gets shot at, and later, he gets framed for the school bus murders and is questioned by the police whom he degrades as incompetent stooges. "Fuck you, Honey," one of the cops shouts at him. Later, Honey and his girlfriend, a taxidermist working on a cure for rectal itch, follow clues that lead them to San Francisco where they find and expose the father and son in their love nest in Chinatown. "Your daughter knew you were fucking your son," Honey says to the father. "And that's why you had her killed." "Eat shit, Honey," says the father, before he takes aim with his pistol. To make the script even weirder, the writer had suggested musical cues which included The Mamas and the Papas' "No Salt on Her Tail," Arnold Schoenberg's "A Survivor from Warsaw" and "Inka Dinka Doo" by Jimmy Durante.

    I could not possibly recommend *Honey,* but it was so weird it was compelling and I wish that I'd made a copy of it. It was a little irritating to read because it kept reminding me of Lakshmi who called people "honey" when she was pissed at them. After I wrote *Honey* up, I remembered I was supposed to "work up a few ideas" for her float for the Pride parade for a meeting after the weekend.

    Taking a break from the scripts, I picked up colored pencils and paper but nothing was coming to me. Part of my block was that I was disgusted by the idea of making Lakshmi a float, one on which she would reign as queen with an explicit banner that told the world just how fabulous she was. I was lounging in bed with Kyle on a Sunday afternoon when I went for the obvious and sketched out something that was not unlike a giant, tiered wedding cake on wheels. On its top tier was a Louis Quatorze chair where Lakshmi would be enthroned. Above the chair would be an oversized halo made from tinsel garland and in back of it would be some giant angel wings. On the other tiers would be eight to ten handsome young men wearing nothing but aprons and chef hats. At the front of the float, I drew an oversized cake where a muscle puppy could pop out and dance as he spread his angel wings.

"Your cake looks like it melted," Kyle said to me. "All the sweet cream icing flowing down."

"Hmm, that's an idea," I said and started humming "MacArthur Park" when the phone rang.

"Hey, Tyler, it's Jeremy."

"What's up, Jer?"

"Oh, just a bit of a shitshow on Sunday morning. Tim showed up at the kitchen and didn't have any towels. He thinks Gene was trying to sabotage him and never ordered them. They had to use Depends."

"*Depends?* Adult diapers?"

"You heard me. One of our clients died and had a bunch of them in his apartment that his mother donated."

"Lovely. Tim's right about sabotage. How did the cowboy hamburgers go over?"

"Really well," said Jeremy. "I told Gene that seven people called to tell us how much they loved them, a record."

"Really? Seven people?"

"No, but that's what I told Gene, just to frost his balls. If he has any."

"If he does they're probably the size of pearl onions."

"I think Pearl Onions is his new drag name."

I laughed to realize that Gene had a growing anti-fan club, that I was not the only one who disliked him for his vicious snobbery.

"Anyway, Lakshmi and Jacob Hellman want to meet with us again on Monday at five at the Center," Jeremy said. "About this little float of hers."

"Lakshmi *and* Jacob? What's Jacob got to do with it?"

"I don't know... maybe he's concerned about the budget. The sign-up list for the float committee is a little lackluster. Word got out about Lakshmi wanting something like Cleopatra's arrival in Rome in that Elizabeth Taylor movie."

"Hmm. Cleopatra. That's not a bad idea," I said. "Maybe we can get some guys to dress up as Nubian slaves and haul her in on a giant sphinx... except it's covered in cookies and cake frosting."

"Or cowboy hamburgers."

"Maybe we should get her an asp she can hold to her breast and sink its teeth in."

"Yeah, a good way to conclude the parade — her corpse rolls down the float and ends up face down in some paper flowers."

The image of a giant parade float made out of sweets raced in my head like a roller coaster. Maybe that was the seed of a new screenplay.

*

"Jacob will be with you in just a minute," said Vonnie leaving us a plate of homemade shortbread as Jeremy and I took seats before Lakshmi's desk. She was polishing up a sentence on her computer screen, perhaps from the book she was writing. "Hi," she said absently as she pressed save and then turned to us. "I hope you're enjoying your time off, Tyler."

"I don't really have time off," I said. "Just other kinds of work, I'm…"

"Then I hope it's giving you time to go to auditions."

"I'm not an actor, I — "

Jacob Hellman burst in without knocking, wearing a beige tie and a white shirt that stretched over his gut. "Sorry I'm late," he said as he gave us his froggy grin and picked up a chair from the corner behind Lakshmi. He did not set his chair with ours to face her, but set it next to hers. I was not the only one who thought this was awkward. She looked at Jacob, startled, and was about to say something before she decided not to. She looked even more miffed when he reached for a cookie.

"Jacob, do you really need that?" she asked.

"What?"

"The cookie," she said as he took a bite.

"I guess I don't need it," he said as he chewed. "I'm just a little hungry."

"Cookies have their consequences, Jacob," she said, scolding him. "Keep in mind that you represent me and this organization before you consume any more needless calories." He shrugged and tossed the rest of the cookie in the trash receptacle.

"Well, then," she said, eyeing the manila envelope in my lap. "I'm excited to see what you came up with, Tyler."

"A couple of ideas," I said. "First one is like the board game Candyland. On the top tier we'd have the Candy Castle and in front of it a throne made of gingerbread where you could sit as the Candy Queen. And then the cute guy volunteers could be like the game pieces along the track that winds through the Lollipop Forest, Gumdrop Mountains and the Root Beer Sea and Ice Cream Islands."

I handed her a sketch I had made with colored pencils. She looked quizzically at it, her mouth to one side. "That's a lot of calories, Tyler," she said. "Even if they're imaginary. What else have you got?"

"The other idea comes from the song MacArthur Park. The float would be like a little park with some grass and flowers and there would be cute guys along the tiers leading up to you on a park bench where you would have a picnic basket and could wave at everybody. At the front of the float we'd have a big melting cake. Occasionally, this hunky angel in a Speedo would pop out of the top layer and shake his groove thing to the Donna Summer version of the song."

She gasped. "MacArthur Park is melting in the dark, all the sweet cream icing flowing down," she sang, and I understood why her career as a cabaret singer had been disappointing. "Tyler, I love that song! But I think maybe the Richard Harris version would be better."

I handed her the sheet and her face lit up. The sketch included the banner she wanted.

"I don't know," Jacob said when he motioned to her to hand him the drawing. "I thought we were thinking about a heavenly theme with handsome guys wearing halos and angel wings."

"That's a little obvious," Lakshmi said.

"Maybe," Jacob said. "But do we really want a big, melting cake on the float?"

"Not an actual cake," I said. "Something made from wood and polyethylene foam, a shell."

"It is just a *little* surreal," Lakshmi said and picked up her Ouija board. She set her fingers on it and the heart-shaped pointer wandered toward "Yes."

"Let's keep thinking about it," Jacob said. "But whatever we do, I'd like to propose something."

We looked at him as he bobbed his head and grinned, stretching the silence.

"What I'd like to propose is that I sit on the float with Lakshmi too. Next to her."

Without smiling, Lakshmi gave a nervous rat-a- tat-tat of a laugh. "You... y-y-you want to ride on m-my float?" she asked.

"Well, I think it should be *our* float. You're chief executive officer and I'm chief operating officer."

"You are?" asked Jeremy, startled. He looked over at me to see that I was just as surprised. Had Jacob been getting a salary? Is that where money had been going?

"I am," Jacob said. "And I'm not trying to diminish Lakshmi's contribution or authority here, but I have had a role to play in this organization."

Lakshmi was shaking her head, her mouth open, gasping before she could find words. "Jacob, this is... this is... very unexpected," she said. "We should have had a discussion about this!"

"We're having one now."

"I mean between the two of us."

He shrugged.

"Listen, you're the yang to my yin, Jacob, and I don't want to diminish the role you have played here. But I don't think you should be sitting next to me on the float as my equal."

"I'm not your equal?" he said.

"Look, honey, I'm not saying we aren't all equal here but I am the one who started this organization."

"No, I'd say *we* started it. You and me and a few others."

"What others?" she shouted.

"The people who came to you with some startup money and asked you to lend your name to an organization that *we* initiated."

"I have done *more* than lend my name, Jacob!"

"Of course you have. But this was never your idea. This was Ganja Stone's idea. The whole concept of Manna is a copy of God's Love We Deliver in New York, including the angel imagery. I mean, I'd like to say it was *my* idea, but I can't. It was Ganja. And it was the GSCLA that got the idea of bringing it to LA."

"The GS *what?*" I asked.

"The Gay Ski Club of Los Angeles."

"This organization would never have happened without me!" Lakshmi shouted. She was up out of her seat and pacing. "It's an extension of the Being Center! A place where we were already offering meals! And you know that, Jacob! And I am sorry to disappoint you, but the amount of work you've done for us *does not warrant* a seat atop our Pride float!"

"I think it does," Jacob said, all too calmly. "When it comes to raising money you've been undervaluing my contribution — especially my recent contribution."

She shook her head, her body trembling as she hyperventilated. "Oh, you would bring that up! Just throwing it in my face! Boys!" she said addressing me and Jeremy. "Jacob wants you to know that he's the one who got the two hundred thousand dollars to pay off Jericho and keep the lights on."

"Out of his own pocket?" I asked.

"Of course not," said Lakshmi. "He went *begging* to a *benefactor*, someone I might add, who is a donor that I cultivated *first*."

Jacob shook his head with a faint smile that suggested this was just another of Lakshmi's little tirades. "Lakshmi, he gave it to *me*," Jacob said. "Because he knew I'd be the one who would be controlling it."

"Oh, you're just *so* financially responsible and *so* successful, aren't you, Jacob, with your house in the Hollywood Hills!" she screeched. "And your BMW! And your weekend place in Palm Springs!"

I looked at Jeremy to see if he was as astonished as I was to be witnessing such a personal argument. He was.

"Don't be jealous, Lakshmi, you'll get there someday," Jacob said.

"Oh, I will," she said. "But while you were raking in money with your in-home nursing business, I was conducting services at funerals and counseling people with AIDS and HIV, people like *you*, Jacob! You were shopping for real estate while I was changing adult diapers!"

"I've changed my share of diapers, Lakshmi," Jacob said. "And I've washed bedpans and mopped up vomit and diarrhea. For that alone I deserve to sit on the float."

"Excuse me," Jeremy interrupted. "I don't mean to interrupt your argument but—"

"We're not arguing!" Lakshmi said.

"Whatever it is, it's out of hand," I said. "And it's embarrassing."

"You're embarrassed, Tyler? *You* are?" she snapped.

"We both are," said Jeremy, his own anger in the open. "And we need to talk about this little float of yours. Only a few volunteers have signed up to build this thing because the growing consensus is that it doesn't represent all the volunteers. We think everyone who wants to march for Manna should be able to do so."

"Jeremy, no, it is wonderful to volunteer and it is an honor to be of service," said Lakshmi, pacing again. "And this float will honor those volunteers. But they don't *all* have to be marching with us."

"Yes, they do," I said. "If the people who show up at the kitchen each day want to march in an apron down Santa Monica Boulevard, we should let them. They deserve that if they've been driving to Downey and peeling garlic and scrubbing burnt rice from the bottom of a pot."

Lakshmi pulled her hair out of her eyes and stared at me with hatred but then her face softened as her eyes flashed left and right — she was getting a vision.

"All right, all right, *Tyler* and *Jeremy*," she said in a mocking tone, as if our very names offended her. "I am going to pray about this. I am getting an indication," she said looking up at the ceiling, as if seeing through it to God in heaven. "An indication that there is a loving and beautiful compromise. I will get back to you on this. Thank you for coming in."

She sat in her chair, spinning it back and forth then grabbed a Kleenex as she wiped at tears and started crying. Jacob was following us out when she waved her tissue at him. "Stay, Jacob. We're not done."

We shut the door and trotted down the stairs. Out on the sidewalk, we heard Lakshmi and Jacob resuming their argument. Her voice, when she got angry, was piercing, like the screeching notes of the violins in *Psycho*.

"So what do you think this compromise is?" I asked Jeremy.

"I don't know, Tyler. But hopefully, Lord willing, Jacob and Lakshmi can rule as homecoming queens together. He'd look so darling with a tiara."

*

"Oh, she's *desperate*," Gene said when I stopped by the kitchen on my way back from De Laurentiis and showed him the plan for the float. "This time she's gone too far. If anybody should be on that float, it should be us — the chefs and the staff."

"I'm surprised to hear you say that," I said. "Lakshmi is *desperate*?"

"Of course she is, just lusting for stardom, addicted to the spotlight," he said as he handed the sheet to Jonnie. "The girl's just got to have it, can never get enough. She dies when no one's looking at her."

Jonnie looked at the sheet. "Gene's right. If anyone should be on this float, it should be the people who run the operation," she said. "I should be on it, and so should you and Tim and the rest of us working here."

"Actually, Lakshmi did ask Jeremy and me to be on the float," I said. "Even though we're both over... you know, thirty."

"She wants you and Jeremy on the float?" said Gene with a hurt, quizzical look.

"She thinks we're cute," I said and shrugged. "But I'm not really the float-riding type."

Gene had that downcast, deflated look as he stared at the floor. Jonnie set her hand on his arm. "Aww, Gene, I'm sure she's going to ask you too," she said. "You're cute."

"If we're going to have a float... it should include the *chef*s!" Gene said. "These meals don't cook themselves."

"So Tim gets to be on the float?" I asked.

Gene's brows furrowed as he wrinkled his nose. "Tyler, no one wants to look at *Tim*," he said.

Koala arrived with a big smile under his oversized, black-rimmed glasses. He was always well-dressed, always in black, and wearing slacks and an Italian leather jacket even though it was warm out. "Hello all!" he sang. "I am so excited to see what you came up with, Tyler. Lakshmi was just raving about it."

"Hi, Koala," I said, offering to shake his hand but he went for the big hug. "Uh, nice of you to take charge of constructing the float."

"It's the least I could do for Lakshmi when she's done so much for, well, all of humanity!"

"So I gather you have experience?" Gene asked, his voice drenched with sarcasm.

"I do! When I was a florist I worked on a few floats for the Rose Parade. One of them, for the City of Monrovia, won the prize for floral presentation!"

"That's *very* impressive," said Gene with his nose up in the air and his wormy smirk. "You'll have to tell us all about it someday."

"Can we count on you to help build it, Tyler?" Koala asked, with irrepressible positivity. "We've got a lot of paper flowers to make and fasten! And I'm sure you, of all hunky people, can inspire others to join our crew!"

"I... I can't commit right now," I said. "I've got a lot of scripts to read and write up. But let's talk again when the dates get closer. So, where are you building this thing?"

"Lakshmi got permission from the church to let us use the back lot here," he said. "I can't wait to get started!"

"So, Koala... will you be on the float?" Gene asked as he eyed Koala's baldness and rail-thin frame.

"I don't know. Am I?" Koala asked, suddenly self-conscious.

"From what I'm hearing you have to be willing to wear a bikini bottom."

"Oh, then I don't think so," he said and blushed.

"I think most people will be fully clothed," I said to rescue Koala from Gene's bitchery as I passed the sheet. "Here's the basic design. Feel free to riff on it but run any big changes past Lakshmi. This is her thing."

Koala bit his index finger and cocked his head as he stared at the drawing and its banner. I was wondering how Koala got his name since he was anything but plump and fuzzy and looked more like a magpie to me. "I can make this work," he said. "But for the banner to be readable, it should be more of a rectangle than a ribbon."

"OK. Gimme a call if you have any questions," I said and took my keys from my pocket to signal I was leaving.

"Tyler," Jonnie said, coming closer to me and looking up in my eyes as I was about to step out. "Since you're here, do you think you could do Pasadena? I know it's far away but we've got five clients out there who are hungry and no one willing to go! The driver canceled because his dog died!"

"Uh, sure," I said, saying goodbye to my afternoon — the dying dog bit had won my sympathies and Pasadena was a nice place to visit. I liked driving that curvy little freeway with its WPA tunnels and its parks full of sycamore trees.

I dropped off meals to one guy in a complex of Green and Green bungalows, one to someone renting a room in a Victorian mansion and one to some lovers who lived in an old, converted gas station. The last delivery was to a crumbling, Mission-style guesthouse behind a dilapidated mansion where there was a chained and snarling German shepherd in the backyard. "Thanks," said the emaciated, purple-spotted man who took the tin full of baked chicken and baby potatoes and threw it to the dog. He picked up his piece of key lime pie and ate it with his fingers.

"Uh, I don't think you should feed your dog chicken bones," I said.

"Not my dog," he said and grinned to reveal a nearly toothless mouth. I waited until the dog had finished eating to make sure he didn't choke. It took about thirty seconds.

After the delivery, I went to a coffee shop on Colorado Boulevard to get some food for myself. It was a restaurant I was strangely drawn to with its broken neon sign that read "Luncheonette and Soda Fountain" in Art Deco letters. The place was no longer a working soda fountain but its decor and fixtures from the 1930s were intact. It had a sleek, steel counter where there were twenty empty canisters for syrups labeled cherry, chocolate, cola and so on with two nozzles that had been jerked for carbonation. The decor celebrated Pasadena's Rose Parade from its early days with walls covered by oversized pictures of floats covered in flowers. The pictures were black-and-white blowups that had been colored with pale photo tints and featured bathing beauties of yore riding on flowery swans, seahorses and peacocks. It was giving me more ideas for some screenplay that was assembling in my unconscious. I picked up a sugar packet with my fingers and suddenly there was a seed in my head, something to plant and water then grow and trim.

Over the next few weeks, I gorged on script reading and made enough money for rent and bills for the month. Then I took a few weeks off to work on a script titled *The Sugar Parade*. It was a period piece set in the early 70's in a factory town based on Lodi, California, where a corporation manufactured cookies, snack cakes and candies. Each year, to promote the town and its products, an annual parade was held in which businesses, churches and civic organizations created floats that had to be covered entirely in sweets. My protagonist, Buzz, was a college dropout who comes home to rescue his grandfather facing eviction from his retirement home. Buzz inspires his friends to take on the building of a float and win the grand prize of

$25,000 so they can revive their dreams, pay off debts and keep his grandpa in the home.

I knew this screenplay was not Oscar material. It was candy corn, empty calories, but funny and feel-good with a lot of heart. I pitched it to my agent as *Breaking Away* meets *Willie Wonka* and she laughed and said she was "intrigued." I was finishing a rough draft of the script on an overcast afternoon in late May when the phone rang.

"Hello, Tyler. It's Koala Cordanno."

"Well, hi, Koala, how ya doing?"

"Truthfully, I'm a little frantic," he said. "We're having an all-hands-on-deck moment for this float, which is supposed to be floating down Santa Monica Boulevard next Sunday. But barely anyone is showing up to help me build it!"

"Sorry to hear that. What's the problem?"

"They decided on who would ride on the float with Lakshmi. And some of these men aren't even volunteers! Granted they're all just *gorgeous*, but some of them have never come near that kitchen!"

I realized I was not going to be one of the float hunks after all, which was a little less than heartbreaking. For one thing, it would have meant being next to Lakshmi for about two hours as a cub scout in her den. And two hours is also a long time to hold your piss.

"Well, that ain't right, Koala," I said when I heard the soft beep of call waiting. "Let me see who that is." I clicked on the cradle button.

"Hey, Tyler, it's Jeremy."

"Hey, I'm on with Koala. What's up, Jer?"

"Lakshmi's freaking out because there's no float. She's called a meeting at four. Can you make it? She asked for you."

I heard another beep.

"Let me call you back." I clicked the phone again. "Hey, Koala."

"No, Tyler, it's Lakshmi."

"Oh, hi... Lakshmi."

Lakshmi?

"I'm hoping you can come to this meeting at four about our entry for the Pride parade."

"I wouldn't miss it," I said. "I'm wrapping something up but I'll get there when I can."

I walked Holden around the block and then drove to the Center where the meeting was underway. About thirty people were standing, not sitting, in the reception room as Lakshmi paced before them. Jeremy, Koala and Jacob Hellman stood in back of her. Nigel was speaking in the musical notes of his upper-crust accent.

"So I do hope you have seen now that the overwhelming feeling here is that this is not the most representative float for all the people that make up Manna. That would be the volunteers, specifically, who we believe this float should honor. What we are proposing is that everyone who wants to march should be able to do so. Those who ride upon the float would be our elderly volunteers, the ones who cannot or should not walk for miles in the hot sun."

"Oh, aren't you just so articulate and aren't you just *so sensitive* and considerate of the elderly," said Lakshmi as she did her strut and fret in some knee-length boots and a tartan skirt. "Those who ride *upon* the float," she said, mocking his plummy accent.

"Thank you," said Nigel, mocking her with a courtly bow. "Very kind of you to say so, Lakshmi, but I assure you I am simply urging you to do the decent and respectful thing here."

"I beg your pardon?" Lakshmi said in disbelief. "The *decent* thing? Are you insinuating that I am *not* decent?"

"He won't but I will," said Ruth of the Jewish Mom's Brigade. "With my fractured hip I can't march but I'm offended I wasn't even invited to."

"I second that," said her friend, Marleen with the rust-colored perm. "Ruthie should be on that float but *you*, Lakshmi, *you*! *You* want to be up there surrounded by a bunch of Chippendale's dancers so you can make an entrance like the Queen of Sheba!"

"Queen of Sheba is right," said Goldie, the blonde from the same group as she pulled up her sleeves with her nails she had painted in the rainbow spectrum in honor of Gay Pride. "Maybe instead of a pickup truck, you should get some *camels* to haul in your caravan."

That got a laugh and Lakshmi turned red.

"All right, all right," she said, making her tamping down motion. "Here's what we're going to do if we get permission from Christopher Street West. We'll have the float... *and* we'll have marchers following after it."

"I believe you are putting the cart before the horse," said Nigel. "The volunteers should come first and then the float follows after."

"Oh, is *thaht* what you believe?" said Lakshmi, wrinkling her nose as she imitated Nigel's accent. "The marchers following ah-fter it."

"Lakshmi, he has a point," said Jacob, quietly. "The volunteers are the lifeblood of this org— "

"Fine... fine!" Lakshmi almost shouted, cutting Jacob off. "The volunteers march in front of the float. Just a reminder, *everyone*, the float is *not* about me, it's not about *you*, it's about Manna from Heaven, something to bring awareness to our organization *and* to our coming fundraiser. I *will* sit on the float with a few friends of mine and we will make room for some seniors and people who can't march. The important thing now is that we get it built." She glanced at Koala who looked peaked with skin the color of an uncooked chicken. "How far have you gotten, Koala?"

"Not far," he said. "But we'll be building all weekend, starting at sunrise, so please, *please* sign up." He passed some clipboards with sign-up sheets around the room.

"I am so glad we could resolve this," Lakshmi said. "Now if you'll excuse me, we've got a fundraiser to work on. Thank you, all. I can't tell you how much I appreciate your work."

When the clipboard reached me, some of the names on it were "Cleopatra of the Nile," "Her Majesty the Queen of Sheba" and "C. U. Next Tuesday."

"Tyler, can I talk to you for a second?" Lakshmi said to me as she turned toward the stairs.

"Sure," I said and followed her up.

"Since you have time off, I'm hoping you can help Koala," she said as she plopped down in her swivel chair and spun left and right as she played with her hair.

"I don't really have time off, I —"

"Tyler, I hired you because I thought you were committed to this organization."

"Of course I am. But I've never built a float before, I have other work now, I'm not on the payroll here, I —"

"Look to God to guide you, Tyler. He will find you the angels you need. Tyler, you do understand that this float is about making us some money. Be sure to incorporate some signage about Celestial Objects and include the dates and the location. Can you do that?"

"I... I think so," I said.

"Koala really needs you and so do I and so do all of our very sick clients. And the sooner we have some money, the sooner you can come back to the kitchen. I know the two of you will do a spectacular job. It's going to be fabulous."

"Fabulous. OK," I said, knowing I had committed myself not just to designing but to *building* a fucking float for Lakshmi Steinmetz. But something, a little rumble in my gut, said something else was about to go wrong — very wrong.

Chapter 21

The sign-up sheet for Marchers for Manna was limited to forty-eight and was immediately filled — the volunteers wanted to parade. One of them was a movie props manager who got us some oversized kitchen utensils to carry down the street including giant egg beaters, cheese graters and whisks. Sign-ups for the float committee were still pretty meager and made up mostly of Lakshmi's most dedicated followers. These volunteers were inconsistent and grew bored with the making of paper flowers, something we did inside the church on the edge of the community room's stage. Among the majority of volunteers there was still the lingering resentment that the float was all about Lakshmi and it was referred to as "MacArthur's Barf."

As for the Barf, its three tiers had been nailed together by a former set designer and their tops were covered in artificial turf. At the peak was a little park bench where Lakshmi would reign, all by herself, under a banner with her name and title above her. Koala had planted mini-gardens of bright, paper flowers shooting up from the turf on bendable wires so that they would bob in the wind. The bottom tier included a tiny pond filled with blue glass pebbles that was surrounded by velveteen cattails. Just in back of this water feature was a park bench where a few "infirm and older" volunteers could sit. The pickup truck that would haul the float would blast "MacArthur Park" from some speakers in the payload.

I was at work on the giant cake with all the "sweet cream icing flowing down" that was on the second tier. The set designer had built a three-tiered square cake made from plywood because a round one was too difficult. He cut some holes in it for air, lined the inside with some pink polyester to avoid splinters, and then I "frosted" it with polyurethane foam that I let drip for a melting effect. I spray-painted the faux frosting with a heavy application of bright pinks and oranges that I let run and smear. Using an open star tip on a pastry bag, I piped some tile caulking and then textured it with a wet sponge to look rained on. The top of the cake had a hinged lid with some fake birthday candles that the muscle puppy could push up so that he could pop out, spread some retractable angel wings and then shake his heavenly ass.

We were running out of time and short on finished flowers, but Koala rejected the notion of using something called floral sheeting "because it was cheap-looking and garish and it's more like plastic sequins than flowers." He insisted on individually made paper roses, daisies and carnations in vivid colors, which had "the dignity of their own creation and would add a richness of textures." Each morning of that week, Koala brought with him a laundry basket of flowers he and his roommates, some other *Way* queens, had labored on through the night. We started fastening them to the chicken wire structure, and as more of the float was completed, it attracted more volunteers — they wanted to be a part of something that was growing more impressive. It was simpler in design than a Rose Parade float but looking almost as professional.

By early Thursday morning, the end was in sight. Another couple hundred flowers would finish covering the lower sides. Once these were fastened, Koala would attach multiple skirts of white vinyl fringe with a matte finish. "We're not doing one of those tacky, tinselly, ones," he said. "This isn't Mardi Gras!" As he carefully stapled the skirts, I went to Kinko's and picked up the banners for the float, one for Lakshmi and a larger one for the back that advertised *Celestial Objects, a Benefit for Manna From Heaven. Join us!* The back banner was a blowup of the poster for the event, which featured some Peter Max art from his early, psychedelic period that his lawyer agreed we could use. The Art Nouveau letters were against a background of hot pink and electric blue planets that revolved around a heart-shaped sun. It fitted well with the "MacArthur Park" theme, a song of overwrought, psychedelic melancholy from the late 60's.

I helped Koala fasten the Celestial banner to the float's back. He thought the edges of the banner were harsh so we took the last hundred paper flowers and made a frame with them. When that was completed, we had the satisfaction of having added something that suddenly tied everything together, which had given the float some "unifying principles."

"It's good," I said. "Really good."

"I think it's... *beautiful*," Koala said, astonished by the final result.

I was suddenly, strangely proud of something that I had thought was ridiculously stupid, something I had designed as a kind of joke, something I had expected Lakshmi would reject. And then in my head I heard whistling, a tune I couldn't quite place. I started to whistle it out loud.

"Why are you whistling *that*?" Koala asked.

"What am I whistling?"

"It's from *Bridge Over the River Kwai*, the *Colonel Bogey March*."

"Oh. Right," I said as the movie's plot came back to me. It was about the building of a railroad bridge by British prisoners of war captured by the Japanese during World War II. Even though the prisoners are grossly mistreated and many of them die from sickness and overwork, they cheer when they complete the bridge and take pride in their accomplishment. Of course the movie does not end there.

Our moment of self-admiration and sense of accomplishment was interrupted when Bryce came running down the stairs, out of breath, and with a panicked look on his face. "Tyler, you should come upstairs to the kitchen."

"What's wrong?"

"It's Tim," he said. "I've never seen him so pissed."

I ran up the stairs to the community room and saw Tim with a crumpled apron in his hand as he argued with Jonnie. Behind him stood his Tipplers.

"It's inexcusable!" he said, shouting but sure of himself, no tremble in his voice as he shook his finger. "He did this to sabotage me!"

"He did not, Tim!" Jonnie shouted back.

"Yes he did! And it's the third time he's done it, the little shit!"

"What's wrong?" I asked.

"Gene did not order towels again!" Tim shouted. "There are no towels here, they did *not* show up at nine! We called them and there is no scheduled delivery of towels until Monday. Monday! You cannot run a kitchen *without kitchen towels*!"

"He's right," I said to Jonnie. "You need fucking towels."

"Tim, I'm just sure he forgot," she said. "Calm down!"

"Forgot on purpose! Don't try and minimize this, Jonnie! I cannot and will not work in conditions like this!"

Tim threw his apron in the laundry bag and started for the stairs.

"You can't just leave, Tim!" Jonnie shouted. "You have a meal to get out!"

"Watch me," Tim said.

"This is all fucked up!" said Wayne the Pain after he lit a cigarette inside the church with his vintage Zippo lighter and blew the smoke east, west, north and south. He took another drag. "Come on, boys. Let's blow this shithole," he said, smoke puffing with every word. After tapping his ash on the floor, he and the other Tipplers pulled off their aprons, dropped them on the floor and followed Tim out.

I walked into the kitchen to see a sparseness of volunteers who had stopped working. They were all looking at me in silence.

Bryce threw me an apron. "Get to work, bitch," he said.

"Where's Gene?"

"She took the day off. Seeing the gynecologist. Her menstruation *has* been irregular."

"And just what are we serving?" I asked. I looked up at the menu board and read "Sauerbraten, Boiled Baby Potatoes, Red Cabbage Salad, Black Forest Cake."

"Sauerbraten?" I said. That was something I had never eaten much less cooked.

"Tim started this on Tuesday... for German Thursdays," Bryce said as he smashed at crumbs in a bowl. "The meat's been marinating."

"*German Thursdays?* And just what are you doing?" I asked.

"I'm crushing ginger snaps. They go in the sauce."

"*Ginger snaps?*"

I went to our copy of Joy of Cooking in the spice cabinet, my go-to for practical, reliable recipes.

"OK," I said. "Fuck. We need to slice this up thin... thin, thin, thin if it's gonna be ready on time. And we're gonna roll it up and braise it in the sauce for like an hour, hour and a half, like braciola. And before it goes in the oven we have to sprinkle it with... brown sugar. Really? Brown fucking sugar?"

As soon as each hotel pan was filled with the sliced, rolled meat and some marinade, we slid them into the oven. Bryce took the remains of the marinade and ran it through a sieve and then added a couple of buckets of sour cream and the crushed ginger snaps before warming it on the stove.

We encouraged Jonnie to have one of her longest prayer circles ever and like "a blessing from heaven," the mime troop returned in whiteface and black-striped shirts to perform a Pridethemed piece. While the beef was braising, I stepped out of the kitchen to watch as two sad, tear-streaked mimes flew kites that got tangled. The entanglement led to the mimes meeting and falling in love, with one of them offering a flower to the other. They rubbed their tears off of each other's faces then walked hand in hand toward two other mimes unfolding a crepe paper rainbow. Under its arch, the mimes detached some sequined hearts from the front of their shirts and exchanged them.

I ran back into the kitchen, muffling my sniggers, when the first pan of beef came out. It was a little chewy and undercooked but it was edible and better with a splash of Bryce's sauce. It was stop-and-go on the assembly line and close to twelve thirty when finally over 350 servings were packed up and sent out along with some vegetarian and vegan meals. We were prepping the Friday meal when Gene appeared near the end of the day in some bright-yellow Lycra, having come straight from his workout session.

"Did you bring any towels?" I asked.

"What's that supposed to mean?"

"He's not actually asking if you brought any towels, bitch," said Bryce.

Gene smirked. "No, I did not bring any towels," he said. "I thought we had enough to last until Monday."

"Oh, is that what you thought," I said. "We're also out of aprons."

"Aprons?"

"Yeah. We've been using them for towels."

"That's very resourceful of you," he said. "If only Tim had thought of that. If he had, you wouldn't be taking over for him and I wouldn't be here on my day off."

"Taking over for him? I am *not* taking over for him."

"We hope you are. He's not coming back."

"I'm sure he's coming back."

"He walked off the job," Gene said. "Tim's let everyone down — our clients most of all."

"Gene, for the third time in the last three months you didn't order any towels for him," I shouted. "That's a hostile act. Pure passive aggression."

"Hostile act?" Gene said, his mouth agape as he feigned shock. "What's hostile is walking off the job!"

"This has happened three times!" I said. "You should have ordered towels! Unless this is what you wanted to happen."

"What are you implying?"

"That you're trying to get rid of him."

Gene was quiet as he stared at me with his pale-green eyes. We were both aware in the silence that the volunteers were listening.

"I didn't want this, Tyler. But I'll be honest with you — I think it's a good thing he's gone."

"He's not gone! He's pissed off!"

"No, he's fired. I've already talked about it with Lakshmi and Jacob. We all know that he has… a problem. We need you to start back full-time. The *clients* need you, Tyler."

I was wordless — sad more than anything — but that was the top layer of some darker feelings.

"How's the float going?" Gene asked, the issue of Tim already in his rearview mirror as he wandered over to the window that looked down on the back lot. "Well, well!" he said. "It's exceeded *my* expectations. It looks like Koala has done a wonderful job."

Koala has done a wonderful job?

"We worked very hard on it," I said. *And you, Gene, are a real fucking cunt.*

As soon as I got home I called Tim. He didn't pick up but I left a message on his machine.

"Tim, it's Tyler," I said. "Please call me. I really need to speak with you. You shouldn't have walked out but they shouldn't have fired you. We need you in that kitchen. Call me."

On Friday morning, I was back in the kitchen at eight thirty. Gene was there, signing a receipt for a delivery of towels and aprons. It was a long, depressing day and I couldn't stop thinking about Tim. For one thing, the volunteers kept asking us where he was. "I'm sorry to say he's no longer with us," I said. A few volunteers who were close to Tim left in anger when they heard he was fired.

On Saturday morning, I was back at the church to meet with Koala and a rep from Christopher Street West who would inspect the float for safety issues. Lakshmi arrived and was joined by some of her handsome male friends, all of them *Way* queens, for a rehearsal of sorts. Her friends were all wearing polo shirts of a light blue-green color that looked familiar and then I realized it was the same color as Tiffany's gift boxes. Lakshmi was wearing a white pantsuit by Valentino, the material of which had a faint suggestion of feathers in its jacquard. "Oh my God!" she exclaimed coming closer to the float on a pair of white, ostrich leather heels. "It's unbelievable! It's gorgeous! Thank you so much!" she said hugging Koala and then me.

Koala was chortling with pride as he gave retractable angel wings to the muscle puppy wearing a blue-green bikini bottom.

The puppy got into the cake then popped out as a test. Using a drawstring, he opened his wings and shook his shapely butt. Koala helped Lakshmi up to her bench and she took a seat, warmly smiling. The music started from the truck and it was the Donna Summer version of "MacArthur Park" which was being used after all since the muscle puppy found it "more danceable" than the original.

I watched the float as it was hauled out slowly and it seemed like I was dreaming or watching a movie. I was struck by how strange my life had become, that it seemed like anyone else's life but mine. AIDS had derailed so many lives, destroyed many others and sent some, like me, on an unexpected trajectory. But as I looked at Lakshmi basking on her float with her polo-shirted hunks, I couldn't deny that I despised her and the sycophants she had appointed to power. And I knew I was not alone.

And soon enough, Lakshmi Steinmetz would learn in a very ugly way that she had enemies in Los Angeles and even more in New York.

Chapter 22

Some suspected it was Jericho. Others thought it might be Tim and the Tipplers led by Wayne the Pain who was, after all, a smoker with a Zippo lighter. Others assumed it was Derrick Vanderven or any number of others who had been hired, humiliated and fired by Lakshmi. Another theory, one that made me laugh, was that it was Jacob Hellman, miffed he hadn't been allowed to ride alongside Lakshmi in what he was overheard calling her "Chariot of the Goddess." None of these men would have done it themselves, it was theorized, but had paid someone to take care of it under cover of night.

    I had set my alarm for six in the morning to meet Gene and Bryce to make mac and cheese for an early delivery so both staff and volunteers of Manna could be done by ten thirty and march in the Pride parade. But the phone rang at five and on the message machine I heard a garbled message and someone in hysterics. "Tyler, come here now," was all I could make out and I realized it was Koala. I pulled on jeans and a T-shirt and was groggy and slapping myself awake as I drove to the church while aching for coffee. It was still dark out when I saw lurid, red lights whirling in the back lot of the church and the tail end of a fire truck. With my heart thumping, I lurched into the first parking place I could find and ran to the float.

Koala, who arrived early to do some touchups, was sitting slumped on the church's back stairs, tears streaming down his face, unable to talk as he sobbed. He just pointed me toward the float. I walked around the fire engine to see the float had burned and imploded before it was doused with water. The Astroturf had melted into globs and had the harsh stink of melted plastic. The chicken wire molding was warped and blackened and the park benches were charred and had fallen through the foundation. The metal stems of the paper flowers were like strange, ugly hairs that strayed from the exoskeleton of some alien monster eaten by acid. Everything was smeared with wet ashes.

The West Hollywood Sheriffs were at the crime scene and one of them was cataloging evidence. Tucked into clear plastic pouches were rectangular cans of Zippo lighting fluid. Any notion that a homeless person was looking for a private place to sleep and smoke a few cigarettes was utterly destroyed by this evidence. The lighter cans seemed intentional, left there as a means of rubbing it in: *Yes, this is arson.*

I went to Koala, hugged him and let him cry on my shoulder. "You just let it out," I said and patted his back. I was surprised by how I felt at first, violated and angry, that this labor of love, even if it was for the glory of Lakshmi Steinmetz, had been destroyed as an act of revenge. But part of me also felt that she deserved it, if Koala did not, that the float had been a tribute to her colossal ego and a waste of time and money — money that might have gone to health insurance for the staff.

I looked over Koala's shoulder to see Bryce arriving with a thermos cup of coffee and raised eyebrows. "Guess I got here too late to make s'mores," he said.

"Koala," I said, looking into his eyes and trying to think of something comforting to say. "We are gonna march today, like this never happened. We have to show the assholes who did this that Manna from Heaven will *not* be intimidated."

I felt stupid after I said that. I had repeated a version of some hackneyed line from a dozen movie and television shows and my execution was wooden.

"You're right, Tyler," he said. "But excuse me if I don't feel like marching at the moment."

"Of course. And whoever did this can't take away the memory of your beautiful work."

He quietly nodded.

"You want to come upstairs? Sit down? Get some water?" I asked. "You're probably in shock."

"No," he said. "I'm just going to drive home and go back to bed. I'll be fine, Tyler."

Both Bryce and I gave Koala a hug before he trudged off. It was total darkness in the kitchen before I flipped on the fluorescent lights. Their electric buzz seemed loud and their light was harsh.

"Bryce... what the fuck?" I whispered as I went to open the supply cage. "Who the fuck did this?'

"I don't know," he said. "But I kinda wanna hug him too."

We both started laughing, the kind of low snicker that comes out of a guilty pleasure. We tried to stop and found we couldn't.

Gene arrived carrying a garment bag of the clothes he would wear for the march. "And what do we find so funny?" he asked.

"It's not funny at all," I said, covering my mouth as it twitched into a smile.

"Nope. Something really fucking *sad* has happened," said Bryce and we burst out laughing again.

"Are you laughing at me?" Gene said, looking at his zipper.

"No."

"Then I'd like to be included."

"It's — it's the float," I said between chuckles.

"What about the float?"

"MacArthur Park has melted in the dark," Bryce said and then we really started laughing — a belly-aching, doubled over, wet-your-pants moment.

Gene went to the back door and looked at the float. He returned a second later, his face turned white. "You... you think this is *funny*?" he said. "Somebody burned our float! It's a malicious act! The flames could have spread and set this whole church on fire!"

Bryce and I straightened up. I cleared my throat. "Sorry, Gene," I said. "Gallows humor. We know it's not funny."

"No, it's not funny," Bryce said, deadly serious. "It's fucking hilarious!"

That started a new round of laughter. Gene was staring at us, his head cocked in disbelief but he was fighting back a grin. "What are we going to do?" he asked. "Lakshmi is going to be devastated."

"The show must go on," Bryce said with mock histrionics. "And Lakshmi will ride." Then, in his own voice he said, "Let's just rework it a little, give the float a martyr theme. We'll tie Lakshmi to a stake, shave her hair off and smear her with ashes for a Joan of Arc look."

Gene tried not to laugh but then squirted snot from a nostril before he doubled over. All three of us were laughing and had to straighten up when the first of the volunteers arrived. As the grating of cheese began, I started some butterscotch nut bars.

The drivers arrived an hour and a half earlier than usual and we hustled to get the meals out by ten. Lakshmi arrived at nine forty five in her white pantsuit with her bevy of hunks in their Tiffany-colored polo shirts plus the muscle puppy in his bikini bottom. All of them had heard the news and looked as if they had arrived at a morgue to identify a corpse. Lakshmi was wearing some pink low tops on her feet but one of the hunks carried the shoe bag that held her Louboutin heels, a pair of kicks the spectators would never get to see. She walked slowly, gravely to Jonnie at her table in the community room and the two of them hugged before pulling apart to wipe each other's tears. We were getting out the last of the mac and cheese when Lakshmi came into the kitchen and stood in the doorway for dramatic effect, her head tilted to the side. She walked slowly to me, her face looking like the mournful Madonna of a Russian icon.

"Tyler, I am so very sorry," she said. "You worked so hard on our float. I would give you a hug, but your apron is stained."

I looked at my apron which had some smears of cookie batter.

"We all worked hard on it," I said. "I'm so sorry... about... what happened, especially sorry for Koala."

"He's just... *destroyed*. Everyone! Everyone, please!" she called while turning in a slow circle to bring the volunteers to her attention. "I know we weren't planning on a prayer circle today to save time," she said in a sad and breaking voice. "But I think we could all use a talk with God right now."

Everyone quieted as she shut her eyes and entered into a prayer fugue.

"God, our Holy Father, we ask that you heal those who were wounded by this hateful act, that you remind those who poured their love and dedication into this float that their efforts did not go unnoticed by you. And God, we know that someone is out there who *really* needs your love and your forgiveness, someone who suffers deeply in his separation from you, someone lost in a labyrinth of hatred. He is someone whose pain is so unbearable that he inflicts it on others in the desperate attempt to feel less alone. That man, the destroyer of this float needs you, God, more than we do, and we ask that you heal him as we forgive him. Amen."

After the kitchen was cleaned and locked up for the day, Gene, Bryce and I got ready to walk down to Santa Monica Boulevard and join the parade. "Let's put on the nice aprons," Gene said and took out the show versions with the Manna logo that we used in publicity shoots.

"Are you sure about this?" I said. "We'll be the only ones wearing them."

"We're the chefs," Gene said. "We deserve a little distinction. Besides, Tyler, you look like you just rolled out of bed. Couldn't you at least have done your hair?"

"I came straight here when I heard the Romans set fire to Cleopatra's barge," I said.

"When do I get an apron?" Bryce asked. "I just made mac and cheese again. For free. And I got here at six fucking o'clock."

"Now that you mention it," Gene said. "We just might have a position if you're interested, Bryce… if you can put your red-hot acting career on hold."

Bryce put his hands on his hips and sneered. "You're so sure I want to work with some fussy bitch pretending she ain't from Tulsa?" he said. "If I come to work here, it's because I can work with Tyler."

Gene chuckled. "That may be exactly what happens," he said. "If you can tame your vicious tongue. I'll be the executive chef and Tyler will take over for Tim and you'll be number three."

"Uh, do I get a say in this?" I said.

"I thought you'd be thrilled," Gene said. "Unless your stellar writing career has suddenly revived."

"Give it time," I said.

"We need you, Bryce, now that Tim is gone," Gene said. "We're only expecting more clients."

"I can't replace Tim," Bryce said, slowly shaking his head.

"Of course you can."

"No, Gene. Tim was great."

"Tim was great? Tim's food was terrible!"

"Sometimes. But Tim was a great *guy*, with a big loving heart. And he wasn't mean-spirited. The volunteers loved him."

"Yes, they did," I said, looking at Gene. "Tim had a real warmth, something you could never —" I stopped myself. "Something the rest of us could only aspire to."

Gene was quiet and had another of those moments in which his arrogance disappeared and in its place was a gaping wound, something plastered on his face that betrayed his longing for adoration. It wasn't long before his vicious smirk reappeared with one eyebrow raised up and his lip curling like a Disney villainess.

"Something *to* which the rest of us could only aspire," Gene said. "I would think that someone who calls himself a writer wouldn't end his sentences with a proposition."

"Now, Gene," I said. "When has that kind of snobbery ever made you more attractive to others?"

"Somebody here thinks her own farts smell like Chanel No. 5," said Bryce. "You'd be very lucky to have me, Missy. I *might* consider working here."

Gene scoffed at that. "Oh, might you," he said. "The two of you might show me a little gratitude for offering you employment. Now let's not be late for the parade," he said and handed me an apron and then, after bobbing his head in faked indecision, he tossed one to Bryce.

"Well, bless your heart," said Bryce as he tied it on.

When we reached the corner of Santa Monica and Fairfax, Lakshmi was in an intense conversation with an organizer from Christopher Street West whose name tag read Ashton. "I understand your float was destroyed," he said with a gentlemanly demeanor as he blinked at her. "But your permit is for forty-eight marchers."

"Yes, and we need everyone who was *riding* on the float to be included among the marchers," she insisted.

"That's a total of nine more?" the organizer said, looking at the hunks in their vivid polo shirts and one in a bikini bottom with some angel wings on his back. They stood in back of Lakshmi, their hands clasped behind them to show off their triceps.

"Nine," she said. "There's plenty of room for them since we don't have a float."

"Well, all right, Lock-shmy," Ashton said. "But that's going to throw off your symmetry. We had six rows of eight and now we have seven rows with one extra person."

"Oh," Lakshmi said, her face brightening. "I'll just walk by myself."

"Behind them? By yourself?" he asked with a quizzical look.

"No, in front of them. I am the founder and CEO," she said with a harsh smile.

Someone else with a clipboard from CSW came over. "Ashton, we've actually got forty-seven now — one of the marchers isn't here, Koala Cordanno."

"Fine," said Ashton. "This little lady here and the men in aqua will make a line of eight in the back."

"In the back?" Lakshmi said.

"In the back," he said, showing her his clipboard. "These are the first eight here, the banner carriers." Lakshmi looked over the page where the names of the first eight people to sign up were printed. Those same eight were looking at her now, two of them being Goldie and Marlene from the Jewish Mom's Brigade. "We got here first," said Goldie to Lakshmi. "And we're carrying the banner."

"You should get in the back," said Marlene.

Lakshmi was pacing, making involuntary gasps again, flustered. "I should get in the *back*?" she said.

"You heard me. I mean who the hell are these guys in the polo shirts?" said Marlene. "Never seen them in the kitchen."

Lakshmi's mouth was open in disbelief. "They're my friends!" she said.

I looked over at Bryce, and like me, his face was red and he was biting his lip as he tried not to laugh. The oversized utensils were being passed out to the marchers. "What row am I?" I asked Ashton. "Last name is St. George."

"Row six, position b from the north," he said. I winked at Goldie and Marlene as someone handed me a giant ice cream scoop. Bryce got a huge rolling pin and Gene got a big spatula as we took our places. A minute later, Lakshmi came to the back of the formation, quiet and sulking. The hunks joined her and took their positions, but they were empty-handed since we had run out of utensils. The dancing boy looked the strangest of all, someone who just happened to be wearing a turquoise bikini and angel wings for the march. Lakshmi was placed in the middle of the row, to distinguish her, but she was a foot shorter than anyone beside her and got buried.

It was the first time I had ever marched in a parade and I'd be lying if I said I wasn't warmed by the two hours of cheers and applause as we made our way west. The Pride parade in those days was less about shirtless men on floats sponsored by bars and discos and was all about different services for people with AIDS. It was an hour longer than it had been in the past and included every hospice where men went to die. Manna from Heaven was a new entry, well regarded, and news of our destroyed float preceded us. Chants of "Manna, Manna, Manna" ran in waves down the boulevard and spectators ran out to hug and kiss us when the parade had to stop. I got more than my share of attention from volunteers and friends in the crowd as well as a few strangers and former customers from JJs Pub. Some ran over to give me a kiss or a hug or a bottle of water. "Well, well. Isn't somebody popular," Gene said.

"It makes up for a torturous high school experience," I said.

Occasionally, I glanced over at Lakshmi who was trying to smile and wave but she looked irritated and impatient and was shielding her eyes from the bright sun with her hand. It was somewhere around La Cienega when I looked in back of me and saw that she was gone. As usual, Lakshmi Steinmetz had left early.

Jonnie apologized for Lakshmi on Monday to Gene and me. "She wasn't feeling well," Jonnie said.

"Not feeling well?" I asked. "She just disappeared."

"No, she had a headache and felt a little... disrespected. Bad vibes from the volunteers."

I was not feeling well either, overwhelmed by the thought of returning to the kitchen full-time. I had a slowly pulsing headache and my every movement felt weighted with lead. Jeremy was filling in the marker board with the number of the day's clients which had shot up to 417. I would have to bake tomorrow's dessert in three batches. Just the thought of it left me wanting to collapse on the floor and sleep. "When can I get a commercial mixer?" I said to Gene.

"After the fundraiser," he said.

The promise of a fundraiser kept me going for the next few weeks. But I wondered if anything would really change. And I was wondering if I was more than just tired all the time.

I had to man up and consider that I might be infected too.

Chapter 23

"This cannot be right," said the Filipina nurse as she looked at the numbers for my blood pressure. "Let us do again."

She pumped up the constrictor around my arm and watched as the mercury fell. "Oh my, my, my, it was right first time. Eighty-nine over fifty-seven. You sure you alive?" she deadpanned.

With a thermometer in my mouth, I shrugged. She removed the thin glass tube and looked surprised. "Have to try this again too," she said, and waved it before putting it back in my mouth. She waited for a full minute to pass. As she looked at her watch, I remembered my old mantra from when I practiced Transcendental Meditation and repeated it mentally. *Shiama, shiama, shiama...*

"It is ninety-two," she said, raising her eyebrows. "Mild hypothermia. In July. Do you drink a lot?"

"I had hepatitis. Twice," I said. "So I might drink once or twice a month."

"Doctor will be right in."

One of the reasons I respected Dr. Machenbaum aka Dr. Mensch is because he was not the type to overprescribe. He encouraged exercise and activity over antidepressants and recommended healthy bedtime habits over Xanax. He was not inclined to prescribe Valium for anxiety and he refused my request for Ritalin when I learned that a number of successful writers credited it with creative spurts. When drugs were absolutely needed, he gave them to me from a store of samples provided by pharmaceutical reps so I didn't have to pay for them. On Saturday mornings, Dr. Machenbaum called his patients to see how they were feeling — the first time he did that I was in disbelief. On the morning of my hypothermia, I could hear him through the walls in the next room, patiently listening and counseling an elderly man who had a miles-long list of ailments. When the doctor entered my examination room, he smiled as he always did and I felt a little better.

"Nice to see you, Tyler," he said, glancing down at the chart. "What brings you in?"

"Hi, Doctor Machenbaum. I'm just so sickly," I said. "Constantly getting colds I can never shake. I never feel *right* anymore. My body feels like one big ache. I get home from work and just want to lie in bed."

"Your temperature is very low," he said. "That's a sign of exhaustion. I'm going to take a stab here and say you're working too much."

"Definitely," I said. "But it feels like more than fatigue. I'm wondering if this is a swollen lymph node."

I pointed to a lump under my jaw which he probed.

"That feels more like a lipoma but I'm not sure. You've never tested for HIV, correct?"

"Correct."

"It's time you do."

My heart started thumping. I am sure if my blood pressure were taken at that moment it would have been 370 over 360.

"Scary," I said.

"Sure it is. But I think we should run a number of blood tests and include that one. You *are* better off knowing. There are treatments now, preventative measures that can at least delay the onset of AIDS."

"OK," I squeaked.

Jesus Christ — the onset of AIDS.

"It takes two weeks for results. In the meantime, get some rest, get plenty of sleep."

It was a typical, sunny afternoon as I drove home along Wilshire Boulevard with its palm trees swaying in the warm breeze. But I felt like I was trudging for miles down the cold stone steps of a castle's winding staircase to a dungeon full of medieval tortures.

"You did what?" Kyle shouted at me as he gathered costumes and props for his new public-access cable show, *Wake Up You Guys!*

"I got an HIV test," I said. "Dr. Machenbaum said it was time."

"Shouldn't you have talked to me about this?"

"Wait, I need *your* permission to decide what to do for *my* health?"

"If you're positive then I'm positive. The bottoms are always more at risk."

"And your point is?"

"That maybe I don't want to know!"

"I *do* want to know. And so should you. We can't run from this."

Kyle started pacing. He was trembling and his forehead broke out in a sweat. He went outside and lit a cigarette. It was his worrying that really got me worried.

On Monday morning, feeling just a little rested, I looked at the marker board and saw that the client list had climbed to 441. I blinked a few times but the numbers did not change. I soon felt a throbbing in my head and chest.

"Oh my God, oh my God," I said as I slumped and dropped the ties of my apron. Jonnie was filling her coffee cup as Gene unloaded the supply cage.

"What's wrong, Tyler?" Jonnie asked. "You went white!"

"Four hundred and forty-one clients?"

"I know. It's a lot."

"A lot? It's impossible!"

"No, it's not, Tyler, it's…"

"You don't work in the kitchen, Jonnie," I said. "You don't know!"

"Tyler, we can't say no. These are all people in need."

"We *can* say no! We can have a wait list! We can prioritize! What we can't do is serve four hundred and forty one people out of this tiny fucking kitchen with a staff of volunteers!"

The dam on my anger was broken and I was shouting. The alcoholics in the community room had suddenly quieted and were eavesdropping on us instead of the other way around. "Just say no," said someone into the microphone to laughter.

Jonnie came over to me. She put her hand on my arm, locked eyes with mine. "Tyler, you're panicking. Tell us what's *really* going on," she said, playing the therapist.

"This work is too fucking hard!" I said with a choke in my voice. "My doctor told me I work too much!"

"I know it's hard work," she said.

"Not hard, it's exhausting!" I turned to Gene. "Don't tell me you're not completely tired at the end of the day, Gene. Especially since Tim left."

He shrugged his shoulders, made the slightest nod. "It's... not easy," he said.

"Tyler," Jonnie said. "We will get you a raise..."

"After the fundraiser," I said with her in unison. "I know. But it's not just money. It's the workload! I worked in restaurants all through college. And I know I'm doing the work of two or three people. And then, like a janitor, I have to clean up at the end of the day! I haul trash down two flights of stairs four times a day because no one else will do it."

"We'll hire Bryce soon," Gene said. "And we'll get you a commercial mixer and another oven and —"

"We need more than Bryce! We need benefits! An AIDS organization should provide health insurance for its employees! I spent six hundred dollars on tests at the doctor's on Friday! Six hundred dollars I don't have! That's two and a half paychecks! I put it on my credit card, which is nearing its limit! In the meantime, our so-called *executives* are sitting around in comfy chairs in air-conditioned offices."

"But Kyle has money," Gene said. "Can't he help you out?"

"Kyle is a working stiff. And neither of us gets a *stipend* from our parents."

Gene frowned and folded his arms.

"I need to worry about my own health now," I said. "And that may mean leaving this job."

"Tyler," Jonnie asked me, inserting a dramatic silence. "Are you HIV-positive?"

"I don't know," I said. "But I'll know soon. Look, we need to meet with Jacob and Lakshmi, have them come in here once in a while, see what it's like to try and make meals for hundreds in this tiny kitchen."

"Lakshmi is way too busy with the fundraiser," Jonnie said. "And she's finishing her book."

"Then let's at least get Jacob in here. Maybe he could volunteer for an hour, see what the fuck it's like."

"Jacob is busy too. Please, please, hang in there. I will pray for you, Tyler. God is going to get us through."

"I don't know," I said.

Jonnie was quiet, got cutesy and pushed my chin up. "I will give Lakshmi a call, Tyler. I will relay your concerns. And I'm going to ask her to do something else for you, something you deserve. You're coming to the fundraiser, aren't you?"

"Maybe. I just might want a night off, I —"

"Of course you're coming!"

"To bartend?"

Jonnie and Gene chuckled. "No, we've got that covered," she said. "Celestial Objects is on a whole new level! We've got food booths from the best restaurants and drink stations from the liquor companies. I want you and Gene there for something else... I just need to discuss it with Lakshmi first."

"I'll see how I feel," I said. I realized that the Friday before the event would be the day I'd get my test results.

The day of the big event would also be the day that a magazine would finally hit the newsstands with an article about a "new age guru in New York and California," a piece that would send her into a rage.

Saint Bryce, as I started to call him, made the two weeks until Celestial Objects a lot more bearable. His latest gig was house-sitting in the hilly neighborhood of Mount Olympus in a mansion he called "Pseudo-Spanish Brady Bunch." He had to be at the house for showings and keep the place tidy but he was otherwise free to volunteer.

"Bryce! You're back again," I said when he showed up at 8 a.m. on a Tuesday, one of the slowest days for volunteers.

"Of course I did, darling. It gets so boring up on Mount Olympus. The other gods are just so tedious and I like slumming with the mortals. Which reminds me, would you like my recipe for ambrosia? I'm not talking about that dreadful fruit salad with the little rainbow marshmallows, I mean the real thing, the elixir of immortality."

Work and Bryce's humor kept my mind off of my HIV results and that fortnight seemed both interminable and fleeting. On the Friday before the big fundraiser, I asked Kyle to sit with me when I made the call to my doctor at four forty-five. Kyle sat across from me in our living room in a tank top and short shorts as I pressed the numbers into our transparent phone that revealed its circuitry.

"Dr. Machenbaum will call you back," said the receptionist. "Before five."

That didn't sound good. We turned on the television and watched the news in silence. The last clip was about Zsa Zsa Gabor starting her three-day sentence for slapping a cop. As she was escorted to the Beverly Hills jail, faux protestors met her with signs of "Fry Zsa Zsa." Somehow we laughed.

At 5:03, the phone rang.

"Hello?"

"Tyler, it's Dr. Machenbaum. I'm sorry, I —"

I'm sorry?

"I got held up. I did get your HIV results and I am glad to report that they are negative. Negative."

I shook with relief and fell into that combination of quiet sobbing and laughing. Kyle looked panicked, unable to read me until I gave him a thumbs up. His face fell in his palms and he bent over, then sat up and wiped at tears.

"I'm seeing a little more bilirubin in your liver panel than I like," the doctor continued. "That's a lingering effect of the hepatitis but it isn't severe and everything else is fine."

"Thank you so much, Doctor," I said. "Thank you, thank you."

"Have a good weekend, Tyler."

"I will have a fantastic weekend. Same to you."

Kyle was looking in the distance after I howled with relief. I fell to the floor on my knees and shook my fists as if I had finally won Wimbledon.

"What about me?" Kyle said with a tremble in his voice.

"What about you?"

"What if I have it?"

"Why would you if I don't? Unless you're not telling me something. Get a test."

"Why should I?"

"So we can start fucking again without condoms. If you've got one I think we should fuck right now."

The sex that afternoon was a cosmic experience, when all sense of self disappears and only bliss remains, when you are gobsmacked by the endless beauty of the universe. My whole world had transformed. Everything looked clean and brightly colored, like the final scenes of a Disney animation with fireworks going off over a kiss at a wedding.

On Saturday morning, I was supposed to show up at the hangar and learn where I was to stand when Lakshmi would introduce me to the crowd. I took a few volunteers to the airport with me so they could have some experience of an event they had not been invited to nor could they afford. Neither Berto, Hector or Slim had a car, but twice a week, they took the bus from Echo Park to work at Manna. They always stayed until the bitter end to wash pots and pans and mop the floor. I suspected all three were HIV-positive so I kept my good news to myself, but as we merged onto the 10 Freeway, I felt like I was rocketing on a popsicle through a sky filled with cotton candy.

The Santa Monica Airport is not beautiful by any means. It's older than LAX and it's for rich people with private planes. Its hangars are utilitarian structures made of rusty, corrugated metal and its tarmac is old, gray and crumbling. But everything about the airport seemed to sparkle that day and everyone seemed warm and engaging. The exterior of Barker Hangar was decorated with banners featuring vintage Peter Max art. The central banner was a sky full of stars and planets with flying angels in electric robes that scattered neon sprinkles. The walkway to the entry was a rainbow-drenched gauntlet of swallow-tailed pennants. As we walked, I felt like of one of Max's figures that strolled through the sky and rained down flowers with every step.

Jeremy and Joffrey were at the reception booth and organizing guest lists when I arrived with the friends. "How's it going?" I said.

"It's a little crazy," said Jeremy. "Go on in, guys, have a look around but it's hot in there. They just turned on the AC."

"They have AC in a *hangar*?" I asked.

"No, but Lakshmi special ordered it. Insisted on it," Jeremy said. He pointed to some cooling machines connected to diesel batteries with accordion hoses that extended to openings in the hangar's walls.

"She doesn't want anyone sweating," Joffrey said. "That is to say, she doesn't want to be seen sweating."

"Cost a damn fortune," Jeremy said.

The four of us entered and saw a stage had been set up and before it was a clearing where the attendees would stand and later dance. Above the stage was a movie screen and to the sides were some concert speakers. Along the sides of the hangar were booths of many kinds where everyone was at work arranging all the "celestial objects" for sale. Famous interior designers like Bobi

Leonard, Michael Kreiss and Waldo Fernandez were auctioning their services and had created rooms that displayed their different styles. Other booths were full of racks of designer clothing and display cases of jewelry. The most interesting booths had paintings and sculptures from the cities' different galleries and one included works by David Hockney and Don Bacardi who were both scheduled to attend that night. A smallish Hockney acrylic of a backyard filled with agave plants and orange trees had a starting bid of $25,000.

 Per my instructions, I went to the stage and spoke with the stage manager who showed me the bright green mark on the floor where I would stand at 9 p.m. "Be backstage at eight forty-five," he said before returning to caucus with the event planners.

 It was hot in the hangar so the four of us wandered outside in search of water and to take in the food booths and drink tents where caterers were setting up. We stopped at the trailer of one caterer who was providing bottled water and a simple lunch of a green salad and pasta for the event's volunteers. I heard a loud and familiar laugh, and further up, I saw Lakshmi seated on a patch of grass under a shade tree where she was surrounded by dozens of adoring followers. She was smiling and laughing, like it was an ether frolic, and did not sit cross-legged but with her bare, smooth legs to one side and her shoes kicked off. I was in such a good mood I was almost happy to see her — my smile that day could not be wiped from my face. She noticed me but ignored my friends. "Tyler, would you bring me some lunch?" she shouted to me. Surrounded by devotees, she was basking in their adoration and unwilling to interrupt her bliss.

She had to notice my face go dark as soon as she asked. I was offended that there was no "hi" or "how are you" or acknowledgment that I was with others.

"I'd get it myself," she said apologetically. "But I've taken my shoes off."

I nodded my head. I walked back to the caterer and filled a paper plate and grabbed some plastic utensils. I wasn't sure why it had pissed me off but realized that this was how she saw me, as a someone who would do for her.

I brought her the plate in silence. "Thank you," she said mirroring my own stern expression before returning to her petting zoo.

I'm not sure when she read Diane Toussaint's Vanity Fair article, but it was definitely before the show got started.

*

I dropped the volunteers off at the tiny bungalow they rented in Echo Park and went home to walk Holden and to shower and change. Holden had been lonelier since the passing of Luna and I wanted to talk to Kyle about getting him a companion for those evenings when neither of us would be home for hours. Kyle was performing with the Comedy Omelette that night and couldn't attend Celestial Objects until later if at all. He likely wouldn't be there when I would be the one on stage, getting a little recognition, and that was perfectly fine as I had little investment in this token gesture. I wanted fair labor practices and health insurance and instead what Lakshmi and Johnnie had offered was a few minutes of attention; they had thrown me a chewed-on, meatless bone. At Jonnie's urging, Lakshmi would introduce Gene as the Executive Chef and then me with my new title of Second Executive Chef. This would happen after she introduced Jacob Hellman and film producer Aaron Sibley as Heavenly Heroes. Gene and I were doing the work for shit money and no benefits, but it was Jacob and Aaron who were the heroes.

Gene had told me to wear a suit, something I didn't own, or at least a sports coat. The only sports coat I owned was a vintage Don Loper from the 1950s, something I bought at Aaardvark's Odd Ark for ten dollars. It was twill with flecks and had padded shoulders, velvet elbow patches and was very Ricky Ricardo from the episodes that took place in Hollywood. I would wear it with some cuffed slacks from the same era and a pair of black wingtips. I showered and worked up my pompadour to its tallest with a few dabs of Brylcreem. When I got out of the bathroom, I saw the flashing light on the answering machine.

"Tyler, sweetums, it's Bryce," he said. "I have some *must* reading for you. The Vanity Fair article is out and *someone* is going to be shitting a hot crowbar."

I walked Holden to the newsstand at the end of the street, bought the magazine and read the article before I got in my car. I was struck by the splash photo of Lakshmi. It was a glamour shot that depicted her as a sex kitten. She was heavily made up with deep red lipstick on a pouty mouth and rouge to heighten her cheekbones. She looked straight into the camera with eyes dramatized by mascara and she was wearing a Hustler pink skirt suit with an open jacket to reveal a black, lace-trimmed camisole. On her feet were some expensive-looking, snakeskin heels and extending from her short, hiked-up skirt were her legs, pulled up and prettily splayed across a dark cushion. It was a good, flattering shot but intriguingly dark and more than a little, well... *slutty*. If she were busty and naked, it could have been a pose for a Playboy centerfold. The photographer, a woman, may have pushed this image to coincide with the content of the article, but clearly, Lakshmi wanted to be seen as an object of desire. It was a provocative photo and by no means a dignified portrait of an "authority." She looked evil, like Joan Collins as Alexis Carrington.

The title was "Lakshmi of Los Angeles Loves You." The summary below it in smaller type read: "Lakshmi Steinmetz is the latest guru to the stars, a new age Mother Theresa doing good works for people with AIDS — but some wonder if her real ambition is to be the biggest star of all."

And bingo was his name-o!

The article was not a puff piece but a good piece of writing that was thoroughly researched and accurate. It detailed Lakshmi's rise from struggling actress and singer to the most prominent authority on *The Way of the Miraculous,* someone who offered "spirituality and a loving God" during the hopelessness of the AIDS crisis. Toussaint described *The Way* as "an alternative to the religions that condemn homosexuality but something that comes from out of them. It is a syncretic belief system that uses terms from Judaism and Christianity but is infused with the mystical traditions and philosophies of the East."

Like so many gay men, Lakshmi, when she was Miriam Steinmetz, described herself as a "hot ball of self-loathing" someone who spent the 70's in a "purple haze of drugs and sex" and wandered from "job to job, city to city and man to man." Deeply unhappy and without direction, she suffered a debilitating depression after the dissolution of a "marriage that was over before the honeymoon began." Years later, after another fizzled romance, an ex gave her a copy of *The Way of the Miraculous*. "It was a consolation gift, a peace offering. The first time I read it, it was like a seed had been planted. When I reread it a year later, the seed had become a fruit-bearing tree. I saw my path clearly now, and knew my life's work was to spread the gospel of *The Way*."

So far I hadn't read anything that Lakshmi hadn't mentioned in the confessional portions of the cassettes that Jonnie had given me. Toussaint described Lakshmi's constant activity: her presiding over funeral rituals, as an officiant at celebrity weddings, and her work as an unofficial counselor to couples and others. But like most articles about controversial people, the story would build her up before it took her down.

Only one person on the West Coast spoke critically of Lakshmi, but New York was quite another thing. I read, to some surprise, that the Being Center of Manhattan was a place of strife and chaos and about to go under — that was news to all of us in California. Unlike in Los Angeles, the celebrities and board members of the NY Center resisted Lakshmi's insertion of God and prayer into their organization. She had fought bitterly with its director, Shannon O'Dea, an actress of note.

Lakshmi had attempted to oust Shannon and had fired another employee facing his own life-threatening illness which deprived him of health insurance benefits at the worst possible time. "Lakshmi Steinmetz is no less than a monster," said one Manhattan

Center employee who would not give his or her name. "She's utterly incompetent, irresponsible with money and goes into a rage when she doesn't get her way. She has no idea how to run an organization and relies on prayers instead of practical measures. Steinmetz has never understood the day-to-day operation of the Center, and her occasional drop-ins here only make things worse. She's jealous of Shannon and can't stand that she gets the credit she deserves and the love of the clients we serve. Steinmetz wants all the love and attention for herself and she can't share power. She may have her board members in LA under her thumb because they're all students of *The Way*, but we're independent in New York. I used to attend her lectures but now I see her as nothing more than a narcissistic hypocrite."

Donors, board members, a fabled film director and his TV journalist wife had already transferred their support from the Being Center to a new organization, one led by O'Dea. "Shannon took her Rolodex and the client and volunteer lists with her," said the unidentified employee. "Without any data, that left the Center a shell of itself."

That sounded familiar.

The article continued with a series of interviews with some show business shoguns who predicted that Lakshmi would soon be on the cover of Time and Newsweek and would be the next big thing, a household word, someone who could "monetize this blend of new age and Christianity." One nameless but "powerful" talent agent said Lakshmi would give "rise to a new religion," a notion that Lakshmi had to dismiss as both a criticism and as being in conflict with the principles of *The Way*. She was compared to Aimee Semple McPherson who had created a new sect of Christianity and also had a penchant for romantic pursuits of younger men. "I don't discuss my love life. And God put me here to lead a social revolution, not to start a new religion," Lakshmi said. "To overturn hatred as our leading dynamic and replace it with peace and love."

"Now that is just a slightly immodest statement," I said out loud.

The article continued with some critiques I welcomed of *The Way* from religious and philosophy scholars who punctured its very premise as being a message from Jesus, a prophecy. One expert on modern religions and cults concluded it was "just the latest California hokum that would be supplanted soon by some other fad." Another called it out as "Nothing new. The idea that the world is all *maya,* an illusion, can be found in religious movements in America and California in the late 1800s like New Thought. *The Way* is a regurgitation of pop psychology and Eastern mysticism with a generous sprinkling of twelve-step programs."

The piece ended with one of Lakshmi's West Coast allies making a backhanded defense of her, film producer Aaron Sibley, who I would be sharing a stage with soon. I remember him, just happening to show up at the kitchen as if he were a volunteer, when Lakshmi was giving Diane Toussaint a tour. Diane had invited Aaron to sit at the edge of the community room's stage where he spoke into the mic of her cassette deck. Now I was learning what he'd said and was imagining that Lakshmi's eyebrows were on fire when she read it.

Aaron recalled partying with Lakshmi on Fire Island in the 70's. "It was in the days before AIDS when she was a...an honorary gay man who snorted poppers and danced until dawn or the blow ran out, whichever came first. Back then, as now, Lakshmi wanted to be loved, to be adored, to be powerful and famous. She tried to sing, she thought she could act, but she realized that a career in show business was just not in the tarot cards. She had to find something and she did when she found *The Way of the Miraculous*. And it was good timing — she found *The Way* when gay people needed a miracle. Lakshmi's made a place for herself as a modern-day shaman. She gives to the community and in return she gets what she's always needed: to be a star, to be loved, to be famous. She's not as venal as Tammy Faye Baker. She's more like Mother Theresa with a taste for Dior and Dolce Gabbana."

Oops.

Aaron had stated the obvious... and what would Lakshmi think of that? I was about to find out.

Chapter 24

The event was crowded by eight o'clock. David Hockney and his entourage arrived, led by his young lover, the bushy-browed Bing, who was wearing a headset and making a path for him. "Make way for Hockney," Bing shouted and the crowd did. Just behind Hockney was the portrait artist Don Bachardy, making a more quiet entry after chaining his bicycle to a pole inside. I ran into Gene who was wearing a black suit and holding a glass of white wine as he watched a slideshow of staff and volunteers dissolving on the screen.

"That's what you're wearing?" he said. "You should have worn a suit."

"I don't own a suit," I said. "Maybe I could afford one if I got a stipend."

Gene smirked. "Maybe you could."

"Besides," I said. "Isn't it a little hot for wool?"

"Just a little. Go get yourself a cool drink. We're supposed to be backstage at eight forty-five, Mr. Ricardo. By the way, where's Lucy?"

"She's performing tonight. Maybe coming later. So... did you read it?"

"Of course I did."

"How's she doing?"

"We don't know. She's gone dark. She'll show up a minute before she's due."

Just then, Aaron Sibley walked past us, ignoring us, in the company of yet another new personal assistant who nodded as Aaron barraged him with a stream of questions. Aaron had a type when it came to assistants: young, pale and nervous-looking with funny eyeglasses.

"Looks like Aaron's got a new slave," I said. "Why bring your assistant to a fundraiser?"

"Who else would go with him?"

"Right. You read what he said about Lakshmi."

Gene smirked. "Well, he knows her from way back."

"Why is he being honored tonight? Sibley's a 'Heavenly Hero?'"

"Don't you know?"

"No."

"Aaron's the one who got the money from Tony Fursten to pay off Jericho, money so we didn't have to close."

"Tony Fursten? The studio head?"

"Yes, Trillionaire Tony. He's here somewhere... but not with that phony-baloney princess he married."

I took a look around. "Tony Fursten kept us open?"

"Yes. Aaron and Tony had a thing a long time ago," Gene continued. "They used to rent a house on Fire Island. Aaron's got quite the snake and then there was this other snake, a real one, a defanged cobra that they brought out at parties and, well, you can guess what got shoved down its mouth and what it got shoved into. Tony's the one who put Aaron into the Betty Ford Center when he was cuckoo for cocoa puffs."

"Cocoa puffs?"

"Nose candy. Miami snow. Bolivian marching powder."

"Right."

Now I understood how Sibley was able to get green lights on all his derivative and mediocre movies. Suddenly, I wanted a drink.

"I think a cocktail might be just what the doctor ordered," I said.

"They're free," Gene said. "Get a couple. I know you're always in search of a bargain. See you backstage, Ricky. Maybe later you could sing "Babalu." Did you bring your congas?"

"It's conga," I said. "Singular, not plural."

I was standing in line at the Finlandia booth with its giant ice sculptures of clashing stags when I noticed someone taking a warm brie and chutney pastry cup from a caterer's tray. He was about to eat it when he noticed me and smiled. From his bald head and short, squat body, I realized it was Tony Fursten, and strangely, he was all by himself. I imagined him with his dick in the mouth of a defanged cobra and smiled back. We'd never met before, but I held some resentment for him. Fursten was the one who had kiboshed my script *Sleepless Nights* after a series of hopeful meetings and an attached director and star. He mistook my smile as an invitation and walked over after dumping his finger food in the trash.

"You're cute," he said offering his hand for a shake.

"Thank you."

"I'm Tony."

"I, I know who you are. I'm... I'm Tyler," I stammered.

"Are you an actor, Tyler?"

"No," I said. "I'm a writer, a screenwriter. But currently I'm one of the chefs at Manna."

"Oh really," he said, his smile broadening.

"Yes, I've got to get backstage soon," I said. "They're introducing us."

He reached into his coat pocket and pulled out a card. "That's my private number," he said with a smile. "Nice to meet you, Tyler."

I was stunned. One of the most powerful men in Hollywood had just given me his number. My heart started racing — not from a rush of sexual attraction, but from the excitement of advancing my career. I looked at the card and hallucinated that its edges were trailing strings— strings that were attached to Tony Fursten's ass.

"Thank you," I said and nervously rushed off as I stuffed the card in my pocket.

The lights dimmed and the crisp, artificially deep voice of a local disc jockey filled the hangar. "Ladies and gentlemen, please welcome to the stage, the executive director of operations for Manna from Heaven, Jonnie Lindley!"

Jonnie stepped out, her hair in an updo and wearing full-length culottes of embroidered silk and a blouse that made the most of her bosomy assets.

"Thank you all *so much* for coming! We are so honored by your presence," she said as some recorded music started. "This is a song I wrote called 'One Door Closes.'"

I had never really heard Jonnie sing before. She was good. She was a little sharp at times, but she sank into her performance and connected to her feelings. The song's lyrics borrowed heavily from Alexander Graham Bell as well as some other pop standards, but the music had a honeyed sadness that captured the audience, me included. The lyrics spoke of the ups and downs of life and especially of a life in show business.

> One door closes
> One door opens
> Regrets, I've quite a few
> Glory fades and
> Glory blossoms
> We're old but think we're new.
>
> One door closes
> One door opens
> Life takes another turn
> Stages full of
> Sights and wonders
> And hopes that crash and burn.
>
> Time to rise up
> Spread my wings
> Shake the ashes free
> Like a phoenix
> Born in fire
> To seek new victory.

One door closes
One door opens
The days are slipping by
The laurels crumble
Sometimes I stumble
But I'll give it one more try.

One door closes
One door opens
At least, it's open now
The day will come
When one door closes
And we take our final bow
We take our final bow.

The audience applauded loud and long. "Thank you, thank you," Jonnie said with a little laugh, chuffed to have connected with everybody. "We can't forget why we're here tonight. We're here for our clients. And here to introduce you to a few of them, we are honored to present the work of photographer Damien Trembley."

The lights got darker and some somber cello music accompanied a stark series of black-and-white photographs projected on the screen above the stage. All of them were men with AIDS, shirtless, and photographed from the chest up with the telltale signs of lipodystrophy and the dark splotches of Kaposi's sarcoma. Most of them had the gauntness of wasting syndrome and all were depicted as what they were: ill and dying. One of them I knew from my deliveries, a former dancer on *The Carol Burnett*

Show who was devastated when his incontinent cat had to be taken from him and put to sleep. I looked at my watch and realized I needed to get backstage.

I climbed the steps to the waiting area where Gene, Jacob and Aaron Sibley were looking at the photos on a TV monitor. I looked over at Damien Trembley who was in the company of a short, chubby man with a shaved head that I realized was his partner, Sir Albert Neumeister, a director who had won an Academy Award for my very favorite movie. The two had met years ago in Andy Warhol's Factory when Damien was doing the actual work of photographing celebrities and then silk-screening over their images with tints before Warhol signed them.

"And here he is, please welcome Damien Trembley," Jonnie said when the portraits concluded. I watched on the monitor as Damien went out to take a bow to steady but subdued applause.

"What the hell was *that*?" I heard and we looked away from the monitor to see Lakshmi had arrived backstage.

"What the hell was *what*?" said Neumeister in his English accent as he stepped toward Lakshmi. She looked at him, flustered, and was perhaps unsure of who he was.

"That was depressing!" she shouted. "Absolutely grim! We're trying to raise money here!"

Damien returned from the stage, having overheard Lakshmi and seeing the shocked look on Albert's face. "What's the problem?" Damien asked.

"It appears Ms. Steinmetz did not care for your photographs," said Albert.

"No, I did not. Who approved this?" she asked, looking at the stage manager with his clipboard. He shrugged his shoulders. "I thought we weren't doing this!" she hissed.

"And just what was wrong with them?" Damien asked, cocking his head with an angry smile.

"They were depressing! We're trying to get people to open their checkbooks, not reach for their Prozac."

"Of course they're depressing!" Damien shouted. "They're people with AIDS! AIDS is depressing! That was the idea, Lakshmi, to remind people of who we're helping!"

Jonnie had just introduced Antoinette Rosamond, the world's most famous actress turned HIV activist, and the audience was giving her a long round of applause.

"They already know who they're helping!" Lakshmi shouted over the noise. "This is supposed to be a fun evening!"

"Oh, it has been glorious fun!" said Damien. "I've never had more fun in my life!"

"I cannot say we feel very appreciated at the moment," said Neumeister. "And we're so very sorry you were unhappy with your depiction in Vanity Fair."

The two men glowered at her before they turned and walked off. Antoinette was addressing the crowd when Lakshmi turned and looked at the four of us. She locked eyes with Aaron Sibley and clenched her teeth as her eyes slit. She stomped toward him in a pair of heels encrusted with rhinestones and almost stood under him since he was a good foot taller.

"Hi... Lakshmi," he said with a weak smile.

"What the hell was that about?" she asked.

"I don't know. I had nothing to do with it."

"I'm not talking about those pictures. I'm talking about what you said to Vanity Fair. Here we are, honoring you! And this is how you talk about me? To the press?"

"Darling, I thought you'd be pleased with it. I was —"

"Don't you 'darling' me. How could I be pleased with what you said?" she shout-whispered. "You've insulted and embarrassed me!"

"I did no such thing!"

"You made it sound like I was some talentless failure who had to resort to some flaky spirituality so I could finally get famous, someone *desperate* to be loved and adored. You called me a shaman!"

"So?"

"So? *So?* I am a serious person, Aaron! You made me sound like fame is all I care about! And in return for my *service* I get to wear some designer labels? And you practically called me a fag hag!"

"I did not!"

"Yes, you did — you called me an 'honorary gay man.' I've heard you use that expression before and then laugh and tell people it's a nice name for 'fag hag.'"

"You're distorting this, Miriam, I was simply —"

"*Do not call me Miriam!*" she almost shouted, aware that she might be heard beyond the stage. "The whole thrust of this vicious article is that I'm some crazy bitch obsessed with fame, someone who throws tantrums when she doesn't get her way!"

Aaron was staring at her, blinking in silence, when he got the same thought we all had — that at this very moment, Lakshmi

Steinmetz was a crazy bitch throwing a tantrum. Aaron started to smile and then he laughed, covering his mouth. Lakshmi made a guttural, mewling sound as she trembled. "Fuck you, Aaron!" she shouted and then stomped away. I looked at the monitor and saw that Antoinette had stopped speaking, and was looking behind her, waiting for the backstage to quiet before she resumed. Jonnie, looking perplexed, ran after Lakshmi as she descended the stairs.

"Lakshmi!" Jonnie stage-whispered. "You're next! You're supposed to go out and introduce the Heavenly Heroes."

"I can't do it," she said. "You'll have to do it for me."

Jonnie's eyes darted back and forth. Antoinette had finished her speech and left the podium to thunderous applause. The music to introduce Lakshmi had started, and strangely, it was a lesbian folk version of "Down by the Riverside."

"What do I do? What do I do?" Jonnie said to herself.

"Just go out there," said the stage manager. "Say what she was going to say."

I looked at the monitor. The stage was empty and I could hear the audience murmuring. "OK, OK," Jonnie said and took a few calming breaths. "Gentlemen, hit your marks."

The four of us followed Jonnie out and I stood over an X of green tape at the far end of the stage. Aaron was doing his best to smile and I was able to grin my brightest when I thought of him with a defanged cobra coiling and uncoiling with its mouth clamped on his cock.

"We'd like to honor these four men tonight, our Heavenly Heroes of Manna for their selfless service," Jonnie sang into the mic.

Wow! Gene and I were heavenly heroes after all.

"First, please welcome film producer Aaron Sibley who —"

Jonnie stopped speaking. There was a loud hubbub in the crowd. In the audience, close to the stage, I could see Damien and Sir Albert inside a circle of others that included Hockney and Don Bachardy as well as the designer Waldo Fernandez with his friend, the songwriter Carol Bayer Sager. They were ignoring Jonnie as they listened to Damien ranting about what had happened to him. "This is a disgrace," Damien shouted. "She's behaved like a complete bitch. We're leaving!" The hangar had quieted and the crowd parted as Damien and Neumeister walked out, their footsteps the only sound. Hockney and his entourage were watching them leave.

Jonnie did her best, smiling and nervously laughing as she continued. "He was heroic when we needed a hero, please welcome film producer Aaron Sibley." Aaron shrugged his shoulders and mugged for the crowd as he stepped forward to the applause. He had broken out in a sweat and his hair had dampened and clung to his forehead in a dark flap. Next, Jacob was introduced as "The hero who raised the first twelve thousand dollars for Manna and since then done so much more." Gene and I were described as "two tireless chefs who inspire our volunteers and delight our clients with their culinary creations." Jonnie had forgotten to introduce Gene as "the executive chef" and I could see that it miffed him. The audience was asked to applaud for all four of us but it was obvious to everyone that something had happened — the room had gone rancid and rumors were spreading in contagious whispers.

The stage manager stepped behind Jonnie and whispered in her ear. "Oh," she said, looking surprised. "And now, will you please welcome the founder and chief executive officer of Manna from Heaven and the Being Centers of Los Angeles and New York, Ms. Lakshmi Steinmetz!"

Gene and I looked at each other as the audience welcomed Lakshmi. "Not like she'd ever give up a chance to be on stage," he said to me behind his cupped hand.

Lakshmi stomped out in her aspect as the stern, reprimanding mother. Starting from stage left, she marched to the podium at stage right. She had picked a cloud white skirt suit, suitable for summer, and her sparkling pumps matched the glittering pendant of her necklace and their matching earrings. She nodded in that grim way as if we were her children who had disobeyed and disappointed her but were doing a little better.

"Thank you, thank you all," she said. "It is because of all of you that Manna from Heaven exists and we are able to serve our clients. How very blessed we are to be the ones who can give. And how blessed are we when we are the ones who are able to forgive others," she continued in a not-so-veiled reference to her grievances that day. "We cannot know peace, we cannot return to God's love until we can offer forgiveness to those who have offended us, a task which can be as painful as the offense itself. But one step in reaching that forgiveness is forgiving ourselves when *we* can't easily forgive, when *we* need God's help in bringing us to that state of grace where *we*, can once again, be generous."

Lakshmi looked over at Aaron, briefly, as he struggled to maintain a flat expression.

"Human beings, myself included, can never achieve perfection," she continued. "But we can be better, we can strive, we can overcome our egos. And one way we do that is to teach others what we most need to learn."

Her words, as usual, were making some kind of sense and rooted in the circular pseudo-logic of *The Way*. And maybe this was an apology? I had to agree she was teaching others what she needed to learn, or rather, to implement.

"And now I would like to ask you for *your* generosity," she continued. "I'm asking you to put yourself first by putting others first. I know that *all* of you will help, and will help yourselves in the process. Thank you."

It was one of the shortest speeches she had ever given. A moment later, a DJ started his set with Black Box's "Everybody, Everybody," but no one took to dancing. Lakshmi had slipped away early, as usual, and I went to get some smoked salmon pizza from the Spago booth. The revved-up crowd was supposed to return to the booths and up their bids in the silent auctions, but a lot of people were filtering out. As I descended from the stage, Kevin Darrington was there to meet me wearing a summer suit of ivory linen that made his tan look deeper, his hair look blonder and his eyes look bluer.

"Hello, Tyler," he said through his infectious smile.

"Why, Kevin Darrington, how are you?"

"Never better. I just had to tell you how handsome you looked up there."

"Right back atcha," I said. "You want to get a drink?"

"I thought you'd never ask."

We stood in line at the Bombay Gin tent and were greeted by someone dressed as Queen Victoria. She gave us a haughty nod and cooled herself with an antique fan of tortoiseshell and mother of pearl.

"So just what happened back there?" Kevin asked me as we got our gin on the rocks.

I looked both ways before speaking. "You didn't hear it from me but... Lakshmi Steinmetz is a malicious bitch. And if someone doesn't stop her, she's going to destroy this organization."

He covered his mouth as he snickered. "So... tell me how you really feel?"

I was filling him in on the VF article and what had happened backstage when Kyle found me. He was wearing his yellow jacket with a metallic sheen and a bolo tie with a clasp of a Colt revolver.

"Well well, Kyle, how are you?" Kevin said. "I was just asking Tyler where you were."

"I had a show," Kyle said.

"A show! Glad to hear you're still trotting it out!"

"I don't have any choice," Kyle said. "Showbiz or nothing."

"Then best of luck with... or rather, break a leg with all that. Say, I just noticed Jonathan Pringle over there and he'll be upset with me if I don't catch him up on the offers on his place. Great to see you both. Tyler, we'll talk soon — I mean that."

"We need to," I said before he walked away.

"So he's doing well," Kyle said, taking a sip of my drink.

"He's doing spectacularly," I said.

"If you're talking about money. I'd rather fail in showbiz than succeed in real estate."

"And that's why we're together, Kyle. How was *your* show?"

"Good. Audience was a little dead. They don't laugh much when it's hot. How did *this* go?"

"Um, not so well. But I got Tony Fursten's phone number."

I showed him the card and he was shocked into silence.

"Tony Fursten? For real?"

"For real."

"Are you gonna call him?"

"I don't *think* so!" I said, scoffing. "Anything he'd do for me would have strings attached to his chunky butt. And I already have a boyfriend. Don't I?"

"Maybe he'd like the two of us," Kyle said with a grin.

"I can't imagine having sex in such a... transactional way. And with him it would be like trying to fuck a rock pile."

"Lots of people have fucked a lot worse than rock piles to get ahead. He's a big bottom, from what I've read. He goes through something like a guy a year and when he gets tired of them, he kicks them out then buys them a condo."

What Kyle was saying was true — we knew one of Tony's cast-offs at the kitchen, a beautiful young man named Slater who looked like a blond surfer and occasionally volunteered. Bryce referred to him as "the Catamite."

I looked at Tony's card again and thought about throwing it away but I stuffed it back in my pocket.

On Monday when I arrived at the kitchen, it was already hot, sunny and stuffy. Jonnie looked worried as she took her phone out of the rolling cage and unwound its cord.

"What's the matter?" I asked.

"Oh, good morning, Tyler," she said, her face grim.

"It's not a good morning. Something's wrong," I said just as Gene arrived.

"I'm not going to lie. The receipts from the fundraiser were disappointing," she said. "We made about a third of what we expected and expenses were higher than projected. Don't ask me what it cost to air condition that hangar!"

"So we won't be getting raises," Gene said.

"Or benefits or a new kitchen," I added.

Jonnie just sighed.

Somehow, someway, I determined I would finish my screenplay. I decided that the float the characters were building in *The Sugar Parade* would be destroyed by fire before they rebuilt it — that would be much more dramatic than the bad guys wrecking it. And if my agent could sell it, I'd leave this damn hot kitchen and its New Age junkies and what I came to think of as Manna from Hell. After we served turkey tetrazinni, I went to work on no-bake cookies to avoid keeping the ovens on when Jonnie rushed into the kitchen with a look of panic.

"Gene, Tyler! Lakshmi's called a meeting for this afternoon. She needs everyone there."

Chapter 25

Staffs of both the Being Center as well as Manna from Heaven were packed into the reception room with some having to stand behind the couches: a gathering audience for the Lakshmi show. Julie Sainsbury was there as well as the "upstairs people" who included the bookkeepers, payroll guy, the facilities manager, as well as the women that scheduled house cleanings and massages for people with AIDS. The last to join us was Elissa, the woman who went to the clients when they were in their final hours to say goodbye, the loneliest ones who had no friends or family, and as usual, she looked to be grieving. We were whispering our concerns — was it all crashing down, like the Being Center in New York? From upstairs we could hear Lakshmi on the phone and she was loud as usual, but she wasn't shouting. Her door was open and she sounded in a good mood, chuckling between breathy exclamations. "Well, of course!" she said, "That's exciting! One door closes, one door opens... love you too."

At 5:31 she trotted down the stairs in flats and workout clothes. Without a smidge of makeup she somehow looked younger and her skin was pink and radiant. Jacob followed her down and stood in back of her as she clasped her hands under her chin.

"Everyone, I have some excellent news to share." She paused again, milking the moment, chuckling to herself when she threw out her hands.

"My book is being published! Through Random House!" she said.

Jonnie, Gene and Julie gasped in awe, their mouths turned to big Os. Jonnie started some applause — it seemed impolite for the rest of us not to clap too. She went to Lakshmi and hugged her and the two of them rocked in each other's arms before they broke away and laughed then cried. Gene had that look on his face where his mouth was stiffly upturned in a smile, but his eyes were dead — he was pierced with an ice-cold spear of envy.

"Thank you, thank you," Lakshmi said as Jonnie returned to her seat. "I know this wasn't what you were expecting to hear from me today. I'm leaving for New York tomorrow and then I'll be working with an editor on a rewrite and after that there will be a tour and book signings etcetera, etcetera. But I assure you I am leaving you in good hands and I will be checking in. Jacob?"

Jacob nodded and gave us one of his Mr. Toad grins. "First, I want to take this moment to thank all of you for making Celestial Objects a success. And it *was* a success," he said. "But the one thing that's true about money is that as soon as you get some, you need to get more. We've renewed our search for a permanent director and are homing in on a few candidates. We are *not* neglecting your concerns and we *are* here for you."

So how did I feel knowing Lakshmi was getting published? I didn't feel anything except miffed that I had to drive in traffic to hear about it and drive in more traffic to get home.

August in LA is my least favorite month with its long, hot days and blinding sunshine. It also has the worst traffic, courtesy of tourists driving around Hollywood with maps to the stars' homes or sitting in open-air buses to glimpse Morgan Fairchild's star on the Walk of Fame. The movie studios dump their shittiest movies in August and boredom sits on the land like an obese, sweaty monster that squashes everything. We wait for school and dances and football games to start, the appearance of Halloween decorations, and the start of the new fall season of television.

In the cool, early mornings before I left for the kitchen, I worked for an hour on polishing *The Sugar Parade*. On the first of September, my self-appointed deadline, I brought twenty copies of it to my agent. She would send it out after Labor Day when "the town" returned from Maui, Provence and the Hamptons. I was experienced enough at that point not to have any expectations and told almost no one about it except a few friends who had read it and gave me notes. I did not attempt to use the "law of attraction" by "seeing my success" and did not go shopping for a new car or a house as a part of that process. I will admit that I checked out *The Rocky Horoscope* in the *LA Weekly,* a titillating astrology column tailored to the hopes of those who struggled in showbiz. My horoscope, as always, was a mixed message: "Trust in your instincts and your own unique perspective. And remember, the Sistine Chapel was painted over seven years while the Starry Night was painted in an afternoon. In some way, you will celebrate something. Don't trip on your cape."

It was not because I hadn't made a visualization board that Shelley called me a week later to say that everyone had passed on my script. The last two holdouts had "loved the writing" but the hesitation was that it was passé, that it was too much like a teen comedy and that era was over. And it was. John Hughes, among others, was no longer making teen comedies. Teens had gone to the small screen in *Beverly Hills 90210* and other shows like it.

But like the temperature in the kitchen that summer, the client count at Manna kept climbing. We had completely run out of storage space but neither Gene nor Jonnie refused the bags and boxes of kitchen odds and ends that people still brought us, stuff like chipped jars of purple horseradish, dusty boxes of My-T-Fine pudding and generic cans of peas and carrots. We began to store supplies as well as donated food in the backstage wings of the community room's stage until the church janitor put a kibosh on that — the homeless were sneaking in to steal it, and worse, they were fighting over it.

The hotter it got, the fewer volunteers we had and that left us with long afternoons that stretched to the evenings. Even Bryce had to back away when the house he was sitting got sold. He took a temp job filling in as private chef to Antoinette Rosamond and made her the English dishes she ate as a child including toad-in-the-hole, shepherd's pie and a suet pudding with the provocative name of spotted dick. He also made her chili from a guarded recipe (she had paid a restaurateur thousands of dollars for it with the promise to keep it secret) that infamously had been flown on a jet to her when she was filming in Turkey in 1960. "You didn't hear it from me," Bryce told me on the phone. "But next time you make chili, add half a bar of Cadbury dark."

I wanted to serve the clients but the work at Manna was just too grueling and my debts were piling up. I was pondering going back to script reading and bartending or maybe returning to an old job in postproduction, something that would give me flextime. I could see if anyone I knew was still at Central Casting and find work again as an extra. And some restaurant somewhere needed a waiter, but I felt too old for that — waiting tables in Los Angeles is for people in their twenties awaiting their big break. And if someone told me they wanted their "dressing on the side," I might just throw it in their face.

Where had the years gone?

September in Los Angeles is even hotter than August when the devil winds, the Santa Anas, blow in. I got home from work on one Wednesday and had to wait until shadows fell on the sidewalk before I could take Holden on a walk that wouldn't burn his paws. We returned just as the phone was ringing.

"Tyler St. George, it's Kevin Darrington! How are you?"

"Well, ya know, Kevin, I'm OK when I count my blessings."

"You have too many to enumerate."

"It's true. I have a fridge full of food, a mostly working car, a good dog and an indoor toilet. Who am I to complain?"

"And you have Kyle."

"Who?"

"Kyle!"

"Oh, you mean that guy who keeps his clothes here. I think his name's Kyle."

He chuckled. "You sound tired, Tyler."

I sighed.

"It's nothing I want to talk about. It's my fault if I don't find a more reasonable job."

"About that. Let's see if we can't make Manna from Heaven a little more reasonable."

"And how would we do that?"

"Jacob may have told you we have a few people interested in the directorship. One of them is qualified but he's a little too good-looking."

"*Too* good -looking?"

"He's a former mayor, Harvard-educated, with a masters in municipal administration. He's also known for some nude photographs taken in the late 70's when he was Chad Morrow."

"Chad Morrow?"

"Yes. A cover model for Stallion magazine, issue number seventeen, their bestseller ever. It's still on sale in every gay bookstore in America. You can get your own copy at A Different Light."

"Wait. You're talking about Robert Bravermann — he was mayor of West Hollywood."

"Yes, as well as Tom of Finland's favorite model. He's still hot as a habanero but what's actually important is that he knows everybody. He knows how this little city of WeHo works because he helped create it. And he has connections from when he worked at LA City Hall. There's only one little problem."

"What's that?"

"Well, two problems. Robert is just... distracting. It's difficult for one not to reach into his pants and revel in what's in there even as he's going through the rigorous details of a business plan. But, seriously, the other thing is that he's not a student of *The Way*."

"So he's smart."

"Very smart. He's got an IQ as big as his cock."

"Who's the other candidate?"

"One of Lakshmi's lackeys, a certain Mr. Edgar Shrimpton. He's a former dancer and an administrator for a ballet company and maybe he could raise some money. But he wouldn't know what the fudge he's doing. In his favor, Lakshmi knows him and likes him because he thinks she's God. But Bravermann's got something else in *his* favor."

"What's that?"

"Jacob Hellman's got a crush on him. He's been stroking off to issue seventeen since 1979."

October was too soon to be roasting turkeys, but Gene had done it for the second time that month.

"Gene, could we please wait on roasting turkeys until the weather turns?" I said when we finally got to mopping, rushing through it to make a five o'clock meeting at the Center. "It takes hours and it's still fricking hot in here."

"But it's popular. And it's cheap."

"Is it popular? Unless it's dark meat, turkey is kinda dry and tasteless. And I hate that lumpy gravy."

"It's comfort food. It's what the clients want."

"Please. Let's wait until Thanksgiving. People with low blood pressure don't tolerate heat well. Can I get a ride with you to the meeting?"

"What's wrong with your car?"

"Nothing. It's just that yours has air conditioning. I'm really looking forward to the meeting today."

"Why?"

"Because the Center has AC."

"All right, Tyler. I get it. No more roast turkey until the weather turns."

"What's this meeting about?"

"I believe we are meeting the new executive director."

"We *are*?"

"Apparently. Lakshmi's Ouija board said 'yes.' She called Jacob from New York and gave him the go-ahead. It's Robert Bravermann."

A few weeks before, after talking to Kevin, I was passing by A Different Light and went in to see if it was true that issue 17 of Stallion was always for sale in the magazine section. It was — there was a stack of them with a banner that read "Twelfth Edition." The original issue date was from over ten years ago and the man on the front had a hairstyle from the era, longer and over the ears with sideburns. Regardless, "Chad Morrow" was indisputably beautiful. He was as handsome as Tom Selleck in his Chaz commercials and like him, Chad had a brushy mustache atop a full mouth and straight white teeth when he smiled. In a close up picture, Chad's eyes were described as "cornflower blue" but they were more jewel-like with the intensity of lapis lazuli and radiating striations of turquoise and aquamarine.

As for the rest of his face, he had high and wide cheekbones, a straight, little nose and a superhero's jawline — all of it was in perfect symmetry. Of course, there were other parts of him that made him Stallion's most popular model. In the 70's, actors and models were thin, even emaciated, and gay men embraced an aesthetic of gauntness. But "Chad Morrow" had a jump on the pumped look that was popular in the 80's when thin meant "wasting disease." Mr. Morrow was hitting the weights in the disco days and had square pecs and muscular arms with a subtle vascularity. His chest and stomach had the right amount of body hair that obscured nothing and heightened everything. His hips narrowed to snakelike but then his thighs bulged to reveal an intrigue of musculature. The magazine had pictures of him riding naked on a horse and in another he was wet and glistening as he stood in some foamy surf at dusk. My favorite pic was one where he was smiling over his shoulder as he raised up a flannel shirt to reveal a tan line and just below it, the perfect male behind: round and high with a sweetly contoured protuberance, like a pair of albino cantaloupes.

Damn.

I am not what is known as a "size queen" but I would be remiss if I didn't mention his other protuberance, which was uniquely spectacular. It wasn't some ridiculous and unwieldy monstrosity but it was both long and thick with a large, showy glans that was like a medieval helmet with a brim. This same issue of Stallion also included some black-and-white drawings of Chad by Tom of Finland. "In Chad I met someone who was the living embodiment of my masculine ideal," said Touko Laaksonen. "He is a man who needs no embellishment, someone who is simply perfect in appearance."

So what did he look like now? Hot as a habanero? The man who was known as Chad Morrow would be in his mid-forties.

When I walked into the reception room, Robert Bravermann was seated, leaning forward and engaging others. He was dressed in a pressed white shirt with a black tie and gray slacks but he needed no color — it only made his eyes look bluer, and in real life they were almost electric. His teeth were as white and straight as in his pictures and they glistened in his easy smile. Standing to shake hands with me he said, "Nice to meet you, Tyler." He had kept the big mustache but had updated his hair to a shorter, military style and in some ways, he was even more attractive, someone who was warm and approachable. He began the meeting by asking everyone to introduce themselves and tell us what they did for the organization. His baritone voice was rich and pleasant and his speaking style was natural, without any theatrics.

"I'm aware that most of you here have concerns and some... *complaints* about the way the organization is run," he said. "And from what I've heard so far, there are some growing pains as the operation gets larger. I'd like to hear from all of you, directly, as to what your concerns are. The first step in solving a problem is identifying it."

I looked around the room and no one was smiling or looked relieved. We were all guarded, looking at each other in mutual skepticism as we gauged this first encounter.

"You may not feel comfortable airing your complaints in a group setting," Bravermann continued. "But please understand that I am available to you on the phone or in person, however you feel most comfortable. Let's make an appointment. I like meeting in person and prefer to interface because a phone conversation can miss certain nuances."

At that point, he picked up his leather-bound eighteen-month planner and opened it. "As for solving what are *our* problems, nothing happens overnight. I'm new to this job but I'm not new to working for a nonprofit. In order to help you, I'm going to need your help. All right. Now before we make some appointments what questions or input do you have for me?"

Who the fuck was this guy? Even as he used a little corporate-speak, he seemed sincere. I wanted to trust him but he seemed too good to be true. He saw the conflict in my face.

"Tyler, you look like you were about to say something."

"Uh, I..."

"Please. Go ahead."

"I hesitate to, I..."

"Well, let me start for you. I understand that the working environment at Manna is a difficult one, that you're all very challenged, especially in the kitchen as the client count grows."

"Absolutely," I said, then cleared my throat. "And it's exacerbated by a sense that we aren't being listened to, that nothing ever changes as the workload just gets worse. We've had what's been called a 'successful fundraiser' but there are no new hires, no pay raises, no improvement in working conditions. And there's always been a feeling here that you could get fired for saying the wrong thing."

He looked around and saw gently nodding heads. Gene looked directly at me, his mouth pinched, as if I had said something I shouldn't have.

"A little background on me," Bravermann said. "I studied history and political science. And I know a lot about the nature of employer-employee relations. It's completely within human nature for one human to exploit another, to wring as much as possible out of someone else and offer the least in return. The enslavement and exploitation of some by others is the history of our species, it's built into us. Our *progress* as humans is the ongoing attempt to treat each other as equals, to make fair deals, to have situations that are win-win. I'm going a long way to make the point that it's natural and expected that even in a small nonprofit like this one, employees have to demand what's fair and employers have to make concessions."

    I looked around the room as we searched each other's faces and saw in them some surprise, a little awe, a bit of relief.

    It was true that Bravermann's IQ was as big as his cock but his heart seemed even bigger. Was a change really coming?

Chapter 26

A few months later, where Lakshmi's float once stood, there was now a portable storage unit. Bravermann stopped by to accept delivery of it himself and then came upstairs to "check in on things." Since his hiring, he had been by the kitchen nearly every day, giving tours of the place to potential donors. He was planning on hiring professional fundraisers to do four events a year, but in the meantime he had turned to foundations he had worked with for grants at other nonprofits. He brought visitors on "site visits" at the peak moment when drivers were arriving and the assembly line was in full swing but before the prayer got started — he had no time for that. He showed visitors the kitchen but did not come into it when we were at our busiest. He might ask the "three chefs to wave," which now included Bryce. The last thing he showed donors was the menu board. The client count stood at four hundred, and would stay at four hundred unless it fell (doubtful) or until we got a new kitchen (no time soon), a policy I very much welcomed.

The monthly meetings returned and were on the last Friday of each month. At the third of them, we officially welcomed another new employee, Tito, whose job it was to set donation cans on the counters of local businesses and then collect them. Tito was a cute, bubble-butted Brazilian who claimed to be straight but he liked to wear full-length, leather chaps in broad daylight and he rode a Harley with a bright red gas tank. The "Manna cans" that filled most quickly were in bars in Silverlake, leather and otherwise, where Robert Bravermann was not unknown and where Tito got a lot of attention. He also knew how to "work West Hollywood," which required a different outfit: 501 jeans that were tight around the ass with a tucked-in polo shirt that hugged his pecs.

"Now, I've been here a few months," Bravermann said and smiled broadly on one cool and rainy afternoon. "And I've discovered a collective martyr complex. I'm astonished to learn that no one here has health insurance. No one. An organization that supports people with AIDS should provide its staff with health care."

"Not because we haven't been asking," said Jeremy.

"We have been told it is simply not affordable," said Nigel. "That the needs of the clients come first."

"We can't afford *not* to take care of our employees, for the sake of our clients," Bravermann said. "This is not up for discussion and it's something I've insisted on to the board. We *will* be providing all of you with a health plan as soon as possible. And all of you are entitled to take the occasional mental health day. We've all taken on this work because we want to help, but we're exposed to death, sickness and suffering on a daily basis. We're more than entitled to get away from it and do something that renews us and brings us some joy."

He then leaned back, folded his arms behind his head and grinned. "Now I need to know something," he said. "For those of you who have been here for at least a year, when the hell are you going to take a vacation?"

"A *paid* vacation?" asked the Baguette.

"Of course a paid vacation! Like I said... martyr complex!"

*

A week later, Gene was a combination of irritable and dejected as we set up that morning. Bunny Glick, one of our older, motherly volunteers, the type Gene liked to bond with, had set him up to have coffee with the other gay man in her life, the one who did her hair.

"I wasn't attracted to him and he wasn't attracted to me," he said with a dead tone. "And besides, he's just a hairdresser."

"Just? I think they're called hair *stylists* now."

"Whatever."

I had forgotten that Madge had predicted Gene's lover would be as famous as Gene would become once he ascended as the spiritual leader to hundreds of thousands.

"Maybe someday he'll be like Jose Eber or Vidal Sassoon," I said. "You know, a hair stylist to the stars."

"I doubt it. You should have seen his own hair. He's got one of those Steven Segal ponytails wrapped with a tube of orange yarn so that it sticks out. And he was wearing these awful glasses with orange lenses."

Bryce arrived at 8:31.

"You're late," Gene said.

"Good morning to you too, Miss Pissy Pants."

"It's not the first time, Bryce. You need to be here on time."

"But I arrived five minutes early yesterday. So I still have a credit of four."

"It doesn't work like that. And stop calling me Miss Pissy Pants, especially in front of the volunteers. You're undermining my authority."

"Now somebody, I won't say who, seems to have flushed her sense of humor down the toilet this morning along with her stink fudge. Tyler, how are you?"

"Oh, I'm just fine" I said but I was lying. I didn't want to tell them that it was my birthday and I was depressed because I was now thirty-five, generally accepted as the cut-off age in Hollywood. I was no longer considered young and promising but as someone who hadn't made it.

"I'm still thinking about that dinner last night," Bryce said to me. "Wasn't it good?"

I hesitated to respond.

"Delish," I said.

"You... the two of you had dinner last night?" Gene asked, his tone betraying that he felt left out.

"We did," Bryce said. "Grilled salmon and asparagus with beurre blanc. And the soup was this intense shrimp bisque. A really good dessert too, a pear poached in Marsala and stuffed with a mixed nut praline and then dipped in dark chocolate."

"Oh? What restaurant?" Gene asked, a tremble in his voice.

"Not a restaurant. You know Murray Rappaport — the guy who volunteers on Wednesdays that owns The Wizard of Bras on La Cienega? He invited us to his house. Beautiful place near Fryman Canyon. And can he *cook*."

"I'm so glad you enjoyed it," Gene said with a brief, stiff smile as the delivery from S.E. Rykoff was hauled up the stairs and piled into the community room. That was another welcome change — we no longer had to take tedious trips to Smart and Final. A sales rep from Rykoff showed up each week with order sheets. Better quality products were brought to us and even hauled up the stairs. When Gene left to sign for the delivery, I whispered to Bryce.

"I don't tell him about stuff he's not invited to," I said.

"I wasn't planning to," said Bryce with a mischievous grin. "But then I had to... to chap his ass."

"It's chapped enough," I said. "He had another shitty date last night."

A second delivery person wearing a yellow baseball cap and a matching shirt entered the kitchen with a shocking bouquet of flowers. It was a massive arrangement that featured scarlet anthuriums with their big, wobbly spikes and thrusting above them were magenta orchids with crenellated beards. All of it was set within a thick cloud of baby's breath.

"Looking for Tyler St. George," said the delivery man.

"That's me," I said.

"Happy birthday. Careful," he said and grunted as he handed it to me. It was heavy and needed both hands.

"It's your birthday?" Bryce asked.

"Shh!"

"Those better be from Kyle."

"They are," I said looking at the card after I set it on the counter.

When Gene came back, he stopped in his tracks when he saw the flowers then made that vicious snarl with his hands on his hips. "Aww! Somebody got penis-on-a-platters."

"I did," I said. "Aren't they beautiful?"

"In the eye of the beholder," he said. "I think anthuriums are a little cheap and plastic-looking. They're kind of vulgar."

That triggered me. I had to refrain myself from going all New Jersey on him and shouting, *Fuck you, you jealous little cunt*! I took a few breaths.

"Now, Gene," I said, moderating my voice. "When you say something like that, does that bring you closer to others or does it push them away?"

"Snotty-snobby ain't pretty," said Bryce, pouring on the Southern accent. "Acting all superior ain't ever gonna git you a man or much of anything else."

"And how would you know?" Gene shot back.

"Oh, I know," Bryce said. "And the reason Kyle sends dick flowers to Tyler is because he likes his dick. You might want to take a powder, Gene. Your complexion looks a little green this morning. When's the last time someone sent *you* flowers?"

Gene's face fell and he was silent.

"Nobody? Well, I'll be sure to send you flowers," Bryce said. "When it's your funeral."

I walked over to the new utility fridge to help Bryce take out the first of two pots of chicken cacciatore that weighed at least one hundred pounds.

"The bitch just asks for it," Bryce whispered.

"I know," I said.

We were setting the pots on the stove and lighting the burners when Bravermann entered with a fresh haircut. "Happy birthday, Tyler," he said with his killer smile, looking like Robert Conrad with a mustache.

"Thanks, Robert. How'd you know?"

"It's my job to know. It may be your birthday but let's not let that complicate what I'm about to ask you and Gene. The both of you deserve a raise, but this month we can afford to take only one of you up by ten percent."

"We can't both get one?" I asked.

"In another two months we'll do a raise for the other guy when some grants are in. I really can't decide which of you needs it more but I do trust you to decide between yourselves. Let me know, please."

Bravermann was down the stairs as Gene looked lost in serious thought. Bryce smirked and said, "Between you, me and Robert Bravermann, I'm the one who should be getting a raise."

"I think you should get one, too," I said to Bryce. "You work as hard as we do."

"Bryce has only been here a few months," Gene said with a sudden bitterness.

"Yeah, but he's been volunteering for a year. Like, lots of volunteering," I said. "And he's very entertaining. The volunteers love him."

"I think I should get the raise," Gene said glancing at me briefly.

"And why's that?"

"Because I've been here the longest."

"I was here before you."

"As a volunteer."

"As a worker," I said.

"And when Jonnie needs a driver, Tyler always says yes," Bryce said. "Not to mention that it's been a long time since I've seen Miss Pissy Pants take trash down that stairway. And Miss P.P. is always cutting out early to get to her workout or her meditation. Not to mention that Tyler's way hotter than you."

Gene smirked. "Bryce, there's going to be a point when I don't think you're funny anymore, when you've crossed the line from court jester to obnoxious queen. Tyler, I should get the raise because you have Kyle."

"*What?*"

"I live by myself. I don't have anyone to share my rent or utilities. Last week you said you and Kyle were looking at a *house* for sale."

"We *looked* at a house... at the end of our block. It doesn't mean we're *buying* a house. We wondered what it would cost, what the down payment would be."

"But together the two of you have disposable income. Kyle just sent you flowers," said Gene, a tremble in his voice as he looked away. I started to pity him.

"Gene, I have been going into debt ever since I started this job," I said. "I watch my pennies. I defaulted on my student loans. We couldn't get a mortgage if we wanted to because my credit is shit. I worked here for nothing when the organization had nothing.

Now that it's got some money, it's only fair I get compensated for some hard frickin' work."

"But you still have Kyle," he said.

I felt the clamp on my anger getting loose.

"And you have your parents!" I shouted. "They gave you a car! A *new* car! And whenever you need money, you just call them up. You're thirty-six years old and you're still getting an allowance!"

"It's a *stipend*," he said. "And it's not that much. Kyle takes you out to sushi dinners... and on trips to Vegas."

"Gene, understand something. It's because of Kyle that I want a raise. I don't want to rely on him. He's not independently wealthy. For his birthday, his mother sent him a shirt from K-Mart — he's got seven siblings and will inherit nothing. As for Vegas, one of the reasons we like it is because we can gamble on the five-cent poker machines for four hours and that gets us a free room. We can see a tits-and-feathers show for fourteen ninety-five that includes dinner! We can drive instead of fly. As long as you don't gamble, it's cheap!"

Gene paused a moment. "Tyler, if you get a ten percent raise, you'll be making almost as much money as I am."

I felt my insides get hotter.

"So that's what this is about?" I said, raising my voice. "It's not about *needing* money but needing to be the one that *gets the most*?"

Gene was quiet, gave the slightest shrug. I felt a sudden disgust for him.

"Well, aren't you just so *spiritual*," I said. "With your detachment from cravings and desires. OK, fine. You can have the raise, Gene. I'll call Bravermann this afternoon and tell him you're the one who really, really needs it, that your whole sense of identity might disappear. The raise is all yours but don't invest too much in it. It won't make you any happier."

Gene kept quiet, his eyes shifting left and right before he raised them to mine. "I suppose you think you're being the more spiritual one by doing this for me."

"No, I *don't*," I said with a derisive laugh. "For one thing, spirituality is not a competition! You've lost the whole point of detachment when you compare yourself to others."

"Oh, and you're just so detached, Tyler, with your screenwriting ambitions. I don't need instruction from *you*," he said. "Not *you*."

"Hi," said a voice from behind us. We turned around to see two chubby guys holding the typical bags of crap that come after cleaning out the pantry. Sticking out of one bag was a box of Betty Crocker instant mashed potatoes and the other had a jar of three bean salad and a cloudy bottle of clam juice. "We wanted to drop off a donation!" said one guy whose chin sprouted a fashionable goatee.

"Thanks so much," I said. "But there's a better place to bring this." I grabbed a copy of my favorite new sheet in a drawer and handed it to them. "The Necessities of Life Program at APLA would love to have your donation. There's a map on here and a phone number."

"Oh. So you won't take them?"

"Sorry, we don't have the room. We send out prepared food. Necessities can stock it and offer it to their clients."

"Oh," they said, shrugging their shoulders, disappointed. They had been expecting sunshine and bubbly gratitude.

"Thanks so much for stopping by," I said.

Gene stared at me after they left. "You were rude to them," he said.

"No, I wasn't."

"Yes, you were. They were excited to come here."

"We can say no Gene. No more martyr complex. It doesn't make you more *spiritual* to suffer."

He made a dramatic sighing sound and turned away.

Kyle did take me to a sushi dinner for my birthday. I waited until we had our hot *sake* to tell him about my day. "So a little good news," I said as I filled his cup. "It'll be a few months but I'm getting a raise."

"A raise?" Kyle said.

"Yep, it's a whole long story, but I..."

Kyle frowned, looked away. "So you plan to keep working at Manna."

"For a while. It's a ten percent raise."

"Yeah, but ten percent of what?" he said and then grimaced as he shook his head. "I... I'm sorry. That's good news. I'm proud of you."

He raised his cup to me. "Happy birthday, Tyler. I have some news, too," he said. But he wasn't smiling.

Chapter 27

Jonnie had brought her black-and-white portable television to work and just before 2 p.m. on a May afternoon she plugged it in. I turned off my new forty-quart mixer full of key lime pie filling and helped her adjust the antennae until the static disappeared. We stood and watched as the audience of the Beverly Lindsay Bromwell Show applauded its eponymous host as she danced out to the synth-bop of a theme by Quincy Jones. In her hand she clutched a book.

"It's booooooook day!" Beverly yodeled. "Reach under your seat and grab your book!" Beverly was out of breath, deeply excited. "For those of you who aren't here, I want you to run, not walk, to your nearest bookstore and purchase your copy of *The Thousand Miracles of Love*. You will experience, as I did, a *miracle* on every page!"

Beverly held up the book to the camera and there, on its cover, was a picture of Lakshmi with her pointy chin cropped out. "Please welcome its author and *my... new... friend,* Lakshmi Steinmetz!"

Lakshmi strutted out in a tailored skirt suit of cerulean blue, white shoes and a white blouse for a very heavenly look. She looked thrilled, confident, and never more happy as at last, she was in millions of living rooms. Her smile was its broadest and she waved to a welcoming audience with the flourish of a Miss America. When they sat in some bucket chairs, Beverly looked at Lakshmi as if she was holding back from a happy cry.

"I've already read this twice," Beverly said, holding up the book again. "And first, what I would like to say is *thank you, Lakshmi*. I've seen something of myself in here, some honest passages about drugs and men and food. And I've seen something else too, a different way to experience the world."

"Beverly, you are a quick learner," Lakshmi said. "But we all have within us the capacity to see the world in a different way, and by doing that, to change it. All of us can experience the world as a manifestation of God as love, as a being who is incapable of mistakes, and see ourselves as a pure expression of his perfect creation."

I looked at Gene whose arms were folded over his apron. His mouth was pinched and his eyebrows were scrunched in that jealous look. Jonnie looked choked up as Lakshmi discoursed on *The Way*, describing illness, death and suffering as an illusion. Bryce had his arms folded and looked amused. To no surprise, Beverly did not ask Lakshmi for any verifiable proof of her statements or question her about the prophetic roots of *The Way of the Miraculous*. "We'll be right back," Beverly said after shaking her head in pure astonishment. The screen cut to a commercial for Little Caesars Pizza Pizza with their new offer of Meatza Meatza: two sausage and pepperoni bedecked pizzas for only $9.99.

"Beverly has just made Lakshmi a best-selling author," Bryce said.

"She's just made her a star," said Gene.

"She *is* a star," Jonnie said and wiped at tears.

I kept quiet. What had struck me was that Beverly Lindsay Bromwell had seen herself in Lakshmi, someone who had been aimless and self-destructive, a kindred spirit who just had to be a star. Beverly had done more than swallow hook, line and sinker the comforting drivel of *The Way* — she had beached herself, belly up, and offered herself in submission to the guru of the moment, one Lakshmi Steinmetz.

"So maybe we'll see even less of her," I said. "I gotta get back to my pies."

A few days later, it was near midnight when I put Holden in the car and we drove to the airport to pick up Kyle from what was his third trip abroad in the last few months. He had been working on some low-budget film productions, courtesy of a new connection through the Comedy Omelette. On this latest trip, he had traveled to Kazakhstan to rework the English dialogue of a German film that had been relocated to Nur-Sultana as a stand-in for Beirut and then he had stopped off in England where he worked with a British screenwriter on some scenes set in London that starred American actors — or I think that's what he told me.

All six feet and four inches of Kyle bounced off the plane and into the waiting area and Holden barked and wagged his tail. Kyle's arms were wide open and his head was thrown back as he grinned and gavotted toward us, putting on a show. His hug was short and perfunctory.

On the drive home, he gabbed on and on about the strangeness and bleakness of Kazakhstan where he had been confined to a rural hotel next to a slaughter yard full of camels, sheep and horses. The Kazakhs had served the crew various kinds of horse meat, honoring the foreign visitors with a special sausage of it as well as a drink of fermented camel's milk. "It's a weird, weird place," he said. "Everyone's drunk, even though most of them are Muslims. And everybody smokes, including children. I bought these from a Russian girl who was a total freak, the only ginger I saw there. She was six and had a lit one in her mouth." He showed me a pack of Belomorkanal cigarettes with the long, cardboard tube that they had instead of a filter and then lit one up and passed it to me. I took a drag and it was harsh. "I had to wait to get to London to buy some decent ciggies," he said.

"How was London?" I asked. For the first time ever, I heard him refer to a redhead as a "ginger" and he was using the word "ciggies" instead of his usual 'smokes.'

He hesitated. "Brilliant."

"Brilliant, OK. So, you're saying 'brilliant' now. When do I get to read this script? Some of it takes place in Beirut and some of it in London?"

"Oh... I don't know. The Germans weren't happy with me. They threw out my draft and offered me half the money," he said. "You hoff done noothing," he said, imitating someone's German accent.

"But they wanted you in London?"

"Yeah, I had to finish my contract."

When Kyle came back from trips, the first thing we usually did was get naked together. I was eager for that, but he stopped me when I went to unbutton his pants. "Don't you want your presents?" he asked, opening his suitcase.

The presents were abundant. The first of them were from Kazakhstan including a hand carved chess set with blue and yellow pieces painted to look like Mongols and black-and-white ones painted to look like a medieval Russian court. There was a bottle of grass liquor in a bottle painted like Genghis Khan and a strange, hand-carved, double-bowled scoop with an exotic filigree of wood burning. Kyle understood my tastes.

"But wait... there's more," he said, quoting from a Ron Popeil commercial. From out of his suitcase came not one but two seven-pound bags of my favorite English candy: black currant boiled sweets with a licorice center. Then he pulled up three brightly colored and checkered short-sleeve shirts, all of which were appealing. After that he handed me a small leather box. Inside it was a striking watch with a deep-blue face and hands that were a lemon yellow. "It lights up," he said and pressed a side button and the face and numbers glowed.

"This is... this is all too much," I said and felt a sudden, numbing sadness as a realization set in. "It's not my birthday or Christmas or our anniversary and Valentine's was months ago. What's up?"

"Nothing," he said. But his face said everything.

On the following day, a Thursday, Gene was having a worse day than me for unknown reasons and was pouting and bitchy all morning. Bryce had been singing and dancing to "Gonna Make You Sweat" by Black Box and I joined him as we waited for the pasta to cook. Gene stared at us out of his glumness and said, "Excuse me... are you being paid to cook or to dance?"

"Oh, sorry, honey," Bryce said. "I've got an extra tampon if you need one."

After we got out spaghetti and meatballs, we were readying fried fish filets and green beans for an unofficial "Catholic Friday" at the request of a dying client when Aidan Rafferty popped in, an up-and-coming playwright. A month earlier, Aidan had invited the three chefs to go with him to a performance of the Bulgarian State Television Female Vocal Choir. Thinking Aidan might be his "famous lover," Gene had pressed him for a date when we were driving back but had been politely rebuffed.

"Hey, Tyler," Aidan said to me, handing me an envelope just as I had washed the stink of fish off my hands. "I've gotta run — things to do — but there's two in here," he whispered. "And you and Bryce are on the list for the after-party."

"Thanks so much," I said quietly.

"Thanks for all you guys do."

"Thanks, Aidan. See you Friday!" Bryce shouted... to chap Gene's ass.

Aidan scooted out without even acknowledging Gene who looked at Bryce and me as if we were the ones who had rejected him. A few minutes later, we started the tedious "frenching" of green beans, which was cutting their ends off, cutting them in half and then slicing down the middle to make them slivers. It was labor-intensive and something Gene insisted on, but I didn't like the resulting texture, which was abrasive. I preferred cutting off their ends with a diagonal cut for smooth, bite-size pieces. On Thursdays, fortunately, we had a full contingent of the Jewish Mom's Brigade who went to work at the task. Unfortunately, we also had Graham "Casting Couch" Stillson with us, a disgraced individual with no place else to go in his life but the kitchen at Manna from Heaven. Graham was standing next to Gene, Bryce and me at the cutting counter when he decided to tell us about his previous evening at a sex club. As Graham was old, gray and built like a Bartlett pear, none of us were all that interested.

"So you know that guy Chris Strickland, the one with the nice legs that always wears the yellow shorts?" said Graham.

"Yeah, he's a driver," I said. "He used to bartend at the Blue Parrot."

"That's him. I ran into him at the Vortex last night."

"*You* were at the Vortex?" Gene asked in disbelief. "The sex club?"

"Yes, I was."

"So I guess they let in anyone who can pay."

Stillson stared at Gene, slack-jawed.

"You were saying?" I said to Graham.

"So I stood behind Chris," Stillson whispered. "And while he was getting serviced, I jerked off on his leg."

That was something neither Gene, Bryce nor I wanted to picture. Bryce and I quietly chuckled but Gene laughed in a scornful way. "Thank you very much for that, Graham," he said. "That's exactly the image I want to carry around in my head this afternoon." I looked over at the Moms Brigade, and thankfully, they were caught up in their own conversation.

"It was hot!" Graham insisted.

"Hot for who?" Gene said.

Graham put down his knife and stared at Gene. "How come all the knives in this place are so dull?" he asked.

"We have a knife sharpener," Gene said. "Knock yourself out."

"And why can't we just cut these beans in the usual way? This takes forever."

"Graham's got a point, Gene," I said. "And I don't like this texture."

"A diagonal cut is better," said Bryce. "And visually more appealing."

"You guys are always looking to get out of here early," Gene responded.

"I'm looking to get things done as efficiently as possible," I said. "Without sacrificing quality."

"Gene, you are just so unpleasant!" Graham said. "The way you speak to people!"

"*I'm* unpleasant?" said Gene in a too-loud voice. "I'm not the one who just told a story about *ejaculating* on someone's leg."

That got the attention of everyone in the kitchen.

"I'd like to speak with you alone!" Graham said, walking toward the community room. Gene rolled his eyes and looked heavenward and then followed Graham out. The kitchen went silent except for the sound of knives dissecting green beans. Suddenly, we heard Graham shouting. "That's appalling! I can't believe this! I'm going to tell everyone what you just said!"

Graham waddled back into the kitchen, his face red with rage. "Listen," he said, getting everyone's attention. "Gene just told me, 'It's Jews like you who make me think Hitler was right.'"

As was often the case, many of the volunteers that afternoon were Jewish. One of them, Bunny Glick, was someone Gene was close to, someone generous with her time and money who had invited us over for tea at her sculpting studio. Bunny was gasping in disbelief. The Jewish Moms Brigade kept silent but had stopped chopping and kept heads down as Gene sheepishly returned to the kitchen. His face was flushed with embarrassment.

"I... I was just... kidding," he said through nervous laughter as he picked up his knife and sliced a bean.

I was stunned — that's all he was going to say? Bryce looked at me and shook his head in disbelief.

"Gene, can I speak with you?" I said.

"Now what?" he answered.

"I said I'd like to speak with you."

We went outside to the landing of the backstairs. Gene crossed his arms over his chest.

"Gene, you have to apologize," I said.

"I already have."

"No, you haven't. Saying 'I was just kidding' is not an apology."

He frowned and sighed.

"Don't tell me *you're* defending Graham Stillson."

"I'm not. He's an obnoxious lech and we should have kicked his ass out of here a long time ago. But what you said to him was fucked up! You offended everybody in that kitchen including me."

"You're not Jewish."

"You don't have to be!"

Jonnie stepped out. "What's going on, guys?"

"Tell her, Gene."

He shook his head again, looking at me as if I had thrust a knife in his gut. He gave with one of his deep, sad sighs.

"I said something I shouldn't have."

"And he owes everyone in there an apology," I said. "Especially the Jews."

Gene looked very childish at the moment as he stuck out his lower lip and slumped.

"Then I think you should do it right now," said Jonnie.

"He should," I said.

The three of us walked back into the kitchen.

"Gene has something he'd like to say," Jonnie announced.

Turning red again, Gene's eyes darted. "I'm sorry," he said, flatly. "What I said to Graham was wrong. It wasn't funny."

His apology struck me as inadequate. From the silence in the room I sensed others felt the same. We worked in silence for the rest of that afternoon. The volunteers left early, leaving Gene, Bryce and me to french the last thousand green beans on our own. Bryce was uncharacteristically quiet until the moment we threw the last of the tortured legumes into the plastic container.

"So, Gene. I figured out your new drag name," he said as he snapped on the lid.

"Oh, *do* tell," said Gene in a tone both mocking and exhausted.

"Annie Semitic."

He stared at Bryce, neither of them smiling when Gene put his hands on his hips and scowled. "Aren't you just *hilarious,*

Bryce. Aren't you just spectacularly funny, always there to provide comic relief. It's so kind of you to just trivialize everything. And I shouldn't have to tell either of you that I haven't got an anti-Semitic bone in my body."

Jeremy walked in and sensed the tension in the room. "Hey y'all. Am I interrupting something?"

"Please. Interrupt," said Bryce.

"Tyler, you can say no, but we've got a monthly meeting next Friday and Bravermann's birthday is just a couple of days later. Can you bake him a cake?"

"Abso-fucking-lutely," I said. "Any fricking cake he likes."

"He likes carrot."

"Carrot it is."

"What's he like to drink?" Bryce asked.

"Irish whiskey. Bushmills."

We wanted to celebrate Bravermann's birthday, were eager to do it. But his party would have an unwelcome guest.

Chapter 28

"A new kitchen is still a ways off, but we've looked at a few facilities and are pricing that out," said Bravermann. "I think we can move to a new building and expand the number of clients by November but we'll do it gradually, in increments. OK, is there anything else or can we get on with our weekend?"

"Yes," said Jeremy who stood and dimmed the lights of the reception room as Joffrey ran out like he really needed to use the bathroom. He reappeared from the kitchenette with the cake I'd made topped by a lit sparkler.

"Oh, shit," Robert said with a laugh. "I was trying to keep that quiet!"

Carrot cakes are usually decorated with a carrot made of orange and green frosting, but instead I'd made a big, chocolate mustache modeled after Bravermann's and he laughed when he saw it. After singing "Happy Birthday," some wrapped gifts appeared as well as some plastic glasses and sparkling wines from Trader Joe's. This was more than some perfunctory office birthday where employees would get a clump of some cheap supermarket sheet cake. We were honoring Bravermann for what he had done for us, done for the organization. He opened Bryce's gift of Bushmills Irish Whiskey first, guessing it was booze from the shape of the box. "It's after five," Bravermann said, looking at his watch, "and it is a Friday," he added before unscrewing the cap and pouring.

Other offerings were a mug that read "World's Greatest Boss" and the Baguette gave him a necktie the same color as Bravermann's eyes, something she said she'd stolen from her father's closet. Jeremy gave Robert some vintage "magic drinking glasses" that featured images of Bravermann from a decade ago wearing a black swimsuit that disappeared when the glasses were filled with a cold liquid. "I forgot all about these," he said and laughed as we tried them out. Nigel gave Bravermann a gift certificate to Book Soup for his reading habit and Vonnie gave him a comforter she had knitted herself. Jonnie and Gene had gotten him a card that they had both signed and featured a drawing of an angel and the caption "Blessings on Your Birthday." Bravermann graciously held it up and showed us its picture as Joffrey, with a mischievous look, pushed over a gift bag from Hickory Farms. Robert pulled out a fat, ten-inch-long summer sausage. "Uh, thanks?" he said. "I don't get it."

"Now you have two," Joffrey said and we howled with laughter. At just that moment, the front door opened and in walked Lakshmi wearing a black sweat suit with her hair pulled back in a scrunchy. We all went quiet. She looked mystified to see a party underway and could see from the looks on our faces that we weren't happy to see her. She readjusted her shoulder bag and looked at the cake and the bottles and then at our faces.

"Lakshmi!" Jonnie shouted with her usual enthusiasm to fill the silence. "You're back early!"

"Hi, Lakshmi. Welcome home," Gene mumbled.

"Thank you," she said in the awkward silence. "I feel like I've interrupted something. Whose birthday is it?"

"I'm afraid it's mine," Robert said and smiled. "Welcome back. Won't you join us?"

"Maybe a little later," she said. "I'm... I'm just getting caught up. I came in to use my computer and write up a few notes for my talk next week. Happy birthday... Robert."

The mood was spoiled. We listened to the sound of her footsteps and the creaking of the stairs. Robert twisted the cap back on what was left of the whiskey and got professional again. "Now that Lakshmi's back, I think it's important that we're all familiar with her work," he said. "If you haven't, I hope you'll attend one of her lectures and learn something about *The Way*."

"Are you a student of *The Way*?" I asked him.

"I'm a student of all religions... or spiritual paths if you will," he said, correcting himself. "But on Sunday mornings I go to mass. And I don't eat breakfast if I'm taking communion," he said with a smile.

Wow. Robert Bravermann was a practicing Roman Catholic.

It was something of a surprise when Lakshmi showed up at the kitchen in a chic, sea-foam pantsuit on Monday, a little after eleven, just as we were readying the assembly line. "Hey, Lakshmi," I said as I frantically stirred forty-quart pans of Chinese chicken and vegetables, waiting for that moment when the sauce got thick and glossy. "This is a surprise."

"It's been so long since I've been here," she said, having a look around at the new industrial fridges and ovens. "I thought I'd come in and get a little dirt under my fingernails."

"Have you met Bryce?" I asked. He was next to me, fluffing tall pots of freshly cooked rice with a paddle.

"I have not," she said. "How long have you been a volunteer, Bryce?"

"Over a year," he said. "Nice to finally meet you."

"Bryce is one of our chefs now," I said.

"A chef?" she said, surprised.

"Yes, he's amazing."

"So... he was hired... while I was gone."

She was irked that someone had gone over her head.

"He's invaluable," I said. "A real help with the workload."

She looked at the menu board and saw the number of clients was at four hundred.

"How long have we been at four hundred?" she asked me.

"We're capped at four hundred, for the last few months now. We won't go above that until we get a new kitchen."

"Who made *that* decision?"

"We requested it," I said. "Four hundred is tough enough in this tiny kitchen. Excuse me, don't want to burn you," I said, pulling on pot holders and lifting the first of the pans to the counter as she stepped away.

"Hello, Lakshmi," Gene moaned to her as he lidded the meals for vegans and vegetarians while chatting with Madge.

"Well, well... if it isn't Lakshmi Steinmetz," Madge said with sarcasm. "Congrats on your book. So you're rich now."

"Thank you," she said with a polite chuckle. "Gene, how are you?"

Gene shrugged and said, "Oh, I'm... just fine." The two spoke quietly, Gene airing his latest disappointment in whispers. Bryce went over to the cassette deck and popped in a mix tape of classic disco. "Shame" came on by Evelyn Champagne King. We revved up the volunteers by blowing on some plastic whistles. "Angels assemble!" I shouted as we took out the tambourines and shook them. Bryce and I did the Hustle while the first scoops of stir fry and rice were plonked into containers.

Lakshmi gave us just the slightest smile and raised her arms to boogie for a moment and I could imagine her as she might have appeared at a tea dance on Fire Island in the 70's, wearing a Halston jumpsuit with a halter-neck and shaking a tambourine. She wandered out to Jonnie who was greeting the drivers with hugs as the rest of the staff was at full tilt getting bags and route sheets ready. "Lakshmi!" I heard Jonnie screech. "What a lovely surprise!"

When the four hundredth meal was packed and bagged, Jonnie called the prayer circle to her attention.

"We better go out there," I said to Bryce, turning off the music, as he cracked eggs to make egg foo young out of the leftover stir fry for the volunteer meal. "Lakshmi's here and we don't want to offend."

"You mean we need to kiss her skinny ass," he said.

Jonnie, Lakshmi and Gene were holding hands as the circle gathered. I took Jonnie's and Bryce's as thirty others joined us.

The room went strangely quiet. Another guru had entered the room.

352

As had been her occasional habit, the woman known as Ma Nerada Matanji, better known as Guru Mama, entered the community room. With her was the famous 60's folk singer, Keith Tandy, whose long hair was down to his waist and now silvery with a blue rinse. Tandy revealed his teeth in a big smile as he always did, but he let Guru Mama do all the talking. With them were some of Mama's other followers including a young man we called the Cookie Bearer who always stood just outside the circle. As usual, the CB was wearing a tight wife beater and had brought with him a wooden plank covered with an assortment of cookies that he balanced on his shoulder. He had a shaved head, tattoos of cobras that twisted up his forearms, and a long mustache that covered his upper lip. His large brown eyes had a sad, worried expression like a puppy in a Margaret Keene painting.

Lakshmi froze as she stared at Guru Mama with contempt. "What is *she* doing here?" Lakshmi whispered to Jonnie.

"She's... she's donating some cookies... again," Jonnie said.

"Egg on my *mustache*!" whispered Lakshmi, sneering. "The false prophet."

Egg on my mustache? What did that mean? Jonnie cleared her throat.

"Thank you, everybody," Jonnie said in her piccolo voice. "We're lucky to have the founder of Manna with us today, Lakshmi Steinmetz!"

Jonnie handed Lakshmi the list of those who have transitioned.

"Thank you, thank you all for your continued good work," Lakshmi said, a stern look on her face. "Really, you are all so amazing.

Today, sadly, we say goodbye today to Zeke Bartholomew Appleby, Alphonso Guttierez, Dennis M. Fitzgerald and Mookie Cougar. Welcome them, God, to their transition, and shower blessings of comfort and love on their grieving friends and family."

Lakshmi, with a tight, angry look on her face glanced at Guru Mama whose arms were making little clinking noises as they were covered up to the elbows with bangles of gold. Mama stood with her chin up, smiling, cocking her head this way, then that way, shaking her curly black hair. As usual, she had a vermillion tilak on her forehead the size of a half dollar. She wore a pendant with a picture of her own teacher, Guru Paravayar, a second one of Lord Shiva the Destroyer, and below it a third one of an enormous sapphire. Her knee length jacket and trousers were of saffron-colored silk and were embroidered with little paisleys made of sequins. I was thinking it must take her a while to get dressed in the morning.

"Thank you, Lakshmi," said Jonnie filling the silence. "Does anyone else request a prayer or have something they'd like to share?"

Volunteers mentioned the names of people who had just been admitted to hospitals or were in their final days or in a bout of suffering. A famous character actor completed a funny story about a dead client's yappy chihuahua that he hated for biting his ankles but was now his own beloved pet. And then Guru Mama spoke... and Lakshmi's face went stiff and white.

"Namaste, which means 'I greet you as I am and as you are,'" Mama said in her squeaky, Brooklyn accent. "Some of you may be wondering, who is this woman with the funny way of talking. I'm the Guru Mama and I can't help how I talk. I've been compared to Edith Bunker and I take that as a compliment. Archieeeee!"

The Edith Bunker comparison wasn't wrong, but her voice reminded me more of Curly from the Three Stooges.

"As for my name, Guru Ma Nerada Matanji, well, guru means 'teacher.' Most people just call me Mama once we're friends, and I want to be friends with everyone," she said, smiling. "I was drawn to Manna from Heaven in the same way I am drawn to love, for there is so much love here. It's something you can see, something that rises up from this church, like the chimney smoke from a warm fire in winter. We stopped by today to bring this offer of love to both your clients and to their loving caretakers. Enjoy."

The Cookie Bearer set down his burden on the table where the AA members put their coffee urns and literature. He unwrapped the plastic on the plank.

"And as ever, all of you, and I mean every one of you, are welcome to join us for prasadam, darshan, and of course, love at our center on South Ogden Drive and Pico this Saturday."

South Ogden Drive and Pico? That was near where I lived.

The Cookie Bearer reached into his saffron-colored shoulder bag decorated with Sanskrit prayers and set some cards with Mama's picture on them next to the free cookies.

"Thank you... Mama," said Jonnie. Lakshmi cupped Jonnie's ear and whispered into it. Jonnie nodded. "In case anyone from the media is here," said Jonnie for Lakshmi, "please note that Manna from Heaven and Ma Nerada Matanji are not associated. And on that note, let us all bow our heads and thank God for the opportunity to serve him, to serve our clients and make each of us more loving and loved. Amen."

The prayer had come to an abrupt end.

Lakshmi was heading for the exit when Mama walked straight toward her. "Lakshmi!" she said. "It's wonderful to see you again. Congratulations on your book."

"Thanks," Lakshmi said and kept walking. "I really don't have time to talk."

"I'm sorry, did I offend you?"

Lakshmi's face was scrunched with anger as she turned to face Mama. She was weighing her words as Keith Tandy, the Cookie Bearer and Mama's other followers stood behind her, a wall of support, looking at Lakshmi and daring her to be disrespectful.

"Look, I get you," Lakshmi said. "I totally understand your energy, but I know who you are, *Denise,* and I know all about you and what happens at your ashram. So don't even *think* about sicking your entity on me. You have no powers here."

You have no powers here. That was a line from *The Wizard of Oz.*

"You're mistaken, Lakshmi," said Mama, shaking her head. "All I've brought here is love."

"Like I said, Denise. I know *who* and *what* you are."

Lakshmi turned and went down the back steps, preferring not to cross Mama's path. Mama shrugged, leading her followers out the other way. Once they were gone, Jonnie tossed the cards the Cookie Bearer had left in the trash. Later, I took one out and read it. Guru Ma Nerada Matanji's center was two blocks from our house. Now I understood why there were so many cars on weekends and Wednesday nights. I took a bite of one of the cookies then tossed it — they were made with Crisco, not butter, and had no flavor.

That evening, I drove to the Beverly Hills Library to return some books and take out some new ones. Before I checked out, I went to the card catalog to see if there were any magazine articles about Ma Nerada Matanji. I found a few and one of them was titled *Egg on My Mustache* from the defunct magazine *New Age Monthly*, and it was written by Baba Sivinanda, formerly known as Joshua Gleeson. Baba was a former promoter of LSD before he became a Shaivite Hindu and a student of Guru Paravayar. In *Egg on my Mustache,* Gleeson chronicled his infatuation with Mama, also a student of Paravayar, who held out the promise that Gleeson could become her equal as a spiritual master. When Baba realized her miracles were sleight of hand and that he had been deceived, he denounced her as a "false prophet." He admitted his vulnerability to her scam stemmed from his being "spiritually avaricious," a phrase I found particularly interesting. One thing Baba did not discuss was why he needed Guru Mama at all, why his original teacher, Paravayar, wasn't enough.

Baba had been "spiritually avaricious," but it made me wonder... had he ever really been spiritually satisfied?

Was anyone ever?

I was all the more interested in attending Mama's darshan on Saturday. And I was surprised to see who else showed up.

Chapter 29

When I lived in Berkeley in the mid 70's, I often visited the ISKCON Center on Sunday, better known as the Hare Krishna Temple. I was amused by the sight of fair skinned Europeans dressed in saris and dhotis but it was also a place of so much beauty. The altar was an ornate and gilded structure that held a variety of deities, some of them primitive and folky with giant painted eyes. At the altar's center was a skillfully rendered idol of dark-skinned Lord Krishna, an incarnation of Vishnu, who held a jeweled flute up to his cherry-colored lips. At his side was his consort Radha, both of them wearing elaborate crowns of gold and uncountable strands of jewelry. Krishna's and Radha's outfits were frequently refreshed, in the same way that my sister used to change the clothes on her Barbie dolls.

Just before the offering of *prasadam,* the free food that attracted Berkeley's professional homeless, the Hare Krishnas danced and drummed and chanted before their deities with men on one side and women on the other. Bare-chested men on the altars waved hairy wands to keep flies away from the deities and fanned them to keep them cool. Carnations dipped in heady perfumes were tossed around and sniffed. It all reached a frantic peak until golden gates descended from the ceiling, the idols were encaged and the lights grew brighter. After worship ended, I sat on the floor with other visitors as devotees distributed paperback copies of the Bhagavad Gita with an insert of color illustrations. We listened to a short talk before the women devotees passed around paper plates of food that was bland, sweet and oily. Unlike most Indian food, it did not include garlic, onions or anything like spice.

In the reception hall of the temple were some paintings I got lost in. They were fairly recent works done by Western artists using the techniques of academic painting. These paintings had a photographic realism but depicted, in one example, the sky-colored Vishnu reclining on a bed of hooded cobras that were afloat on an ocean of foamy milk. Vishnu had four arms that held different items and one of them pointed up and had something like a rotary saw blade around his fingertip. He wore, as all Hindu deities do, an elaborate crown with a halo of a gold plate attached to its back and behind that was a second halo of light. The cobras that made up Vishnu's boat all had their own golden crowns.

Male devotees of the temple were glad to explain these paintings to male visitors and impart bits and pieces of the Hindu cosmology, something of endless complexity, which involved numerous ages, or *yugas*. "Time is like, totally infinite," said a devotee named Arjun who sounded like a surfer from the San Fernando Valley. He had very blue eyes and blond nubs on his head as well as the little lock of hair by which he would someday be yanked up to paradise. "This universe was preceded by another and will be followed by an infinite number of universes after that," he said as I admired a different painting of Vishnu. In this one, the Preserver was young, handsome and bare chested with closed eyes as he floated in the blackness of space surrounded by planets and spiral galaxies. The caption read "Lord Vishnu Dreaming the World."

"Infinite universes," I said, struck by the concept. "Really."

"Rilly," Arjun said with a chuckle of astonishment. "For like, three hundred trillion years... and then it like, totally repeats itself."

"So life is but a dream," I said. "Like in that song about rowing your boat."

"Totally."

"And why does this appeal to you?"

"Because for one thing, it's the truth! And for another, I like knowing that I'm never really gonna die." And then he chuckled again in relief from his worries.

I have to admit that I thought Arjun would have been cute if his head wasn't shaved and he didn't have a V-shaped slash of mud from the Ganges painted atop his nose.

"So, how do you guys feel about homosexuality?" I asked, pondering the homoerotic nature of the image. "Is that allowed?"

"Oh, no, dude. I mean, sex is for one thing only and that's making nice children raised in Krishna consciousness. As Prabhupada said, 'The homosexual appetite of a man for another man is demoniac and is not for any sane male in the ordinary course of life.'"

*

Upon seeing Ma Nerada Matanji at her *darshan* in my neighbor's backyard, I knew she had a different approach to gay people. After paying a voluntary ten dollars (like Lakshmi, Guru Mama did not turn anyone away who couldn't pay), I made my way through a crowded house built in the Spanish Revival style of the 1920s. The kitchen was full of cooks in maroon robes and included the Cookie Bearer. They were at work preparing vegetarian finger food: fried okra and eggplant, kofta balls, rice and lentil cutlets, and something like a pink fudge that I think was flavored with rosewater. The CB was laying out typical American cookies that included peanut butter, chocolate chip and oatmeal raisin. Everybody smiled at me, a new face, and wished me welcome, the typical "love bombing" that happens when a newbie checks out a cult. When I got to the very crowded backyard, Mama was sitting next to a square firepit and adding sticks to its blaze as well as occasional ladles of clarified butter as a sacrifice to the fire god, Agni. A male couple in embroidered dhotis with matching kurtas were circling the firepit with a sash of tulle that tied them together. It was a gay Hindu wedding.

Maybe half of the crowd were gay men and more than a few of them looked to have AIDS. Guru Mama returned to her usual place, on a mat in front of an outdoor altar, where she had a microphone. This altar was less colorful and less gilded than the ones at a Hare Krishna temple and it was filled with darker, brass idols. A dancing Shiva in a circle of fire was the largest and most prominent idol, but up on the left was a framed picture of Jesus kneeling to God in a beam of light. On the right wall was a black-and-white picture of Sai Baba, something of a nod to Islam. Around her neck, Mama had some different pendants that day including a diamond-studded Star of David. As musicians played a harmonium and tablas, she led the crowd in a *kirtan*, a call-and-response chant to Lord Shiva. Sannyasins brought out platters of food and offered them to the idols first before setting them on some picnic tables. The wedded couple took seats on the floor next to Mama and were wearing garlands of tuberoses that I could smell from where I stood.

"Gary and Gary have loved each other for so long," Mama squeaked in her comical accent. "And today, each of them has planted seeds in the field of each other that they will cultivate and harvest for a shared prosperity, a food that ends the hunger that is loneliness. The Garys have tied a knot that binds them, but it is a rope that is long enough to let them walk their own paths, a rope they can tug on when they need each other. There is nothing more holy than service, and the Garys will fulfill the holy duty of serving each other as well as of serving the world."

I winced — not at the sentiment of what Mama said, but of who else she sounded like with these circular sentences. Mama smiled as she picked up an antique silver platter with a cloche. "The last part of this ritual usually involves the tossing of rice over the married couple as a fertility blessing, but I think in this case, these are the right food options."

The Garys removed the cloche and held up a pair of bananas and everyone laughed, me included. After they peeled them, one Gary did a bit of fellatio on the other's banana to an uproar before they each took a bite. They looked to be deeply in love, very happy, and I was moved by their devotion. It made me long for a wedding and a more devoted partner of my own.

"Enjoy the feast! Om Shri Shiva," Mama shouted and the crowd, which included many less-than-hygienic homeless people, converged on the food. I was wiping at my eyes when someone said, "Are you crying, Tyler?"

I looked over to see Gene coming toward me, with the usual, condescending smirk on his face. He looked triumphant, as if he'd caught me at something.

"I love weddings," I said. "And rituals of all kinds. They make me cry."

"Do they, now? I'm a little... *surprised* to see you here."

"I was gonna say the same."

"Why?"

"Because you already have a guru."

I wanted to say gurus, plural, but I held back.

"There are many paths to actualization," he said. "Mama is a guide on just one of them. So why *are* you here?"

"She's my neighbor. Getting to know my neighbors."

"Just look at how she serves our community," he said in awe as we watched the passing of plates of food to a couple hundred people.

"She's kind of like Lakshmi," I said. "She offers religion to people who've been rejected by the one they were brought up in."

"Spirituality, Tyler. Mama says it again and again: 'This is not a religion, this is an interfaith spirituality.'"

"OK, spirituality," I said and a silence passed. "So does Lakshmi know you come here?"

"No," Gene said. "And we *don't* need to tell her. "

We were quiet, taking in the crowd, when a middle-aged woman in a tie-dye outfit walked past us and smiled and nodded.

She was wearing a large pearl-encrusted crucifix which reminded me of something I wanted to ask Gene.

"Gene, were you surprised to find out Bravermann is Catholic?"

"No," he said with a derisive laugh. "I knew that."

"You did?"

"Yes. We go to the same church." His smirk was back on. "I know other things about him, too."

I didn't like the sound of that.

And on top of everything else he believed in, Gene was also Catholic?

When I got home, Kyle was on the phone. On the table was an opened wedding invitation, one of those elaborate, embossed kind with an envelope inside an envelope.

"He just walked in," Kyle said. "OK, Bart. I'll tell him. Bye."

"Tell me what?"

"We're invited to a wedding. My cousin Margaret Anne who lives in Patchagoola."

"*We're* invited? To a wedding in *Alabama*?"

"My parents want to meet you," he said.

"*Your* parents."

"Yes."

"So they know you're gay and I'm gay and that I launch my pork rocket into your fudge tunnel."

"Yeah, I told my dad you're pretty good at it. He sounded interested."

"I don't know," I said. "Aren't they all Baptists?"

364

"This branch are Southern Methodists — but that's practically the same thing down there."

"Sounds like a trap," I said. "How do you know they won't drag us to some remote hunting cabin and tie us up while some preacher attempts to cast out our devils? And shoot us through the head if it fails?"

"If it works then we'll finally be cured." Kyle shrugged his shoulders. "Tyler, I figured we go to this wedding then drive to New Orleans and have some real fun. It's Mardi Gras. We'll eat beignets and pralines and take tours of old plantations."

I was still absorbing this. After twelve years, I was finally going to meet Kyle's parents and not as his roommate, but as his romantic partner. His mother listened to Rush Limbaugh every day. His father, as an air force pilot, had dropped napalm and bombs on the North Vietnamese.

"All right," I said, sighing with apprehension. "I guess we should start shopping for dresses and some matching bags and heels. We don't want to disappoint them."

"Yeah, but let's not look too twinsy."

Once in a while, Kyle *could* make me laugh.

Chapter 30

It was a Thursday in February when some weird shit happened.

I was leaving on Friday for a week — a paid vacation! — and looking forward to some time off and a little adventure in the Deep South. Incidentally, Manna was sending out Southern fried chicken for the first time, a request from a few clients, and something Bryce assured us he could do for four hundred if we used our deep roasting pans as the fryers. "I used to work at Popeye's," he said, "and I know how to make it extra greasy." He and a couple of other volunteers were wearing goggles to guard against splatters as they tended the first two hundred breasts. The snap, crackle, pop of all that frying was intense, something we'd never heard in the kitchen on that level. Gene was super sullen that morning as he slid the side dish into the ovens: pans of baby red potatoes rubbed with olive oil and rosemary. He had been on the phone whispering to someone about something and looked relieved when Madge showed up to volunteer.

I went over to the community room's stage to check up on the volunteers packaging slices of pecan pie when Gene and Madge entered. They went to the other end of the stage and took a seat on the bench behind the piano and whispered in privacy. As usual, Madge was comforting him, her hand rubbing his back as she listened to him while nodding her head. Bryce burst through the swinging door.

"Oh, Miss Pee-Pee! Did you forget something?"

"What?"

"Your potatoes? The ovens are kind of... you know... cold when they're not turned on."

"Oh shit!" Gene said, and we all ran in. It was eleven fifteen — ten minutes was not long enough to bake potatoes.

"Pressure cookers," Gene said.

We grabbed some volunteers and ran down to the storage unit and brought up four, beat-up and tubby pressure cookers that had been donated by a defunct restaurant. They were heavy and their lids had scary-looking pressure gauges on top with cracked knobs. We scrambled to transfer the uncooked potatoes into them, filled them with water, then screwed on their lids and hoped for the best as we set them on the flames of the stoves.

"That one's too full," I said to Gene, as the last of them was filled to the brim.

"Then we'll open it last," he said, annoyed with me. "If they don't cook, then fine, not everyone gets potatoes today."

We told Jonnie to "pad the prayer" and at eleven forty-five, we turned off the flame of the first cooker, released its steam, and then unscrewed its lid to find some slightly underdone potatoes. We dumped them out, drained them, then poured some melted butter on top and the assembly began. We were at about the three hundred mark when we heard a loud, rattling noise and then a hiss of steam that turned to a whistle. We watched at the last pressure cooker shook and spun on the stove.

"Shit! That back burner's still on! It's gonna blow!" Bryce shouted.

"Turn it off!" Gene said.

"You do it!"

"Everybody, out of the kitchen!" I shouted as the rattling got louder.

As the volunteers exited, I crouched as I approached the stove and turned off the flame just as the cooker exploded. The lid blew off and up, smashing into the ceiling and through it, puncturing the sprinkler system. Potatoes splattered across the ceiling and the walls. Water from the ceiling poured into the pans of hot oil and exploded into steam clouds. Plummeting potatoes landed in the oil and sent up little geysers. The sizzling sounded like a hundred angry beehives. I was backing away when the lid fell out of the ceiling and flipped one of the frying tubs. The hot oil raced over the linoleum, scorching it, and sending up smoke and a toxic stink. In a great *whoosh*, a grease fire flared from the stove, one that licked at the ceiling. The water dripping on the fire spread it to the next stove and the flames were like whack-a-moles that danced and hissed.

Bryce grabbed the fire extinguisher, but he slipped and fell in the hot oil. "Fuck," he screamed when the hot oil soaked through his pants and singed him. He held tight to the extinguisher, pulled the safety pin, and aiming up at the stove, he managed to douse the flames with clouds of yellow powder.

"No, *The Sorcerer's Apprentice* by Paul Dukas. It's today's theme music." He jerked his head towards Gene. "Too bad our evil sorceress couldn't come back and fix it all with a wave of her magic wand."

"Well, I hope you and the sorceress have a fun week," I said. "I'm off to the land of Southern fried chicken."

"How dare you!" Bryce said, like he was Scarlett O'Hara.

"How dare I what?"

"Leave me alone for a week with Miss Pissy Pants! You, sir, are no gentleman."

The rehearsal dinner for Kyle's cousin Margaret took place in the backyard of a renovated plantation home. It was a gathering of the blondest people I have ever seen. With my light brown hair, I was the darkest of them except for Eric, a handsome Jewish guy who had married into the extended family. His wife, Becky, was one of Kyle's other cousins, and having heard "some homosexuals from Los Angeles would be in attendance" they sought us out. "We figured you'd be the only other Democrats," Becky said.

"You figured right," I said with relief. "I'm Tyler, a *feigele* from the decadent fleshpots of Hollywood, California"

"Eric," said her husband with a warm smile and a handshake. "A bagel eater from Jew York City"

"Oh, you're the other guy that's getting lynched."

We got in line for the evening's repast, something called Brunswick stew that included tomato sauce and corn kernels. Traditionally it was made with squirrels, rabbits or possums, but the Douglas family's version was to make it with local venison. Kyle's

I turned around and saw that through the indoor windows, a crowd in the community room was watching the spectacle. Their looks turned from concerned to amused as they took in our wet clothes and hair and an epic mess that was everywhere. Triggered by a smoke alarm, the fire department arrived. The first fireman to enter slipped on the greasy floor before we could warn him and he fell on his ass. One of his fellow firemen slipped when he helped him up. Water continued to pour from the ceiling then spread across the floor and into the community room then down the front and back steps. Nigel ran for Felix, the custodian, eating a burger down the street and he hurried back to turn off the main valve.

The last one hundred meals were ruined as they were soggy with water or covered in a wet powder of monoammonium phosphate. One thing we could send out was the dessert and salad along with cans of Ensure protein drink. The three of us spent lunchtime on our hands and knees mopping up oil and water with a week's worth of towels. After the drivers left, we couldn't prep the Friday meal or do much of anything since we had no water. Felix came in and announced, "No one is to use the toilets until further notice." We put some of the afternoon volunteers to work at wiping potatoes from the walls and ceiling as we waited for the plumber. He called at five and told Jonnie, "It's gonna be tomorrow." It was near six when we had contained the mess and were finally locking up the supply cage. Bryce started singing the bassoon line from a familia symphony and then its tune. I joined him in it, but couldn't place it

"What are we singing?" I asked. "Theme from Alfre Hitchcock?"

uncle by marriage was Alton Douglas, the portly descendant of carpetbaggers who had bought up the local cotton plantations after the "War of Northern Aggression." Alton had converted his land from growing cotton to fast-growing pine trees which he sold to a Canadian paper mill that was a town over and spewed a terrible stink. He also owned the local power plant and the motel where we were staying. His hobby was hunting and he had shot and butchered the deer that was in the stew. In the foyer of his very traditional home were some glass gun cabinets that displayed both antique and modern weapons.

"Welcome, welcome all," Alton said to us with a handshake. "Get yourself a drink over at the bar then bring a bowl to my nigger, Melvin, and he'll get you fixed up with some stew." He pointed to a Black man tending a cauldron over a fire pit.

"You're *what?*" I said to Alton.

"We'll do that, thank you," Kyle said and pushed me in the direction of the bar.

"What fucking century are we in?" I said as we got in line for mint juleps. "Did you hear what he said? He's a racist asshole!"

"Shh!"

"And I am not eating Brunswick stew with *venison.*"

"Why not?"

"Because it's like eating Bambi."

"You're in the South," he said. "You eat what you're offered."

We extended our bowls to the Black employee, a middle-aged man wearing overalls and a John Deere cap. He ladled some brown goop into our bowls that made a sound like a soft bowel movement and was not dissimilar in appearance. "Some corn bread, sir?" Melvin asked.

"Yes, sir," I said and he dropped a buttered, gritty cube atop the dark brown mess. Kyle's pretty cousin, Margaret, someone he hadn't seen in ten years, came over to us, all smiles and femininity, just as we were spooning up.

"So nice of you to come all the way from California," she said. "Now, Kyle, what keeps you out *there*?"

"Showbiz," Kyle said.

"Showbiz! Now that sounds interesting. And you, Tyler?"

"Same. I'm a screenwriter."

"A screenwriter? Now, what, please tell me, is that exactly?"

"We write the scripts for movies and TV shows — you know, the stories and the dialogue for the actors. At the moment I'm working as a chef."

"A chef! At a restaurant?"

"No, I work for a nonprofit. We make food for people who are homebound with AIDS."

"Oh!" she gasped and looked stricken. The A word had come up. "Well, that is *very* interesting! And Los Angeles... you *like* living there? How's that working out for you?"

"We love it," I said. "It's a fascinating place, maybe the most cosmopolitan city in the world. And California's got everything — mountains, beaches, deserts. It's just spectacular. You'll just have to visit sometime."

I wanted to ask her how she liked living in a shithole like Patchagoola but my own Southern mother raised me better than that.

"Well, to each his own," she said with a little laugh. "You know, when we heard you were coming, well... we didn't know what to expect. But now that I've met you, I just want to say that y'all are just *so* sweet."

"Likewise," I said.

In the morning, we took a drive before the wedding which convinced me that Patchagoola was a shithole's shithole. The motel was at the end of Main Street which had a series of old, stately mansions but between their lots were tiny little shacks that I first mistook for dog houses since their roofs were too low to stand under. I realized these had been the sleeping shelters of slaves. The surrounding areas were a hodgepodge of mobile homes, prefab houses and plenty of shabby, shotgun shacks with sinking roofs and wobbly porches. Many of these houses had old, rusting cars with their tires removed that were perched atop piles of cinder blocks. Yards were cluttered with rusting appliances, broken furniture and old mattresses with jutting springs. Washing machines were on front porches and clothes were hung to dry on lines. As there was no municipal trash collection, refuse was hauled out to piles in the woods and we saw some bristly, feral pigs rummaging through the garbage.

We went into something like a supermarket and found tall jars of pig's feet, pig's ears and pig's knuckles in red vinegar at the manager's counter where you could buy cigarettes and liquor. Kyle got some Marlboro Lights while I examined the sweets, which included ugly discs of peanuts glued together by a red gunk and cheap cookies with an unnaturally yellow icing called Stage Planks. The slovenly, mostly toothless man in front of us slapped a plug of chewing tobacco on the counter along with a Dr. Pepper, a bag of beans and a hunk of fatback. Without his having to ask, the clerk added a pint of Early Times to the order. The man counted the coins of his change and realized he had enough to toss in a banana Moon Pie.

As we drove around, we saw lots of portable signs on wheels with an arrow at the top that pointed toward a home business of some kind. Some of them were advertising pecans or puppies or Christian day care but most were for boiled peanuts. We spent a dollar on a plastic bag full of them and discovered that when peanuts are boiled they taste like mushy black-eyed peas and are just as disgusting.

The wedding was at a plain but well-maintained church, a white, wooden structure with a few stained glass windows. The window behind the altar depicted a blond Jesus as a shepherd with a lamb in one hand, a crook in the other and a flock of sheep behind him. The ceremony was unremarkable except for a stern-looking man in a kilt who played "Amazing Grace" on a bagpipe; it was a nod to the groom's Scottish heritage and a reminder that all of us, until we are saved, are wretches.

As there was nothing like a decent hotel in the area or an upscale restaurant, the reception was held in the same backyard as the rehearsal dinner. The meal was a cliché of Southern cuisine: fried chicken, chicken fried steak, candied sweet potatoes, collard greens and mac and cheese. The canapés were little sandwiches of pimento cheese or tomatoes and butter on crustless white bread. All of it was prepared and served by a staff of Black women who kept in the back of a smaller, second kitchen that was behind the main one. Kyle and I filled our plates, and for the first time, I would be joining him and both his parents at the same dinner table as well as some of his siblings. I took a deep breath.

I had met Kyle's dad Gunther once before, a retired air force colonel, when he was staying in Los Angeles for a couple of nights to attend a Christian men's conference. He had taken us to Marie Callender's for dinner and asked us to join hands and pray with him after we returned with our chilled plates from the salad bar. After that, he asked me what I thought about last night's Lakers game and that "crazy coach of theirs who gets so upset." When I told him I didn't follow basketball, the rest of the dinner was all too quiet. Before the entrees came, Gunther combed his hair at the table after licking his comb to moisten it.

In Patchagoola, I learned Kyle's mom, Mary Louise, was the talker in the family. I had heard her voice once before, when she sent Kyle a cassette tape of the time she made it on to Rush Limbaugh's radio show as a call-in guest, a very proud moment for her. She had asked Limbaugh to elaborate on his idea that the existence of gorillas disproved the theory of evolution. Pleasantly plump with pink skin and large blue eyes that were always searching, Mary Louise had been raised in Patchagoola and was the fourth daughter of a Baptist minister. She thought it was her job to run the conversation, which she did in a circular fashion. She peppered everyone with unrelenting questions about their flights and how they had slept, interrupting them before they could finish. I wondered if Kyle had inherited his own "loquaciousness" from her. Mostly I wanted her to shut the fuck up. The faces around the table were glum as we endured her bland interrogation. "Tyler," she said, getting to me again. "How was the weather in California when you left?"

"Sunny," I said, "but we're hoping for a little rain next week, we—"

"Oh, that's good," she said, turning to the one daughter in the family. "Lorena, what was it like in Spokane?"

"A little chilly," said Lorena, as Mary Louise moved on to get the next weather report from the fourth of her six sons, Elias.

"Excuse me," I said loudly, asserting myself. "Mary Louise, you've been asking a lot of questions. I have one for you. Why are all the houses here on stilts?"

She looked at me, blinking in the silence. Kyle jerked with discomfort — I had broken some protocol.

"I don't know," she said.

"Maybe it's because it floods a lot?" I said. "I imagine they get a lot of rain since I think Alabama's climate is classified as humid subtropical. Isn't it?"

"I don't know that either."

"Patchagoola sounds like a Native American name. Do you know the name of the tribe that lived here before the European settlers? Were they Cherokees or Choctaws? Seminoles? The Alibamu?"

"Well, I just don't know, Tyler, I —"

"The interesting story is that some thought the tribes in Alabama were the descendants of Aztecs who had fled Cortez and the Spanish in Mexico. But I don't think that's something historians or anthropologists buy into."

"Why, I have no idea," she said, absently blinking. Around the table, the others were looking at me with a sideways glare and Gunther was giving me the stink-eye. I knew I was being rude and superior, but at last the chitchat had stopped.

"Oh, look," Kyle said to fill the silence. "They're cutting the cake."

"Thank Jayzus," I said with a Southern accent, grateful for the chance to leave the table.

"Kyle, breakfast tomorrow is at eight," his father said. "At the Kintuckett Inn."

"I'm sorry, Gunther," I said. "We already made plans for breakfast."

"We did?" Kyle whispered.

"We did."

Kyle walked with me toward the wedding cake as plates and a fancy cutter came out. The bride and groom arrived to cut the first piece. The photographer readied his shot for the moment Margaret would likely smear her new husband's face with frosting when they fed each other.

"We have breakfast plans tomorrow?" Kyle whispered to me.

"Yeah," I said. "I'm asking Betty and Eric to join us at a place called Let's Get the Fuck Outta Here. Oh, there they are, let me ask them."

Betty and Eric were glad to join us for breakfast at the Kintuckett which was the only restaurant in town, a former inn with walls decorated with beaver traps and mounted stag heads. The four of us who were "Yankee trash" managed to discuss the latest Amy Tan novel, the rudderless presidency of George Bush, and a real-life court case that Eric had worked on that inspired an episode of *L.A. Law,* my favorite show at the time. Betty and Eric were curious about the Halloween parade in West Hollywood and shared stories about the one in South Beach. They were telling us about one of their friends, a fellow lawyer, whose weekend life was as a fabled drag queen, a nurse named Anna Phylactic Shock.

We were laughing when Kyle's family filtered in, all dressed up for church. The men were wearing coats and neckties, the women were wearing dresses.

"Will we see you later at church?" Gunther asked us, taking in our casual attire.

"I don't think so, Dad," Kyle said. "We've got to hit the road."

We chatted briefly with Kyle's parents who hugged both of us in the parking lot before we drove off in our rental car and they left for services. "We love you," said his dad to us both. When they were in the rearview mirror, I exhaled.

"So Mom just told me we're invited to another wedding soon," Kyle said. "Elias is getting married. In Idaho."

"Oh, joy," I said.

"You don't want to go?"

"No, I don't want to go — which is different from saying I *won't* go."

He looked over at me and frowned.

"You don't like my family."

I shrugged.

"Is your mom always like that?"

"Like what?"

"She's sweet, but she just took over the conversation. Who put her in charge?"

"She was just happy to see everybody, to have us all together."

"But its yak-yak-yak, a bunch of boring chitchat. She didn't let us talk with each other. She was kind of driving me crazy."

Kyle was quiet before he looked at me with a hurt expression.

"You're talking about my mom," he said.

"I know but I can't pretend that I liked spending time with her. And if you looked around the table, no one else was enjoying it either. They were just *enduring* her."

Kyle gave the slightest nod. "She can be a little... oppressive."

"More than a little. And, I'm sorry... but their religion, their politics, their lack of curiosity. They don't read books or go to movies. And lest we forget... your father dropped napalm on the Vietnamese."

"We don't talk about that," Kyle shouted. "He did his duty. They're my parents, Tyler. And I got a lot of love from them."

"They don't love *you*. They don't know who *you* are. They didn't know you were gay until a few months ago."

"Just cool your jets, mister. This was supposed to be a fun trip."

"Yeah, well, maybe I should be like you and your mom and just pretend everything's fine and smile and blab blab blab all the time. Look at me," I said, stretching my lips in a smile to reveal my molars. "I'm so happy! Let's just make a bunch of stupid jokes and stick our heads in the sand when we don't want to deal with shit like burning children from the sky."

"Asshole," Kyle said, shaking his head. He stepped on the accelerator as we sped past another sign for boiled peanuts. I was still choked with anger, the source of which we had yet to discuss.

We had loved New Orleans the first time we visited. Outside of the tourist traps of Bourbon Street, we found the French Quarter to be charming and quaint and enjoyed the fried and fattening food, the music clubs in basements, the Voodoo and Mardi Gras museums, and the aboveground cemeteries crammed with tombs and mausoleums. We'd also taken a swamp tour and eaten fried alligator (very fishy and not worth the chewing) under a bald cypress tree with some shy Japanese tourists. We determined to come back for Mardi Gras but I did not anticipate what a very different city The Big Easy is during its most famous festival. The traffic into the city that Sunday afternoon was horrendous and it took two hours to reach our hotel once we got off the highway. The streets were overrun with tourists whose only interest was in drinking and getting laid. In our hotel lobby was a throng of loud, drunk frat types wearing T-shirts that read "Beer is God" and "Free Mustache Rides." They chugged from bottles and to-go cups as they gathered to attend a wet t-shirt contest with loaded water pistols.

After we checked in, we bought a couple of strands of overpriced plastic beads from a street vendor to show everyone we were there to party. The French Quarter was stuffed with revelers and in its second- and third-story windows were women lifting up their tops to shake their boobs in return for beads. It took a while before we could squeeze ourselves over the Lavender Line near St. Anne Street, an area mobbed with drunken homosexuals.

It was a little cold, in the lower fifties, but Kyle took off his shirt and tied it around his waist to show the world what he'd been working on at the gym. Up in these windows it was men who were beckoning passersby to drop their pants, display their junk, then lavish them with *throws*. After Kyle got a few beers in him, he shucked his pants more than a few times. Using his long arms, he plucked the beads out of the air, stealing some from his competition. When he shuffled a few lengths with his pants down, he got a downpour of cheap jewelry. As we walked, some men attempted to pull him into circles where they might get a touch and a taste of him. Soon he had a ridiculous number of beads around his neck, a pile that extended a foot off his chest. He looked like some giant, iridescent pigeon.

As I was looking at him, I felt like we were having two completely separate experiences. He was reveling in the attention, happily drunk, and caught up in the spirit of Mardi Gras. I was sober after drinking half of a single, sickeningly sweet hurricane that had very little booze in it. I had a strange and sudden feeling of plunging and of the world going dark. As I looked at Kyle draped in green, purple and yellow necklaces, he was like some bizarre apparition, a grotesque, glittering entity from another world. I felt like I was watching him from afar, through a tear in the space-time continuum. He had become a garish demon with an insatiable hunger for attention. I imagined he had a pointed tail that extended from the bottom of his spine and that his feet had turned into hooves. He looked satanic as he leered at me with yellowed goat teeth.

"You don't have many beads," he said.

I took the single strand of beads from around my neck and tossed them to him. "Here," I said. "You need these more than I do." I turned my back and left.

"Where are you going?" he shouted.

"Away from you," I said. "You don't want me here. And I don't want to be here."

I tried to read in our hotel room but I couldn't concentrate — I was a prisoner of my angry gloom. I turned on the television and watched local coverage of Mardi Gras events and endless commercials for cheap, fried food. One offer, for $2.99, included hush puppies, chicken fingers, french fries and double-battered shrimp with a beignet for dessert. A news story covered the Baptist protesters, a very well-fed group of men, who stood on St. Anne with their signs reading "Fags Burn in Hell" and "Love the Sinner, Hate the Sin." They were taunted by drag queens who offered them beads and sniffs of poppers. A few hours later, around 1 a.m., Kyle showed up. He stood quietly in the doorway, drunk and wobbling, and still wearing his glittering treasures: the material proof that he was an object of desire.

"I came back," he said, shrugging before he closed the door.

"So what's his name?" I asked.

"Whose name?"

"The one you're having an affair with. He's in London? An English bloke?"

He was quiet.

"I'm not happy," he said. "I'm not happy with you. I haven't been for a while."

"I know."

"I have to shut down around you," he said with a terrible sadness, on the verge of sobbing. "I can't be myself."

"Sometimes *you* should shut down. It's hard to be around somebody who's always on. It's embarrassing."

"Embarrassing. Really."

"Yeah, embarrassing to be with someone so needy. You turn every social situation into the Kyle Show. And it's not *our* show. You push me into the audience."

I jumped out of bed and danced, frantically throwing out my arms. "Hey, everybody, I'm here! I'm Kyle! Look at me, look at me, look at me! Like me, like me, like me! Laugh at my jokes! I'm funny! Pay attention to *meeeeee*! Look how many beads I have!"

He was quiet, looking at me with tears in his eyes but my anger was unstoppable. Everything I'd ever held back was gushing from my mouth now, a fire hose that had no valve.

"I don't like to going to parties and dinners with you," I shouted, collapsing into a chair. "You start doing your act, all these planned jokes and bad puns, and a lot of it is just lame. It makes me uncomfortable. And you're loud! It hurts my ears to listen to you."

He stared at me with a wounded look.

"I am not loud!"

"You're excruciatingly loud! And you don't include me in your conversations, or introduce me as your boyfriend. When I *am* talking, you get belligerent and interrupt me until the attention is back on you. It's oppressive!"

He was breathing heavily under his mass of beads, sniffling as he wiped at a tear racing down his cheek.

"Oppressive. Really."

"Yeah. It's like being around your mother."

He shook his head and slumped. "You are just... so fucking hurtful."

"I'm truthful," I said. "And the truth hurts." He lit a cigarette.

"Well, you're no fun anymore," he said. "You haven't been for years. You squash all my fun and I am just *over* it."

Silence passed. I was resenting the stink of the cigarette but I also wanted one.

"So does he think you're funny?" I asked.

"Who?"

"This guy you're seeing on your trips abroad. Does he laugh at your jokes?"

"I am not seeing anybody!"

"I ask because that's how you picked your past boyfriends. You told me that once — 'Dirk and Noah were both kind of dull but they thought I was funny.' Same with your friends — you pick people because they're a good audience."

We were quiet again. Kyle went to the bathroom and I heard the sound of beads falling on the floor after he took a long piss. I had that feeling of being clamped by anger, a steel trap of it around my head and neck.

"You know, you're the one who's needy," he said, stepping out with his new offensive.

"Oh, am I?"

"You're always home. Whenever I get home, there you are, waiting for me."

"It's my home! You're my boyfriend. Where else am I supposed to be? Who else am I supposed to wait for?"

"But you're home all the time. You're a homebody."

"I'm a *homebody*? I'm *out* all the time! I do things with other people! Sometimes I go to plays and movies by myself because you're never around. I make a point of getting home in time to see you before bed!"

"But you need me too much. I walk in the door and you're all over me. I can't meet those expectations."

"Listen to me, Kyle. If I were never home, you'd complain about *that*. I won't battle you to stay in this relationship. If you're unhappy, then *leave*! Get the fuck out. Whatever you're going through, I am *not* the source of your misery."

"Don't be so sure."

"Well, I guess you'll find out soon enough, won't you?"

I knew what I had to say next should not be shouted.

"Look, I'm not dealing with someone who's rational," I said. "I'm tired of being resented, tired of being blamed for your shit, tired of being hated. You *want* me to fight with you, you *want* to play out some drama."

He sat down at the edge of the bed and wiped at tears. "So where did you get your doctorate?" he said. "The one that qualifies you to psychoanalyze me?"

"If you don't look inward, somebody has to. Kyle, the best thing that ever happened to this relationship was the AIDS crisis. We were forced to be monogamous and the fighting ended. I liked it, the peace that followed... I felt safe with you. All this shit coming up now is like those old days... you needing to be adored."

"That's bullshit."

"No, it's not. I'm sorry I don't make much money. I'm sorry I'm not a big-time screenwriter or a director who could help you with your career. Maybe that's who you need. But admit it, if I was that guy, you'd be jealous of me. You'd resent my success even if you had your own. We're not on the same team, Kyle, we never were. You want to win and you want me to lose. You're jealous of *everyone* who gets ahead."

He looked at me in silence as he lit another cigarette. "I thought it was gonna be you," he said, using his pensive voice. "You've got friends who made it, friends who aren't as talented as you. But you gave up. You're working as a *chef*."

The way he said "chef" made it sound like it was another word for dog shit.

"I have *not* given up," I said. "I have not stopped writing."

I could hear his cigarette burning in the silence. He was looking away from me, lost in thought. I imagined he was planning how he could take his revenge. He'd probably go back out to Mardi Gras and *really* enjoy himself.

"Can you give me a ride tomorrow?" I asked.

"A ride?"

"To the airport."

"We fly back on Thursday."

"*You* fly back on Thursday. I'm going home tomorrow."

At the airport, I exchanged my ticket for a night flight that would get in after midnight — it would be a long day of sitting around but at least I wouldn't be at Mardi Gras. At the airport bookstore, I was looking for something light to read. I bought a book with a bright, cartoony cover of teenage witches and wizards aiming their magic wands at each other over a cauldron full of ghosts. The title was *Mordecai's Academy of the Dark Arts* and it was the story of a young warlock arriving for instruction in sorcery at a floating castle in the clouds. The academy was divided into different houses: rival factions that competed in jousting tournaments on winged horses when they weren't learning spells and potions. The student body was made up of witches, warlocks, wizards, mages, sorcerers, sorceresses, fays, fairies, brownies, and pixies, and some of them were more popular and magical than others. Some, like the hero, struggled to prove himself. It was supposed to be funny but I found it shallow and soon lost interest.

Once I'd put the book down, the melody of *The Sorcerer's Apprentice* was back in my head. I chuckled to remember that last day in the kitchen when each solution to a problem triggered a new one.

The Sorcerer's Apprentice...

The version in Disney's *Fantasia* was set in an old castle. What if I wrote a screenplay that reset the story in the American suburbs? And made it about a boy with a single mom and a little sister he took care of, and all of them were menaced by bullies? I could get Spielberg interested in that. I needed a theme — some bigger meaning if it was going to have any depth. I remembered something Lakshmi had said about Dinesh, that he was a "low-grade sorcerer" who flaunted his powers in public instead of keeping them secret. I started writing it all down on a pad I got from the flight attendant. The next day I would be at my computer and writing for the rest of my paid vacation to distract me from my pending breakup with Kyle — or so I thought.

The house we rented had a sad, eerie emptiness to it when I walked in — all too silent without Holden to greet me. The answering machine was flashing with a record number of fourteen messages. The first one was from Jeremy.

"Hey Tyler. I know you're on vacay, but call me as soon as you get this message. Shit's happening. They fired Bravermann."

I had released the years of anger and resentment I had felt toward Kyle in New Orleans, a geyser that could not be capped. And soon I would be doing the same in Los Angeles.

Chapter 31

"What are you doing here?" Gene asked me when I showed up at the kitchen as he and Bryce set up for the morning. "You're supposed to be at Mardi Gras."

"Why was Bravermann fired?"

Bryce had been filling the coffee maker when he shut off the water to listen. We both stared at Gene who went quiet, shrugging before he finally spoke.

"He was insubordinate."

"Who says? To who?"

"To *whom*. Lakshmi... and Jacob."

"Insubordinate how?"

"They told him to do things... that he didn't do."

"Yeah, that's the definition of insubordination. What didn't he do?"

Gene was quiet again. Bryce and I looked at each other with eyebrows raised in skepticism.

"We need specifics or this is all bullshit," I shouted. "How was he insubordinate?"

"Why are you so angry?" Gene asked.

"Why aren't you?" I shot back. "Bravermann got you a raise and benefits and a paid vacation. He stabilized this organization."

"I'm sure Lakshmi had her reasons."

"Like what?" I shouted.

Gene shook his head, exhaling noisily as he rolled his eyes.

"Can we please have this conversation without all this anger?"

"I'm pissed off!" I shouted. "We should all be angry! Lakshmi has fucked up again!"

"She's done no such thing," Gene said. "And I think you should go, Tyler. You're not scheduled today."

Bryce and I looked at each other and shook our heads in silent agreement.

"So what's it taste like, Gene?" Bryce said.

"What?" Gene responded.

"Lakshmi's asshole. You're too gay to lick her pussy but I bet you can really get your tongue up her rectum."

"That is *so* disrespectful," Gene said, but with the slightest grin.

"Disrespectful?" Bryce said. "We should respect *her*? We all know the reason that witch fired Bravermann. He stole her spotlight."

"Exactly," I said. "She can't stand it that we like him."

"I'm sure you both *love* him," Gene said as his eyebrows crunched and his mouth thinned to a sneer. "I'm sure you're both hoping to get an invitation to his dungeon."

"His what?" I asked.

"His sex dungeon. Everyone knows he has one."

"No, everyone does not," I said. "And I don't give a shit about his sex life. At least he has one, unlike some people."

Gene's face fell. I'd wounded him, and I'd wanted to.

"If you think we're defending Bravermann because he's beautiful you are sadly mistaken," I said. "You are just fucking sad. And if you don't stand up for him, you're just a tool — a gullible tool of some new age charlatan."

"*Charlatan*? Who are you calling a charlatan?"

"Miriam Steinmetz… also known as Lakshmi."

"Lakshmi started this organization," he said. "How dare you speak like that about her!"

"I'm calling her out for what she is — a phony, a snake oil saleswoman. She's no better than a televangelist, flaunting her charity while milking all the stupid sheep for their money. *The Way* is bullshit."

"*The Way* is bullshit?" Gene said, his mouth agape.

"Total bullshit! It's not a prophecy from God or Jesus. There is no such thing as prophecy! There never has been. There's no such thing as God."

Gene looked away from me as he gasped. "And I thought you were spiritual," he said. "You're a nihilist!"

"I'm an atheist," I said, saying it out loud for the first time. "And you're a child looking for Mommy… instead of becoming your own adult."

He stopped midway as he took a colander out of the supply cage and held it to his chest.

"I didn't realize how little respect you have for Lakshmi... or for me."

"I have zero respect for her and will have none for you if you don't stand up for Bravermann."

"How do *you* know what Bravermann did or didn't do?"

"We both know what he *did do* you fucking ingrate! If Bravermann's done something wrong, they'd tell us what it is! Don't be so gullible! That's the problem with your whole stupid life, Gene — you're so fucking gullible! Lakshmi is no different than Dinesh or any of these other frauds you're hoping will spring you from your misery."

Gene looked like he was going to cry.

"You can't talk to me like this," he said, a tremble in his voice. "I'm your superior!"

"You are not superior to me in any way. Unlike you, I do my own thinking."

Gene was wordless, frozen. He was still holding the colander against his chest. Jonnie entered the room, cocking her head in a scolding way.

"Well, good morning, Tyler," she said, surprised to see me. "What's all this yelling about?"

"It is *not* a good morning," I said, then turned to Bryce. "Bryce, I'll call you later. We're meeting Bravermann for breakfast."

"Give him my *love* and my *respect*," Bryce said. "And tell him thanks, that I had the best time last night at the *dungeon*."

I joined Jeremy, Joffrey, Nigel and Tinka at a booth at Hugo's.

"Glad you could join us, Tyler," Jeremy said. "You... you came back early."

"Uh, yeah," I said shrugging. "I had enough beads and beer. If you've seen one of those parades you've seen 'em all."

Next to our table I heard a pair of screenwriters pitching to a development exec and his D-girl, a story about a stranded alien from another planet that's mistaken for a baby, gets taken in by an orphanage, and ends up being adopted by the lonely wife of the mayor of New York. Apparently, John Ritter was attached to play the mayor but Donald Trump was also interested and would raise some money if they gave him the part. And it was a musical, with songs by Air Supply.

Bravermann arrived, dressed in a button-down and slacks but no tie. He was not smiling but he was composed and stoic and asked each of us how we were. After we ordered and the waiter left, he set his palms on the table.

"Thank you all for coming this morning. I have yet to sign a nondisclosure agreement so this is my one chance to speak to you in a freer way."

"So they fired you because you were insubordinate," I said.

"That is what they're saying."

"Did they give you an example?" Nigel asked.

"No. I told them I wanted our fundraisers to be modeled after the ones for God's Love in New York. Lakshmi said no, that we didn't need that, and she didn't want anyone getting rich off of the AIDS crisis."

"Isn't that rich," I said. "Did you hire someone? Go behind her back?"

"Of course not. But I asked her what *her* plan was... how she would raise money. We went around and around on it. She said she'd have to pray on it, that God would provide, that we didn't need a business plan. She was waiting for a 'revelation' and she would get one when the time was right."

"What about Jacob?" Nigel asked. "Supposedly he's got a knack for business."

"Oh, he runs a few businesses. And Lakshmi's been his meal ticket. But Jacob's the one who fired me."

"Jacob did?" Jeremy asked.

"Yes. Lakshmi wasn't even in the office. She didn't want to be there. She'd been planning it for weeks, ever since she came back."

"And saw how well things were going," Jeremy said.

"Without her," said the Baguette.

"Did you try talking to Jacob?" asked Joffrey. "Ask him what this was really about?"

"No, Jacob doesn't want to piss her off by taking anyone's side but hers. She's the rainmaker and he…"

"Sucks up the crumbs," said the Baguette. "A bottom feeder."

Bravermann's forehead got furrowed. "And Jacob's kind of… a woman scorned," he said.

"He is?" asked Joffrey.

Bravermann shrugged. "He kept asking me out, inviting me to his place for dinner. Once he asked me what my favorite meal was. I told him it was pork chops and apple sauce. He said he'd make it for me. I told him 'no way' and that he needed to start acting more professionally."

"So Jacob has a crush on you," said the Baguette. "The fat little toad who thought he could get the hottie."

"Pretty much," Bravermann said. "And my lawyer will be bringing that up when we discuss my severance."

"Robert," I said. "I think I speak for everyone when I say we won't let this happen without a fight."

"Don't lose your own job," he said.

"I don't care if I do."

"Here's what I think you should do," Bravermann said spreading his hands on the table. "Unionize. It's what I encouraged them to do at the California Aids Project before I left. The people who are drawn to this kind of work don't always fend for themselves. They're self-sacrificing, vulnerable to exploitation. They want to be their mamma's good boys... and girls. Believe me, a year from now if Manna survives, it will be run like a corporation. Its director will be making two hundred and fifty thousand a year. And it will grow and move to a larger building and it won't depend on volunteers. And that will be a good thing for the clients."

Because Bravermann had suggested all of us attend one of Lakshmi's lectures and learn more about *The Way,* I decided I'd do just that on Thursday evening. And I'd reach for the mic at question time. I had something I was just dying to ask Lakshmi in front of her adoring followers.

I never needed to ask Lakshmi why she fired Bravermann.

Early on Thursday evening, I covered up my hair with a replica of the billed cap worn by the crew of the Nostromo from the movie *Alien.* I put on Kyle's aviator jacket that was too large and hid my body. The last part of my disguise was some gold-rimmed, nonprescription glasses, something that I wore to meetings with development execs to look intelligent. I waited until the last minute to walk into the Harmony Gold theater on Sunset Boulevard where

I handed a woman a ten-dollar bill who wished me "a beautiful evening." Keeping my head down, I took a seat in the back row as the lights dimmed.

"Ladies and gentlemen," said a voice through the loudspeakers. "Please welcome Lakshmi Steinmetz."

It was Pissed Off Lakshmi who took the stage that night, strutting out in black heels with red soles and wearing a blood-colored jacket over a black skirt. She put her hand over her eyes and squinted as she looked up at the control booth.

"Excuse me," she said when the applause died down. "Whoever is up in that booth, you're burning my eyes out."

The spotlight softened.

"Thank you all so much for coming," she began, her snarl turning to a smile. "A little bit of housekeeping first before we start our prayer. Some good news first — the paperback of *The Thousand Miracles of Love* will be out in June."

The audience applauded as someone two chairs over from me took a seat. Without looking directly at him, I saw it was Jacob Hellman. Had he spotted me?

"And now for some... other news," she said through an angry smile. "You may have heard that things are in flux at Manna from Heaven and the Being Centers. You may have heard that we let go of Robert Bravermann." She shrugged. "He's Catholic, he doesn't get it."

He's Catholic?

"We're looking for a new director who's a student of *The Way*, someone who is aligned with our spiritual values. This is, after all, a spiritual organization, and its mission continues and will not be interrupted. I can promise you *that*."

And there it was, an admission as to why Bravermann was terminated. Lakshmi was jealous of him, surely, but her reasoning, her official justification was that he didn't accept her as his spiritual authority. The only way in which he had been "insubordinate" was in his rejection of her new religion rebranded as "spirituality."

Bravermann had a case for religious discrimination.

I sat through the whole talk, just in case she brought up Bravermann again, even the passing of the mic where Betsy, poor, lovelorn Betsy, told the story of being involved with yet another man who wanted the milk but didn't want to buy the cow. Occasionally flashbulbs went off and I realized someone was taking pictures that night. As I was leaving, I noticed Duncan McKenna drifting out with the crowd, a notebook in one hand and a cassette recorder in the other. He was saying goodbye to a man with the camera when he noticed me and stopped in his tracks, trying to figure out who I was.

"Duncan, it's Tyler," I whispered. "I'm kinda incognito."

"Tyler! What are you doing *here*?"

"Long story. And you? Don't tell me you've converted."

"Fuck no. People magazine wants a story about Hollywood's glitzy guru," he said.

"Then I think you should buy me a drink."

Chapter 32

We were on high alert the following Monday. Weeks ago, a publicist had arranged for Eleanor Landon, a tele-journalist, to do a puff piece on Lakshmi for a prime-time news show. Lakshmi was arriving that morning to show Eleanor the kitchen of Manna for a story timed to air with the paperback release of The Thousand Miracles of Love. When I walked into the community room, Jonnie and Gene were circling around Joffrey's computer with a lit smudge stick. The smoky air had the sharp stink of burning sage as they nodded to the computer, then turned and bowed to the four ordinal points. Joffrey stood, his arms folded, looking at them with an amused skepticism. Gene was dressed in slacks, a button-down shirt and had on black leather dress shoes. He and Jonnie continued the ritual by doing a combination of what looked like Reiki and a "laying of hands" on the computer but their healing was directed at the monitor instead of the tower.

"Thank you, guys," Joffrey said. "But I think we should just bring it in for a repair. I've got a backup printout from yesterday so... we're good."

Gene was chanting "*Nam myoho renge kyo*," and Jonnie was muttering "send your healing vibes to this computer, God, so that it may continue to serve you and our mission. Amen."

I stared at Gene and Jonnie, trying not to laugh, as Gene took a seat at the table next to her.

"Good morning, Gene. You look nice today," I said in hopes that he would explain his clothing and seating choice.

"Thank you," he said, avoiding eye contact.

"You got dressed up to be on camera?"

"No, Tyler," he said, as if I were so dense. "I'm the executive chef now. I won't be in the kitchen anymore."

"You won't?"

"No. That's yours and Bryce's job now."

I was wordless but he could read from my face that I wasn't happy.

"Why are you looking at me like that?"

"You're not going to be in the *kitchen*?" I asked. "You won't actually be *cooking*? Taking out *trash*? *Mopping* at the end of the day?"

"No," he said, as if he were disgusted. "You're in charge now. In the kitchen anyway. I thought you'd be thrilled."

"Not really."

I went into the kitchen where Bryce was unlocking the supply cage. He jerked his head toward Gene. "Did you get a load of her?" he said. "In her male business drag?"

"At least he'll be out there."

Gene did not look at us when he came into the kitchen and went to the marker board to fill out the day's menu. And then, for the first time in months, he adjusted the client number to 428.

"Uh, four hundred and *twenty eight*?" I said to him. He shrugged his shoulders and raised his chin in his haughty way.

"I talked about it with Lakshmi and we're ending the cap. We can serve a few more clients."

"No, we can't," I said.

"Yes, we can. And we will."

He raised his eyebrows in triumph before he turned and walked out.

"Bitch is trying to make you quit," Bryce said.

"Not doing it. Then I can't get unemployment."

Gene returned to the table where he did nothing except sit and watch us, occasionally chatting with Jonnie, with the catalog from Rykoff opened to the same page and an empty order sheet. At one point he actually put his feet up on the table.

With the exception of Gene, we had not glammed up ourselves or the kitchen as we had done for the reporter from Vanity Fair. But Lakshmi and Eleanor Landon showed up in a cloud of glamour, sharply dressed and at the very worst time. Bryce and I were hard at work and timing the cooking of buttered noodles with the baking of Swedish meatballs. They were a childhood favorite of mine and a dish I had initiated, but it was the first time we had attempted it and it was not well made. Some of the meatballs had fallen apart and they were all different sizes, which gave them different cooking times. Unable to send out uncooked meat for safety reasons, we erred in overcooking them. The last step was to simmer them in a cream sauce, which was splitting because we had to use half and half when we realized that the heavy cream had spoiled.

Through the indoor windows of the community room, we watched the TV crew arrive. There was a segment producer, two cameramen, a sound man, some gofers and both a hair and makeup person. Eleanor and Lakshmi rehearsed walking into an area of the kitchen with the most flattering light and hit marks that had been taped on the floor. The hair and makeup guys stepped toward them and touched up lipstick and tamed stray hairs. Eleanor was one of those people who looked more like a star athlete than a serious journalist. Her thick blonde hair was perfectly coiffed upward and back to reveal strong, square features. She was wearing flats while Lakshmi was wearing three-inch heels so that they were closer in height.

Bryce and I were making the best of the meatballs as we assembled the volunteers for assembly. Bryce gave some parsley to the volunteers to de-stem and chop and then sprinkle as a cosmetic to give the end product some appeal. Lakshmi and Eleanor stood near the end of the assembly as Lakshmi explained our mission using her actressy, plum-in-the-mouth voice. The shooting stopped when they had to adjust for a sound check and review the audio.

"Hello, everyone," Lakshmi said to the busy volunteers during the pause. "Thank you all for your help today. Hello, Tyler."

"Hi," I said, not looking at her as I removed another pan of meatballs, shoveled them into a basin and then mixed cream through the drippings.

"Hi, Bryce," she said. "How are you?"

"Busy," he said, and turned back to the stove and the noodles, fishing one out to see if it was *al dente*.

"Thanks for letting us come by today," she said. "I brought some copies of my book if you'd like one."

"Nooooo, thank you," I said.

"I have enough asswipe at home," Bryce whispered to me and we shared a private laugh. Lakshmi stared at us with a combination of hurt and anger. The volunteers weren't happy to see her either and ignored her. Most of them knew Bravermann and had been charmed by his almost daily appearances. And they were well aware of how Bryce and I felt about Lakshmi, something written in dark ink on our faces. She was not among her faithful and not basking in adoration.

"Eleanor, we've come at a busy time," Lakshmi said. "Perhaps we should shoot this elsewhere, maybe out in the community room with the kitchen in the background."

"I think that's a wonderful idea," said Eleanor.

Just as the two of them and the crew left, Magdalena walked in wearing the same blue jeans and work shirt she had worn for the last year. I wondered if she'd ever owned a bra. She and Gene had obviously had a conversation and she was looking at me with contempt as she stood at the end of the assembly line. "Swedish meatballs?" she said. "This looks more like dog food."

"You would know," I said.

She was glowering at us when Jonnie teetered in. "Tyler," she said to me. "Is everything all right?"

"We're very busy," I said. "We're a little shorthanded since Gene decided he needs to park his ass at the same table as you."

"Lakshmi's worried about you and Bryce. She says there's a really bad vibe in here."

"She's right," I said. "The vibes *are* really bad. And she can take responsibility for them. Do you and Lakshmi want to help?"

"Of course we do."

"Then stay out of the fucking kitchen."

The bad vibes were about to get worse.

I was exhausted when I got home, but was determined to write something other than a screenplay when I got some rest. I was coming back from a walk with Holden when an airport shuttle stopped in front of our house. Kyle stepped out with his luggage.

Holden wagged his tail and strained on his leash. Kyle bent down to pick Holden up and let him lick his face. Kyle looked both sad and contrite as he looked into my eyes. After he set Holden down, he grabbed me for a deep, warm hug.

"I've wanted to do that for a while," he said, and I felt a strange and ugly jumble of emotions. I was glad Kyle was home because I had missed him, but I had been missing him for a while — we lived in the same house, but were seldom together. And when we were, he was distant or annoyed and yearned to be elsewhere. I was burning with hatred and hurt, but once we got in the house, we went straight to bed where I rolled on a condom and gave him the angry, punishing fuck he wanted. When he started crying, I asked him if I should stop but he shouted "No!" over his shoulder as if I were stupid for asking. When it was over, he fell asleep and appeared to me like some sad, freakishly oversized baby. I felt a strange, deepening sorrow for him and accepted that perhaps he was ruled by urges he couldn't control. To distract myself, I went to my computer, the one Kyle had so generously given me for my birthday, and worked on a letter to Lakshmi.

When he woke up, Kyle asked me to order a pizza for dinner, something I was glad to do and he was happy to pay for. I went to the phone and saw I'd missed my phone messages.

"Tyler, hi, my name is Emma Stern, I'm a journalist from the LA Times. I got your number from Duncan McKenna. I'm doing a story on Lakshmi Steinmetz and I'm wondering if you would give me a call."

Hell, yes.

I played the next message. "Hello, Tyler, this is James Ogridowsky from the United Food and Commercial Workers returning your call. Let's get you scheduled for a face-to-face with one of our reps."

Most definitely.

The last call was from Jeremy. "Hey, Tyler. Got a weather report for you — cloudy with a chance of shitstorm. Jacob's called an emergency meeting for tomorrow. Little bitchface might be there. She tried to get you fired."

Chapter 33

Bryce and I were sweaty, greasy and exhausted after a busy Tuesday but we drove together to the Being Center with our hands stinking from bleach. With Gene's butt glued to a chair outside of the kitchen, the days were longer and we were late when we entered the reception room to find its couches crowded with all the employees of the Center and Manna. Julie Sainsbury was not there. Both she and her felonious husband had quietly disappeared while Bravermann had been boss and Lakshmi was away. There was one new face, a man seated next to Jacob Hellman. One significant female face was missing.

"I'm Ben Gumport," said the new face, a man of average appearance and average height who stood to shake hands with Bryce and me. "I'm the interim director. You must be Tyler and Bryce."

Gumport was not warm or smiling. He had an intensity to him and the remnants of a Southern accent with a tone that always sounded like he was exhausted, being put upon, a perpetual victim.

He looked Bryce and me up and down and noticed my Swatch with its image of the Star Child from *2001 A Space Odyssey*. He took in the jewels of the ear studs Bryce wore then looked directly at our rings to evaluate Bryce's Navajo turquoise and the silver elephant I had bought in Tijuana for four dollars in 1980. I looked at Gumport's dark blond hair and saw he peroxided its top. His cheeks had acne scars and he was wearing a little bit of makeup — his complexion reminded me of a teenager wearing tinted Clearasil. I could smell that he was a smoker and heard it in his voice.

Bryce and I squeezed onto the couch next to Jeremy, Joffrey, Nigel and the Baguette. Jonnie and Gene were seated on the opposite side, next to Jacob... we had taken sides. The Center's employees were sitting on the other couches.

"Just about everybody's here," Hellman said. "Before we get started, I want to say that all of you are welcome to express your honest opinions this afternoon. You're welcome to say, 'Fuck you, Jacob Hellman, you're a real piece of shit' because this meeting is about clearing the air and getting our mission back on track."

I wanted to say, "Fuck you, Jacob Hellman, you're a real piece of shit" but held back.

"We'll start as soon as Lakshmi gets here," Gumport said after glancing at his watch. In the background, we could hear Lakshmi behind her door screaming on the phone at someone. Jacob signaled to Vonnie to nudge Lakshmi. "We're ready for you, Lakshmi," Vonnie said on the phone when she got to her desk. "Yes, everyone is here... just waiting for you. No, Lakshmi, no. Jacob asked me to. I am just telling you that the meeting is about to begin and we hope you can join us." Vonnie shook her head in annoyance as she hung up and took her seat. We waited in silence when we heard a door open and then the slow pitter-patter of what sounded like a child coming down the stairs.

Lakshmi was in plain mode — no makeup and wearing dark, loose workout clothing. Her hair kept falling over her face and she used her thumbs to pull it back. She looked around the room at our faces with a hurt look. "Hello," was all she said, with a terrible sadness, as if she'd just gotten a cancer diagnosis. Jacob brought her a wooden chair from the kitchenette and she sat just outside the room in the hallway, a position that put her at the top of the circle like the gemstone of a ring. She extended her hands to the right and left for a prayer circle and threw back her head. "Let us pray," she said.

"Lakshmi, no," said Gumport. "We should not start an employee meeting with a prayer."

Lakshmi went rigid, her mouth clenched and her eyes slitting.

"We talked about this," Jacob said to her.

"All right, all right," she said. "I will just say it is *very* difficult for me to leave God out of important matters."

"Noted," said Gumport. "But we're going to take some steps in a different, more professional direction as a part of this organization's growth."

I didn't know or trust this guy — but I liked this development.

"As Jacob mentioned, we want to have a frank discussion with all of you about your concerns for Manna and the Center," Gumport said as he looked at faces around the room. "This is a project that needs to change to serve its clients, to serve *more* clients and to make its employees feel safe and valued. We've learned that some of you are interested in unionizing."

"Are you opposed to our unionizing?" I asked.

"I am not," Gumport said.

"I'm completely opposed to unionizing, it's inappropriate!" Lakshmi said, raising her voice. "This is a nonprofit!"

"Is it?" I said. "A lot of people profit from this organization."

"Just what are you insinuating?" she snapped at me.

"In the spirit of honesty, Lakshmi, you use Manna to promote your book. It's printed on the back cover, isn't it? 'Lakshmi Steinmetz is the founder and chief executive officer of Manna from Heaven'... and isn't she a saint."

"I'm promoting Manna *with* my book," she said.

"The organization doesn't need your book, it needs leadership," I shot back. "And Jacob gets paid to be COO. What's your salary, Jacob? I bet you make more money than anybody else here," I said, staring at him. "Jacob also gets access to our client list, something he exploits for his nursing business. And before Bravermann, money for this organization just disappeared, vaporizing like *Mexican gas*, a result of *somebody's* poor choices. Lakshmi, why doesn't Julie work for you anymore? And what happened to her husband, the, uh, felon? Is he still on the board? No?"

"How dare you! I will not be slandered!" Lakshmi said, standing and thrusting her finger at me. "That is a series of lies and distortions!"

"No, it's not," Jeremy said. "Bravermann told us the bookkeeping here was a complete joke before he took over — no accountability, no reporting, and no oversight."

"We don't need oversight at the Being Center!" Lakshmi shouted. "*I* am the oversight! And I don't need to hear the opinions of Robert Bravermann!"

"Yeah, you do," I said.

"Robert Bravermann was the worst thing to have ever happened to this organization!"

"Bullshit!" I yelled at her. "He was the best thing to happen to it!"

"Tyler, stop yelling at Lakshmi!" Jacob shouted.

"If she can yell at us, we can yell at her. I thought we were being honest!"

"All right, stop!" Gumport said, making a tamping down motion with his hands. "Let's not yell and let's please discuss. What I understand, and correct me if I'm wrong, is that the majority of employees here were happy with Mr. Bravermann as director. They were opposed to his firing."

"You're darn fuckin' tootin,'" said the Baguette as heads nodded around the room.

"And beyond that," said Nigel, "we are extremely dissatisfied with the explanation for his termination. All we have been told is that he was insubordinate. We were given no specifics as to any actual transgressions or to their negative outcomes."

Lakshmi was wrinkling her nose and pinching her lips as Nigel spoke, her nails digging into the palms of her hands.

"Would you please, at this moment," Nigel continued, looking at Lakshmi, "give us an honest explanation of what he did or did not do that resulted in his dismissal."

Lakshmi was silent, twisting her hair around her fingers.

"We await your answer," Nigel said.

"I know the answer," I said.

"You do *not*," Lakshmi shouted.

"We all know why...it's obvious!" I said. "You're *jealous* of him! For all your newfound fame as an author, you still want *all* the attention."

"This is outrageous!" she shouted at me, her finger a dagger that stabbed the air as she stood. "That is a personal attack!" She turned to Gumport. "Really, Ben, I'm just supposed to take this? To stand here and be insulted? I want this *thing* out of here *now*!" she said pointing at me. "He no longer works here!"

"No, Lakshmi," Gumport said as she stood and paced. "You don't fire anybody, and if you do, you're firing me. We're working toward an environment where job safety is not endangered by honest engagement."

"What I said is the fucking truth," I shouted as I stood, connecting with an anger that blazed inside me. "But I also heard your explanation at Harmony Gold on Thursday, the one you made in front of hundreds of your *sheep*... I mean your followers."

"What are you talking about?" she said, as she stopped her pacing.

"I was there and so was a writer from People magazine," I shouted through gritted teeth. "You said, 'He's Catholic, he doesn't get it. This is a spiritual organization and I'm looking for a director who's a student of *The Way*.'"

She was grimacing as her face went red.

"Let's knock this down a decibel or two," said Gumport. "Lakshmi, Tyler, I need you both to take a seat."

"I'll sit down when she sits down," I said.

It was quiet for a moment when Jacob spoke up. "Look, Lakshmi does have a point," he said quietly. "This is a spiritual organization, right?"

"Is it?" I said, still standing. "I signed up to cook and deliver food to people with AIDS. Are you telling me that to work here I have to believe in the bullshit of *The Way of the Miraculous*?"

"The *bullshit* of *The Way?*" Lakshmi shouted. "How dare you denigrate my entire belief system!"

"I'm asking you a question, Jacob," I said, looking at him. "I'm not Catholic or spiritual. I'm an atheist. Do I get fired too, for my lack of religious beliefs? Or rather, my lack of *spiritual* beliefs, which is what Lakshmi calls her brand of snake oil... do I?"

Jacob started to speak and stopped. He took a breath. "Tyler, this is unacceptable. What you're doing now is so rude, it is so inappropriate."

"You said we could be honest," I shouted. "I am being fucking honest!"

Jacob drew a breath and exhaled long and loud through his nose. "Listen, there were other reasons for firing Robert," he said. "Some sensitive issues we can't really discuss."

"You're lying," I said pointing my finger at him.

"Tyler, sit down," Gumport shouted.

"I'll sit when Lakshmi sits!"

A tense silence filled the room. Lakshmi took her chair, crossing her legs, her foot nervously twitching as her eyes scanned the ceiling. I sat down at the edge of my seat and gave her a sideways glare.

"Jacob, I have a question for you," said the Baguette, a strange and sudden surprise in the tension.

"What?" he said.

"Did you ever ask Robert out on a date?"

Jacob stiffened. "Of course not."

"You sure, Jacob? You didn't ask him to come over to your place for dinner? We heard you were going to make him pork chops and apple sauce."

A low giggle rippled through the room as Jacob turned red. Gumport bit his lip in the attempt not to grin. Lakshmi was out of her chair again, pacing. "I have had enough of this!" she shouted.

"So have we," said Joffrey. "And we have a demand. We want Bravermann back."

"That is *never* going to happen!" Lakshmi barked, halting to face us. "All of you are ridiculous! You have no idea what goes on at this organization, the challenges we face, how hard I've worked to keep this place going. And I am *appalled* at how you have treated me, the disrespect!"

"I have *no* respect for you," I said. "I put up with your new age bullshit because I believed in Manna. I never believed in *you*."

"We reject your decision to fire Bravermann," Jeremy said. "And you better do something about it. We've already spoken to a reporter at the Times and he's very interested in what happens next."

Lakshmi glared at Jeremy as her hair fell over her face again. "You're telling *me* what to do?" she shouted. "*Fuck* that, Jeremy. And *fuck* Robert Bravermann! He is never coming back here!"

And then, weirdly, Lakshmi stood on her chair, shaking her finger like an old-time preacher. "None of you tell *me* what to do! You are *all* insubordinate! Goddamn it! I don't have to take this shit! I'm famous! And none of you are to talk to reporters, none of you! Do you understand me? You will not fuck with my livelihood!"

Lakshmi started trembling and burst into angry sobbing as her arms flew out. And then she did something that is forever burned into my memory. Like a child throwing a tantrum, she made fists, bobbed in place, and threw back her head to make a shrieking, ear-puncturing, primal scream. She sounded like she was spitting out her own lungs when her voice gave out, tearing her vocal cords. She clutched her throat, jumped off the chair, then ran upstairs and slammed her door. We heard items fly from her desk and what sounded like choking and coughing mixed with sobbing.

We were stunned into silence but I turned to look at Bryce who had the faintest little grin. And then, like in a John Hughes movie, he started a slow clap and we joined him, bursting into applause then outright laughter. Gene and Jacob had folded their arms and looked frozen with contempt for us, unable to speak. Jonnie, looking ashen, was shaking her head in disgust. "I'm glad you all think this is funny!" she said and then ran upstairs. Jacob followed after her.

Gumport was quiet, trying and failing to look neutral. It was silent but for the muffled sounds of Jonnie and Jacob comforting Lakshmi behind her closed door.

"All right," Gumport said, nodding, trying to return to normalcy. "I can see why we might have had some problems here." He wasn't trying to be funny, but that also got a howl.

I looked at my watch. I would need to leave soon for my dinner date with a reporter from the LA Times.

I admit it was kind of fun to meet Emma Stern at Cantor's Deli where she was finishing up Lakshmi's book. It felt a little like being in a movie, like being a spy secreted into Russia or a stool pigeon ratting out a crime boss. When Emma ordered "caw-fee" I knew she was from New Jersey. We had grown up just a few miles away from each other, exits 8 and 9 off the Turnpike, and we talked about the Carvel ice cream stand on Route 18. We both liked the dipped vanilla cones.

"Do you mind if I record this?" she said, taking out her cassette deck.

"Not at all," I said. "Glad to go on record since I'm losing my job at any moment. But I need to know... is this a puff piece? Are you a member of the New Age community, a fan of Lakshmi's?"

"No, and definitely not a fan after reading this," she said, picking up *The Thousand Miracles of Love*. "A little about me. Jewish but secular, a religious skeptic. We celebrated Christmas at our house because we liked the tree. My beats are the entertainment industry and the New Age movement which often intersect." She paused a moment. "Have you read this?"

"Not interested. I've heard her lectures."

"This thing about a miracle being a 'shift in awareness'... people are really buying into that?"

"They do. But it's more that they're buying into Lakshmi. *The Way* is nothing without her. Others have tried to promote it, but she's the one that's convincing, the new Saint Paul. More than anyone, she knows that gnawing hole in people, the emptiness, that abyss that people stare into when their dreams don't come true or even if they do."

"Interesting," Emma said and smiled. "So tell me your story, Tyler. How did a religious skeptic get involved with Steinmetz?"

Two hours later, I added to the generous tip that Emma had left our waitress. "I used to be a waiter," I said. "We're what's called 'campers' since this table should have turned a while ago. Oh, and before I forget — this is for you."

I handed her an envelope.

"It's a draft of a letter we're sending Lakshmi and the board," I said. "Not finalized yet, but I'll get you a signed copy when it is."

"And this is for you," she said, handing me Lakshmi's book. "We have copies at the office. You should read it."

"Why?"

"Everything you've told me was foreshadowed. She's repeating a pattern. I'll tell you, Tyler, the word that keeps coming up around this woman is 'bitch.' Read it. It's loaded with ammunition."

I got home to a new batch of phone messages. "Tyler, it's Jeremy. Just got off the phone with Bravermann. Benjamin Gumport is a union buster. Robert says he's a professional liar and not to trust anything he says."

The next message was from Gumport. "Hello, Tyler, Ben Gumport here. Very nice to meet you today. Would you give me a call at your earliest convenience? I'd like to meet with you, have a chat."

Returning that call could wait. Reading *The Thousand Miracles of Love* could not.

Emma was right. Lakshmi's book was as much of an autobiography as it was a collection of her thoughts and superstitions. Nothing I read about her past was that surprising and I was familiar with some of it. She did not go into the most personal details, but she had suffered nervous breakdowns after a broken engagement and later, a weeklong marriage with an Atlanta businessman. There were long bouts of depression following other romantic disappointments including an infatuation with a gay man, a junkie, and an actor who lost interest once his star was rising. And though she did not go into any humiliating details, there were numerous references to an unsuccessful work and business life. She alluded to being fired, to "another chapter of chaos and another chapter 11" and to "conflagrations at work when the bitch popped out and I couldn't stuff her back in her box." She also referred to "another of my fine messes" and "one more of Lakshmi's catastrophes" and "setting off a new chain of disasters."

As she'd mentioned in her lectures, Lakshmi had tried different cities where she thought she would flourish, but finally accepted that "my problems followed me everywhere I went, sneaking into my luggage like gremlins. I'd open my suitcase, and there they were, snickering after they had ripped up all my plans for happiness." More than once, Lakshmi referred to using her "Get Out of Jail Card" when she was broke: phone calls to "my loving father. Later, I realized I had been making the wrong call. I needed to call the Loving Father."

That made me shake my head with disgust: her dependence on Daddy and a pattern of getting others to bail her out. When they did, it was faith in God that got the credit. And why would you need a business plan when the Heavenly Father did you favors, just in his own good time? Emma was right — *The Way of the Miraculous* had not transformed Lakshmi from a spoiled child to a responsible adult. She was the same, impossible brat she had always been, a chaos agent who left others to clean up her nuclear messes. The phone rang and I looked at my watch. Who was calling me at eleven on a Tuesday evening?

"Tyler, you're holding out on me."

"Hey, Duncan."

"Goddamn it, I don't have to take this shit! I'm famous! You will not fuck with my livelihood!"

"You talked to Emma," I said. "I was planning on telling you but she scooped you. Do journalists really use that expression? Scoop?"

"We traded quotes so we can both use it. Emma gets to use 'He's Catholic, he doesn't get it' in her article. I just have to hear the 'I'm famous' line from someone who was there. And she did this standing on a chair?"

"Yeah. You might have heard her scream after that. The whole city did before her vocal cords came out of her nose. When's this article coming out?"

"Maybe next week, as soon as we get a fact check."

But some messy, stenchy shit would hit the kitchen fan before either article was published.

Chapter 34

On Wednesday morning, Gene was glaring at me from his seat outside the kitchen, arms folded over his chest. Without saying a word to him, I went over to the indoor windows with their frosted glass and slammed them shut. Jonnie came into the kitchen, a look of concern on her face as she balanced on her stilettos. She stepped back when I took out a cleaver and a chopping board.

"Tyler," she said. "We need to have a discussion."

"After work," I said.

"I'd like to speak with you now."

"Go ahead," I said as I helped Bryce take the first of three vats of Carolina chicken mull out of the fridge and set it on the stove to warm.

"In private," she said as a few volunteers popped in.

"You might have noticed we're busy," I said.

"Then let's talk at lunch."

"Can't. We have a meeting with our union rep at twelve. *You* should be at that."

"All right. Then we'll talk after work."

"We'll be getting done after five... I think. Sooner if Queen Gene wants to get off his royal buttocks and actually do his job."

She sighed. "Just what's happened here?"

"That's a rhetorical question, Jonnie. You know exactly what's happened."

"I'll see you at five. At the Center."

"I am going to say something I've never said to you before, Jonnie. No. No, no, no. I am not driving to the Center after a long day of work and wasting my gasoline. Not like you've ever done me any favors."

She blinked at me in silence.

"OK, Tyler. We'll meet here after five."

Jeremy and Joffrey strode in a little after ten when the kitchen was in full swing. "Lakshmi is so damn pissed," Joffrey whispered, showing me his earplugs. "Nonstop screaming since nine this morning. It's toxic over there."

"She talked to Emma Stern, that reporter from the Times," Jeremy said. "She read Lakshmi your letter that demanded her resignation. Did you sign our names to that?"

"I did not. I typed them. And I told the reporter it was a draft, that I'd get her a copy of the complete letter."

"Gene's telling everyone you signed our names."

I was annoyed with Emma but furious with Gene. I pushed through the swinging door and nearly lunged at him as he sat chatting with Jonnie.

"Stop telling people I signed their names to a letter," I shouted at him, drawing everyone's attention. "It was a draft and I *typed* their names. We'll complete the letter this week and everyone who wants to sign it will. Do you understand me? If you don't, then ask your father, the lawyer, what the word 'slander' means."

He was quiet as I stared at him, then he paled and shook. After I returned to the kitchen, he left for the day.

When the chicken was out and the prayer was over, Bryce and I put a meager number of volunteers to the labor-intensive work of making ratatouille for 450. That was a side dish Gene had picked as one of his typical, passive-aggressive moves as it involved the slicing, dicing and seeding of multiple vegetables and then softening them in batches in hot oil. A little before twelve, a stout lesbian Latina with a pompadour came into the kitchen. "I'm Camilla," she said. "The rep from the UFCW. Are you Tyler?"

"I am," I said. "Welcome."

"We have the same haircut," she said, smiling as we shook hands.

"Looks better on you," I said, and managed a grin as staff from the Being Center arrived. We were making a circle of metal folding chairs in the northeast corner of the community room as the Women's Stag AA group set up theirs in the northwest. "Excuse me," said their leader, the one with the asymmetrical bob whose eyebrows were still scrunched with anger. "But you are too close to our meeting."

"No, you are too close to *our* meeting," I said.

She gasped. "Sir, I am just asking you to move."

"No, you didn't ask. We have a meeting too, you might have noticed. Why don't you move? The stage is free. You can bring your chairs up there. If you want, you can close the curtains for all the fucking privacy you want."

"Language!" she muttered as the women stared at me. "That was so rude!"

"I was rude?" I said. "For the last two years, you have assumed the worst about me because I'm a man. You've never said hello or shown me any common courtesy. I am sick of your dirty looks and sick of your hostility. And I am not going to apologize to you or anyone else because I have a dick. Maybe men have treated you like shit but that does not give you, whoever the fuck you are, any right to treat me so poorly."

All of them were slack-jawed, but a moment later, they picked up their chairs and took them to the empty stage.

"Wow. Interesting start," Camilla said with a bemused smile and then passed us all a pamphlet that included a ballot on the back.

"Sorry," I said. "I'm just so over their bullshit."

"It's cool. I like your *agallas*," she said. "Spunk."

Camilla walked us through the pamphlet's points and talked about the protections and advantages of collective bargaining.

"From what I hear, you guys've already got Benjamin Gumport trying to bust you up. He'll make a few changes, make some promises, and then you'll be vulnerable, you'll trust him. But these guys are snakes in the grass, working for a bonus when they get their outcome. I'm telling you, do this and vote quick. They won't fire you until they've got your replacements, and believe me, they are working on your replacements now."

Before the meeting ended we took a straw vote, not an official one, and it was a unanimous yes since Gene and Jonnie did not attend. Bryce stood on his chair with a sheet that had the word UNION written on it. And then, like Sally Field in the movie *Norma Rae*, he pivoted to everybody watching. We returned to the interminable task of ratatouille and were relieved see Snake Hips Steve had tied on an apron and was already at work.

We had innumerable volunteers named Steve but Snake Hips was one of our favorites. He had a blond mullet that reached to the middle of his back and wore unbelted Levi 501s that bragged of his thirty-inch waist. Sinewy with blue eyes that popped from his tanned face, he was good-looking and good at institutional cooking. He also had stories of growing up in Reno and working backstage with the likes of Liberace, Al Martino, Rip Taylor and Joey Heatherton.

"Can we put you in charge of the pork chops, Steve?" I asked. "With a garlic herb butter?"

"Sure, but I hate pork chops," he said with his Western accent. "We made 'em all the time when I worked at Circus Circus, thousands of 'em every Friday."

"You worked at the Circus Circus... in Reno?" Bryce asked, incredulous.

"Cheapest buffet in the city. All you can keep down for a buck. On Friday, we sent out plain pork chops. On Tuesday, the ones that weren't eaten were 'smothered in onions.' By Thursday, when they got old and dry, we covered them in red gunk and sent them out as 'barbecued pork.' The ones that remained by Saturday were cut up into little pieces and put in the chop suey. I haven't eaten a pork chop since."

Johnnie came back to the kitchen at five ten. We were still in the process of softening sliced eggplant in oil before we could mix it into the vats with the other vegetables. It was five thirty before we were done cooking and started the process of sponging and mopping. Jonnie popped in to check on our progress and I noticed that she had a little metal tab clipped to her collar with the number 2 on it.

"How's it going, Tyler?" she asked.

"Still working."

"I see."

"You could help," I said. "Grab a sponge, grab a mop."

"I'll just wait out here."

"How was the museum?"

"I beg your pardon?"

"LACMA," I said, pointing to the collar tab. "Did you see the Mexican Splendors? Or the German Degenerate art? Who'd you go with?"

She shrugged her shoulders and nervously laughed. "I don't know what you're talking about."

"Yes you do. And now I know that I shouldn't trust you — you're a liar."

By the time we got done mopping, it was getting dark in the community room as some twelve-steppers set up their Debtors Anonymous meeting. A couple of the debtors were arguing about how much money had been spent on cookies. "Joanna, I can't believe this!" shouted an unhappy woman. "You bought Pepperidge Farm? That is *so* extravagant!"

Jonnie and I retreated to the corner behind the piano after I switched on some stingy, yellow lights. She took the bench and I opened up a folding chair to face her. As usual, she was trying to be warm, trying to be open, playing both sides.

"So... just what do you want, Tyler. What are you trying to do here?"

"You know what we're trying to do."

"Is this about money?"

"Money?" I said, raising my voice. "This is not about fucking *money*. You couldn't pay me off with a billion dollars. Don't insult me."

"Then what's this about?"

"It's about fairness, Jonnie, about decency. It's about Lakshmi fucking up and fucking someone over. We're sick of her fucking chaos and we're sick of her hurting people. She knows and *you* know that firing Bravermann was wrong."

Jonnie shook her head and sighed. "It *was* wrong," she said.

"Then what are *you* going to do about it?"

"Me? I can't do anything."

"Yes, you can. Stand up to her and to Jacob Hellman and tell them *you* don't accept it. And if you don't, then this shit will be on you, too. You'll be nothing but a coward, a stooge of Lakshmi Steinmetz, used by a user. And you won't deserve anyone's respect, including your own."

She was quiet as the debtors argued over the quality of the coffee. "Joanna, I told you to get Folgers! We can't afford freshly ground!"

"Tyler, we... there may be factors we're unaware of as to why Robert was fired, we —"

"Jonnie, he was doing a *great* job!" I said, getting loud again. "She fired him because he doesn't buy into her con — because he doesn't kiss her phony ass and because he eclipsed her. She isn't interested in friends or colleagues or partners — she's only interested in followers who worship her."

"You know, it's really scary when you start shouting like that."

"I don't care. Lakshmi has been scaring us since the beginning. You need to pick a side, Jonnie. You can be one of the good guys, or you can be the toilet paper that Lakshmi uses to wipe her skinny ass."

"Tyler, you know you're a hair away from losing your job."

"I don't give a shit. I can get a better job — one that treats me like a human being. Look, Jonnie, I know Lakshmi bestowed this little ministry on you, a chance to twinkle, twinkle little star. But is your time on this sad, little stage more important than doing what's right?"

She drew in a breath then clucked.

"That was mean, Tyler! Mean."

"What's mean is not backing up Bravermann. Now I need to get the fuck out of here. I'm exhausted."

And then I turned back when I had one final thought.

"Let me ask you something," I said as she picked up her shoulder bag. "Just *what* do you do here that makes you indispensable? Other than leading everyone in prayers to an imaginary friend while the food gets cold, just what *is* your function?"

She looked away from me, wounded, and I regretted being so frank. I'd meant every word I'd said, but it didn't make me feel better. I was down the stairs when I saw Snake Hips waiting outside for me.

"Tyler, can I walk you to your car?"

"Sure, Steve. What's up?"

He looked around to make sure no one was listening to us. Some alcoholics were near the yuccas, sucking on their cigarettes.

"Gene offered me a job."

"Do you want it?"

"I do. Right now I'm just temping. I'm driving around Barry Manilow's lyricist to do errands because he doesn't have a license. Yesterday I drove him to Baskin-Robbins. This guy doesn't need an assistant, he's just lonely. The one time the phone rang and I had to pretend to be the receptionist, it was Julio Iglesias."

I laughed.

"Take the job, Steve. We told Gene to hire you a long time ago."

"Did you? Thank you."

"I'd say I'd be glad to work with you but I'm not gonna be around for long."

"I figured that. That's why I brought it up."

"The only thing I would caution you about is... you'll have to work with Gene."

Ben Gumport invited me to his town house in WeHo near Marix Tex Mex restaurant for a 6 p.m. one-on-one the following day, a meeting he was having with every individual employee. The town house he lived in was one of those depressing, utilitarian boxes built in the 70's with cheap, frameless windows. Its only flourish was its thick application of stucco in the egregious cake-frosting style of the era. The inside of his place was completely lacking in personality, devoid of paintings, and filled with the kind of cheap, unfinished furniture that was sold on street corners or at stores with names like The Pine Mine. The only thing of color that caught my eye was a pink Barbie dollhouse, or rather, a ski chalet on the living room floor. Barbie was outside in a teal-colored snowsuit with skis fastened to her feet. Midge was upstairs in the triangular room wearing a blue fur coat and matching hat as she sat before a vanity. A super blond Ken was waving behind the bar, wearing a pink and green mylar T-shirt that exposed his bulging biceps. In front of him were two tiny cocktails.

"Yours?" I asked as I took a seat and pointed at the chalet. With his bleached hair, Gumport looked like someone aspiring to be Ken. He wouldn't have been the first gay man I ever met who collected Barbies and their accoutrements.

"Oh, no," he said, loosening his tie. "It's my daughter's."

"How many kids do you have?" I asked.

"Two. The younger one visits on weekends. She's getting a little old for Barbie now. She's starting to ask about makeup."

"So you're divorced."

"For obvious reasons. It takes some of us a little longer to figure things out."

"So, what would you like to discuss, Ben?"

"I'll be direct with you," he said. "Lakshmi Steinmetz is not good for Manna from Heaven."

I held my breath — this was surprising.

"No, she's not," I said after I exhaled "She's mercurial and unprofessional and doesn't know what the fuck she's doing."

"I don't disagree," he said. "And between you and me, I'm sick of all these fag hags exploiting the AIDS crisis for fame and fortune and warm fuzzies."

"OK," I said, even more surprised. "I don't disagree with you."

"At the same time, I have friends that I would drive to her stupid lectures or to a Love-a-Thon or a darshan if it gives them some comfort."

"Understandable. So in the spirit of being direct... we know you were hired to bust our union."

"I was not, Tyler. I was hired to restructure your organization."

"We want Bravermann back."

"I don't think he'd come back. We're coming to some very generous terms with him. And you don't want him back."

"Yes, we do."

"Bravermann screws up everything he gets involved in. He left the California Aids Project a complete mess."

"They seem fine to me — better after the staff unionized with the Health Care Workers."

"Believe me, Robert left a mess that took years to clean up. And I know, because I was the one who cleaned it up."

"From what I've learned, CAP had a similar trajectory to us — a grassroots organization and everyone working for pennies. And then it stabilized, got funded and executives started paying themselves fancy salaries while the employees were still making shit."

"That's Robert's version."

"Why would the employees unionize if they thought they were being treated well?"

"Because the one thing we all want is more. Smoke?" he said and offered me a Marlboro Light.

"No, thanks."

"Do you mind if I do?"

"No. I like the smell of smoke," I said. "At first. It stinks after a while. But I like to look at it, curling up then disappearing and coming out of people's noses and mouths, like they're dragons."

He grinned for the first time and lit up.

"So, what do they pay you, Ben?"

"I can't discuss that."

"You know what I make, but I don't know what your deal is. We heard you're getting a hundred grand for two months work."

"It's a lot but it's not that much."

"Isn't it a shame that all this money for severance pay and an interim director couldn't go to serve more clients?"

"It's the cost of change, Tyler. Things get messy."

"So would you do what I do for seventeen thousand a year?"

"Certainly not," he said with a chuckle. "But I wouldn't want to pay union dues either. I'll promise you something today, Tyler. We will find a good director and we will stabilize Manna. One thing we may do is spin off the Being Center. Its services are not essential. They're duplicated at other agencies."

"Interesting," I said.

"And we don't need that New Age witch doctor as our CEO. She's destructive and she bleeds money."

The doorbell rang.

"That's my six thirty," Gumport said. "I'll see you Saturday. We can talk then if you like." The smoke from his cigarette had turned from aromatic and pleasant to bitter and sickening. He stubbed it out.

"Saturday?" I asked.

"At the volunteer party."

"Right. You're coming to that?"

"I was invited." He was referring to the Thank You Volunteers Party, something that Bravermann had organized with a wealthy friend who was opening up his house in the Hollywood Hills to the staff and volunteers of Manna.

"Hug, Tyler," Gumport said to me as he stood, opening his arms. I should have offered just to shake hands but we slapped each other's backs and briefly embraced. I opened up the door where Gene was waiting on the stoop. We glanced briefly at each other and said nothing.

Berto, Hector and Slim asked me to drive them to the Thank You Party. Berto wanted to go as her drag persona, La Reina del Universo, and asked me if she could walk in on my arm. I said I'd be thrilled. "Then we have to get there a little late," he said, "if La Reina is going to make *una gran entrada*." Berto told me that Hector would also be dressing as a woman and Slim would be her escort.

Berto asked me to wear a red shirt and black pants to match her outfit and I complied. I completed my look with one of Kyle's better leather jackets, a black one that cinched at the waist and fit me better than him. When I arrived at the Silverlake bungalow and knocked, the door opened, as if by magic, and then La Reina del Universo stepped out from behind it. She was dressed in a fiery red dress with spaghetti straps, a train and a split hemline that revealed her shaved legs and pumps decorated with florets of faux rubies. From the hallway, I saw a lacy Spanish fan snap open before yards of purple chiffon pushed out and Hector appeared. She told me her name for the evening was Quincey Anera. She was wearing a full-length gown that was a shocking lavender with a lacy bodice. Tulle was layered over a train covered with artificial flowers in different shades of purple. "It's the dress I might have worn at my *quinceañera*," she said. "If I could have had one." Both ladies had glittering tiaras that were nearly five inches tall. Slim appeared last and was dressed like a riverboat gambler with a white vest under a Victorian tailcoat. He looked handsome and devilish with slicked-back hair and a pointy goatee that glistened with pomade.

The Regency-style house in the Hollywood Hills appeared small and unimpressive from the outside, but it was four spacious stories that descended down the precipitous hillside. We left my car with a valet and walked through the tall double doors. La Reina del Universo was thrilled to land on a marble platform with a cascade of rounded steps that descended to a large and crowded living room. Everyone was looking up at us as she linked my arm, a sudden burst of red in the room. We slowly took the stairs as she craned her neck, her Adam's apple hidden by a choker of garnets. La Reina had everyone's attention and I enjoyed the curiosity it incited, the sudden silence in the room. Quincy Anera and Slim waited until we were at the bottom of the stairs before they took the platform for their own entrance. Quincy acted like she had been crowned Miss World and waved to the crowd and blew kisses with her fan. Slim leaned on his walking stick with a fanged snake head ornament and refused to smile and looked badass. When we got to the bottom of the stairs, we were converged on by volunteers who came to hug me and to gawk at La Reina and Quincy. "Let's get a drink," I said and looked around. Lakshmi was nowhere in sight.

We went out to the bar on a vast deck that had a pool and a view of the lit-up L.A. Basin. As we waited in line for drinks, friends and volunteers came up to me, hugged me, kissed my cheeks and called my name. The Jewish Moms Brigade, with husbands and adult children in tow, were pulling me into hugs, introducing me to their families. That's when I noticed Ben Gumport, across the pool, smoking and observing me. Kevin Darrington, who I hadn't talked to in weeks, joined Gumport and got a light from him for his own cigarette. I waved to Kevin who smiled and waved back as he tilted his head and exhaled smoke. I decided at that moment that I was going to have a good time that night, a *great* time. I'd have a few drinks and bribe the DJ to play my favorite songs for what I knew was a farewell party. Bryce and Snake Hips found me and we hugged.

"Is Witchiepoo here?" I asked Bryce.

"No. We heard she's not coming. Gene snuck out when he heard you got here."

Bryce took a joint out of his front pocket. "Care to join me?"

After we smoked, we gave the DJ a ten then took to the floor and he launched from Janet Jackson's "Rhythm Nation" to a decade back with the Bee Gees' "Night Fever." Bryce and I did the old line dance with the kickball change and four reaches for the sky. A few others joined us and it was amazing how quickly those old steps came back. Everyone got on the floor when the DJ launched into KC and the Sunshine Band's "That's the Way I Like It." The party had really started.

After an hour of dancing, I decided I'd see the rest of this interesting, whimsical house. It was like a Mexican cathedral had collided with Pee Wee's Playhouse, a glorious collection of religious folk art and mid-century kitsch. I wandered down to the bottom story which had a collection of vintage attractions from old carnivals including a working shooting gallery with ducks going round on a loop. Someone dressed as an old-time carny handed me a loaded pump-action BB gun. When my turn came, I missed every shot.

"I guess this means I don't get a kewpie doll," said a voice behind me.

"Mr. Darrington, how are you?" I said, turning to see Kevin.

"Drunk! So not bad at all!"

"Should we get our fortunes from Esmerelda?" I said, motioning to the fortune telling machine. "On me," I said handing him one of the free tokens. The gypsy inside came to life and pointed as a card dropped in the slot.

"Well," Kevin said, improvising. "Esmerelda says, 'Someday your prince really will come.'"

I picked up my card. "Mine says 'You will be looking for a job soon.'"

"No, you won't," Kevin said.

"Yes, I will be. Not sure what you've heard, but I'm not gonna be cheffing at Manna much longer."

"Not according to Gumport. He's noticed you're very popular. He doesn't want to risk an uprising."

"I don't trust that slimy parasite — he's about as authentic as his hair color."

"Noted. You know Lakshmi kicked me off the board," he said.

"I did not."

"She's kicked off everyone who isn't a disciple. A few others quit — we're the 'infidels,'" he said with a laugh.

"That's fucked up, Kevin."

"It was expected. But we have a few cards left to play. It's not about whether we stay on the board. It's about keeping Manna going."

Jeremy and Joffrey were walking toward me with grins on their faces.

"Been looking for you, Tyler," Joffrey said.

"Now we know why Laxative didn't show up," said Jeremy. "It's out."

"What is?"

"The Times article," said Joffrey with a grin, as he took a newspaper out from under his arm. "The Sunday paper comes out on Saturday evening."

Joffrey handed me The Calendar, the entertainment section, which is printed in tabloid format on Sundays. On its front page was an unflattering picture of Lakshmi in one of her prayer slumps with her eyes closed. The headline was "Hollywood's Glitzy Guru" and the subheading read "With Her New Time Religion, Lakshmi Steinmetz Has Taken a Star Turn... and Turned Off Many Others."

Emma Stern had not taken a light hand in her portrait of Lakshmi.

The following morning, I looked through my desk drawer for something I couldn't find right away, a card that I stared at, put away, took back out, then threw in the trash. I took Holden for an extra walk as I rethought my decision, changed my mind again, then changed it back. "Fuck it, Tyler, just do it," I said to myself then took out the card and punched its number on my phone.

Two rings later, someone picked up.

"Hello."

"Is this Tony Fursten?"

"Yes, it is."

"Tony, my name's Tyler St. George. You gave me your number a while ago at Celestial Objects. I'm one of the chefs at Manna from Heaven."

"Right. Glad you called, Tyler."

"Tony, I... I was very flattered to get your number, but I don't want to mislead you. I'm calling about something that's important to both of us, that's important to our community."

"I'm listening."

"Did you read today's Calendar section?"

Chapter 35

The article about Lakshmi in People magazine came out a day later, on Monday, for a one-two punch. She didn't ask me for my advice on how to deal with two scathing exposés but I might have told her to look to God and his healing love and to make a "shift in awareness."

Emma Stern's LA Times piece included a short history of similar religious movements that preceded *The Way* in California, a place that had always been a "hotbed of religious and personal reinvention." Those movements included New Thought and its outgrowth, the Church of Religious Science, both of which shared the notion that illness is a mental state, something that could be changed by different thinking. Emma tied the principles of *The Way* back to Quimbyism and to Christian Science and connected it to another more popular mutation, the Reverend Norman Vincent Peale's *Power of Positive Thinking*. All of these were rooted in the pseudoscience of the law of attraction: positive thoughts, including prayer, attract positive outcomes.

Emma connected *The Way's* emphasis on "shifts in awareness" to Hindu notions of maya, so sickness and suffering and anything else that is inconvenient can be dismissed as an illusion. She noted that Lakshmi's lectures had first gathered steam at the Theosophy Lodge in Los Angeles — *The Way of the Miraculous* was a natural partner to Madame Blavatsky's religion that also blended the faiths of the East and West. Their big difference was that Blavatsky's syncretism confirmed reincarnation and Lakshmi's did not. Lakshmi was open to the possibility of transmigration, for practical reasons, but she touted an afterlife, a "transition to another plane of existence." That was something, Emma conjectured, that was more appealing to people dying from AIDS than the notion of being reborn again in another fragile body. Emma noted that the imagery and language of Manna From Heaven were rife with angels in paradise, a promise of what we become and where we go when we die.

Emma's take on *The Way* was that there was nothing new about what Lakshmi preached, and its appeal came from Lakshmi herself. She was a convincing performer who included relatable moments in her lectures and a familiar message of "all you need is love." But then Emma detailed how Hollywood's "biggest guru since Werner Erhard" was described by many as less than loving and as an angry, hateful hypocrite who treated others poorly. Many called her a "bitch" although someone called her a "mega-bitch" and "others used an even more coarse anatomical word." In response to Emma's bringing this up, Lakshmi rebranded herself as "a bitch for God," a statement she would later try to claw back as a joke. She defended herself as having the "highest standards" and as a victim of "sexism and jealous resentment." She compared herself to other powerful women who were accused of "witchcraft and worse." One of her rivals, Selina Dandry, a former actress with her own moneymaking new age ministry, said Lakshmi's description of herself as "a bitch for God" was "two words too many. Lakshmi's an egomaniac and her boards deal more with her childish demands for attention than they do in running an effective charity."

The article rehashed the feud that was ending the Being Center in New York and then focused on the current fights raging at Manna from Heaven. Emma included interviews from employees who Lakshmi had "forbidden to speak to the press" but openly defied her in their defense of Robert Bravermann, a man she had publicly dismissed at one of her lectures with the quote, "He's Catholic. He doesn't get it." She was also quoted on her explicit desire to find a new executive who was a "student of *The Way*," which was incontrovertible proof of religious discrimination.

Emma went on to quote ex-board members, dubbing themselves "the infidels" who claimed their removal was for support of Bravermann or for slighting Lakshmi or for not embracing her teachings. "Not all of us are her disciples," said Kevin Darrington, a Beverly Hills realtor. "And I suspect I'll be out by the time this article is printed. Lakshmi is a starf-cker and in her quest for her own stardom, she's forgotten who asked her to get involved in an organization she neither conceived nor organized. Manna from Heaven was grafted onto the Being Center but it soon outgrew it, something Steinmetz doesn't want to acknowledge. Her biggest contribution to it is that she gave it a cute name."

And then Emma quoted some of the fired employees we had referred her to. "It's *The Way* or the highway," said former director

Derrick Vanderven, "which includes respecting her as its highest authority. Lakshmi doesn't want a director to actually run what she sees as *her* operation, to cede them the power to make decisions. Instead she calls on her higher power to advise her, and good Lord, her HP gives her just the worst advice." The last quote was from Jericho. "Lakshmi jokes about herself but she'll rip your dick off if you joke about her. Nobody takes herself more seriously. You don't make fun of Jesus and you don't make fun of Steinmetz. She sees herself as the next savior and she wants to be bigger than Jesus."

The People magazine article would be even less soothing for its subject. Duncan cowrote it with a New York-based writer and quotes were pulled from alienated employees and board members on both coasts. One of them from the NY Being Center called Lakshmi the "spoiled child of a wealthy lawyer, someone who is still throwing temper tantrums, a tiny terror on the verge of middle age but stuck in the terrible twos. In the end, it's her bitchery that does her in, whether it's running a nonprofit or dating a man. She's impossible. An artist with real talent might be able to get away with being a bitch from hell, but it's just Lakshmi, a New Age quack. For someone who talks about love all the time, she inspires a lot of hatred."

A former employer of Lakshmi, a biographer of note, described her as "crying all the time, desperately unhappy and addicted to her Ouija board. She could be sweet and engaging in one moment and furious or deeply sad a second later. She had no idea what to do with herself but the one thing she refused to be was ignored."

The last half of the People article dealt with the tumult at Manna from Heaven, starting with the disappointing proceeds from Celestial Objects, an event that suffered from Lakshmi's "micromanagement and inexperience as well as conflicts with the celebrities that enabled her rise." The humorous controversy of the Pride float was mentioned as "a portent of an ego out of control" that culminated in a rebellion when Bravermann was fired and the board was purged of its self-described "infidels." Jacob Hellman refuted that board members were pushed out for their lack of pliancy or belief in *The Way*. "They simply weren't doing their jobs and neither was Bravermann," he said. When asked if he had shown romantic interest in Robert, Jacob said, "I won't dignify the question."

Duncan recapped the last, explosive staff meeting and included the full quote of her final outburst: "Goddamn it! I don't have to take this shit! I'm famous! You will not f-ck with my livelihood!" The summation of the article left readers with the impression that Lakshmi was a huckster, the leader of a religious movement she had relabeled as "spirituality" and it was something she intended to profit from. The picture of Lakshmi inserted at the end was a two-shot where she looked angry and condescending as she berated lovelorn, stoop-shouldered Betsy who cringed from another public humiliation.

Other articles were to follow in the next two weeks, most in magazines like Premiere and Entertainment Weekly where the newly christened "Bitch for God" was covered more as a show business phenomenon than as serious news. Her celebrity was treated as the latest frivolous excess of Hollywood's self-indulgent stars for whom fame and fortune were not enough. They were described as "the glitterati who hungered for more, for some deeper satisfaction that eluded them, and looking to a former nightclub singer to help them find it." In these articles, the celebs and stars who had flocked to her were no longer inclined to lavish praise or identify themselves as one of Lakshmi's faithful. One previously inspired mogul had changed his tune from "she's the miracle worker of West Hollywood" to "someone doing some good work." In the same piece, Joni Mitchell referred to Lakshmi as "this woman who wants people to stop and listen to her when she prays at parties."

Another journalist on the religious beat for *The New York Times* interviewed an expert on cults who called Lakshmi a cult leader. "Her cult is not as dangerous as the Moonies or the People's Temple, not for the moment, but it's still a cult whose members offer their submission and contribute their dollars. They believe in prophecy and magic and of contact between their leader and God. Steinmetz is typical of cult leaders in that her authority cannot be questioned and those who do are expelled from her organization. Her followers are not asked to give up their private lives to join her at a commune and that makes her less powerful, less dangerous. And as a woman surrounding herself with gay men, she's not guilty of being a sexual predator like Jim Jones or Joseph Smith. But like every cult leader, Steinmetz burnishes her reputation by providing a charitable service, a giveaway, something she does with one hand while inviting adoration and allegiance with the other. As her cult grows and faces scrutiny, a few of her followers have come to the painful realization that Lakshmi Steinmetz is not as invested in God or love as she is in fame and power, the typical aspirations of any charismatic leader of a cult."

Those next two weeks were difficult for Lakshmi, we were told, who was not inured to criticism. "She's wounded," said Joffrey, the employee who jockeyed the most between the kitchen at Manna and the offices at the Center as we sipped our coffee one morning. "She's always crying, with the door locked, and leaving early so she can be with her daughter. Yesterday she was walking out the door, lugging her computer home, and I asked if I could give her a hand. She said, 'Yes, take the knives out of my back... and return one to Jacob.'"

"To *Jacob*?" I asked.

"They're feuding. They run into each other's offices, screaming and slamming doors. You didn't hear it from me," Joffrey said after looking both ways. "But I think they're pushing her out."

"Who is?"

"Gumport and Jacob."

"Jacob?" I said. "*Jacob Hellman* wants Lakshmi out? She's his cash cow."

"They *are* pushing her out," Jeremy whispered. "Jacob is taking her place, something he arranged with Gumport when he brought him in. Jacob wants to be CEO."

"Jacob's a social climber," said Joffrey. "He's as desperate for attention as Lakshmi. He's a would-be star fucker... if anyone wanted to fuck him back."

"So maybe we'll be building him a float," I said.

"I'm all in," said Bryce. "But let's not set it on fire until his pudgy little ass is sitting on top of it."

"Why would Lakshmi leave?" I asked.

"Because we're two months away from running out of money," said Jeremy. "Gumport's fee is wiping us out and Lakshmi is toxic now. If she leaves, well... we have an unidentified donor waiting to step in, that's the condition he's set. It's someone who floated us through our last crisis."

"Oh really?" I said and tried not to smile.

"Tyler," said Bryce. "Just what are you grinning about? Did you just eat some shit?"

"Excuse me," Gene said, from across the community room. "Bryce, Tyler! I think you're needed in the kitchen."

"So are you," I shouted.

On Thursday, Gumport summoned us to a meeting at the Center. Bryce and I groaned about going, about driving through rush hour traffic after another draining day in the kitchen. Manna was no longer a place of dance music and tambourines, no longer a happy party with volunteers who chatted and flirted as they set to their tasks. Tension increased between Lakshmi's lackeys and those who detested her. The work was even harder with the number we were serving, something Gene ratcheted up as a tool to torment Bryce and me. I had lost my patience with some of the more difficult volunteers, the ones who were needy for attention or were bossy know-it-alls or who wanted to read me their poetry while I was trying to cook. "This pie tastes like sour cream," said Terrence, an older, effete guy with his nose in the air, someone who bragged about his time as a sous chef in the Kennedy White House.

"I would hope to hell so," I snapped at him. "Since it's a *lemon sour cream pie*. Now do you want to package it or do you want to find someplace else to volunteer?"

Once again, Bryce and I were the last to arrive in the reception room at the Center. Gumport looked pleased with himself as we squeezed in on the couches. Next to him was the latest new face, a mildly attractive and serious-looking male with a thick head of gray hair and wearing the usual black slacks, white shirt and solid tie.

"Welcome, Bryce, Tyler. Let's begin," said Gumport. "I have a favor to ask all of you. A *favor*. I want you to keep what I tell you to yourselves for a while. We don't want to blast this to the press. Lakshmi has decided to leave the organization. She's a famous author now and has a book tour to complete and a new book to write. The decision was hers, and before leaving, she will make a very generous gift to Manna at a time when it's needed."

"Like to pay you for your services," said the Baguette.

"More like to underwrite our next fundraiser," said Gumport. "But you are correct, Tinka. I am not inexpensive but I am worth every penny. The end result of my work here will be an organization that can sustain itself and grow."

He loosened his tie. "Now...I understand why all of you were motivated to unionize... but," he said, looking around at our faces. "I want you to consider that the need is gone, that it's left with Lakshmi's departure. And I want you also to consider that Manna is going to be more attractive to donors if its employees are not unionized, if donors don't see their dollars going to bloated salaries."

"No one here has anything like a bloated salary," I said. "Except Jacob, maybe. Nor do they expect one."

"They do not, Tyler. They dooooo not," he said, sounding like a folksy Sheriff Andy Taylor. "And to that end, we want to pay you, all of you, fairly for your good, hard work. At this time, I have the honor of introducing you to our new executive director, Evan MacNamee."

"Hello," said the stranger who nodded his head. That was all he had to say for the next thirty minutes.

Jeremy called me at home that night and filled me in on the leaked details of Lakshmi's departure, something that was arranged by her lawyer.

"The BFG had to leave," Jeremy told me. "Bravermann was about to file a suit against her that claimed religious discrimination, something she couldn't deny given what she said at Harmony Gold. Her terms were that she remain as an honorary member of the board and that she would always be credited as the founder of Manna."

"As ever, Miriam is just the height of modesty."

I honestly don't know what else Lakshmi arranged, but I am sure she took some satisfaction in what happened next.

Chapter 36

On Friday, we met at noon to take a vote on unionizing. It was a meeting Gumport had encouraged but was not allowed to attend. "We just don't need to do it," said Vonnie. "Gumport's taken care of her. The BFG is gone and she can't come back."

"Guys, listen to me," I said. "My gut is telling me *don't trust Gumport.* Bravermann doesn't. Gumport has no compunctions about taking money earmarked for charity. He's a sweet-talking snake but his fangs are poisoned. As soon as we reject this union, they'll fire our asses."

Only Bryce was with me. The union was voted down.

An hour later, Vonnie reported our decision to Gumport. She called to tell me that he raised his fist and shook it in triumph and went immediately into Jacob's office to shout the good news. "And I heard them howl with laughter and the pop of a champagne cork," she said. "That's when I felt my stomach drop."

"Mine just dropped too," I said.

On Monday, I arrived to the sight of Snake Hips Steve starting his first day as an employed chef in the kitchen. Gene was giving him a set of keys and then made a show of hugging him as he looked my way. "Welcome, Steve," Gene said in his loudest voice. "We are so glad to have you in our family." And then Gene looked at me with his high, witchy eyebrows and sneered, as if seeing in his magic mirror that Snow White was dead.

On Tuesday night, I couldn't concentrate on anything, not even television, and felt a sudden malaise: a flatness and lack of interest in anything. I went to bed early and woke from a dream of being cut up and fried like a chicken in hot grease. I realized I had a fever, a sore throat, and a feeling like rats were tunneling through my intestines.

"I've got the flu," I said to Gene when I called in sick. "I doubt I'll be in for the next few days."

"I'm sure you won't," he said.

I was still wobbly and low energy when I returned to work on Monday. It was close to eleven and we were ready to serve up Bryce's famous mac and cheese when Madge came into the kitchen. "So, Tyler," she said to me, with an accusing stare. "How was your trip to Las Vegas?"

"My what?"

"We all know where you were last week."

"I was home in bed."

"Oh, sure you were. You win any money at the Sands?"

She walked out to the community room to get her bags from Tinka. I was enraged and followed her out.

"Listen to me, lady. I was home sick!" I shouted at Madge. "I was not in Las Vegas! You owe me an apology!"

My shouting had grabbed everyone's attention.

"You better get a hold of your anger," said Madge.

"You better get a hold of your psychic bullshit!" I yelled from deep inside me. "If you had any powers, you'd have seen me sick in bed with a fever."

The kitchen was quiet when I returned. The only sounds were of the plunking and sealing of food into containers.

After lunch was out and the leftovers were served, Jeremy pulled me aside.

"Tyler, you know Magdalena shows up every time we need a driver."

"I don't care. She accused me of something that's total bullshit. I'm sick of her shit, and Gene's shit. They're conspiring against me, always off in some corner, smirking while they whisper. If I'm getting fired, fine, they should do it already."

That afternoon I was up in the pantry looking for cornstarch when I found the KitchenAid mixer I hadn't used in months. It was covered with dust and in the bottom of the bowl were some dead insects. *I deserve this mixer,* I thought. I brought it out to the community room where Gene was ordering from the Rykoff rep. "Can I borrow this?" I asked him. "I'm, uh, baking this weekend."

"Yes," he said. "Take it. Evan MacNamee is coming by at five. He wants to talk to you."

Gene and I had a deal.

The new director arrived at five sharp and handed me an envelope with my paycheck for the week and a separate one for the following. "We value our volunteers, Mr. St. George," Evan said. "And we can't abide their abuse by employees."

"I can't abide being abused by my employers anymore. Keep this," I said, returning the check that had 'severance pay' written in the lower left. "This is not a fair compensation. I'll be suing you to get one."

"I got fired," I said to Kyle when I walked into the house. He was working on a screenplay.

"You did? What's that?" he asked, referring to the KitchenAid in my hands.

"It's part of my compensation. I always wanted one."

"Cool." He checked his watch. "Let's celebrate. You want to get some Thai food?"

For the next few days, I felt like I was sniffing carpet cleaner. I was still getting over the flu, aching all over, and my head was a globe full of gas-soaked cotton. I went to work on my screenplay but the words wouldn't flow — I couldn't "connect." I picked up Kyle's Game Boy, something I disdained as a time suck, and played my first game of Tetris. An hour later, I was addicted although I knew my only reward for reaching the highest level would be an animated image of Cossacks dancing around St. Basil's Cathedral. I screened lots of phone calls, most of them coming from consoling volunteers. Kyle had just finished reading John Grisham's *The Firm* and gave it to me to read before he left for another trip to London. "It's good," he said.

"I don't read books like this," I said. "A thriller?"

"Have a little fun. They're making it into a movie."

The Firm had a compelling story and whisked me away to another world, a corporate one plagued with paranoia. "My life is nothing like this," I muttered to myself when I got to the part where Mitch, the young lawyer, hires a private investigator to look into the mysterious death of one of his associates. And then my phone rang.

"Hey, Tyler," Jeremy said as I screened him. "Shit's going on and there's something you should know. I was —"

I picked up the phone.

"Hey, Jeremy."

"Hey. So you know, Lakshmi hired a private investigator."

"For what?"

"To look into your criminal past."

I laughed but my heart started beating faster.

"Oh, the drama," I said, and looked out the picture window to see if there was a menacing black van on the street with men inside it conducting a stakeout. "Do you think I'll get sent to prison for not paying my student loans?"

"No, but they're fighting you on paying unemployment."

"What? That was the whole point of getting fired. If you quit, you can't get benefits."

"Yeah. So, I hate to say this, Tyler, but — "

"What?"

"You were right. They fired me, they fired all the dissidents. They said we were 'inessential.' Gumport hates Bravermann for unionizing the Aids Project."

"And for not letting him suck his fat cock."

"Likely. Bleach Blondie's finally gotten his revenge."

"Wow. So for Gumport this is all some stupid fucking game."

"Yeah, if you can't get laid, you can at least have the fun of being a shitty person. I think Gumport and Gene hatched this little plot to get you fired. They had a meeting the day before you got into an argument with Miss Claire Voyant."

"You know what's best served cold," I said.

"Revenge?"

"Oh, Jeremy. I think you and I are too decent to ever take revenge. But we do know reporters at the Times."

Chapter 37

Emma Stern put us in touch with Bruce Prendergast, a news reporter from the Times's city desk. He bought us pumpkin pancakes at Hugo's and after we told him some colorful stories about Ouija boards and fired telephone psychics, he grinned. "Thank you very much," he said. He had something juicy to work with.

Out of the blue, a lawyer called me that afternoon and said he'd file a suit for wrongful termination if I put half up front. His fee was $20,000 — I told him I hadn't made that in a year. A second lawyer called me an hour later and said he'd take the case on contingency. I met him in the apartment that was also his office. On his living room wall, weirdly, was the colorized xerox of Madonna that had been auctioned at Heavenly Objects.

Part of the process of suing Manna from Heaven was for medical reasons due to "the stress of an unhealthful work environment." I could use some rest, but for the next few weeks, part of this shameful deal was going to appointments with a chiropractor that were pleasurable but unneeded. I also had to see a second doctor for an examination to detect soft tissue damage through magnetic resonance imaging, a costly and unnecessary process. Later, I had to get psychological evaluations from the two sides. Manna's psychologist was a shy and attractive Italian immigrant who smiled the entire time we chatted. I had the impulse to ask him out. He asked me if I had a history of "using inappropriate language in the workplace" as if reading from a script. When I got back from that evaluation, I had a message on my machine from Evan MacNamee. "Tyler, give me a call, let's make an appointment and see if we can't get you back to work at Manna." I called Vonnie to see what was up.

"It's kind of a crap storm since you left, Tyler," she said. "Volunteers have vanished and Bryce gave notice. They were short twelve drivers today. They brought in this other pastry chef and she quit after three days. They want you back."

Ugh! Go back to work with Gene?

"Tell Evan to call my lawyer and we'll consider his offer. Vonnie, just how are they justifying firing me? Because I yelled at Gene's psychic?"

"Tyler, I'm mailing you something," she said. "It's a copy of a letter Gene sent to Jacob and the board. You didn't get it from me."

A couple of days later, I got a copy of Gene's letter that stated the reason I should be terminated. It had been dictated to the Baguette and typed up by her. In the letter, it said that I had accosted one of our volunteers, Magdalena Quacinella, and screamed "Fuck you, you fucking bitch and fuck your psychic bullshit."

"Why didn't you tell me about this?" I asked Tinka when I got her on the phone. She was working her new job as a receptionist at Sapphic Tattoo.

"They told me not to tell you."

"Who did?"

"Gene and Jonnie."

"I need you to write me something," I said.

The next Sunday morning, I opened up the *LA Times*. Splashed across the front page of the Metropolitan section was the headline "Manna from Heaven Rocked by Feuds." I knew the slant was going our way when I saw a picture of Gene, shot at an angle that made his eyes look like they were melded together and that accentuated his double chin. The article recapped Lakshmi's histrionics and Jacob was described by former employees "as a mendacious social climber who had arranged his own high-paying salary." Manna's financial woes were reiterated, including its recent bank balance. "Benjamin Gumport was paid an outrageous sum of money to bust our union then fire the dissidents and replace them with staff that's friendly to Hellman," said Jeremy Pindor. "This was a nonprofit with the best intentions and now it's being sucked dry by some greedy parasites." The article chronicled the new age antics that affected the workplace, including sage ceremonies for a slow computer and my argument with a "former telephone psychic with a Svengali-type hold over head chef, Gene Sitz."

Bryce called me from the kitchen around ten, his last day there. "I won't say who," he said gleefully. "But some stuffy bitch is having a very bad day."

"Tell Gene the picture's not as bad as he thinks," I said. "Tell him I said that he looks like a flounder... but in a good way."

"Flounder is right," Bryce said. "One that's been split up the middle and gutted. Bitch just begged me not to leave. Mildred is back in the kitchen and stinking of pies and grease and working like a common frump."

Some say there's no such thing as bad publicity. I don't agree with that, but on Monday, my boss from my old post-production job called me. "Hey, Tyler, if you aren't playing black jack at Caesar's Palace this weekend, do you want to work a few shifts?"

"Sure," I said.

That afternoon my agent called. "Hi, Tyler! I heard from Lindy Menenos at New World. She read about you yesterday and it reminded her of how much she liked *The Sugar Parade*. She wants to talk to you about a project she thinks you're just perfect to rewrite."

"What's the project?"

"It's about some working-class kids who live in a mountain resort. It's *Breaking Away* on skis. Have you ever skied?"

"I'm doing it right now. What's it pay?"

"It's ten grand. It'll take you a few weeks."

And as for $10,000, that's the paltry amount I got a few months later when my lawyer settled with Jacob Hellman. When I got that check, I used part of it to buy Gene a subscription to *Skeptical Inquirer*, something that would remind him of me on a bimonthly basis. And then I wrote a letter to the board of directors and sent each of them a copy.

Dear Board of Directors of Manna from Heaven and others,

I loved working at Manna and embraced its mission to feed people with AIDS. I never expected to make a fortune from it although others certainly have. It was with deep regret that I sued our organization to be compensated for my wrongful dismissal. I was accused of shouting obscenities at Magdalena Quacinella, an avowed psychic, who is a close friend to Gene Sitz. Using her so-called powers, Quacinella told Gene that one day he would have a famous lover and a future as a spiritual leader to hundreds of thousands. She also predicted he would own a luxury German automobile and a home off of Mulholland Drive.

Ms. Quacinella, in a very public way, accused me of skipping work to play in Las Vegas while I was at home in bed with the flu. I called her on her "psychic bullshit." I did not use the word "fuck" or "fucking" or "bitch" in my argument with her. Attached is a letter from former employee Tinka Tomkowski who vouches for my account.

I was fired for "alienating a volunteer in an organization that relies on them," according to Mr. MacNamee. If anyone should be fired for alienating the volunteers, it is Mr. Sitz. He constantly offended both employees and volunteers. One of the most egregious instances was on a Thursday afternoon in March of 1991. Sitz, a gentile, and Graham Stillson, a Jewish volunteer, were arguing in the community room. At the end of the argument, Stillson entered the kitchen in a rage. "I'm going to tell everyone what you just said!" he shouted. "Gene just told me, 'It's Jews like you who make me think that Hitler was right.'" Among those present that day were a number of the Jewish volunteers we relied on including Bunny Glick, Marlene Plotkin, Ruth Schwartzman and Goldie Gottlieb. Mr. Sitz made a weak apology only after I encouraged him to do so.

I wish all of you and everyone who works at Manna the greatest success in fulfilling our mission to serve people with AIDS. It is unfortunate that this once-beautiful, grassroots organization has been exploited as a means of self-promotion and profit-making, but it is also completely expected. I wish you the very best as you transform Manna into a professional nonprofit that is stable, self-sustaining and secular.

Sincerely,

Tyler St. George

cc: Lakshmi Steinmetz, Jacob Hellman, Evan MacNamee

I didn't know if this letter would get Gene fired. But I knew it would chap his ass. His idol, Lakshmi, would never look at him in the same way again.

I went back to work on *The Sorcerer's Protege,* something I wanted to finish before rewriting *Rocky Mountain High,* the ski movie. With *Protege,* I had a feeling that I was on the cusp of something that would be wildly successful: a story about a young man on the verge of adolescence that discovers he has the powers of a sorcerer. His dead father, he learns, was also a sorcerer, one who lost a battle to an evil warlock who breaks out of his spell-cage to take his revenge. That would be a screenplay I could sell!

A few months later, I was at the dentist's when I read an article about Lakshmi buried in the middle of Entertainment Weekly. "The press has chased me out of Los Angeles," she said in the lobby of a Seattle hotel where she continued her book tour. "And perhaps I need to work on my relational style. I know I've chafed a few people. I was criticized for how I ran my organizations, but please! They were something I started at my kitchen table. What did I know about managing a charity?"

That was something of an admission but it was not an apology. The responsibility of the press is to be accurate and they can't be blamed for who Lakshmi is or how she behaved.

And someday, I knew, when she was fleeing another mess of her own creation, Steinmetz would be back in Los Angeles... with the biggest plans of all.

Chapter 38

Madge's prediction of my future as a hugely successful screenwriter didn't come true. Maybe when she said it "would all just explode" she meant it would be blown to smithereens but that wasn't quite true either. The Sorcerer's Protege was roundly rejected in the long, tepid wake of movies like Willow, Legend and Labyrinth. "Everyone likes your writing, and they're blown away by your imagination," my agent told me. "But in Hollywood, fantasy is still the f-word." I never sold that million-dollar spec screenplay, but I did get steady work as a script doctor, writer for hire and as a ghostwriter. Later, I had a gig doing adaptations of Israeli novels. Only a few of the scripts I worked on were ever made and I can't be proud of any of them. They are what a friend calls "corpse lipsticks," which is shorthand for "You can't bring a corpse to life but you can put a little lipstick on it."

Kyle and I went into relationship counseling with a psychologist for a second time to "salvage or bring closure" to our union. Kyle chose closure when he moved out while I was away at a softball tournament, but then he invited me to join him in the parsonage he rented from the same church that leased its kitchen to Manna. I turned him down after I found a letter from the doctor he was seeing in London. I then made the mistake of falling in love with Adrian, a magazine writer, who had been in the cult of the Church Universal and Triumphant for most of his adult life. Adrian was in therapy with a psychologist and his angry ex was also a psychologist, and before their breakup, they had been in counseling with the same psychologist that Kyle and I had seen. For a few weeks, I saw my own psychologist, Eli, a Jungian, who screamed at me in our sessions and encouraged me to buy Star Wars figurines and Barbie dolls in order to recreate my traumas. I later learned Eli was the head of his own mini-cult, one in which his followers, some other psychologists, believed they were the "Water-Bearing Illuminati of a global spiritual movement." The WBI would take gay people from shame and marginalization to their rightful place as the vanguards of the Human Transformation Movement. They believed Eli, an Aquarius, was "The Ascended Spiritual Master who would unite the planet" and reign over it in the Aquarian Age.

  After getting Kyle, Adrian and Eli out of my life, I used my experience to write a play that was produced within months of my finishing it. *Therapy Junkies* was a comedy that had a few good runs and won an award. It was a spectacular satisfaction to present something exactly as I had written it, something an extraordinary director enhanced by another 20 percent with his own imagination. The success of the play triggered a new round of writing gigs including a TV series that lasted one season, some tedious but well-paying industrials, and the novelization of a blockbuster movie.

Later, I got work as a writer on "reality" or "unscripted" television which obviously is neither. It was around that time that some successful screenwriting friends of mine, known as the Davids, called me with some... *encouraging* news.

"Tyler, we were just sent this book that we might get to adapt," said David. "It's called *Harry Potter and the Sorcerer's Stone* and it's gonna be huge! It's so much like that screenplay you wrote about the boy sorcerer."

"You were just early," said Dave. "You have to keep going, Tyler. One day you'll write that spec that'll put you over the top."

Fantasy was no longer the f-word and more like the fuck-yeah! word. Sigh. But self-pity is so unattractive and all my disappointments were self-inflicted. I don't know if J. K. Rowling ever read *Mordechai's Academy of the Dark Arts* and she certainly never read my screenplay. She did write a brilliant allegorical series that exploited the dynamics of going to a new school, finding your identity and celebrating your otherness. One thing I got better at was weathering defeats. Like a cold or flu, I knew the pain of rejection would pass and life would resume with its many comforts and abundant pleasures.

When the manager of my apartment complex got fired for rewriting the rent checks to himself, I offered my services to my landlord with the idea I'd get the time to write my own stuff. For years, I had pondered the writing of a science fiction book series. Living frugally, I did research for a year then took two more to write the first book. It was a successful indie novel and later it was acquired by a Big Five publisher who contracted with me to write its sequels. The Davids optioned my books for a screen project and got it to the top rung of the ladder before it took the usual, bone-shattering fall. My novel offended more than a few people with its excoriation of religion and its misuses but it attracted something of a readership. At long last, I had achieved the status of... a minor figure.

As for being an apartment manager, well, that was what really exploded. I started managing another building, and then three more after that as well as some vacation rentals in Hawaii, Los Angeles and Palm Springs. That led to flipping houses, an enterprise to which gay men are biologically predisposed. It's something I do on weekends with my adorable, moral and reliable partner, Miles, who works in TV as a composer. The realtor we work with is my good friend, Kevin Darrington, who moved himself and his business to Palm Springs when he married the man he fell in love with, another realtor who had once been a film student.

And what happened to everyone else?

A few weeks after Bruce Prendergast's devastating Times article, Bryce and I went to the Pride parade in WeHo on a sunny Sunday in June of '91. We cheered the Dykes on Bikes and the Gay Scientists in their lab coats. We booed the Log Cabin Republicans and chuckled when we saw the Gay Mormons dressed up as pioneers and riding on a Conestoga wagon. Behind the Mormons were marchers from Manna from Heaven. Gene was among those who carried oversized kitchen utensils and he tried hiding his face from us behind a giant strainer. And though Manna had just "laid off redundant staff due to financial difficulties," someone found the money to build a float, one that hadn't been torched by an arsonist. The float was covered with white floral sheeting and had sky-blue trim for a heavenly effect with a banner on its side that credited Lakshmi as the founder of Manna. Sitting on top of it and grinning like a homecoming queen on ecstasy was Jacob Hellman. He was wearing some angel wings attached to his shoulders. I watched his paunch jiggle when the float bumped over a pothole. That's when I remembered his invitation at a meeting from a couple of months back. "Fuck you, Jacob Hellman!" I shouted. "You're a real piece of shit!"

He turned toward us, his face fallen. "Lose some weight!" Bryce shouted before he threw his opened can of Diet Coke. The can landed on the float and spilled its sudsy, brown contents down the tiers and left what looked like a diaper stain.

Bryce moved to the Bay Area when he got accepted at UC Berkeley. To this day, we are very close friends and we still get together to cook and eat. In 1996, he visited me with his partner, Adam, and we accepted Snake Hips Steve's invitation to tour the new facility for Manna from Heaven.

Manna had become exactly what Bravermann had predicted. Its building was a sizable two-story structure, a former ballroom on Sunset Boulevard in Hollywood. The lower floor was an immense kitchen with walls of walk-in refrigerators and rows of industrial stoves. The upper floor included close to twenty offices for executives and a staff of professional fundraisers. Out in a spacious parking lot was a fleet of new vans with wraps of Manna's logo on their sides. A token crew of volunteers still offered their services, but most of the work was done by a paid staff of twenty drivers and more than thirty kitchen workers. They made thousands of meals a day. Jacob Hellman and Jonnie had left years before when their services were "no longer needed."

As he showed us the place, Steve admitted he wasn't convinced of the necessity of Manna now that a cocktail of drugs had ended the AIDS crisis. "I see some of our clients at my gym," he said. "And they're more buffed than I am." He explained the organization had corporate partnerships with health insurance companies that used Manna's services to send out meals tailored to people's medical conditions. Fattening desserts were no longer on the menu since no one was suffering from wasting disease and patients getting fatter was the bigger concern. "We do send some meals to people who can't feed or shop for themselves. But no one's dying of AIDS anymore," Steve said. "Manna is just another self-perpetuating institution. It's not exactly a nonprofit."

We walked past Gene's cubicle with its glass walls, where he was sitting at his computer, reading glasses on, and pretending to be involved with something on his screen. Bryce knocked on the glass and then pressed his nose and opened mouth against it to make a smashed monster face. Then he turned around and rubbed his butt on the glass as Gene turned red.

"Gene's been having a rough few years," Steve whispered.

"We heard," I said.

More than a few people had called to tell me that a year after the dissidents were fired, a new volunteer had arrived at the old church kitchen, somebody who "had rocked Gene's world." Marc-Francois said he was from Delaware and that he was a Dupont. He had come to Hollywood to pursue his dream of acting, something he said his family did not support, financially or otherwise. In the kitchen, he lavished Gene with compliments and told him he was "very handsome" and "an amazing chef" and "just so spiritual." It was an instant and powerful romance, as at long last, Gene had found love. Just a few months later, Marc-Francois moved in with Gene. When Marc asked Gene to buy him a pickup truck, Gene complied. He also complied with the request to open a bank account together as well as apply for some joint credit cards.

It was not long before this scion of the Duponts made more requests of Gene. When these were denied, the verbal abuse began and this was followed by physical abuse. The police had to get involved, but it was not before Gene's bank account was depleted and his credit cards were maxed out. When Marc-Francois, whose real name was Dwayne Wadley, realized it was time to find a new victim, he loaded up his truck with Gene's stuff and drove it over the Mexican border.

I would be lying if I said I'm incapable of schadenfreude, but this story made me sad, as Gene always had. Some people will always be susceptible to the flattery and charisma of con artists, whether they are brazen opportunists posing as lovers or as spiritual gurus from Sri Lanka, Atlanta or the Bronx.

As for the Bronx guru, sometime around 1995, she got her own punishing Vanity Fair article that focused on her ashram in Florida. Guru Mama, who was childless, arranged marriages for her devotees then took their children to raise as her own. Those who attempted to leave her ashram were threatened with blindness or infertility, something she said she could inflict by appealing to the goddess Kali. Before her death, Mama was plagued with numerous scandals and lawsuits and she was prosecuted as a tax cheat.

The Sri Lankan guru, Dinesh Carvalho is still around. He's still lecturing and posts videos on You Tube, Instagram and TikTok.

He also writes books that instruct his readers on how to "shift their awareness." And for a modest donation of a thousand dollars, Dinesh still blows the blue light of consciousness into those who are ready to receive it. He defended taking the millions he made to casinos which he said was "an exercise in detachment from money. It is easy come, it is easy go. It is just money and its only value is in how we perceive it."

As for someone who had received the blue light, it was a decade later in 2013 when I spoke to Jonnie again. I saw her often, walking alone in West Hollywood, or waiting in line at CVS pharmacy, but she never seemed to recognize me. One afternoon Miles and I arrived to eat lunch at Kings Road Cafe and we were seated next to her. She was alone, as usual, and had just paid her check.

"Hi, Jonnie," I said.

"Well, hello," she said, not using my name.

"How ya been?" I asked. She had updated her hair to something shorter and contemporary. She was still a blonde, but her gray roots were showing. As usual, she wore a shiny blue blouse and her lashes were thickened with black mascara.

"I'm just fabulous," she said. "It just gets better."

"This is my partner, Miles," I said.

"Nice to meet you, Miles. Say, I've started a new ministry," she said as she reached into her giant purse. She handed us calling cards with her picture on them and her expression, as usual, was of happy astonishment. The card read "Jonnie Lindley lecturing on *The Way of the Miraculous*" and it had both a website and a physical address. "You should come by!" she sang. "It's very fulfilling"

"Uh, well, thank you," I said, and politely pocketed her card.

Had she forgotten who I was and our conflict from years ago? She seemed too independent to be suffering from Alzheimer's. When Miles excused himself to use the bathroom, she put her hand gently on my forearm then looked at me with an intense expression.

"Can I ask you something?" she said. I was reminded of all the ridiculous errands I had run for her and wondered if she was going to ask me to drive some meals to Torrance.

"Never hurts to ask," I said.

She cleared her throat.

"Do I... do I look *good*?"

I was wordless.

"Jonnie... you look... you look fantastic," I finally said as a chuckle escaped. "And what is more important than that?"

Jonnie's ministry never took root and grew. The place where she offered a free lunch to homeless people was re-rented to a nail salon. Only one person was ever able to capitalize on *The Way of the Miraculous* and she was doing it again years later in Los Angeles. But Lakshmi had much larger ambitions beyond getting more followers and shifting their awareness.

In 2014, two people I knew were running for public office in Los Angeles. One of them was Robert Bravermann, in a bid to be a member of the LA Board of Education. An article about his candidacy appeared in the Times and featured a current picture of him with his famous mustache. In the comments section online, no one discussed the issues he raised or his qualifications but they did bring up his appearance. "He's still hot," and "Take your shirt off, Robby," were among the posts. It was a reminder that men, too, can be objectified and that seriously good-looking people are not always taken seriously.

Over the years, Robert and I bumped into each other at bars and parties and fundraisers. He was perpetually handsome and had taken to wearing a turquoise stud in one ear. One night we were chatting at the Roosterfish in Venice when I informed him we had both dated the same guy. We agreed that the guy, Clint, was sensationally cute and lots of fun in bed but he was "not one for the long haul." I didn't bring up to Robert what I had learned about him from Clint — that after seven years in the job, Robert had left his position as chief administrator for one of the city's biggest hospitals. He had clashed with corporate heads when they pressured him to "fudge the numbers," something he would never do. It was one more time in his life when morality and integrity had resulted in the punishment of Robert Bravermann.

I voted for Robert for the school board but he lost to a well-funded opponent. Robert's occupation was listed as "Teacher." Another person on the ballot that year was described as "Author."

I needn't have worried about Lakshmi's run for Congress. She was attempting to follow in the footsteps of a rock star of the Watergate era, Hank Scharffenberger, a man who was one of the Democrats' most powerful and accomplished politicians, somebody who was reelected eighteen times from one of the wealthiest and most influential districts in the United States.

In her run for representative, Lakshmi held numerous rallies that featured famous actors and musicians. One singer-songwriter even penned her a campaign song. The rallies were attended by as many as two hundred people, but as one reporter from the LA Times noted, the attendees appeared to be the same two hundred carrying the same signs. They were likely the same two hundred that attended her lectures on Tuesday nights at an old movie theater. I saw from a picture on Facebook that one of her supporters was Koala — he was still hanging in there for her.

Miles and I attended a fundraiser for one of Lakshmi's opponents at a home in Bel-Air where I shook hands once again with Tony Fursten. He said "Nice to meet you, Taylor," and showed no interest in me or Miles. The candidate, Kenneth Leung, was a decorated colonel in the Air Force and an active member of its reserve. By 2012, Colonel Leung had served in both California's State Assembly and its State Senate. He had bachelor degrees in political and computer science from Princeton and a doctor of jurisprudence from Yale. He had been a student of Miles's cousin, a professor emeritus in New Haven, who told us "Kenneth Leung may be the first Asian American president" and encouraged us to donate to his campaign. We did.

Southern California may be a hotbed of New Age foolishness, but most of us who live here are sensible. Leung never held a single rally but he ran away with the election after Scharffenberger and the Democratic party endorsed him. Lakshmi came in a distant fourth. "This is not the time to give in to depression or discouragement," she wrote on Facebook which was some very kind advice to her followers who had to be hurting as much as she was.

And she wasn't discouraged. Her defeat did not stop her from running for president six years later in 2020 and raising some money from her followers to do it. Some accused her of running to revive her celebrity and to sell more books, but I suspect that part of her believed that God had told her to run, in the same way that Allah had commanded Mohammed to recite, or the angel Maroni had told Joseph Smith to translate the golden plates. Maybe she believed she could win, as after all, she was the only candidate promoting love, sweet love, which is something, you know, that the world needs now.

One evening, someone called me from Steinmetz for President headquarters. "Hello, Tyler," said a volunteer with an actressy thrill in her voice. "I want to urge you to consider making a contribution to Lakshmi Steinmetz for president! Now more than ever, America needs her message of love."

"You're in a cult," I said and hung up. After that, I did a Google search to see what had happened to Lakshmi following her *hejira* in the early 90's.

I knew the BFG had been back in LA for a while because I'd run into her a couple of awkward times in the early aughts. The first was when I got a complaint about a noisy Oscar party at one of my tenants. When the tenant didn't pick up her phone, I had to drive over. I was looking through the screen door when I heard a familiar voice screeching, "Just what the fuck is she wearing!" as Gwyneth Paltrow, in an excessively sheer top, introduced the next category. I knocked on the door and there was Lakshmi, glaring at me over a balloon glass of red wine.

"I need you guys to keep it down, maybe close the door," I said to my tenant. "Have fun, but the neighbors are complaining about someone who is *really* loud."

The second awkward time was when I discovered Lakshmi and I had the same dermatologist. I was in the waiting room, reading on my iPhone, when she stepped out and made her next appointment, her face freshly injected with fillers and dotted with the punctures from a Botox needle. We pretended not to see each other.

While I waited for my own procedure, I did a Google search and learned that Lakshmi had moved to Minneapolis in the mid-90's where she was the minister of a New Thought mega-church. Her ministry there had lasted four years — pretty lengthy for Lakshmi — but it was "rampant with controversies and financial improprieties." In her final months, before she was pressured to resign, she laid off three-quarters of the church's staff to deal with a deepening deficit. It all sounded just the slightest bit familiar. In an interview from the same period, Lakshmi admitted that she faced financial problems of her own. She had lost not one but two multi-million dollar investment properties.

The woman just wasn't good with money — not her own and not other people's. Perhaps she was just a bad Quimbyist, someone who hadn't properly visualized her success. The article mentioned that she was returning to Los Angeles to "test the waters and resume a ministry not attached to a physical church."

She must have made up with Jacob Hellman and film producer Aaron Sibley who both got involved in her congressional and presidential campaigns. Jacob had been organizing her revived lectures on *The Way* and handled the gate at different repurposed movie theaters around the city. Not to go quietly into obscurity, Jacob had written his own book in partnership with a controversial psychiatrist, the death fetishist Alicia Goertzen, the "doctor of dying" who had her own New Age tendencies and infamously described a tour that an "entity" had given her of the afterlife. Now Goertzen was in the years long process of dying herself and Jacob was determined to take over her legacy when she did.

Both Jacob and Lakshmi's books were distributed by Eloise Clayman's publishing company, Clayman House, which included a roster of new age writers that advocated for Ayurvedic medicine, thinking yourself to wellness, and the "magic of believing" to bring love and prosperity into your life. Naturally, they all blurbed each other. None of them mentioned that the way they had attracted prosperity into their own lives was to write books about attracting prosperity.

In 2020, the Divine Ms. Steinmetz created quite a sensation when she qualified for the debate stage with the Democrats' presidential candidates. In her first appearance, she fumbled and was widely ridiculed. She had become a national punchline and was parodied on Saturday Night Live as a New Age witch who lived in a different dimension. But at the second debate, Lakshmi "connected" as actors refer to it, and with a flourish of fluttering fingers, she came up with some applause lines. The eldest son of the Republican incumbent tweeted "Lakshmi Steinmetz has won this debate."

Her reversal happened only a day later when she appeared on CNN and was interviewed by its handsome prime-time star. After complimenting her on her performance, he confronted her with visuals of her embarrassing tweets, one of which was anti-vaccination and others that were a refutation of science and dismissed

AIDS and mental illness as "illusions." The anchor accused Lakshmi of being "irresponsible" and the two argued on live television. She accused him of "undermining my spiritual authority." When he asked her "what university or institution qualified you as a spiritual authority?" she replied that he had "orchestrated an ambush." Her campaign crumbled after that. Some candid footage was released of her as she tearfully lamented she would not get to debate the Republican. She had planned on demanding that he "embrace love and reject fear" because, you know, all you need is love, love, love is all you need.

Two months after a Democrat other than Lakshmi became president-elect, the New York Times did a follow-up article on her. Lakshmi's revived book sales had brought her some cash flow and she moved to Washington, DC as a base for her third run for office. Her new apartment was less than a mile away from the White House where an even more dangerous narcissist had fomented violence in his last weeks in office. The article included a quote from the national chairman of the Democratic party who compared her to Jill Stein and called Lakshmi "the most dangerous woman in America. She's a wild card with the potential to overturn everything, a bomb waiting to explode with a fuse lit by Republicans and a campaign chest filled by Russians."

Coming to her defense at the end of the piece was Lakshmi's daughter, Ananda, a low-profile figure who was married and studying French literature in Paris. "I don't understand these attacks on my mom," she said. "She's just running a business." That was not a description I disagreed with. Ananda did not defend her mother as a thinker or politician or even as a "spiritual authority."

Money had never been as important as fame to Lakshmi, but deep down, she always knew she was selling something, whether it was her books or exposure to herself as a channel to the divine. "You will not fuck with my livelihood!" she had screamed at all of us, words that echo to this day.

Soon after Lakshmi announced her second run for president in 2023, a dozen staff members from her 2020 campaign contacted the press and collectively warned other politicos not to get involved with her. Warning of "verbal abuse and emotional torment," they exposed her sudden rages and spoke of being "traumatized and reduced to tears." Several spoke of having her phone thrown in their faces and one recalled driving Lakshmi to the hospital after she put her fist through the drywall of a motel room when it didn't have a bathtub. One staffer had the specific task of carrying nondisclosure agreements in her briefcase to pay and silence the taxi drivers, hotel clerks and restaurant staff that witnessed Lakshmi's degrading outbursts. Another staffer spoke of the devastating disappointment in learning his hero was "the worst hypocrite, the antithesis of a loving and forgiving human being. A decent person doesn't need an endless supply of nondisclosure agreements."

As of the time of this writing, Lakshmi is demanding that the incumbent meet her on the debate stage where she can counter him with the depth of her "spiritually informed platform." Of course, another platform is what she's really interested in, one with national television coverage, and one more chance to be a star. As of this writing, she has implied she may run as a third party candidate if the incumbent refuses to debate her. As for continuing this campaign, let me address her directly.

I get you, girlfriend, I totally understand your energy. It's late in life, and you want to cement a more spectacular legacy, you want to "heal the world" of its perpetual sorrows and take credit for it. But don't run for president, *honey*. Don't waste other people's money on another vanity campaign. You'll never be president, but you might sabotage the Democrat and throw it to a Republican who will end a woman's right to choose, who will let the Russians take Ukraine and who will end programs to fight climate change as our cities go underwater. You can do the right thing, Miriam, and *quietly* raise money for politicians who can win. If you get another autocratic Republican elected, that will be a catastrophic mess that neither your father nor your Heavenly Father can bail you out of. It might mean the end of democracy in America... and the world.

And as for attention, readers may be asking, so what about you, Tyler St. George? Aren't you just a fame whore too, lusting for more readers and more recognition? Why did you publish this book instead of just leaving it on your computer? Isn't it more than trying to end someone's run for president with its potential for igniting global catastrophes?

It's not. It's my responsibility to write this book. But I will admit I've enjoyed my little sips of fame. I'm not averse to admiration if I've earned it, but that's not why I write. I like when people connect with my work, which is a form of love, an antidote to our universal loneliness. I also enjoy making people think and pissing them off when I show them the God they believe in is the biggest fame whore of all. That God did not create a safe, happy humanity free from death and suffering. That God is needy — someone who demands recognition and must be worshipped before he ends a bloody and unjust war, cures a child's cancer or frees us of the "ego addiction" that brings so much pain. That God is infamously jealous of other gods and he always has been.

Let me admit that Lakshmi and I have always had some important similarities — something I knew from our first conversation. Both of us write fiction but only one of us will call it that. We both have escaped into the paintings of Maxfield Parrish. And like me, I am sure Lakshmi still sends little checks to Save the Children and Operation Smile and whatever else shows up in her mailbox. To her credit, Lakshmi is not like those other attention junkies that I really loathe, the ones who exploit hate and fear and stoke resentment; the right-wing performance artists like Milo, MTG, Ann Coulter and the worst one of all, Donald Fucking Trump.

I wish for Lakshmi what I wish for all the other humans that inhabit this planet: the peace and deep satisfaction that comes from loving others and being loved back. She is absolutely right about love and so were the millions before her who promoted the same message. I also wish her freedom from the painful trap of self-obsession as well as a greater capacity for honesty, rational thinking and treating others well and fairly. I do wish Lakshmi would apologize to those she has harmed, to take Step Nine of the Twelve and make amends. But wishes, like prayers, are not what makes a thing come true.

About the Author

Clark T. Carlton is the award winning author of the science fiction/fantasy series *Antasy*, published through Harper Collins Voyager which includes the novels *Prophets of the Ghost Ants*, *The Prophet of the Termite God* and *The Ghost Ants of Grylladesh*. He is also the author of the play *Self-Help or the Tower of Psychobabble* and the screenwriter of projects he hopes are long forgotten. He was born in the South, was raised in the North, went to school in the East and lives with his family in the West.

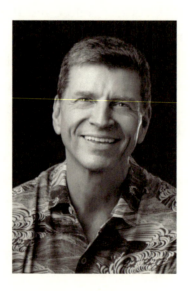

Made in the USA
Thornton, CO
08/30/23 17:08:16

15a1b8e4-386a-4c71-9f24-e8e526d9f24eR01